DARK DESTROYER

A MEDIEVAL ROMANCE
PART OF THE DE WOLFE PACK /
GREAT MARCHER LORDS OF DE LARA

BY KATHRYN LE VEQUE

Copyright 2015 by Kathryn Le Veque
Print Edition

All rights reserved. No part of this book may be used or reproduced in any manner whatsoever without written permission, except in the case of brief quotations embodied in critical articles or reviews.

Printed by Kathryn Le Veque Novels in the United States of America

Text copyright 2015 by Kathryn Le Veque
Cover copyright 2015 by Kathryn Le Veque

KATHRYN LE VEQUE NOVELS

Medieval Romance:

The de Russe Legacy:
The White Lord of Wellesbourne
The Dark One: Dark Knight
Beast
Lord of War: Black Angel
The Falls of Erith

The de Lohr Dynasty:
While Angels Slept (Lords of East Anglia)
Rise of the Defender
Spectre of the Sword
Unending Love
Archangel
Steelheart

Great Lords of le Bec:
Great Protector
To the Lady Born (House of de Royans)

Lords of Eire:
The Darkland (Master Knights of Connaught)
Black Sword
Echoes of Ancient Dreams (time travel)

De Wolfe Pack Series:
The Wolfe
Serpent
Scorpion (Saxon Lords of Hage – Also related to The Questing)
Walls of Babylon
The Lion of the North
Dark Destroyer

Ancient Kings of Anglecynn:
The Whispering Night
Netherworld

Battle Lords of de Velt:
The Dark Lord
Devil's Dominion

Reign of the House of de Winter:
Lespada
Swords and Shields (also related to The Questing, While Angels Slept)

De Reyne Domination:
Guardian of Darkness
The Fallen One (part of Dragonblade Series)

Unrelated characters or family groups:
The Gorgon (Also related to Lords of Thunder)
The Warrior Poet (St. John and de Gare)
Tender is the Knight (House of d'Vant)
Lord of Light
The Questing (related to The Dark Lord, Scorpion)
The Legend (House of Summerlin)

The Dragonblade Series: (Great Marcher Lords of de Lara)
Dragonblade
Island of Glass (House of St. Hever)
The Savage Curtain (Lords of Pembury)
The Fallen One (De Reyne Domination)
Fragments of Grace (House of St. Hever)
Lord of the Shadows
Queen of Lost Stars (House of St. Hever)

Lords of Thunder: The de Shera Brotherhood Trilogy
The Thunder Lord
The Thunder Warrior
The Thunder Knight

Time Travel Romance: (Saxon Lords of Hage)
The Crusader
Kingdom Come

Contemporary Romance:

Kathlyn Trent/Marcus Burton Series:
Valley of the Shadow
The Eden Factor
Canyon of the Sphinx

The American Heroes Series:
Resurrection
Fires of Autumn
Evenshade

Sea of Dreams
Purgatory

Other Contemporary Romance:
Lady of Heaven
Darkling, I Listen

Multi-author Collections/Anthologies:
With Dreams Only of You (USA Today bestseller)
Sirens of the Northern Seas (Viking romance)

Note: All Kathryn's novels are designed to be read as stand-alones, although many have cross-over characters or cross-over family groups. Novels that are grouped together have related characters or family groups.

Series are clearly marked. All series contain the same characters or family groups except the American Heroes Series, which is an anthology with unrelated characters.

There is NO particular chronological order for any of the novels because they can all be read as stand-alones, even the series.

For more information, find it in **A Reader's Guide to the Medieval World of Le Veque.**

Author's Note

This novel is different from the usual Le Veque rock 'em, sock 'em battle tales. This one is a simple but powerful love story....

In Celtic mythology, the term "Dark Destroyer" is synonymous with "rogue" or "rake", hence Gates de Wolfe's nickname. He's not a wicked man by any means (no de Wolfe ever could be), but he is definitely the love 'em and leave 'em type when it comes to the ladies. A ladies' man? Absolutely! But you'll find out why we like him so much (isn't that half the fun of a good tale?)!

Still, Gates is a very different Le Veque hero. He's in no way perfect. At some points, he's really not even likable. But he's human, and he's a de Wolfe, which means he has great capacity for change. In fact, you're going to see a big change in him from the beginning of the novel to the end, where he really comes to terms with what he's done in his life that he's not proud of and how difficult it is to live up to the de Wolfe name. He's got some demons. But I really fell in love with him in spite of his flaws.

Things to note – in the beginning of the story, there is a mention of St. Milburga's Priory in the village of Ludlow along the Welsh Marches. It is an actual place. Although a very old priory with a rich history, having been built in the Dark Ages, St. Milburga's was eventually a Cluniac priory for men only. In this novel, I have taken artistic license to make it a woman-only healing order. Also, none of the castles in this novel exist. I have taken artistic license with them as well. But I've made them real enough that you would think that they actually do exist!

As for the family ties in the novel – because it wouldn't be a Le Veque novel without family ties – Jasper de Lara is the son of Liam de Lara, who is Tate de Lara's (DRAGONBLADE) adoptive brother.

Jasper's wife is a du Bois from Rhys du Bois' mother's family (SPEC-TRE OF THE SWORD). There are de Lohrs in this novel and one in particular I think you'll like – a young knight named Alexander de Lohr. He will undoubtedly receive his own novel at some point. Also, there is a minor character named Tobias Aston, who is the grandson of Dallas Aston (THE FALLS OF ERITH).

No huge politics in this book, or big battles, famous historical characters, or even deaths (surprise, I know!). There's really no battle action at all. This novel is simply a roundabout love story between two people who couldn't possibly be more different, and the entire story focuses on their world. It comes from the heart, not the sex organs. It reads like a soap opera. It's a different kind of romance but one that I hope will have you cheering in the end.

A simple love story? You be the judge.

Enjoy!

Big hugs,
Kathryn

TABLE OF CONTENTS

Prologue... 1

The Ballad of the Dark Destroyer 11

Chapter One 12

Chapter Two 26

Chapter Three 42

Chapter Four 68

Chapter Five 78

Chapter Six 85

Chapter Seven 123

Chapter Eight 141

Chapter Nine 155

Chapter Ten 174

Chapter Eleven 190

Chapter Twelve 205

Chapter Thirteen 216

Chapter Fourteen 230

Chapter Fifteen 244

Chapter Sixteen 261

Chapter Seventeen 280

Chapter Eighteen 292

Chapter Nineteen 305

Chapter Twenty 317

Chapter Twenty-One 325

Chapter Twenty-Two 341

Epilogue 353

About Kathryn Le Veque 360

PROLOGUE

~ "YOUR SINS WILL FIND YOU OUT!" ~

England, 1357 A.D.
January

"I DID NOT think you would come!"

A young woman, rather homely in face but with a figure that would make Aphrodite proud, raced from the barn entrance towards a figure standing back in the shadows amongst the hay and horses that were crowding the structure.

It was snowing outside, meaning that most of the animals that usually spent their time outside were now crammed into the warm spaces of the barn, absolutely packed to the rafters with hay that had been well covered to keep the moisture from it. Back amongst these big clusters of hay, and back behind the crowded animals, a very big man opened his arms to the woman.

"I told you I would," he said, brushing the dusting of snow off her shoulders. "Did you not believe me?"

The woman was overwrought with joy. Her homely features had chased most men away from her, but not this man; he had been kind to her when they'd met in town on this day. He was passing through on his return home from France but he'd sent his men ahead as he'd remained in town, slogging through the dirty piles of snow to strike up a conversation with her.

The woman had never seen such a handsome man, with hazel-gold eyes, dark hair, and a grimly square jaw with a big dimple in the center of his chin. He was a knight of the highest order with his expensive weapons, soaring height, big muscles, and brilliant white-toothed smile. She could never have known that it was that smile, that wildly alluring gesture, which had sent every maiden's heart fluttering between Brighton and Edinburgh.

He was a de Wolfe, and a wolf, in every sense of the word.

The man was a predator.

Gates de Wolfe, he'd introduced himself, son of the Earl of Warenton and member of the legendary de Wolfe family. And Lady Mary, daughter of the richest man in the town of Halford near the Welsh Marches, was thrilled to have the attention of so handsome and prestigious a knight. She was so thrilled that she had agreed to meet him in the barn on her family's estate, well away from her protective father and three older brothers. With them around, no man would come near her, or at least that is what her family told her. It had nothing to do with the fact that she had a face like the hind end of a goat.

A face-like-an-ass or not, Gates wasn't particularly looking at her face. He was looking at the full bosom and slender waist, the only things he'd been looking at all along. He liked his women full and luscious, and Lady Marie – or Mary – or whatever her name was (because he really didn't care) fit that bill. He was only interested in what lay beneath her surcoat. Moreover, she had been most eager to his attentions and Gates knew that, once again, he'd found a willing victim. Or partner. Aye, he preferred to look at her as a partner because in his experience, the women were always quite eager to do whatever he wanted to do.

Whatever would satisfy his needs.

He'd been through this kind of routine before, too many times to count. He found a woman with whom he physically lusted after and there would be no sating that lust until he'd found his release inside the warm recesses of her body. Gates was the perfect knight, intelligent and powerful and brave, and he was the life of any gathering. He was humorous and generous, and had more friends than he could count. He was also a natural leader, one that men looked to for confidence and direction. But he had one big weakness – the female body. Women were his downfall and he knew it.

So did most of England.

But Lady Mary hadn't heard of his unsavory reputation, thankfully, so in the guise of pretending to remove her cloak, Gates ended up pulling it over her head so he wouldn't have to look at her butt-face. Then, he threw her back onto the hay in a darkened corner. Lady Mary giggled, and he pretended to laugh as if it was all a big joke, but the truth was that Gates didn't want to look at that face.

For his purposes, it would only serve to deter him and his physical needs were so strong at the moment that he would not be discouraged. It had been months since he'd had a woman because the ravaged countryside of France, particularly around Poitiers that had just seen a major battle, did not have an abundance of women in general.

Gates knew that for a fact because he'd fought that battle. He'd spent months in France, dealing with mud as deep as his waist, hunger, cold, general poverty, and very little female companionship. He'd had to wait to return home to England to once again sample well-fed female flesh and, at this point, he didn't care what she looked like. Well, not much. Therefore, he pretended to play a game as he covered Lady Mary's face with her cloak.

He was already undressing her as she tried to pull the cloak off her head, but Gates, being slick and clever, prevented her from removing it. "Nay," he breathed, kissing her full, quivering bosom exposed above the top of her surcoat. "Leave it there. Covering the eyes heightens the senses, my lady. Trust me when I tell you that this will make your experience as grand as you can imagine."

Lady Mary continued to giggle but she stopped trying to tug the cloak off. "As you say," she said. "But... may I at least pull it off at some point to gaze upon you? I do so wish to gaze upon you."

But I do not wish to gaze upon you, he thought dismally. "In a moment," he murmured, kissing the top of her bosom again, like great creamy mounds of softness. "Let me guide you through this wondrous world where the only limits are your imagination. *Trust me.*"

Lady Mary settled down admirably at that point. "I do," she whispered sincerely. "Oh, I do!"

Gates went to work, quickly. He wasn't sure how much time they had and he didn't want to waste it. As the horses snorted and shifted in the stall beside them, and the smell of animal dung and damp hay sat heavily upon the air, Gates pulled back the neckline of Lady Mary's expensive surcoat. There were lacings across her breasts and he quickly loosened them, allowing him access to her big, warm breasts.

He nursed furiously against her nipples, causing the woman to gasp and buck, and then his naughty hands snaked beneath her gown, tossing aside layers of fabric, so he could get to the jewel beneath. He ran expert hands up and down her soft thighs, feeling her quiver, before tossing back the final layer of material to reveal her perfect womanhood nestled between her legs.

Gates took a moment in his frenzied quest to look at her from the waist down; she was indeed spectacular, which was rather unfair considering one had to get past that face in order to see her true beauty. He slowed a bit at this point, gently touching her inner thighs and then delicately blowing on her woman's core, heated breath which caused Lady Mary to shriek with pleasure and surprise.

God, she's beautiful, he thought to himself as he carefully touched the thick outer lips, covered with a fine matting of dark curls, stroking them lightly, blowing heated air on her, and greatly exciting himself in the process. His erection was already hard as a rock. Grasping her thighs, he parted her legs wide to reveal the unfurling pink flower between them.

Lady Mary writhed and gasped as Gates fingered her delicate woman's center. It was rare to see such untouched perfection and he felt most fortunate. Dastardly, but fortunate. He bent over, depositing tender kisses just above the dark fringe of curls, stroking the woman and feeling the moisture from her body. She was becoming maddeningly wet and he was loath to wait any longer to put his stone-hard shaft where it belonged – deep in this virginal body that was calling to him, demanding his love and his seed. If he closed his eyes, he could almost hear the breathy whispers…

… take me now!

He always had been one to obey a woman, whether her words were spoken or not. He was greatly attuned to them. With care, he inserted a finger into Lady Mary's core, listening to her cry and gasp. The sensual intrusion had frightened her. He kissed the flat belly in his view.

"Relax, love," he said softly. "Relax. You shall enjoy this, I swear it."

Lady Mary was trying to find her way out from all of the fabric over her face. Not only had the cloak been thrown over her, but her skirts were up around her head as well. She was starting to suffocate.

"I want to see you now," she begged, sounding timid. "May I please?"

Gates looked up to see that she had the cloak and skirts half-off her face. He could see that pimpled forehead and hairy brow of hers, particularly the brow – it was a solid bushy line of hair from one temple to the other. *Good Christ!* He tossed the fabric back over her head so he would not lose his erection.

"Not yet," he said patiently. "Your senses will be heightened if you cannot see. Are you enjoying this so far?"

Lady Mary sounded disappointed. "Aye."

Gates grinned. "Excellent," he said as he began to untie his breeches. "You will enjoy this more in a moment. Be patient."

Lady Mary sighed heavily, with sadness, from beneath the piles of fabric over her face. This was all so new and exciting and thrilling to her, but she was also starting to feel some frustration that she had to keep her head covered simply for the blind experience he promised her. She wasn't entirely sure her senses were heightened because she could not see what he was doing, but there was a certain amount of anticipation as to what his next move would be. She liked what he was doing so far. It was exciting and made her feel quite womanly.

She simply wished that she could watch him.

But Gates was firm that she keep the cloak over her head. In fact, she tried to lower it slightly, simply so she could peep one eye out to watch him, but he had quickly put it back over her head and then he had leaned on it with one big arm, anchoring it down over her face so she couldn't move it at all. Meanwhile, his free hand was at the junction between her legs, stroking her so that she eventually forgot about the fact that she could hardly breathe.

And then, she felt it.

Something big and heavy was against her woman's core; she could feel it, warm and smooth and pushing into her. He was pushing into her slowly, rubbing at the nub of pleasure buried deep in her woman's center as he did so, and she forgot all about the cloak over her face as her body started to twitch and jerk with pleasure. The brisk rubbing he was doing against her was making her legs quiver uncontrollably. She could feel his body as it entered hers but she was so overcome by the other sensations he was creating with her that all she could do was lay there like a mindless, boneless lump of flesh. She couldn't respond in any way. She could feel his body pushing more deeply into hers and she waited for the flash of pain that would signal the end of her maidenhood, but he was rubbing her tender core so briskly that she almost didn't care.

"Marrrrrrrrrrrrrrrrrrry!"

A voice over the heavy breathing, from outside the barn, carried upon the cold air. Gates came to an immediate halt, his head shooting up, as Lady Mary propped herself up on the hay, the cloak and skirts still over her head. Clumsily, she yanked them off.

"My father!" she gasped. "He is looking for me!"

Gates was already securing his breeches, having to fold his erection back painfully as he did so. *Damnation!* He cursed silently. He'd been too slow in doing what he needed to do and now he was caught with his....

"Marrrrrrrrrrrrrrrrrrrrrrrrrrrrrry!"

The voice was closer now. Breeches secured, Gates was already on the move, leaving the way he'd come. There was a big grove of trees to the south of the barn and he'd tethered his horse there, sheltered from the snow beneath the heavy canopy. He was already running away as Lady Mary tried to grasp at him.

"Wait!" she cried softly. "Please… when will I see you again?"

Gates paused by the gap in the slats he had slipped in through, one leg out into the snowy night beyond. Looking at her mono-brow and pimpled face, he suddenly couldn't remember what had him so excited about the woman to begin with. She certainly wasn't worth risking his life over when it came to an angry father. He smiled wanly.

"In your dreams, love," he said, blowing her a kiss purely for effect. "You will see me in your dreams. *Adieu!*"

With that, he disappeared out into the snowing darkness beyond, leaving Lady Mary flustered and as frustrated as she could possibly be. As she gasped and grunted with disappointment, trying to straighten out the clothing that Gates had thrown askew, her father and two older brothers entered the barn.

"Mary!" her father barked. "Did ye not hear me callin' to ye, lass?"

Lady Mary was agitated as she tried to cover herself up. "I heard you," she said, obviously unwilling to explain the real reason behind her presence in the barn on this cold and frozen night. "I… I did not want to answer you."

Her father and two brothers came to a halt, eyeing her as she sat, open-legged, on the hay stack. "Why not?" her father demanded, wondering why his daughter's clothing was all pulled apart. "What are ye doing out here?"

Mary wouldn't look at any of them, trying to fasten up the top of her surcoat where Gates has ripped the laces out. "I… I wanted to be alone," she said petulantly. "There is nowhere to be alone in that big house so I came out here to be by myself."

Her father was increasingly confused. "Alone?" he repeated, looking at his equally confused sons. "Ye have yer own chamber, lass. Ye could have spent time alone in there. Why did ye have to come out here to… ah… *God's Bones*, Mary! Now I understand!"

Lady Mary looked up from tying off the top of her bodice, puzzled at her father's tone. "What do you understand, Father?"

Her father had an expression that suggested complete and utter disgust. "Ye… ye wicked girl!"

Lady Mary cocked her head curiously. "Wicked?" she repeated what he had said. "Why am I wicked?"

Her father grew red in the face, suddenly quite flustered. He shoved at his sons. "Get back in the house," he said. "Get back… go, I say! This is not for ye to hear!"

Now it was Lady Mary who was increasingly confused. "What on earth is the matter with you, Father?"

Her father jabbed a fat finger at her. "Enough!" he said. "Ye… ye vile creature. Yer clothes are… and yer bosom is untied… ye came out here to… to…!"

Lady Mary threw up her hands. "To *what*?"

"Gah!" the father threw his hands over his ears. "I cannot say it! Ye… ye came to pleasure yerself where ye would not be seen! Ye wicked, wicked girl! The priest will have something to say about this!"

It occurred to Lady Mary what her father thought, and it was far from the truth. The man thought she'd come out there to touch herself in inappropriate ways, at least as the church viewed it. She'd done that to herself, of course, but this time, it was a man who had shown her pleasure. She suddenly felt quite ashamed that her father thought she had come all the way out to the barn to pleasure herself and she shook her head furiously. She had to confess everything lest she find herself at the mercy of the parish priest, who was a lascivious and dirty old man. Nay, it would be better for her father to believe she was a harlot rather than a masturbator because, under no circumstances, did she want to face their priest.

"Nay, Father," she insisted. "I… I was not alone. There was a man with me. A knight. But he is long gone and you cannot find him. We… we only kissed, Father, I swear it."

Her father began to roar again, hands still haphazardly over his ears. "Lies," he hissed. "No man would sneak away to kiss ye, Mary. 'Tis time ye realized that. And no man would risk my wrath for the likes of ye. Come with me, Daughter. We will see the priest this evening so he can purge ye of this… this wicked desire ye have. Yer sins will find ye out, Daughter!"

Lady Mary found herself being hauled up from the hay, being dragged out into the night by her father. She struggled against him, and even pleaded with him, but the man was resolute. His wife having died years earlier, he had been the sole parent to Lady Mary and it was clear he had failed miserably if the girl was out in the barn pleasuring herself and then inventing imaginary lovers to cover her dirty actions.

As Lady Mary was dragged off to the priest who sent her father out of the room as he spanked the girl's naked buttocks with a switch, and enjoyed every strike in a most peculiar fashion, Gates was on his mighty steed, riding north through the snowy trees, heading for his army which was, at best, only a few hours ahead of him.

He'd brought one thousand two hundred and eight-seven men with him back from France, men who served the Lord of the Trilateral Castles, the Earl of Trelystan. Jasper de Lara was a strong supporter of Prince Edward and his wars in France, so much so that he had sent his best knights to France for the past fifteen months. Now, it was their time to return home.

Riding hard into that frozen night, Gates quickly forgot about Lady Mary and his inability to complete what he had started with her. Instead, he found himself looking forward to returning home again. He knew of several local ladies, at least he had fifteen months ago, and he hoped to see them again. In fact, he hoped to see a great deal of them. Already, he was calculating which lady he would see first. Those were thoughts that made him press his horse even faster.

It was back to the Marches once more and the hope for continued romantic possibilities.

~ THE BALLAD OF THE DARK DESTROYER ~

On moonlit nights,

When Shadows wane,

The Dark Destroyer lingers in the mist.

Eyes of flame,

Heart of steel,

His love for one woman

Became his Achilles' heel.

Kathi, he called her,

His maiden fair

But her heart the Dark Destroyer was never meant to bear.

No longer eyes of flame,

No longer a heart of steel,

The man once known as the Dark Destroyer

Finally learned what it meant to feel…

Love.

CHAPTER ONE

February

L ORD JASPER DE Lara came from a long line of quality knights, men who had fought and died for the crown of England. His own father, Liam de Lara, had fought for both Edward II as a young knight and Edward III for most of his adulthood, and his adopted uncle was none other than the great Tate de Lara, the bastard son of Edward I. Therefore, Jasper knew what it was to fight for the crown and to provide the king with what was necessary in order to advance his cause, one way or the other.

The latest cause had been France but, then again, France had been a cause since before he was born. It was the continuous cause as far as Jasper was concerned and the need to claim regions of France for England had drained coffers all across the country. But, as one of the king's most powerful warlords, Jasper could not refuse the request for coinage or manpower, and he had often supplied both.

As Lord of the Trilaterals – three castles along the Welsh Marches that maintained the volatile border between Craven Arms to the south and Welshpool to the north, the House of de Lara commanded a good deal of power. Edward leaned heavily upon it while Jasper, not unlike his father before him, was increasingly disillusioned about the crown and its agenda across the sea. Money and men were contributed with no real results. Stagnation made for cynicism.

But that disillusionment had seen some relief since the return of Jasper's army from France and the news of a major English victory. He'd only lost three hundred men and, after the story relayed to him by his commanders – Gates de Wolfe, Alexander de Lohr, Tobias Aston, and Stephan d'Avignon – Jasper thought that his losses were rather low considering what they had faced back in September near the town of Poitiers. The English had triumphed against superior French forces and even now, three weeks after the return of his army, Jasper forced his men to tell him nightly of the Battle of Poitiers so that Jasper didn't miss any of the details. Every night, he learned something new from a different perspective. He knew his knights were growing weary of repeating the tale constantly, but Jasper would continue to demand the stories until he was satisfied.

And tonight would be no different. Jasper, his household, and his army were in shelter at Hyssington Castle, the biggest of his three holdings along the Welsh Marches, mostly because winters here seemed to be less severe than at the mountainous Trelystan Castle, which was the biggest of the three, or Caradoc Castle, the smallest of the three and also the one that was the most difficult to reach through a rocky pass. If the pass got snowed in, they would be stuck there until the thaw, which was an unpleasant thought. Therefore, the de Laras always wintered at Hyssington as she sat atop a gentle slope surrounded by a somewhat flat valley. The view was for miles all around, now a great white landscape that glistened magically under the rarity of sunlight.

But being sequestered at Hyssington made for crowded conditions with the returning army crammed in with the rest of the de Lara subjects. Hyssington had a single-storied troop house, a three-storied keep that was squat and large, plus a gatehouse that also had living quarters in it. It was three-storied as well, larger than the keep, and had one room on each side on the second floor, with the portcullis in between, and then the top floor had four big chambers that also included murder holes in one of the rooms. Soldiers mostly used those holes for a garderobe, which Lady de Lara tried to discourage because she didn't like human waste pouring out right at the entrance to the gatehouse where it could be tracked all over the castle. In fact, she had been known to yell at men for such a thing.

The great hall of Hyssington was a massive structure that could easily hold eight hundred men or more and these days, in the midst of the snowy winter, it slept hundreds while across the bailey, the troop house contained those who weren't sleeping in the hall. On this evening well after sunset, the great hall was full of men and smoke, with not one but two hearths, at opposite sides of the hall, billowing out heat and flame and smoke in an attempt to stave off the cold winter's night.

Gates was coming from the gatehouse where he had just set posts for the night. Now that he had been back for three weeks, it was as if he'd never left. Jasper, who had been loaned the services of a pair of knights from the Earl of Worcester, Henry de Lohr, had been happy to return de Lohr's knights in favor of de Wolfe and his regular knights as soon as they had returned. It wasn't that he hadn't been grateful to the earl for the loan of the de Lohr knights, for he was quite grateful. In fact, Worcester's son, Alexander, had gone to France with the de Lara army, so their men were fairly intermingled.

Even now, Alexander was at Hyssington, staying a few weeks to rest before heading back to his father's seat of Lioncross Abbey. Nay, Jasper hadn't been ungrateful to de Lohr for the loan of the knights, but now it was more that he wanted to regain a sense of normalcy within his own ranks, which had been disoriented when all four knights had left to France. There was something about his captain, Gates de Wolfe, that held men together, an aura and strength about the man that was as legendary as his family name. Jasper had always relied heavily on the man and to lose him to Edward's wars in France had been a painful separation. Now that de Wolfe was back, Jasper wanted things to return to normal.

It was what he had prayed for.

Gates knew what his liege had prayed for. He knew how important it was for Gates and his other knights to return from what Jasper often termed "Edward's foolery". Gates had served Jasper since he had been a page, coming to serve the House of de Lara. He'd never left. He had grown up on the Marches and had proven himself as the great fighter and commander they knew today.

But Gates also knew that Jasper was somewhat over dependent on him, something that had been evident the first day they'd arrived back at Hyssington. It was as if something went out of Jasper when his senior knights returned and for the past three weeks, he'd done nothing but remain in his chamber as others ran the daily accounts for his properties.

As Gates approached the great hall with tendrils of smoke escaping through the thatched ceiling and bright, warm light emitting from the doorway and lancet windows, he wasn't entirely sure he could take another evening recounting the stories from Poitiers. Jasper had demanded tales nightly and Gates wasn't certain that he could sit through more of the revelry. As he considered his options, he saw his three subordinate knights approach from the troop house on the north side of the bailey. He slowed his pace as he and his men joined up.

"Greetings, de Wolfe," Alexander de Lohr was the first to speak. "So we are in for another night of Tales from the Bloody Mud? Who shall go first this night? I can tell you with confidence that it will not be me. I am all talked out."

Gates looked at the tall, blond knight who had become a close friend. Alexander had the de Lohr sky-blue eyes, golden hair, and infectious smile. He was also quite handsome and had been known to compete for female attention against Gates. So far, their record was nearly even in conquests although Alexander didn't have the sordid reputation that Gates did. He had been private with his female victories whilst Gates really didn't give a lick what people thought of his personal life. Still, Gates and Alexander were as close as brothers and Gates grinned at Alexander's statement.

"As am I," he said, glancing to the other two knights standing next to Alexander. "To be truthful, I am not entirely sure I can stand for any more stories of Poitiers. I do not see them as tales of glory as Jasper does. I see them as the loss of friends and of devastation in general. De Lara has no idea how horrible the conditions were even though we have tried to tell him. Still, he only sees knightly glamour and victory."

The knight standing next to Alexander snorted. Tobias Aston was a young knight from a good family with a muscular, sinewy build and long blond hair he kept tied at the back of his head. He was attractive, and skilled, and Gates had never seen a faster man in all his life. Tobias Aston, literally, moved like lightning.

"De Lara comes from a long line of great knights," Tobias said, "yet he has not seen a battlefield in years. He lives through our tales and has ever since his elder son was killed."

They all knew that. Roget de Lara, the shining star of the House of de Lara, had been killed at the Battle of Crècy ten years earlier whilst leading the de Lara army to victory. Jasper had taken the field at that time and after carrying Roget's body off the field of battle, the man never took up a sword ever again. He'd never even touched one as far as they knew. Therefore, even though their liege could be annoying, there was sympathy for the man and what he had lost.

"He still has his younger son, Jeffrey," Gates reminded them of what they already knew. "The lad is a knight but spends all of his time at court with Edward because Jasper believes he is safer there. Personally, I think the lad would be safer in a pit of vipers, but no one has asked for my opinion."

The other three knights laughed softly at Gates' quip. "And no one will," said the last knight, Stephan d'Avignon. A massive man with cropped, curly brown hair known as "Bear", Stephan came from a very old and battle-scarred family. He was no-nonsense and somewhat curt at times, but he was a knight to be trusted and admired. "The man sends his son to live in London, away from battle, and he sends his daughter to live in a convent. He is doing all he can to keep his children safe from the ills of the world."

"Yet he demands tales of battle," Gates said. "He wants to know the excitement of it without participating. "

That was a very true statement as far as they were concerned. Alexander sighed heavily. "De Lara is waiting for us right now to fill his head with more tales of battle and you know he will come looking for us if we do not make an appearance soon," he said. "It is therefore my suggestion that we swallow whatever distaste we have for telling the man stories of battle and simply get on with it."

Stephan made a face of displeasure. "What more can we possibly tell him?" he wanted to know. "We have told him everything we possibly can."

Gates eyed the burly knight. "*We* have told more stories than you have," he pointed out. "It is your turn to speak first this night, Bear. It is time for you to lay yourself open as the rest of us have."

Stephan threw up his hands. "But I do not have as many stories as you three have," he said. "I was holding the line while you were all off trying to outfight one another. The man with the greatest score of victories to impress the women with, eh?"

Gates and Alexander waved him off irritably as the four of them began moving towards the glowing entry to the hall. "There is nothing wrong with impressing women with tales of victory," Gates insisted, "and if I do not have any, I simply make them up. I do not need to outfight anyone, and especially not you three whelps."

Alexander cast him a long glance. "Then it must have been someone else I rode to help when his horse became mired in the mud at Poitiers."

Gates scratched his chin. "You only imagined such a thing."

"Did I?"

"If I say you did, then you did."

Alexander laughed softly. "Next time, I shall let you sink."

Gates grinned but didn't respond; he didn't acknowledge that Alexander had been forced to help him at Poitiers when he became stuck in the epic mud and quite possibly saved his life in doing so. The weather had been raining off and on for the past month and had created horrendous conditions at times, so to save his pride and not discuss what they all knew about de Lohr's heroics, Gates changed the subject.

"What do you think de Lara will say if you tell him that I had my tongue cut out today?" he asked. "Do you think he will believe you and therefore not demand more stories from me since I will clearly be unable to speak?"

As Alexander and Stephan shook their heads, Tobias spoke in his youthful and animated way. "He would make you write them down if you lost the ability to speak," he said. "He would make you draw pictures in the ashes. A missing tongue would not deter him from demanding stories."

Gates grunted. "Then we must take control of the conversation," he said as the entry to the hall loomed directly ahead now. "Do you think I can regale him with humorous tales instead?"

Alexander snorted. "You do *not* tell humorous tales, Gates."

"I do so."

Alexander rolled his eyes. "In case you have not yet discovered this about yourself, my darling lad, you are about as humorous as a barrel of dead babies," he said. Then, he sighed heavily. "There is no hope for us tonight. God's Bones, I think I feel an aching head coming on."

"And I am quite positive that I have contracted the plague," Alexander grumbled.

Stephan suddenly came to a halt and bent over, coughing violently although it was obvious that it was forced. "And I am, quite simply, dying," he said as he stood up, putting a hand over his chest. "Give my apologies to Lord de Lara. Tell him that I may not make it through the night."

It was a last-ditch effort from the knights to avoid going into the hall, now with the door right in front of them. Gates balled a fist at Stephan.

"And that outlook is guaranteed if you do not make your way into that hall under your own power," he said, looking at Tobias and pointing to the open door. "Go. Your liege awaits and your foolish excuses will not prevent the inevitable."

Stephan and Tobias made their way to the door as Gates and Alexander followed, although Alexander was dragging his feet. He was moving so slowly that he was holding Gates back, who put his hand on the man's back and finally pushed.

"Move," he growled. "Let us get this over with."

Alexander grunted unhappily but complied. The great oak door swung open and he followed Stephan and Tobias into the hall, hit in the face, as they all were, with the warm, stale heat that came from overworked hearths and too many bodies.

The smell, like dogs and unwashed men, did nothing to deter the appetite. Already, there was a great deal of feasting happening at the two long, overused feasting tables and over near one of the two blazing hearths, men were playing a game of strength. There were two teams, men on each team all latched on to each other and then somewhere in the middle, the two teams came together by one man from each team grabbing hold of a man on the opposite team.

Then, they began to pull in a great tug-of-war, each team trying to pull the other team off its feet. As the knights wound their way deeper into the hall, they could see that one team had pulled the other team straight into the hearth, laughing when clothes were lit on fire.

Stephan pointed at the men who were beating the flames out of their sleeves and hair, grinning, as Gates and Alexander shook their head in disapproval. But the game was catching on, and more and more men were tugging at each other, trying to throw one another into the flames. Gates simply walked past it all, followed by Alexander, as Stephan and Tobias observed the antics. But then Alexander realized they were lagging behind because they didn't want to sit with de Lara, so Alexander whistled between his teeth, catching their attention, and cast them a threatening expression that forced them to follow him. Soon, all four knights were approaching their liege.

The man was sitting at the end of the larger feasting table, gorging himself on boiled mutton that comprised the evening's meal. His wife was not with him, as was usual, as Lady de Lara preferred to take her meals in her room and away from the loud and smelly men. She wasn't one for socializing, anyway, and other than a glimpse now and again, no one had really ever seen her. She kept well to herself. Jasper de Lara, however, very much enjoyed the company of his men. He was still a handsome man at his advanced age, with graying blond hair and a bushy white and gray beard, now with spots of gravy on it. He was dressed heavily against the cold, in woolen tunics and a fur robe, and he smiled brightly when he saw his knights approach. He waved them forward.

"Ah!" he called out to them happily. "Come and sit, all of you. I thought you would never arrive! *Wine!*"

He bellowed the last word so loudly that Alexander, the closest to him, turned away and rubbed at his left ear, positive the eardrum was ruptured. Servants were running at the table from all directions, bringing cups and pitchers of the dark red wine that Jasper favored.

The knights sat around their liege as cups were placed in front of them and quickly filled, splashing red droplets onto the tabletop. Gates was just lifting his cup to his lips when he happened to catch movement next to his right arm. Turning, he found himself looking into familiar, sad, doggy eyes.

"Good evening to you, Jean," he said to the massive black dog with a head the size of a cow's skull. "I trust you have stayed away from the men trying to throw one another into the fire?"

He drank his wine as Jasper, across the table, laughed. "I named my dog after the French king so that I can order him about and be cruel to him," he said, affectionately eyeing the mutt that weighed more than most grown women. "But I love Jean more than my own family, unfortunately. He is a loyal and true friend. He seems to have taken a great liking to you, Gates. He has seemed most attentive to you since your return."

Gates eyed the dog, who was gazing back at him hopefully – hopeful that Gates would give him a scrap of food. Gates chuckled at the dog. "The dog has good taste," he said, reaching out to pet the big, black head. "I had a dog once, as a lad. A Wolfhound, of course."

He grinned at the play on his surname and the others chuckled. "My mother hates dogs," Alexander said flatly, already nearly done with his first cup of wine. "We had cats and horses. Lots and lots of cats and horses."

Jasper motioned for Alexander's cup to be refilled immediately. "And your father did not take a stand against your mother?" he asked. "I find that astonishing. No house should be without dogs."

Alexander held up his cup for his second helping of wine. "I agree," he said. "Which is why when I inherit Lioncross Abbey, I will flood it with dogs. There will be herds of them all about the place and if my wife doesn't like it, then she can go find accommodations elsewhere."

Jasper banged on the table. "Here, here," he declared firmly. "I applaud your attitude. A house without dogs is no house at all."

He drank deeply to his own toast as servants brought around the trenchers for the knights. The men dug into their food with gusto; in addition to the boiled mutton, which was heavily seasoned with pepper gravy, there were boiled carrots and a great portion of beans cooked in some kind of sauce. Along with the fresh bread and butter, it made for a fine meal and Gates was well into his food when he noticed a big dog head that was quite interested in his food as well. With a heavy sigh, Gates tore off mutton from the bone and fed it to Jean, one dog-bite for every two or three of his.

"Alexander, do you intend to leave for Lioncross soon?" Jasper asked as his men devoured their meal. "Your father loaned me about five hundred men last year when I was having some trouble with the Welsh. He also loaned me about fifty archers and some big wagons to carry supplies back and forth between my properties because the Welsh burned the last supply train I sent out. I should probably send the wagons and the men back to him when you leave."

Alexander was slopping up peppery gravy with his bread. "I was planning on leaving as soon as the weather clears a bit," he said. "It is a four-day ride to Lioncross but I would hate to get caught in a snow-storm. When it looks as if there will be more than a day of clear, I will take the chance and leave."

Gates fed Jean the last of the fat off the bone. "I can go with you to help with the men and wagons," he said. "I should like to pay my respects to your father and convey Lord de Lara's thanks for the generous loan of the men."

Before Alexander could reply, Jasper shook his head. "Nay, Gates," he said. "I have other plans for you."

Gates looked up from petting the dog on the side of his big head. "What is that?"

Jasper suddenly didn't seem so jovial. His manner took a sharp turn and he seemed rather frustrated, in truth. He swallowed a mouthful of wine before speaking.

"My wife wants me to send men to St. Milburga's Priory to retrieve our daughter," he said. "Gates, do you remember Kathalin? Of course you do not. A foolish question. She had been sent to foster before you ever entered my service. Do you ever remember me telling you of her?"

Gates shook his head. "Nay, my lord," he replied. "Other than a few mentions now and again, I do not know much about your daughter."

Jasper grunted, scratching his ear in a decidedly unhappy gesture. "Nor do I," he admitted. "She has been gone from me so long that I do not much remember the lass. My wife sent her away because she was never much good with young children around. Any manner of screaming or childhood drama would send the woman into fits, so, much as her brothers were, Kathalin was sent away to foster at five years of age. That was fourteen years ago. We have sent yearly dona-tions to St. Milburga's, of course, and we have paid well for her education there by the nuns, but we received a missive several months ago from the Abbess at St. Milburga's informing us that Kathalin wishes to commit herself to the cloister. She asked for our blessing and permission to do so."

The knights were listening with some interest because it was surprising to them that Jasper was speaking on something other than Poitiers and the wars in France. It was diversified dinner conversation that was a relief to them all.

"She wishes to become a nun?" Gates clarified. "It seems to me that if your daughter has been in a convent all of these years, then taking her vows would be a natural progression."

Jasper lifted his eyebrows, holding up his cup to the nearest servant for more wine. "That was my thought as well," he said, "although I had hoped to make a political match with her, marry her to a warlord somewhere. I suppose it is just as well that she remains in the convent and I do not have to supply her with a dowry. However, my wife does not want her to take her vows and has demanded I bring her home. Now, suddenly, she wants to be a mother to the girl. It is a stupid notion, I think. We do not even know the girl though she be our daughter. It seems like bringing a stranger back home."

That was evidently the basis for the frustration he felt in the situation because he slurped up his wine and demanded more food, his manner growing agitated. Jasper only seemed fond of his dogs and sons and men, never the womenfolk in the family. It was apparent that he viewed his daughter's return as the introduction of an unwanted element at Hyssington. He had little tolerance for women and their drama. Gates glanced at Alexander and Stephan before speaking.

"So you want me to ride to St. Milburga's and escort her home?" he asked. "There is a St. Milburga's in Ludlow, I believe."

Jasper was already nodding. "That is where she is," he said. "Take Stephan with you and fifty men. As you know, the Welsh have been launching raids along the Marches to steal what they can because of the harsh winter and I'll not have my daughter become a captive in exchange for all of my food stores. I should have her well protected by an escort."

Gates simply nodded. "Aye, my lord," he said. "When shall I go?"

"Immediately. For all I know, she may have already taken her vows, so there is no more time to waste."

"And if she has taken her vows, my lord?"

Jasper cast him a long look. "Get her out of that convent," he said. "I do not care how you do it, but vows or no vows, she is to come home. This is not open to negotiation."

Gates understood. He looked at Alexander. "My escort and I can come with you as far as Knighton where we will turn east for Ludlow," he said. "Mayhap it would be best if we got an early start on the morrow."

Just then, a roar of laughter and yelling rose up in the room and the knights turned to see that several soldiers had been pulled into one of the hearths. One man was running through the hall with his hair on fire whilst his friends tried to douse it. Alexander simply shook his head at the antics as he turned back to Gates.

"Mayhap we should make it the day after tomorrow," he said, eyeing the room of drunken, and in some cases burning, soldiers. "I do not think my men will be in any shape to travel come the morrow."

Gates could see his point. He turned back to his cup of wine, petting the dog next to him absently and coming to realize that he had just been given orders to violate the sanctity of a convent should Jasper's daughter have already taken her vows. Not that it particularly bothered him; he'd done many things in his life that he wasn't particularly proud of, actions that were a means to an end. But violating the sanctity of a priory was something altogether different.

Gates found himself hoping that the de Lara girl hadn't taken her vows simply so he wouldn't have to go through the trouble of breaking down the door to get at her. As he sat there and pondered what the future might bring, Jasper spoke up.

"Enough foolish talk," he declared, his mood swinging back in the direction of joviality. "Let us speak on far more entertaining things, like Poitiers. Who will tell me more tales tonight? Bear, I have not heard nearly enough from you. What will you tell me of the last phase of fighting when both Jean and his son, Philip, were on the field? Where were you during this time?"

Stephan struggled not to show any measure of displeasure at his liege's expected request. Dutifully, he thought back to that brutal and bloody day, thinking back to the friends he lost, to a close friend that had fought with him almost to the end only to be accidentally cut down by an English archer. It was a memory he did not wish to share but one that had him increasingly frustrated as de Lara pushed him for stories. Without the tact that his fellow knights had, Stephan was untried in keeping his thoughts buried.

Therefore, as de Lara pushed him beyond endurance, the entire story of his close friend dying in his arms with an arrow to the back of the neck came out and the disgust in the Battle of Poitiers was made clear by a man who did not wish to relive it, not even to his liege. It was a harrowing and painful story that emerged, one without humor and by the time Stephan was finished telling it, de Lara was gazing back at him with a measure of shock and sorrow. Suddenly, there was no more joy in demanding stories from Poitiers for Jasper de Lara. Beyond the glory of the English victory were the stories of grief. That was what men on the battlefield truly felt.

Jasper learned, after that night, not to demand any more tales of Poitiers lest he hear stories like the one d'Avignon told him. Inevitably, it reminded Jasper of Roget's death ten years earlier as the man had been impaled by a pike upon the muddy, violent fields of Crècy, a raw wound to Jasper's memory that had never properly healed.

After that night and tales of Stephan's dying friend, the raw wound bled openly once again.

And so did a father's grieving heart.

CHAPTER TWO

St. Milburga's Priory
Ludlow

CLANG!
That was what the iron pot in her hand sounded like when it came into contact with a human skull. Trapped in the kitchen as an influx of Welsh raiders ran amok through the wing of the cloister, she'd had no choice but to fight back with the only weapons she could find. The Welsh didn't seem to be interested in the women in particular, but more in the food or any valuables they could find. They shoved nuns aside or, in one case, barricaded the Mother Prioress in a closet by blocking the door, and ran through the cloister taking anything they could carry. On this day at St. Milburga's, chaos reigned.

Until they came to the kitchen. A big, rectangular-shaped room with a dirt floor and enormous, bricked hearth, it was stocked with winter stores and there was a woman inside that had decided to fight back. Backed into a corner with a handled iron pot in her hand, the young woman in charge of the kitchen was dressed in the rough, brown woolen garments of a novice nun but possessed silky dark hair and brilliant blue eyes that lauded astounding beauty normally not usually seen in the cloister. But that beauty was marred with anger on this day and she had swung the pot at the invaders for all she was worth. *Smack!* A hit against a hand and men would howl.

The raiders were trying to relieve the kitchen, and the priory, of barrels of dried beans and vegetables, items intended to keep the priory supplied throughout the winter, but the young woman with the pot in her hand would not permit it. St. Milburga's Priory had known raids before from the Welsh, especially when food was scarce, but this raid was particularly bad. There were many starving Welshmen who wanted what the priory had, and the nuns and wards of the priory found themselves fending off a fairly serious invasion of men intent to plunder their meager resources. Even Welsh children were involved this time, making it harder to fight back for the healing order of nuns.

Even so, the Welsh could not be permitted to steal the food that the priory needed in order to survive, which meant the nuns found themselves on the defensive, most especially the young woman in the kitchen. When the pot became too heavy for her to bear, she collected a big piece of wood stacked neatly near the hearth and began using it like a club.

"Go away!" she shouted. "Go away or be damned! God will punish you for this, do you hear?"

The Welsh mostly spoke their native tongue and did not completely understand her, although a few of them understood her words quite clearly when she brained them with the wood. The tall lass was not beyond aiming for the heads, and sometimes the buttocks, of the Welsh who were trying to steal from her. Oddly enough, however, they didn't try to fight back – they grabbed for items from the kitchen, whatever foodstuffs they could get their hands on, and the young woman would chase them down with her wooden club.

However, not all of them would allow her to chase them away. One Welshman, young and big, grabbed at a barrel of barley, which was quite heavy. When the young woman rushed him with her club, he reached out a hand to shove her back, nearly pushing her into the hearth. This only seemed to infuriate her and she leapt to her feet, exchanging the wood for a long iron spit that they used to roast meat on. It had a pointed edge, like a dagger, and she went after the man with it.

The Welshman had his back to her as he tried to flee, only catching a glimpse of the spit in her hands at the last moment. Since he had the barrel of barley in his arms, he had to drop the thing in order to defend himself and prevent the young woman from goring him. The wooden barrel fell to the dirt floor and exploded, sending barley everywhere.

The Welshman and the young woman wrestled with the iron spit for a few moments; he was trying to take it from her and she was trying not to let him. But he was much stronger and managed to yank it from her hands, injuring her palms as he jerked it free. Just as he managed to wrest it from her, his cohorts began to yell in their harsh language, their shouts echoing against the cloister, and the Welshman with the spit bolted from the kitchen, still holding the spit. Enraged that he'd taken her weapon, and now with bloodied palms, the young woman ran back to the hearth to reclaim her wooden club.

Racing to the kitchen door, she came to a sudden halt as she heard the sounds of heavy fighting going on outside of the kitchen. Instead of simply screams and running feet, she could now hear weapons clashing, metal against metal. Someone, somehow, had brought weapons into this raid and she could hear the sounds of a battle quite clearly now, growing worse.

The main entry in and out of the kitchen opened into the cloister, a covered walkway that joined the Servery, or dormitory for the nuns, to the kitchen and to the refectory and the rest of the priory. Beyond the cloister, in the center of the collection of buildings, was an open grassy area, called The Garth, where the novice nuns and wards often performed their lessons.

It was in The Garth that the young woman in the kitchen seemed to hear most of the fighting going on. Her rage cooled and she began to feel a hint of fear as she peeked around the side of the open door to see The Garth beyond. Immediately, she could see soldiers with weapons, battling the poorly-dressed Welsh, and she caught a glimpse of at least one heavily-armed knight as he rode his big, armored steed beneath the covered cloister. The knight seemed to be chasing the Welsh with his enormous broadsword and as she watched, he caught up to one and gored the man when he tried to fight back.

Now, dead Welsh were littering The Garth as a serious battle went on inside the walls of St. Milburga's. The young woman's anger at the raiders fled; now she was terrified for her safety and she pulled back into the kitchen and slammed the heavy, worn oak door, which had a broken iron bolt on it. The Mother Prioress had never seen the need to repair it, so now the young woman had no real means of protecting herself should the knight, or armed soldiers, decide to invade the kitchen.

But she had her wooden club and she looked at the thing, knowing it would not be enough against an armored knight. She needed something heavier, something that could do damage against the well-protected warrior.

Racing back over to the hearth, she picked up the handled iron pot again, knowing it would be the only true defense against such a man. Moreover, she had to strike first, to stun him or even knock him unconscious so she could run away and have a fighting chance against the madness going on around her.

Rushing back to the kitchen door, now closed, she positioned herself against the wall next to the panel so that when it was opened, she would be behind it and not be seen. She would at least have a few moments to come up behind whoever entered the kitchen and smash them over the head. God forgive her for truly hurting the man, but she would not be taken prisoner, or worse.

She had to fight.

As the sounds of battle continued outside her door, the young woman pressed against the wall and listened, praying fervently that no one would make any attempt to open the kitchen door. She prayed that they would simply bypass the kitchen but she knew that was a foolish hope; the kitchen contained most of the value of St. Milburga's. It was what the Welsh were after and as she clutched the iron pot to her chest, she looked around the kitchen at the damage done by the raiders.

The burst barrel of barley was on the floor near the door. She wasn't particularly worried about that, as the barley could be swept up. A few bags of dried beans had been taken, and a slab of precious pork that had been hanging from the ceiling rafters, but in all, they hadn't lost too much. She wanted to keep it that way but she wasn't entirely sure she could fight off hordes of men with swords. The Welsh hadn't been armed, at least not that she could see, but the second group of men that were in The Garth… they were armed, and heavily so.

She was jolted from her thoughts when something heavily bumped against the old oak door. The door rattled and young woman jumped, shrieking with fright, before quickly biting her lips together. She didn't want to be heard. *Sweet Jesus, do not let me be heard!* she prayed, but it was too late. Someone had evidently heard her cry of fear. The door lurched again and abruptly opened, spilling forth an enormous knight in expensive and well-used armor.

Terror seized the young woman. The knight was barely through the door when she ran up behind him and hit him as hard as she could on the back of his helmed head with her iron pot. He fell like a stone and she pounced, beating him with the iron pot rather haphazardly, trying to strike him on the head again but the pot was so heavy that she ended up hitting him in the neck and shoulders and back with it. The knight, face-down on the dirt floor, grunted in pain.

"You beast!" she shrieked. "How dare you invade our home! I will beat you to a bloody pulp, do you hear?"

She was straddling his back at this point, trying to pin him down with her insignificant weight as she beat him with the pot. Unfortunately, her arms grew quite tired very quickly as the knight put up a hand to try to protect his head.

"I am not here to harm or harass you," he said, his voice muffled against his faceplate. "I swear I mean you no harm, Sister."

The young woman wasn't convinced but her arms were so weary that she could hardly lift the pot anymore. She ended up putting it on his head so that it was engulfing most of his helm as she leaned forward and put all of her weight on it, attempting to keep his head down.

"Then who are you?" she demanded. "What are you doing here?"

The knight was amply protected against her assault but the pot on his head had him in an awkward position, especially with her leaning on it.

"My name is Gates de Wolfe," he said evenly. "I serve the Earl of Trelystan."

The young woman's features rippled with confusion and, bewildered, she backed off the pressure on his head. "The Earl of Trelystan?" she repeated, mulling over his surprising statement. But when she realized she was no longer nearly lying on his head, she pushed her weight forward again, onto the pot, to keep him down. "Lies! You are not from Trelystan!"

The knight beneath her had, so far, made no move to fight back. He simply lay on the cold dirt floor and let her beat on him.

"I am, I swear this to you," he said. "Lord de Lara has sent me but when we came upon St. Milburga's, we walked right into a raid. We have managed to subdue them, Sister. You need not be afraid any longer."

His explanation made a good deal of sense about the Welsh and a second group of armed men appearing in The Garth. Now the young woman was coming to understand somewhat, but she was still frightened and bewildered. In her confusion, she eased the pressure upon his head once more.

"Have they gone?" she asked. "The Welsh, I mean. Are they gone?"

Gates sensed that she had relaxed and he was quick to take advantage of it. He didn't have time to fool around with a frightened nun. Quick as lightning, he pushed himself up, pushed her off, and flipped her over onto her back. Suddenly, he was on top of her with her arms pinned over her head with one hand. As his body weight and one hand kept her wrists immobile, he used his other hand to lift his visor and look at her.

The truth was that he had fully expected to see a nun beneath him – one who wore woolen clothing to chafe her skin and remind her of the vanity of the flesh, one who did not bathe regularly, and one who shaved her head to do away with worldly beauty. He knew she was young by the sound of her voice but other than the usual expectations, he had nothing beyond that.

Therefore, the fact that he had expected something unspectacular and crude somehow made the shock of the opposite that much stronger. Lifting his visor to gain a clear look at the nun who had assaulted him, he was literally jolted with surprise as his gaze fell upon beauty so angelic and unearthly that he could hardly believe what he was seeing. The woman had skin like cream, full and rosy lips, nearly black hair that was now covered with dirt from the floor of the kitchen, and the most brilliant blue eyes he had ever seen.

It was like finding a rose amongst sewage or a white dove amongst ravens. For such beauty to be found amongst the confines of a priory made no sense to him at all. Stunned, Gates had to literally catch his breath, make a conscious effort to swallow, and then resume breathing before venturing to speak.

"Who *are* you?" he finally asked, his voice sounding strangely raspy.

The young woman was frightened but trying not to show it. "Please," she asked softly, "do not hurt me."

Gates couldn't help but watch her lush lips as she spoke, feeling oddly flushed at the sound of her whispery, sweet voice. "I told you that I would not harm you," he said, lifting a dark eyebrow. "But *you* tried to take my head off. I want your vow that you will not try anything so foolish again if I release you. Do I have your promise, Sister?"

The young woman shook her head, her dark hair brushing against the dirt of the floor. "I am not a sister."

Her reply did nothing to abate his puzzlement. "Then what are you?"

"A ward," she said. "That is, I hope to be a novice very soon. I have lived here most of my life. You said that the Earl of Trelystan sent you?"

Gates nodded. "He did."

"Prove this to me. What is his name?"

Her question confused him even more. "Why should I?"

"Because I have asked this of you," she said, forcing her bravery. "You told me that I need not be afraid. If you want me to trust your word, then tell me his name."

It was rather demanding but he almost found it amusing. Here she was, pinned beneath him, and in spite of her obvious fear, she was still prepared to make demands. He saw no harm in answering her.

"Jasper de Lara."

The woman seemed to ease somewhat; he could feel her body relax beneath him, which would have been quite arousing under different circumstances.

"Aye, it is," she finally said.

"And how do you know?"

"Because I am his daughter."

Gates wasn't even aware that his jaw dropped. *I am his daughter.* God's Bones, was it even possible that in the great labyrinth of the cloister, he happened upon the one thing he was actually looking for? He could hardly believe his fortune.

When he and his men had ridden up to the priory swarming with Welsh, he truly hadn't known if he'd find any female flesh still intact much less the exact lady he was looking for. But here she was and evidently unharmed. Still... as he gazed at the woman, a more selfish thought crossed his mind – was it actually possible that old Jasper de Lara bred such fineness out of his fat, worn body and this glorious creature was actually a de Lara? The mere thought boggled the mind.

But the fact remained that identity had been established. Without any reason to keep her pinned, Gates let go of the woman and climbed off of her.

"Lady Kathalin, I presume?"

Lady Kathalin Elizabeth du Bois de Lara slowly pushed herself up from the hard-packed earth, rubbing her elbow where she had bruised it when the big knight had flipped her onto her back.

"Aye," she said. "Did my father send you with a message?"

Gates reached down to help her, assisting the woman to her feet, inspecting her closely as she stood up. She was somewhat tall for a woman, and rather slender, but now that he was seeing her in full view, he realized that he'd never seen such magnificence. He was quite in awe of her, struggling to keep his composure at the surprise of the entire situation.

"I will tell you why I have come, but first you will tell me something," he said. "Were you injured in the raid? Are you sound and whole?"

Kathalin nodded. "I am well," she said, unwilling to mention the bruised elbow she was still rubbing. "They did not hurt me but it would seem that you arrived just in time."

As the volatile situation between them eased, Gates unlatched his helm and pushed it up off of his face so that the bottom of it rested on his forehead. He wiped at his sweaty, stubbled face.

"I would agree with that statement," he said. "But what about the garrison at Ludlow Castle? They are not far away. Why did you not send word to them?"

Kathalin shook her head. "It is possible that word was sent," she said. "I would not know. I have been in the kitchen since the assault began, trying to prevent the Welsh from stealing our food stores."

That made some sense to Gates as he scratched at his neck. "I see," he said. "I have heard of the Welsh raiding villages, but to raid a priory is bold even for them. How long have they been here?"

Kathalin shook her head, eyeing the very big knight. He had hazel-gold eyes, dark hair from what she could see of it tucked underneath his helm, and a granite-square jaw with a pronounced cleft in his chin. He was tall, too – quite tall, with shoulders nearly as wide as the door frame. And the hands he lifted to wipe his face were the size of trenchers. She'd never seen so handsome, nor so big, a man at close range and she had to admit that it was both frightening and strangely alluring. But she would never admit the last part, of course. Future nuns were not to be enticed by men, but if they were, this one might fit that bill.

Her heart fluttered a bit, giddy.

"Not long," she replied belatedly to his question. "Mayhap less than an hour before you fortuitously arrived. You said that my father sent you? Do you come with a message?"

She was asking the question again, the one he'd failed to answer the first time. Gates finished scratching his face and neck, pulling his helm down over his head again.

"The message I bring is that your father wants you returned home, Lady Kathalin," he said, finding some pleasure in that statement because it would mean escorting the woman, and staying close to her, for the return journey. "Your mother and father have recalled you to be with them."

Kathalin's brow furrowed in confusion. "Why?"

Gates shrugged. "This, I would not know," he said, eyeing her, and in particular, her clothing. "You said that you were not a sister?"

Kathalin shook her head. "Not yet," she said. "The Mother Prioress sent my father a missive back in the summer asking his permission but my father has not yet answered. That is why I thought you had come bearing a message from him, an answer to the Mother Prioress' query. But instead, he sends you to bring me back to Trelystan?"

Gates nodded. "Your parents are wintering at Hyssington Castle, my lady," he said, addressing her properly now that he knew, much to his relief, that she was not yet a nun. "If you will gather your possessions, we must return immediately."

Kathalin's furrowed brow turned into a full-blown frown. "Why?" she asked, exasperation in her tone. "This is my home, Sir Knight. I do not wish to return to my parents."

Gates hoped he wasn't going to have a problem with her. The last thing he wanted to do was carry her, kicking and screaming, out of the priory in his quest to carry out his orders.

"You will forgive me, my lady, for suggesting that your concerns are something you must discuss with your father," he said. "I am only the messenger. I have my orders and I would ask politely that you help me to complete them."

Kathalin eyed the enormous man, her first reaction one of refusal. However, she suspected that refusal would not be well met and she didn't want to find herself bound and gagged, thrown across the back of his horse for transport to her family's home. Although Gates de Wolfe seemed polite and had not been aggressive towards her even when she was beating him in the head with her pot, she was fairly certain that she didn't want to provoke him. It would not end well, for either one of them. Therefore, she took a step back from him, away from arm's reach.

"But I do not want to go," she said quietly. "I appreciate that you have your orders, but I do not want to go. This is where I live. I manage the kitchens and every day, I teach some of the children in the village the good words from the Holy Scripture. My entire life is here and I hope you can understand that I do not wish to answer a summons by my father, who is a stranger to me. He is my father in name only."

Gates could see that she was trying to reason with him but the fact remained that he had his orders. "My lady, I can appreciate your position," he said patiently, "but this is something you must discuss with your father. I cannot make any decision for or against you. You must come with me and after discussing these things with your father, it is up to him whether or not he will permit you to return."

Kathalin pondered his response. She was terrified that if she allowed him to take her home, her father might not ever let her return to St. Milburga's. She had no idea why the man was summoning her after fourteen years of virtual silence; it was the first such summons in all of that time. She had lived at St. Milburga's quite happily since leaving her parents, people who were ghosts to her. She forgot she even had parents most of the time because they had made it clear they had no use for their only daughter. At least, they had no use up until now. But something had prompted her father to call her home and she didn't like it one bit. Uncertainty made her very apprehensive.

I do not want to leave my home!

"But why?" she finally asked, feeling tears sting her eyes. "Why does he want me to come home?"

Even though Gates knew why, he wasn't sure how much to tell her. Still, he felt as if he should tell her something. He could see that she was quite upset by the unexpected summons.

"It is my understanding that your mother wants you to come home," he said quietly. Then, he gestured towards the door. "If you please, my lady? I should like to leave as soon as possible."

Kathalin sighed heavily, turning away from him, despondent. "My mother," she repeated, disgust in her tone. "I have not seen my mother in fourteen years, Sir Knight. I do not even know her. Do you know what my last memory of her is? When she screamed at me for something, something I do not even recall, and then she slapped me across the mouth. The next day, I was bundled up and sent away with two soldiers for escort, one of which kept pinching my... well, suffice it to say he pinched something he should not have. Dear God, I was only five years old at the time. What kind of man would do that? And what kind of mother would send her child away like that?"

Gates was listening to her with some sympathy. But he was mostly watching her delicious backside when she turned away from him, a shapely back that flared into hips that disappeared beneath layers of brown wool. He found himself wondering what she looked like underneath all of that fabric but when she finished her impassioned speech and turned to him, expecting an answer, he was caught daydreaming about her shapely behind. Embarrassed, he cleared his throat, trying to cover his blunder.

"My lady, I cannot pretend to know your mother's mind," he said. "All I know is that I was ordered to bring you to your parents. Will you please come with me?"

Kathalin was hoping for a bit more compassion from the man.

"And if I refuse?"

Gates met her intense gaze with intensity of his own. "I hope you will not."

"If I do?"

"Then I have been ordered to bring you home by any means necessary."

So he revealed his true determination that she should come with him. She smiled thinly. "Then all of this politeness from you was a ruse," she said. "You are going to take me whether or not I comply with your requests. Why not tell me that from the start?"

"Because I was hoping I would not have to."

Kathalin opened her mouth to reply when a Welsh raider, evidently fleeing English pursuers, suddenly bolted in through the door. Kathalin screamed at the sight of him and Gates, spurred by her scream, acted on his training; quick as a flash, he threw his big shoulder against the door, slamming the Welshman between the door jamb and the door panel, hitting him so hard that the Welshman hit his head on the door itself. It was enough to stun him so that the two English soldiers chasing him were able to grab the man and haul him, dazed, away.

Kathalin stood there, hand to her mouth in fright, as Gates watched his soldiers drag the man off. He also passed a practiced eye over The Garth, noting that nearly all of the Welsh had been commanded to sit on the muddy ground whilst his men corralled them. Stephan, astride his big, red war horse, was ordering the wounded gathered in one spot. After several moments of watching the activity, Gates finally returned his attention to Kathalin.

"Well, my lady?" he asked. "Will you come peacefully or will you and I have to slug it out? The choice is yours."

Shaken by the abrupt appearance of the errant Welshman, Kathalin struggled to appear as if she wasn't shaken in the least. But it was more than that; when de Wolfe had charged the door and thrown his weight against it to disable the man, she could see in that brief moment exactly how powerful the knight was. He was unstoppable, as strong as a bull, and she could only imagine his skill with a blade was equal. He was not one to be trifled with and her fear of him made a return.

It was strength that could be turned against her.

Still, it didn't lessen her determination not to go with him. She had been unable to reason her way out of it and it was obvious he had no compassion about her position. He would essentially be dragging her out of her home, taking her to strangers who had control over her life. Strangers who had discarded her at a very young age. Knowing reason or brute strength would be no good against the knight, she had to be more clever than he was. A battle of wits was her last defense against him.

She had to try because, Sweet Jesus, she truly did not wish to leave St. Milburga's.

She didn't want to go.

"I wish to speak with the Mother Prioress," she said. "Is that too much to ask?"

Gates shook his head. "Not at all, my lady," he said, smiling to give her a glimpse of those de Wolfe dimples. It was a calculated move on his part, hoping to dazzle her a bit. "You and I will go and find her together, although I cannot imagine where she would be in the midst of this mess. Do you have any thoughts on the matter?"

Kathalin wasn't particularly moved by the dimples, although it made the handsome man ever more handsome. She was too caught up in her own turmoil to appreciate the glorious gesture. Moreover, she wasn't sure where the Prioress was but she intended to hunt the woman down. There was a very specific question she wanted to ask her, the woman who had been more of a mother to her than her own ever was. She wasn't going to leave without seeing the woman one last time and pleading for her intervention. At this point, it was Kathalin's last hope.

Will you offer me sanctuary, Mother Benedicta, so I may remain at St. Milburga's?

Aye, it was a calculated question. Silently, she left the kitchen with Gates right behind her, quite possibly tailing her closely so that in case she decided to run, he could quickly curtail the action. But Kathalin didn't have a mind to run, at least not yet. She wanted to find the Mother Prioress first, a woman who went by the name of Mother Benedicta.

The first big dormitory-like room they came to was called the Refectory where the sick were usually housed, but at the moment it only had a few frightened nuns huddled in it and no Mother Prioress, so they continued on through chambers with names like the Warming Room and the Day Room. Continuing through the cloister to see that the Welsh had, indeed, torn the place apart in their search for possessions of value, they came to a room called the Prioress' Seat and, following the peculiar sounds of banging, found the woman locked up in a small wardrobe.

The Mother Prioress, a tall and rather wide woman, was very glad to see Kathalin but very puzzled to see the enormous knight accompanying her. Even when Gates explained who he was, the Prioress was still not entirely accepting of him. She was more interested in the state of her priory than in the big English knight, which didn't help her attitude in the least, not even with Kathalin told the woman that it was the English knights who had saved them from the Welsh.

Gates stood by while Kathalin followed the flustered Mother Prioress around, collecting the nuns and wards and servants, and even a few children, and gathering them all together in the sanctuary to count heads and offer prayers for their safety and health. He even stood by while they prayed, standing in the back of the cavernous sanctuary that smelled of dirt and heavily-fatted incense, and he was eventually joined by Stephan who informed him that they had forty-four Welsh prisoners as a result of the raid.

Gates certainly hadn't expected the burden of prisoners when he'd come to collect Kathalin de Lara but that was exactly what he found himself with, and his frustration began to surface. Mostly, it was centered around Kathalin and the fact that she seemed to find the need for very long prayers on this day.

As he watched the entire priory pray, keeping an eye on Kathalin's dark head, Gates told Stephan to take the Welsh to Ludlow Castle, only a couple of miles away, where they could better handle the prisoners. Gates, however, didn't go himself; he wanted to remain close to the source of his increasing frustration because something told him not to let Kathalin out of his sight.

It was an instinct that proved to be correct. When prayers were over and the Mother Prioress informed him that Kathalin was not allowed to leave with him because she had been granted sanctuary on the basis of escaping parental abuse and a genuine desire to serve God, Gates unhappily carried out his orders down to the letter and extracted Kathalin de Lara from St. Milburga's Priory by force.

In the end, he did what he hadn't wanted to do – he ended up carrying a struggling woman, bound hand and foot, out of the only home she had ever known.

CHAPTER THREE

H^{ATE.}

H Kathalin wasn't familiar with the feeling much but she knew that every time she looked at Gates de Wolfe, that was exactly what she felt.

Hate.

Any man who could so coldly and callously pull her from her home was a man to be hated. He'd dragged her out of St. Milburga's as the Mother Prioress wailed, creating a truly chaotic and distressing situation, and the knight had kept her bound and seated in front of him as they made their way north through snow-white landscape and freezing winds that knocked the snow from the trees. As they had traveled along, they could hear the clumps of snow hitting the wet, slushy road around them.

He had shown his true character as he'd pulled her from the priory, a man of brutality and cruelty. Kathalin prayed that one of the snow clumps would fly off the tree and hit de Wolfe in the head as punishment for his actions, unfamiliar feelings of vengeance and hate filling her for what he had done. She should have felt guilty for such emotions but she couldn't manage to feel that way.

All she could feel at the moment was utter devastation at what had happened and the fear of an unknown future. All of it, thanks to de Wolfe. He rode silently behind her, his big right arm around her torso to steady them both on the saddle, but since leaving the priory, he'd not said a word to her. She hadn't said a word to him, either, so they traveled together in tense and terrible silence.

It made for an uncomfortable ride until sunset when clouds rolled in and the winds increased, and Kathalin was so cold that her lips were blue. De Wolfe hadn't noticed because of her position in front of him and, with layers of protection between her body and his, he couldn't feel her trembling with the cold. Only when the other knight, a burly beast of man with a great brown beard who had been introduced as Stephan d'Avignon, pointed out the fact that the lady was cold did de Wolfe react. He had someone bring him a rain cloak because it was really all they had and while he held her steady, the bear-like knight covered her up adequately with it.

The cloak hadn't provided much warmth but it had at least provided protection against the cold winds. Exhausted, and distraught, Kathalin continued to ride in cold silence, refusing to utter a sound, well into the night until they reached the large village of Craven Arms where de Wolfe sent d'Avignon to secure lodgings for the night. As de Wolfe wait with a half-frozen woman and his escort on the edge of town, the burly knight returned within an hour to inform them that he had secured two rooms in a tavern and that he'd also found a livery for the men to sleep in, which they gladly did.

The warm haven of the tavern turned out to be a nightmare.

Unfortunately, the establishment was very loud, smelly, and full of people nearly all night long and the two rooms the knight had secured were nothing more than small chambers off the kitchen that the servants usually slept in. The tavern keeper had rented them out, however, with the lure of money to make, so Kathalin and de Wolfe crammed into one room whilst d'Avignon took the second room.

It made an awkward situation worse when Kathalin realized de Wolfe intended to sleep in the same chamber with her even though he politely yet professionally informed her that it was simply to prevent her from escaping.

Frustrated and fighting off tears, Kathalin refused to lay on the bed at all, embarrassed at the impropriety of it. De Wolfe, seeing how distressed she was, untied her hands and allowed her to relieve herself and stretch her muscles, but he didn't trust the woman and ended up tying her to the only chair in the chamber because she wouldn't lie down on the bed. Kathalin's first night away from St. Milburga's was spent trussed up to a broken chair.

It was a barbaric situation to say the least. Kathalin wept quietly most of the night, knowing that de Wolfe was watching her but hardly caring. She was so distraught and drained that she could hardly think straight. But she fell asleep at some point because de Wolfe woke her up before sunrise to ask her if she was hungry. Kathalin simply shook her head and looked away, unwilling to speak with him in any fashion, so de Wolfe untied her long enough to allow her to relieve herself again but the ropes went back on before they continued on their journey.

Hate.

That was all she could manage to feel for the man and the next day of travel was even more miserable. Kathalin only had the rain cloak for protection, wearing the same uncomfortable brown wool she had been wearing when Gates hauled her out of the priory and even though the wool was warm, it wasn't enough against the icy temperatures.

Wrapped up in the cloak, d'Avignon had put her on Gates' horse, seated behind the man this time, but her hands were still bound and Gates held the end of the rope in case she decided to jump off and run. She wouldn't go far if she tried. It was quite clear she was a prisoner to anyone observing the situation. The earl's daughter was now evidently a captive.

The snow returned as they traveled on the second day, first in a light dusting but then increasing in intensity every hour. By the time mid-afternoon rolled around, it was nearly blizzard conditions and Gates knew he had to find shelter before they all froze to death, so he stopped at the very next village they came to.

There were a few homes, two or three businesses that could be seen near the town's well, and a small inn near the north end of the town. It was a *very* small inn, no bigger than a home to be truthful, but that was his destination and he didn't care how crowded it was. As the whiteout from the snow began to blur everything around them, the tiny inn was to be their shelter for the night.

The escort came to a halt in the snow-covered street and Stephan ordered the men to find the nearest livery to safely store the wagon and the horses for the night as Gates pulled Kathalin from his steed. The heavy-boned war horse went with the soldiers towards shelter while Gates and Stephan, followed by Kathalin being led by the rope around her wrists, headed for the inn.

Predictably, the structure was full to the rafters. As Gates, Kathalin, and Stephan entered the place, the smoky and cramped inn wasn't particularly inviting. But it was dry and that was all that really mattered. Initial observations of the room showed that it had a loft above the common room where bodies were already piled in and sleeping. Further investigation showed two additional sleeping rooms upstairs that were barely big enough for a man to move around it.

It didn't matter, however, and Gates ended up paying the innkeeper a very valuable gold crown for the privilege of the loft and the two rooms, enough so most of his men had a warm, dry place to sleep and he and Kathalin and d'Avignon had sleeping rooms. The majority of his men crowded into the inn to get out of the snow, pushing out heavy-clothed patrons and roughing up those who resisted. Gates instructed the innkeeper and the two frightened wenches by his side to feed his men and make them comfortable for the night. He tossed a few more silver groats at the man to make it worth his while and with that, he pulled Kathalin up the stairs behind him.

The de Lara army had taken over the inn for the night.

Only one of the sleeping rooms, the larger of the two, had two beds and a window that overlooked the snowy street below. The second room was windowless except for a very small hole in the wall up near the ceiling for ventilation, and was barely big enough for the small bed that was jammed into it.

A wide-open hole in the wall served as a hearth, shared with the loft on the other side of the wall so the hearth was open on both sides, and the chamber was exceedingly warm, which was a relief considering how cold it was outside. Gates inspected the chamber and realized that, other than the door, there was no way to escape unless one wanted to leap through the flames to the loft on the other side. He hoped Kathalin wasn't that foolish. He pushed the door open wide and indicated for her to enter.

"My lady," he said emotionlessly. "If you please."

Half-frozen, disheveled, and exhausted, Kathalin didn't even look at him as she did as she was told and entered the chamber. But Gates stopped her just inside the door and silently untied the ropes around her wrists. When he pulled the rope off, he could see that the skin beneath them was chaffed and bleeding. Her wrists were badly irritated and he tried not to feel guilty about it.

He was coming to realize the woman had been traveling in terrible conditions for the past two days and had never uttered a word of complaint. He supposed he had known of her discomfort from the onset but was only now willing to acknowledge it as tempers cooled, mostly his. Her lack of complaint both impressed him and made him feel moderately ashamed of his callous treatment of her. She was a lady, after all, and he should have been more chivalrous, but it seemed that his chivalry fled the moment she fought him tooth and nail when he removed her from St. Milburga's.

In fact, if he thought hard on it, perhaps it was because she had damaged his pride. No lady in recent memory had ever denied him his wants, and even though he'd not been romantically pursuing Lady Kathalin, she had still denied him his wishes. He had tried to use the de Wolfe charm on her and it hadn't worked. She had refused his wishes and, truth be told, he was insulted by that. Now, he was starting to feel like a fool.

A fool that had let his pride get in the way of his better judgment.

"I will not bind you in this chamber," he told her. "There is no way for you to escape unless you want to leap through flames to do it, and I do not believe you are that stupid. However, know that this door will be guarded and if you make any move to open it, I will replace the ropes on your wrists and tie you to the bed. Is this in any way unclear?"

Kathalin wouldn't look at him, rubbing her raw skin where the rope had injured her. "It is clear," she muttered.

She didn't say any more than that. Frankly, Gates didn't expect her to. She was beaten and subdued, thanks to him. That's what he wanted, wasn't it? Perhaps it was, once, but now he was coming to feel pity for her. He had been professional yet harsh in completing his orders, and he had come out on top in their dispute. And complete victory was exactly what he wanted.

... wasn't it?

Gates' gaze lingered on Kathalin for a moment before quietly shutting the door and putting two of his best men to guard it. He gave them explicit instructions about keeping the door shut and not letting the lady out, no matter what, before heading down to the common room to seek out the innkeeper. Passing Stephan at the bottom of the stairs as the man slurped his way through a cup of hot ale, Gates went on the hunt.

The innkeeper wasn't difficult to find, back in the kitchens preparing food for dozens of unexpected and demanding guests. Gates exchanged a few words with the man, wanting information on the businesses in town even though they were closed. When he took Kathalin from St. Milburga's, it was without any clothing or possessions whatsoever. A rain cloak had been the only thing she'd had for two days to keep her warm and it clearly wasn't adequate. She needed more.

Therefore, Gates knew the only decent thing to do was to purchase the woman a few necessities because she literally had nothing and maybe if he did that, he wouldn't feel so bloody guilty for treating her so poorly. For acting like a barbarian because his pride was hurt because she hadn't folded to his will, swooning over the flashing de

Wolfe dimples.

Obtaining the name of a merchant who carried all manner of general goods, Gates took a few of his men with him as he ventured out into the snowy night. The snow was blowing vertically as he and four of his men entered the streets of the town. Snow was already gathering in big drifts against the front of the buildings and he counted five doors before he came to the one the innkeeper told him about. He had his helm on and his visor lowered to keep the snow out of his eyes, and he rapped heavily on the door, several times, before a light appeared in the small window next to the door and a man's voice shouted at him to go away.

Standing out in the blizzard, and quite unhappy about it, Gates gave the man a choice – opening the door or kicking it open, to which the man wisely opened it. Gates and his soldiers pushed their way into a small but comfortable room, well appointed, where Gates explained his needs to the terrified elderly man and woman he had just roused right out of their beds.

Goods, he needed. *Any manner of ladies' goods.* He even produced his coin purse and put a handful of silver coins on the nearest table to prove two things – he wasn't there to rob them and he was serious about obtaining ladies' necessities. When the couple saw the money, they were a little less fearful, enough so that the man opened up a smaller door that led to his adjoining merchant business and admitted Gates inside. The wife followed, carrying a lit taper and asked what, exactly, Gates had in mind.

Peering down at the tiny old woman dressed in heavy robes and a sleeping cap, Gates wasn't exactly sure how to answer. Other than an occasional trinket, he'd never really shopped for a woman before so he wasn't entirely certain. He told the old woman that the lady he was escorting had absolutely nothing by way of possessions, clothing included, and he told the woman that she needed things that a proper young lady would have.

There wasn't much more he could say, considering he really had no idea what, in fact, a young lady would have, but the old woman seemed to know. When she asked Gates how tall the lady was, Gates held up a hand to mark the top of Lady Kathalin's head against him and described her as a slender woman. With his brief explanation, the old woman set the taper down and went to work.

Gates watched her curiously as she collected a large woven basket from the floor that contained some kind of trinkets and dumped it over, spilling the items onto the ground. She then proceeded to walk through the shop with the empty basket, in the near dark, pulling things off shelves, digging into other baskets, and opening a case or two.

Gates couldn't really see the woman in the darkness as she banged around, and at times muttered to herself, but suddenly she appeared out of the shadows with a full basket in one hand and a cloak thrown over her shoulder. The old woman approached Gates and took the cloak off her shoulder, handing it to him.

"That is a fine piece of goods, my lord," she said, indicating the cloak that he was already examining. "Blue wool with fox lining. It should be quite warm against this weather, but mind you don't get it too wet. The wool will smell and the fur will rot."

It was actually a beautiful cloak and well made. Gates peered closely at the careful stitching, noting the quality. "You carry goods such as this?" he asked, surprised.

"I do, my lord."

He lifted his eyebrows in mild shock. "I have only seen shops for women's garments like this in London," he said. "I did not expect to find a shop such as this in a small village."

The old woman grinned. "I make them myself," she said proudly. "We have many travelers from Hereford and Shrewsbury. I can always find buyers for what I produce. I personally sew for the Countess of Shrewsbury. She buys all of her clothing from me. Have you not heard of Gerta Black, the seamstress? That would be me."

Gates was impressed. "I am afraid that I have not heard of you," he said, moving from the cloak to the basket. "But that would make sense considering that I do not purchase women's clothing as a habit. What do you have in the basket?"

The old woman shifted her basket to the nearest table, which had neat stacks of woolen fabric on it, and she began to pull items forth out of the basket.

"You said the lady had no clothing with her," she said, indicating the garments she pulled out. "I loosely sew together gowns and surcoats and shifts so that they may be finished off by fine ladies to suit their size, so I have a good deal of unfinished garments that are mostly made. From what you described of your lady, I believe these will fit her. Can she sew?"

Gates shrugged. "I do not know but I would assume so."

Gerta began to lay out what was in the basket; two soft, eggshell-colored shifts were pulled forth, unhemmed so that they were very long, as well as an exquisite, blue damask surcoat that, upon closer inspection, had different types of blue fabric that comprised the bodice of the garment, making it a patchwork-type design but exceedingly becoming with the lace-up front and long, belled sleeves.

There was a second woolen garment in a shade of lavender, simple in design with long sleeves and a snug bodice, and then there was heavy linen that hadn't been dyed. It remained an off-white color but the old seamstress had sewn white rabbit fur around the neckline and at the wrists of the long sleeves. It had a lace-up bodice with no fastening, but the laces were on the sides of the bodice so one could make it as tight, or as loose, as one wanted. It was exquisite.

As Gates examined the surcoats, the old woman pulled two pairs of hose out of the basket along with two big shawls, basically big blocks of material that the lady could wrap around her shoulders and drape over her head for modesty and warmth. She also pulled forth two pairs of slippers, both silk, and one that was lined with fur. Gates saw the shoes and picked one of them up, inspecting it, uncertain how big the lady's foot was but assuming it wasn't too large. He'd caught a glimpse of her feet as he'd hauled her out of the priory over his shoulder, and he didn't think her feet were overly large.

As he studied the quality of the slippers, the old woman removed the final items of the booty – a sewing kit in a small wooden box, two bars of lumpy white soap that smelled of rosemary, some kind of oil in a phial to ease rough skin, a comb made from a tortoise shell, and a small sack of iron hair pins.

"There," she said decisively, pointing to the entire cache. "Your lady will be well supplied for her journey, my lord. What else did you wish for her?"

Gates looked at the goods; there was a lot of it and it was expensive, but he naturally assumed that Lord de Lara would want his daughter well clothed, as the offspring of an earl, so he didn't barter with the woman about the price. He simply had her pack everything neatly back into the basket.

"I left you several silver marks on your eating table," he said, throwing his thumb in the direction they had come from. "Is that enough for all of this?"

The old man quickly retreated back into the cottage, followed by his wife, to collect the coinage and count it. Hovered over the table where Gates had dropped the coins, with only a taper to light the darkness, he counted seventeen silver marks.

"Aye," he said, pleased at the profit they should make. "Are you sure there is nothing else for the lady?"

Gates shook his head, handing the basket over to one of the soldiers that had accompanied him. "Nay," he said. "But if the lady does decide she requires more, I will come and see you tomorrow before I leave."

"Excellent, my lord."

Gates headed for the door but paused before he quit the cottage entirely. "If she requires a different size in shoes, do you have something more she can see?"

The old woman nodded. "I have a few more silk slippers for her to see, my lord," she replied. "A woman in Hereford makes them for me and the Welsh women seem to like them a great deal, so I keep a few here at the shop."

"Readily made?"

"Readily made."

Such a thing as readily-made shoes was almost unheard of and Gates was properly surprised. "Astonishing," he said. Then he tried to think of anything else he needed when he suddenly remembered the red, raw chaffing that the rope had given Kathalin's wrists. It prompted him to ask, "You wouldn't happen to have any medicaments for skin that is raw and bleeding, would you?"

The old woman cocked her head thoughtfully and scurried back into the shop. She emerged a few moments later with a small alabaster pot that was tightly wrapped up with twine made from hemp. She thrust it at Gates.

"Calendula paste," she said. "The petals of the flower are mashed in fat. It should help."

Gates was grateful. In fact, he was quite surprised at how helpful the couple had been, especially since he had threatened to kick their door in. In his gratitude, he tossed a few more coins onto their table and nodded his head in silent thanks before quitting the cottage and heading out into the snowy night.

Fighting his way through blinding snow and armed with possessions that were as much an apology from him as they were a necessity, Gates was rather expecting Lady Kathalin to be quite grateful towards him. In fact, he was confident she would forget the past few days, the distress and fear, and become a pleasant traveling companion.

After all, he'd plied a few women with gifts before and it always worked wonders to the feminine vanity. Even though Lady Kathalin had been living in a convent for the past fourteen years, surely there was a true lady buried underneath, waiting to be coaxed forth. And Gates was most willing to do the coaxing.

He was usually correct, but in this case, only time would tell.

He very much wanted to be correct.

WITH CHAPPED, BLEEDING skin around her wrists, exhausted, and ravenously hungry, Kathalin was trying to count her blessings at the moment. At least she was warm in this tiny, windowless room as a fire raged in the open-end hearth, and at least she had a roof over her head as the storm raged. Those were the things she was grateful for but they were sorely outnumbered by the things she was ungrateful for.

After de Wolfe had left her, the first thing she had done was peer into the hearth to see if there was a way through the flames to escape, but the more she thought on the actual escape, the more she realized that it would be foolish to try. *Stupid,* de Wolfe had called it. With snow blowing sideways outside and impossible traveling conditions, she wouldn't make it to the edge of the village before she froze to death. She was ill-equipped to do anything or go anywhere, much less run off. She didn't even know what direction to travel in. In that instance, de Wolfe had her. There was nowhere for her to go.

She was officially trapped.

So she moved away from the hearth and tried to be thankful that she was at least warm and out of the elements. She was the least bit curious about her surroundings, much better than the accommodations from the previous night, but a close inspection of the bed showed it to be crawling with vermin. Disgusted, she sat on the floor near the hearth and inspected the red welts around her wrists.

Hate.

Somehow, she equated that word with de Wolfe but now that she was warm, and the situation was at least settling a bit, the hate she had built up for de Wolfe since leaving the priory was starting to ease somewhat. She knew the man was only doing as he'd been ordered, as he'd told her, but the fact remained that he was the catalyst for her upheaval. It was difficult to forgive him for that. As she sat and lifted her hands up to the fire, warming them, she began to notice movement in the room beyond the hearth.

Through the flames, she could see de Wolfe's men making themselves comfortable in the loft on the other side. They had their possessions and were finding a place to lie down and rest. Several of them were crowded up by the hearth, but because there was no light in her room other than firelight, they couldn't see her on the other side. But she could certainly see them and she saw quite clearly when one soldier laid a wench on her back right in front of the hearth.

Curious, Kathalin peered through the flames as the woman lay on her back and giggled at the man, who was just out of her view. But Kathalin's curiosity turned to astonishment when the man suddenly threw himself down on top of the woman and fumbled with her skirts, lifting them, whilst also fussing with his breeches until they slid halfway down his buttocks. As his companions yelled encouragement to him, the man spread the woman's legs and, to her giggles and moans, thrust himself into her waiting body.

Shocked, Kathalin quickly turned away, averting her gaze as the soldier made love to the wench in full view of her and in full view of his companions. Some of the soldiers were laughing, drinking, calling to the soldier and belittling his manhood while still others began to crowd around the pair, observing. It soon became evident that they were waiting their turn with the wench because more than one of them already had a great arousal evident through their breeches. One man was even stroking himself.

But Kathalin still wasn't looking; she was embarrassed and shocked by what was going on and she moved from her position near the hearth to the wall across the room, tucked back into the corner where she couldn't see anything, but she could certainly hear the grunts of pleasure. She covered her ears but that only muffled the sounds; she could still hear them.

Having grown up in the convent, she had been separated from men, insulated from their lust by the great priory walls. It had been a very safe place to be even though she had wondered about men from time to time, wondering what it would be like to be married to one. Wondering what it would be like to be in love with one. But here she was, now exposed to the worldly wickedness that Mother Benedicta had tried to protect her from, and the fear and shame of it made Kathalin want to return to the shielding walls more than ever. The world, what she was seeing of it, was a perverse and evil place.

More grunting and moaning filled her ears, bringing back a memory that reminded her that she wasn't being entirely honest about the sanctity of the priory. Last year, she had been in the dormitory when she'd heard similar moaning. Thinking someone had been ill, she followed the sounds and came across two novice nuns lying in a bed together, covered with heavy woolen blankets, and when Kathalin had pulled the covers off to see who was in distress, she found one woman with her fingers in the other woman's body, stuffed in between her legs.

It had been shocking and terrible, and Kathalin had fled the dormitory but had not gone to tell the Mother Prioress. She simply wanted to forget about what she had seen and wouldn't even talk to one of the offenders when the woman came into the kitchen to try and speak with her. She'd ignored the girl who, because of a completely different violation a few months later, had been sent away. But the second woman had remained at St. Milburga's and Kathalin went out of her way to avoid her. They never spoke nor did they even look at one another. Therefore, it was true that St. Milburga's wasn't an entirely pristine haven.

It had its wicked moments as well.

She took her hands away from her ears, listening to the sounds of fornication and hating the fact that her world had changed so much in the past few days. She was disoriented and bewildered, fearful of seeing her father and fearful of his reasons for extracting her from St. Milburga's. In fact, she was fearful of life in general at the moment, hating this new world she found herself a part of.

A knock on the door startled her, rousing her from her thoughts. She was terrified of who was on the other side of the door, terrified that it was a soldier wanting to know if she wanted to join in their wickedness. When the door opened, she was fully prepared to scream, but instead of a lustful soldier, de Wolfe appeared. He had a large basket in his arms and some kind of fabric or coverlet thrown over one shoulder. He frowned when he saw her on the ground.

"What are you doing down there, my lady?" he asked, concerned. "Surely it is cold down there. Are you ill?"

Oddly enough, she was relieved to see him. At least it wasn't a lustful soldier. "Nay," she replied. "I am not ill."

His bewilderment grew. "Then why are you down there?"

She sighed heavily. "Because the bed is covered with vermin," she said. "I will not sleep on it."

Gates' brow furrowed and he set the basket down next to the hearth even though his focus was on the bed. It was clear that he intended to see what she was talking about. But the moment he set the basket down, he had a clear view through the open hearth of the sexual adventures happening on the other side and his eyes narrowed dangerously. He hadn't noticed the grunting noises until now, realizing where they were coming from. His first instinct was to berate his men for doing such a thing in full view of Lady Kathalin but the dirty bed still had his attention.

As long as it was crawling with bugs, the lady couldn't, and wouldn't, lay on it and he didn't blame her. With a grunt of pure frustration, he picked up the entire bed and shoved it through the doorjamb as the soldiers outside the door moved to help him. But he pushed those men aside as he made his way to the loft where the carnal activities were happening. Using deep and threatening tones, he snarled at his men for their passionate display.

The wench, still lying in front of the hearth with her legs spread, was unceremoniously hauled to her feet by one of the soldiers not participating in the activity and chased off as Gates berated his men for their behavior. Like scolded children, the lascivious – and nearly drunk – soldiers backed off and cowered away from de Wolfe's rage, for certainly, no one wanted to enrage him. He was a fair and affable man most of the time, but this was not one of those times. In moments like this, he was a man to be feared and obeyed.

Inside the tiny chamber, Kathalin heard de Wolfe's scathing cut-down of his men. Curious, she peered through the hearth to see men scrambling on the other side, moving away from de Wolfe, who was standing there with the entire bed still in his hands. She could see the foot of the bed as he held it. Then, he disappeared and his men gathered in quiet groups, muttering amongst themselves now that they no longer were permitted the evening's activities.

The situation quieted down in a hurry and Kathalin wasn't quite sure what to think of any of it. With no bed in the now-empty room, the big basket de Wolfe had been carrying was now by the door. The coverlet or garment he'd had thrown over his shoulder was tossed on top of the basket and, hesitantly, she peered at the garment to see what it was. Unable to make a determination, and wondering if de Wolfe would be cross at her for her curiosity, she backed off, unwilling to provoke the man who could wield a bed so easily. She knew he was a man of tremendous strength, as he'd demonstrated from the beginning, but it would seem his strength and determination knew no boundaries. That had been clear from the start. With that thought, she huddled back into her corner and waited. For what, she wasn't sure, but something told her de Wolfe would be back.

She was right.

Close to an hour after he left, Kathalin heard muffled conversation on the other side of the chamber door. She had been dozing, head back against the wall, when she heard the buzz of conversation and by the time she lifted her head, the door was opening and de Wolfe was reappearing. Behind him came a serving wench, tray in hand, and behind her came the innkeeper and another man, obviously a servant from the manner in which he was dressed. As Kathalin watched with great interest, de Wolfe directed the people into her chamber.

The wench went straight to Kathalin and set her tray down at the woman's feet before scurrying out. Meanwhile, the innkeeper and the servant were carrying great bundles between them and as they laid them out on the floor where the bed had once been, Kathalin could see that there was a mattress of sorts and bed clothes. The bed frame was gone, but there was a big, full mattress on the floor now. There were also at least four heavy blankets that she could see and the innkeeper assured de Wolfe, who was standing near the hearth with his big arms folded imposingly, that these bed things were without vermin. He apologized profusely that the original bed had been so unacceptable. Then the man said something about a bath before fleeing the room with his servants. It was a word that had Kathalin's full attention.

A bath meant warm water.

Heat.

"A bath?" she said as the door closed behind the innkeeper. "Is there a bathing room here?"

It was the first time during the entire journey that she had spoken more than just a couple of words and Gates turned to see the expression of hope in her face. He shook his head.

"There is no bathing room in this establishment that I am aware of, my lady," he said. "But he has a barrel that has been used for bathing in the past and he will be bringing it up here to you. I thought that mayhap a bath would be in order since you have been afforded little luxury on this trip. In fact, since we left St. Milburga's without your possessions, I have purchased a few things that you can possibly use."

As Kathalin watched, he went to the big basket he had brought in earlier and picked up the garment that was strewn across it. He held it up for her to see.

"I found a merchant in town who sells all manner of goods," he said, shaking out the cloak. "His wife is a seamstress and she had this cloak available for sale. It is wool and lined with fox, but she says we should not get it too wet lest the fox fur will rot."

There was a hook on the back of the chamber door and he hung the cloak up, removing the lid of the basket, and proceeded to pull out the dark blue garment and the lavender one. He held them up for her inspection.

"I took the liberty of purchasing three surcoats for you," he said. "The seamstress does not finish the garments and she said that you could, according to your fit. She even included a sewing kit. There are shifts and hose and shoes, and there is even soap. You can use it when you bathe."

By this time, Kathalin's mouth was hanging open somewhat as Gates pulled out the shifts and the hose, all of it draping over his enormous arms as he tried to show her what he had purchased for her. Stunned, she looked rather bewildered at the items he was holding up for her.

"These…," she said hesitantly. "These are for me?"

He nodded, still looking in the basket at the shoes at the bottom. "You have nothing," he said. "I thought you might need these things."

Kathalin had no idea what to say or how to react. She looked down at the dirty brown wool she was wearing. "I…," she started, stopped, and started again, evidently very confused about the entire situation. "I do not need those fine things. I have no use for them."

Gates looked at her. "The garment you are wearing is soiled," he said. "Surely you would like to wear something clean and warm."

She was still looking at the clothing she was wearing. "I can wash this," she said. "Mayhap… mayhap after I bathe, I will wash this in the bath water and hang it before the fire. It should be dry by morning."

Gates couldn't quite figure out why she wasn't incredibly excited over new clothing. "But these garments are much nicer," he said. "Would you not like to wear something pretty? Those garments you are wearing do nothing for your beauty, my lady. In these new clothes, you would look every bit an earl's daughter."

She looked at him, then, utterly perplexed. "Beauty is a worldly and sinful thing," she said, her voice faint but insistent. "I should not like to accentuate it."

Now, it was starting to occur to Gates why she wasn't thrilled with her new clothes. Raised in a priory, she more than likely had never seen such finery and if she had, then he could only guess that it was frowned upon. He had to remind himself that all she had ever known was a simple life and lived in simple, undistinguished clothing. Pride in earthly possessions had no place inside a convent.

"That is what you have been taught, is it not?" he asked softly.

Her brow furrowed as she thought on an answer, uncertain how to reply. "We are taught to reject worldly vanities, for they are evil," she said. "The world is an evil place. It is only safe within the walls of St. Milburga's."

Poor child, he thought. *So she was raised like an animal.* All that aside, however, he was glad that she was speaking to him for it gave him a chance to at least establish a rapport with her. They hadn't had that in two days. Perhaps it would ease the tension between them if he were to draw her out in conversation.

"May I ask a question, my lady?" he asked, watching her nod hesitantly. He continued. "Do you think God created the world to be an evil place?"

She was thoughtful in her reply. "He did not create it to be evil, but Mankind is evil," she said. "They have created an evil world."

"All of it?"

"Most of it."

"How would you know this if you have never been out of the convent?"

She pondered his question. "I have been told that by people I trust," she said. "By Mother Benedicta."

"The Prioress?"

"Aye."

He cocked his head curiously. "Don't you think you should find out for yourself if it is evil or not?" he asked. "There are thousands of people in the world and they all cannot be evil. Mayhap you should learn for yourself before making a judgement."

She shrugged, looking back to her rough woolen clothing. "I have never wanted to learn for myself."

"Why not?"

Again, she shrugged. "I have no one to ask other than Mother Benedicta," she said. "She would not lie to me."

A faint smile on his lips, Gates leaned against the wall behind him in a casual position even though he still had surcoats draped over his arms.

"Neither would I," he said. "I am a knight. I come from a long line of knights. My great-great-grandfather was the greatest knight who has ever lived. Therefore, I do not fabricate and I will tell you the truth about everything, should you ask. I am beyond contestation. Why not ask me about the world?"

Kathalin had to admit, it was tempting. Frightening, but tempting. As she sat there, indecisive and fidgeting with her dirty clothing, Gates pulled one of the feather-soft shifts out of the basket and tossed it to her. It landed over her head and she yanked it off, irritated, but the moment she touched it, something in her expression changed. Gates was sharp enough to see it.

"Do you feel that wonderful garment?" he asked quietly. "How in the world can that be wicked? Imagine how warm and lovely it would feel against your skin. Would you not like to wear it instead of the scratchy garment you are wearing now that feels more like tree bark than clothing?"

Kathalin was inspecting the shift quite seriously. Timidly, she rubbed it against her cheek. "It feels like a cloud."

Gates smiled at her interest. "It does," he said, looking into the basket. "There is another one just like it and hose for your legs that are soft as well. How can these things be wicked, Lady Kathalin? It is not wicked to be warm and comfortable, and that is why I brought you these things. I realize you have spent your entire life wearing woolen garments and believing that the discomfort of it was the will of God, but let me assure you God makes some very fine things as well. I would like to believe that He would be happy for you to be warm and comfortable."

Kathalin was still rubbing the shift on her cheek, enchanted with the feel of something she had never known to exist. Gates pushed himself off the wall and made his way over to her, crouching down and holding up his arms again so she could see the fine surcoats he had draped over them. He could see the awe and wonder in her expression and he thought it all quite sweet as well as pathetic; the young woman had grown up without any luxuries at all and had been told that such things were wicked. Well, they weren't. He decided at that moment that he was going to show her things of comfort and luxury that weren't wicked at all.

Much like educating a baby on how to talk, he could see that Kathalin needed much of an education on life outside of the priory walls and, oddly enough, his determination to educate her had nothing to do with making another conquest. Quite the contrary; under the circumstances, he would feel ashamed in doing so and he was quite certain that Jasper would have his hide, so he considered Lady Kathalin off-limits. More than that, there was something too pristine and lovely about her to want to soil her in any fashion. It was a shocking realization to a man who usually thought only of himself.

"I... I have only always made my own clothing," Kathalin said, breaking his train of thought. "We have herds of sheep that we sheer in the spring and in the fall, and then there are sisters who spin the wool and others who weave the fabric. I was one of the ones who would sew the clothing for the others."

Gates watched her as she moved from rubbing the shift against her cheek to fingering the lavender wool. "So you learned how to sew and how to manage the kitchen," he said. "Surely you were taught more than that?"

Kathalin nodded, setting the shift aside so she could inspect the workmanship on the blue patchwork dress. "I have been taught to read and to write in Latin and in French," she said. "I have copied many pages of the Prioress' Bible, the one her father gave to her."

He watched her very pretty hands as they moved over the garment.

"Were you taught to do things other young ladies do?" he asked. "Poetry and painting and drawing?"

She shook her head. "Nay," she replied. "Why on earth would I be taught such vain things?"

"Because God created art and literature and it is quite beautiful."

She looked at him, thinking on his words, as she drew her hand away from the blue surcoat. "That is true," she said. "But I would have no use for them as a nun."

He stood up, moving back to the basket and carefully putting the garments back inside, but not before taking out the pot of calendula salve that the seamstress had given him.

"Why do you want to be a nun so badly?" he asked. "Does the world scare you so much that you would hide from it?"

Kathalin considered his question. "It does not frighten me," she said. "But why would I not want to live my life in a place of blessing and piety and joy. Why would I not want to serve God?"

He turned to look at her. "You were happy there?"

She nodded, thinking on St. Milburga's and trying not to tear up. "Aye," she said. "My friends are there. It is my home."

She hung her head and he could see that the conversation was about to take a downward turn. Quickly, he sought to distract her. "I am sure your parents will be very happy to see you," he said. "I have served your father for many years. In fact, I came into his service as a squire shortly after you were sent away to foster. I was fifteen years of age and attached to a knight who had seen to my education for about six years. When he came into de Lara's service, I did, too."

Kathalin looked up at him, blinking, and he could see that her eyes were still moist from thoughts of St. Milburga's. "The knight was your master?"

"Aye."

"Is he still with my father?"

Gates shook his head. "Nay," he replied. "He died in France about ten years ago and I received a battlefield commission to fight in his stead. Being knighted in the midst of a battle is quite harrowing."

"That is how you became a knight?"

"Indeed it is."

Kathalin was becoming interested in this enormous knight whose manner had returned to the man she had first met at St. Milburga's, the man who had saved her from the Welsh. This side of him seemed quite kind and considerate. In spite of her sworn hatred towards him, she seemed to have conveniently forgotten about that at the moment.

"Have you fought many battles, then?" she asked.

He nodded, casually scratching at his stubbled chin. "Enough," he said. "I only just returned from France where I have been for the past several months. I was at Poitiers, in fact."

"What is at Poitiers?"

He looked at her, thinking it very strange that she should not know about the major battles going on, but then he reminded himself of the fact that the woman had been living in a convent. Current battles and politics were probably not among the things they knew about in their insulated little world.

"There was a very big battle there back in September," he told her. "The English were triumphant over the French king."

It was a simple explanation for a much more complex situation, but it seemed to satisfy her. Her gaze moved over his body, the red de Lara tunic and the portions of mail and plate armor beneath. He didn't wear a full suit of armor, merely pieces on his forearms and chest that were fastened on with leather straps.

"I suppose you have seen a good deal of evil in your time," she said quietly. "Men are evil to one another."

He nodded. "An excellent summation of a much more complicated world," he said. "But as I said before, there are many people in this world and not all are evil. I have seen many good men in my time."

"But you kill," she said, regarding him carefully. "You kill because you are ordered to kill."

He lifted his eyebrows as if to concede her point. "I kill because some men need killing," he said. "I kill because men are trying to kill *me*. I kill because it must be done and for no other reason than that."

He didn't sound as if he enjoyed it, which eased Kathalin somewhat. She knew that there were wars and killing, and she furthermore knew that knights such as de Wolfe were ultimately sworn to the church and to God. But she wondered if that was really true. She wondered if their service to God won out over their pride as warriors. Increasingly, she was curious about de Wolfe and his background, and she also found herself just a bit more curious about the world in general. Now that he'd brought it up, she couldn't help but wonder.

"Then... then mayhap you will tell me of your travels and battles sometime," she said. "Since we are evidently to spend some time together, I would like to hear of the world as you know it. Mayhap it will not seem so evil from your perspective."

He smiled at her, the de Wolfe dimples running deep. "I would be honored, my lady," he said. "But first, will you please do something for me?"

She was somewhat wary. "What is that?"

He pointed to the basket full of clothing. "Will you please do me the favor of dressing in something very warm and comfortable for the remainder of our journey?" he asked. "I should not like to return you to your parents bedraggled, cold, and possibly ill. Your father will think I have failed at my duty to protect you and I should not wish for that to happen. I am not one to fail at my duties, under any circumstances."

Kathalin looked at the basket, remembering the soft feel of the shift against her cheek. She could feel herself relenting as she was given the choice between something soft and lovely, and something scratchy and dirty.

Soft and lovely won out.

"Aye," she said reluctantly. "I will do that."

His smile broadened and he suddenly remembered that he was still holding the calendula salve in his hand. He extended it to her. "You have my thanks," he said, "and this is a salve that will help heal the welts

65

around your wrists. I am very sorry I tied them so tightly, but I could not take the chance that you would escape me. My apologies if I have been less than chivalrous towards you. I never meant you harm."

Hate.

Kathalin wasn't so sure she was feeling that any longer. De Wolfe was doing everything he could to make up for the poor travel and the uncomfortable conditions. He was behaving civilized again, like he had when she had first met him at St. Milburga's, before everything took a turn for the worse. She had been belligerent and resistant, that was true, but two days later, she was mostly resigned. She knew that escape was futile and it would be foolish to try, so she put that thought out of her mind. It was that thought that had brought about red, bleeding wrists. Even if she managed to run back to St. Milburga's, he would only track her down and bring her back.

Faintly, she sighed.

"You did not harm me," she said. "But I would be grateful if you did not tie my hands together any longer. I promise that I will not try to escape if you will simply leave the ropes off."

He regarded her a moment, not entirely certain he believed her. It seemed like too rapid a change in behavior for him, but he would not insult her with a contradiction. "If I have your word as a lady," he said quietly, "then I will not bind you."

"You have it," she said, eyeing her wrists. "Besides… I do not think my skin can take those ropes for another day. Surely my hands will fall off if I have to endure anymore."

Gates didn't say anything more at that point because there was a soft knock on the door and he opened it to find the innkeeper and hot water on the other side. As the male servant in the ratty clothing dragged in, literally, half of a barrel lined with linen, the serving wenches were lugging buckets of hot water behind him. It took several trips from the kitchen to fill the barrel up to a bathing level but when it was adequately filled, Gates chased everyone from the chamber to allow Kathalin her privacy, for which she was grateful.

When Gates himself left, Kathalin leapt from her position in the corner and stuck her finger into the water, delighted that it was very hot. Exhibiting energy she hadn't shown in two days, she realized that she had forgotten about the food that the serving wench had brought earlier and she ripped off the cloth that covered it, digging in to the bread even as she struggled to undress with one hand. But she couldn't do it with only one hand so she shoved the brown, gritty bread into her mouth and yanked off her dirty clothing.

Food and warmth. She was almost giddy with it. She was about to climb into the barrel, still with bread in her mouth, when she remembered that Gates had mentioned he'd procured some soap for her. She found the soap in the bottom of the basket, smelling like sweet rosemary, and she climbed into the hot barrel of water, blissfully, and submerged herself completely. After two days of hell, the experience was pure heaven.

And thoughts of Gates de Wolfe were no longer filled with hate. She had no idea why she felt like smiling every time she looked at the basket full of clothing, but she did.

CHAPTER FOUR

Lioncross Abbey Castle
30 miles south of Hyssington

THE CASTLE KNOWN as Lioncross Abbey was something of a legend in the disputed Marches of Wales and England.

Originally, portions of it had been built by the Romans as an outpost back in the days of the Great Empire but when the Romans left and the Dark Ages came about, the Roman ruins were transformed into a Cistercian abbey by holy men from Kildare. They lived there in relative peace until the Normans came. Noting the prime spot on a massive, flat-topped rise overlooking the River Arrow to the north, the Holme Marsh valley to the east, Wales to the west, the Normans decided that it was a perfect spot for a garrison. A man by the name of d'Evereux and his army stormed the abbey, chased off the priests, and claimed it for his own. Such was the Norman way when it came to acquiring real estate.

But d'Evereux had a plan. He began to build, using the old Roman ruins that had been transformed into the abbey as the basis for his castle. He attached a cavernous three-storied keep to it unlike any of the keeps that were being built at that time. He put the great hall in the keep, attached the kitchens to it, and then built a semi-tower with living quarters that was attached to all of that. Everything ended up in one contiguous building. The result was a very big structure that had corridors, mural staircases, and multiple rooms on every level. D'Evereux also put a massive wall around the place, enclosing a massive ward that included a section used for training soldiers. Because his family's crest was a lion holding a cross, the great and mighty fortress of Lioncross Abbey Castle was born.

D'Evereux was very proud of his mighty castle and had acquired quite a reputation for himself, so much so that he married a great Norman warlord's daughter and she bore him seven daughters and one son, but the son had died soon after birth, leaving d'Evereux with no heirs. His eldest daughter, a fine and true woman, married a Saxon man of noble origins named Barringdon, and Lioncross Abbey remained in the custody of the House of Barringdon for three generations until the Barringdon heiress, named in the family Bible as Lady Dustin Mary Catherine Barringdon, married the great Sir Christopher de Lohr in eleven hundred and ninety-two.

Lioncross Abbey had therefore been held by the House of de Lohr for one hundred and sixty-five years, making it part of the fabric of the family. The old stone walls were in de Lohr blood and de Lohr blood was in the walls. The name Lioncross or "The Abbey" was synonymous with the de Lohr name. In the great hall of Lioncross, seat of the de Lohrs, the current earl now sat. Henry de Lohr, Earl of Worcester, sat impatiently awaiting the appearance of his son, whom he'd not seen in almost a year and a half.

His son had only been home for four days and in that time, Alexander had mostly slept. The man was exhausted and Henry, thrilled that his son was back under his roof, had let the man live his life the way he wanted to, and if that meant sleeping most of the time, he would permit it. But the truth was that he was very eager to speak with his son and as the days passed and Alexander remained in seclusion, Henry was having a very difficult time of it. His wife, a Teutonic princess named Elreda Augustine von Anhalt, had begged him to be patient with Alexander considering the man had been away for so long and was more than likely well due his rest.

So Henry waited, sitting in his usual chair on this cold evening as the snow outside blew in great cloud bursts, hoping that Alexander would wake up from his three-day-long nap and come to see his father. It wasn't often that Henry was able to see one of his children, considering both daughters were married and his youngest son, Baxter, was in France somewhere with Prince Edward much as Alexander had been. At least he had his eldest son home and he was nearing the limits of his patience to speak with the man.

"Here," Lady Elreda said in her heavy Germanic accent, coming up behind him and setting a cup of wine in front of him. "Drink. Alexander will be here soon."

Henry grunted in disagreement as he picked up the cup and drank deeply of the sweet red wine. He smacked his lips.

"Why has he slept so much?" he demanded. "Why is he so exhausted? He acts as if he crawled all the way from France on his hands and knees."

Elreda patted him on the shoulder patiently. "It was a long journey," she said. "And the weather is terrible. He has probably hardly slept at all."

Henry made a face at her. "That is not why," he said. "Shall I tell you what he has been doing? He has been with Gates de Wolfe and they have been leaving a trail of soiled women all the way from Paris. How many little French bastards am I to have on my doorstep come spring? How many fathers will I have to pay off simply to keep them from roping my son to a stake and burning him to cinder?"

Elreda continued to pat his shoulder. "You worry overly," she said. "Alexander is not like Gates, although you know you love Gates as you would a son. Why must you speak so poorly of him?"

Henry rolled his eyes. "Because he is a wild, vain creature who has no control when it comes to women," he said. Then he shook his head and grumbled. "The Dark Destroyer, they call him. He is dark and destructive, all right, and all of his bad habits have spilled over onto Alexander. I shudder to think just how many women Alexander has compromised since he has been away."

"At least one hundred."

Henry and Elreda turned sharply to see Alexander entering the great hall. He looked sleepy but alert, and there was a big smile on his face as he approached his parents, seated at the scrubbed feasting table.

"Is that what you have been doing since I've been away?" he asked, lifting an eyebrow. "Speaking terribly of me? Slandering your own son?"

Henry stood up and hugged his boy tightly. It was a great, satisfying embrace. "Since when is the truth slander?" he asked, kissing his son on both cheeks. "And is it really one hundred women? Must I worry about one hundred irate fathers trying to burn my castle down in their attempts to get to you?"

Alexander snickered as he sat down, patting his mother's arms when she came up behind him to embrace him. "More than likely," he said. "But you have an iron portcullis that they cannot burn, so I would not worry overly. Still, how much money do you have in the coffers? We had better make plans now."

Henry glanced at his wife, a droll expression on his face. "And this is the child you told me not to drown at birth," he said. "I should not have listened to you."

Elreda laughed softly. "Sit, Henry," she said. "Sit and shut your mouth before you make a fool of yourself. I will send for food. Alexander, you must be famished."

Alexander nodded, raking his fingers through his blond hair. "I am," he admitted. "I am sorry I have slept so much. I did not realize I was so exhausted until I lay down on my childhood bed. Then, it was as if I could not keep my eyes open."

Henry smiled at his son, suddenly no longer so irritated with him, and pushed the half-empty cup of wine at him. Alexander gladly took it and drained it. "Not to worry, my son," Henry said. "Surely your trip from France was quite difficult and you have had little sleep as a result. Your mother and I understand."

Elreda, hearing her words echoed in Henry's statement, rolled her eyes at his falsity. The man had been as impatient as a cat for three long days, now pretending he had been relaxed the entire time. Still, she kept her mouth shut as she sat down next to her husband.

"It *was* difficult," Alexander said as servants began to appear from a door at the far end of the hall with food and drink. "The past fifteen months have been quite difficult. Father, I assume you have heard what happened at Poitiers?"

Henry nodded. "A traveling merchant who sought shelter here one night told us what he had heard in London," he said. "Were you there?"

Alexander nodded. "I was," he said. "So was Baxter."

Elreda suddenly grasped Henry's arm as if terrified. "And your brother?" she gasped. "He is well?"

Alexander could see her fear and he nodded quickly, "Aye, Mama, he is well the last that I saw of him," he assured her. "That was two days after the battle and he was with Salisbury's men. You know that he serves de Montacute now?"

Elreda really didn't but Henry nodded. "I do," he said. "Baxter wrote to us and told us that Oxford, his former liege, gifted him to de Montacute in payment for a debt. So you saw your brother and he is well?"

The parents needed reassurance that their youngest son was fine and Alexander nodded again. "He was very well the last time I saw him," he said. "I am sure he will be home soon to tell you himself. There is much change in France currently and many English are coming back home. It has been a very long campaign the past year. Long indeed."

Servants were placing food and drink in front of him so he quieted for a few moments as wine, bread, butter, stewed apples and brawn beef were placed in front of him. He began stuffing his face before speaking again.

"Before you ask, Father, suffice it to say that the battle at Poitiers was very terrible and very bloody," he said, chewing. "I will tell you more later but to be truthful, I have spoken all I wish to speak about it to Jasper de Lara. The man demanded battle stories every damnable night when I was there. I am sick to death of speaking of it right now."

Henry was disappointed; he knew that Alexander had spent some time at Hyssington Castle because when he returned three days ago, it was with a small army of men that Henry had loaned Jasper. He frowned.

"So de Lara gets all of your stories and I get nothing?" he asked, looking at his wife. "Do you hear your son? I am to get nothing."

Elreda shushed him. "Will you at least tell us of your journey, Alexander?" she asked. "Did you see many new and great things on your travels?"

Alexander looked at his mother, mouth full. "Great and new things in France?" he said. "Preposterous. There is nothing new and great in France other than the terrible death that swept it a few years ago seems to have gone away. So many dead has left the entire country a mass graveyard. When you do come across people these days, they hold cloths in front of their faces still, warding off whatever disease they think others may carry. France is not a pleasant place to visit these days."

Elreda sobered at the thought but Henry spoke. "Nor is England," he said. "We had our share of the great disease that swept the nation but the de Lohrs were fortunately spared. Will you at least tell me who rules France now? The traveling merchant told us that King Jean was captured."

Alexander nodded as he buttered his bread. "He was," he replied. "He was captured along with both of his sons and a host of French nobility. It was an utter and complete victory for Edward and for the prince. If you want to know who rules France now, it is the English. The French army, and the aristocracy, is crippled. They lost nearly everyone and everything on that field at Poitiers."

It was a summation of the results of the battle at Poitiers, which was the truth. France was crippled now as a result of that decisive battle and

England was once again in charge. Henry was quite pleased to hear it.

"Then you shall not be going back to France?" he asked. "It sounds as if there is no longer a need."

Alexander bit into his bread. "There will always be a need, Papa," he said. "There has been a need longer than you have been alive. This is not the end, I fear, nor will it ever be, but for now it is my opinion that the situation will be quiet for a while."

Both Henry and Elreda were pleased to hear such things from their son. They had never liked the idea of both of their sons fighting in France for a vanity war, wars that only benefitted the monarchy and those in control. At least, that was how they both looked at it in times when they would discuss such things.

"Quiet," Elreda murmured, her hand draped on her husband's arm. "Is it really true? Is it possible that you will be able to live your life peacefully and enjoy home and a family of your own?"

Alexander swallowed his bread, nearly choking. "Mama," he said, drinking his wine to wash down the lump of bread. "Who said anything about a family of my own?"

Elreda grinned at her son. "I did," she said. "You are nearly thirty years of age. It is time for you to consider such things, Alexander. A wife and then children of your own. Your father could make a wonderful match for you, you know. Now that you are home, you must allow him to do this. You will command a fine bride, my son."

Alexander frowned. "I have been home four days and already you are broaching the subject of a wife," he said, looking at his father as he pushed his food aside, suddenly no longer hungry. "Did you put her up to this?"

Henry held up his hands as if to ward off his son's anger. "I did no such thing," he said, "although you are at an age where you must consider such things. It is time for you to do your duty as the future Earl of Worcester. You owe the family an heir, Alex, and a legitimate one at that with a woman you are actually married to."

Alexander rolled his eyes. "Not now."

"Why not?"

"Because I have only just returned home," Alexander stressed. "Will you at least give me a few weeks before you are both trying to saddle me with a wife?"

Elreda pretended as if she hadn't heard him. "Your papa's garrison commander at Bronllys Castle has a beautiful daughter," she said. "Her name is Anwyn de Titouan and she is nearly seventeen years old. A beautiful girl with dark hair and blue eyes. She is quite accomplished, I am told, and I should like for you to meet her. We thought mayhap to secure a contract with her for either you or Baxter, but you are the eldest, Alexander. You must marry first."

Alexander laid his head, face-down, on the table and began softly banging his head against the tabletop as his parents began arguing over the suitability of a garrison commander's daughter for the future earl. It truly seemed not to matter how he felt about the situation; his parents were determined to marry him off. Finally, he lifted his head, with his forehead skin red from where he had banged it against the table, and put up his hands.

"Please," he roared softly, causing his parents to look at him. "I will find my own wife, or at least I will have the final approval on the woman I marry. This is not your decision to make."

Elreda, normally a very even-tempered woman, frowned at her eldest son. "I would be happy to agree with that statement but for the fact if left up to you, I would be in my grave before you decided to marry," she said unhappily. "Let me at least find you a selection of good and true women to decide upon. Let me go to my grave knowing you have a wonderful woman to take care of you."

As Alexander geared up for an argument, the entry door of Lioncross' enormous hall opened and a soldier entered, snow on his shoulders and on his helm from the storm outside. The winds howled in after him as harried servants struggled to close the door and the soldier rushed straight into the hall where, already, Alexander and his parents had turned to look at the man. Henry spoke first.

"What is it?" he demanded.

The soldier's face was pinched red from the cold outside. "We just received a message from Ludlow Castle, my lord," he said. "The Welsh attacked St. Milburga's Priory several days ago. There is also word that they have attacked Woofferton and ransacked the town. Ludlow asks for reinforcements against these attacks."

The words filled the air with instant tension but, given the seasoned nature of both Henry and Alexander, they didn't react with panic or fear. Henry was an excellent commander and an excellent strategist, and possessed the supreme de Lohr trait; the more critical the situation, the calmer he became. In battle, that characteristic had served him well. He calmly stood up from the table, as did Alexander, who was interested in the information but for different reasons than his father was.

"St. Milburga's was attacked?" he clarified.

The soldier nodded, rubbing at his freezing nose. "Aye, my lord."

Alexander's expression grew serious. "Do we know the end result?" he asked. "Did they destroy the priory?"

The soldier shook his head. "I will bring the Ludlow messenger to you, my lord," he said. "You may ask him that question, for I do not know the answer."

Henry reached out and put a hand on his son's arm. "Why such interest in St. Milburga's?"

Alexander looked at his father. "Because Gates is there," he said. "Or, at least, he was heading there. Gates and a fifty-man escort had been directed by de Lara to go to St. Milburga's to retrieve de Lara's daughter, who is a ward there. Gates and his escort traveled south with me from Hyssington but we split off at the road for Ludlow. I continued south and he headed to Ludlow. He has been to St. Milburga's within the past few days which makes me very concerned that he and his escort may have run into trouble from the Welsh."

Henry could see what had his son so worried. "Indeed," he said. "Then you must go immediately to make sure he was not injured or worse, especially if they had de Lara's daughter with them. With the

Welsh raiding all over the Marches this winter, even a fifty-man escort is not safe. I am surprised Jasper sent so few men to collect his daughter."

Alexander was already on the move, deeply concerned for Gates and the trouble the man might be in. "I am taking five hundred men with me, Father," he said. "I will go to Ludlow and leave off two hundred and fifty men with them, and if Gates is not at St. Milburga's, I will continue on to Hyssington to see if he is there."

Henry was following him, as was the soldier, all of them heading to the hall entry. "Take more men than that," he said. "I have almost two thousand men here with me, tucked away out of the snow and growing fat. Take more of them with you to reinforce Ludlow's garrison."

Alexander nodded, feeling the surge of battle once again in his veins. He was conditioned that way. His mother spoke of living a peaceful life but the truth was that warfare and battle were the norm for knights like Alexander de Lohr. It was what he did best, what he thrived upon, and with the possibility that Gates could be in grave danger, Alexander was determined to help him.

Therefore, before sunrise the next day in the midst of a snowstorm, Alexander and nine hundred de Lohr men departed Lioncross Abbey for Ludlow. Later that day, however, they had their first run-in with a large group Welsh raiders heading for Lioncross and Alexander suffered his first taste of battle in three years on English soil.

It was a nasty and short skirmish that saw ten de Lohr soldiers injured and nearly twenty Welsh either injured or killed. The Welsh were desperate, which meant they were reckless, and Alexander sent the wounded back to Lioncross with that message.

Beware the reckless raiders.

Meanwhile, Alexander pushed through and made haste for Ludlow.

CHAPTER FIVE

~ THE CHANGING HEART ~

Hyssington Castle

THE LIGHT IN the chamber was low, but that was to be expected. It was always low because Lady de Lara liked it that way. Shut up in her chamber day and night, the four stone walls of the room plus a small dressing alcove were her entire world and it was a precisely controlled world. Even Jasper knew that; he was only allowed to see his wife when she summoned him and this night, she had summoned him.

His wife was on the third floor of the keep, high above the castle grounds where she could watch everything going on. That was how she knew the soldiers were using the gatehouse murder holes for a garderobe and, in turn, sent her maid to relay her message for them to stop pissing on the main entry to the castle. She was a very observant woman in her secluded little world, very conscious of what was going on outside of the walls. There was little the woman missed.

But she did miss her husband because of his predilection for staying away from her as much as possible. It was his choice, something she had grown resigned to because she had no choice in the matter. Jasper had seen to that. Entering his wife's chamber, he was greeted with the heavy smells of rosemary and clove. They were incredibly strong scents that always made him sneeze. By the second sneeze, he heard his wife's voice.

"Jasper?" she called. "Is that you?"

Jasper turned towards the canopied bed, a massive piece of furniture surrounded by an initial layer of heavy brocaded curtains, red in color, and then a second layer of a gauzy fabric that one could nearly see through. It was filmy and cloudy in nature. It was through this second layer that Lady de Lara was viewed. No one except for her maid, and occasionally her husband, ever saw her more than that.

"Aye, Rosamund," he said, moving in the direction of the bed. "It is me."

Through the gauzy muslin, Jasper could see the shape of his wife, the former Rosamund du Bois. She was part of the prominent de Titouan and de Llion family, intermingled with the House of du Bois and the prominent House of de Lohr, whose military presence was very heavy along the Marches. In fact, de Lohr, de Titouan, and de Llion were considered synonymous with the Welsh Marches. In her youth, Rosamund had been a stunning example of beauty with her dark hair and bright blue eyes. But that beauty had been covered up for many years and now Rosamund moved about her chamber in heavy scarves and wimples, covering her head and face. Only her eyes were visible. She had to do that, unfortunately, because a horrible disease had robbed her of her beauty long ago. Scaly skin, lesions, and horrific bumps and pustules on her face. It was a curse and something terrible to behold.

Leper.

It was a terrible word. Jasper couldn't even bring himself to say it, not even when the physics from Gloucester and London had diagnosed her those years ago. It was a word never uttered within Hyssington or anywhere else for fear of spreading panic, and when the House of de Lara moved from castle to castle as the weather dictated, Lady de Lara was always transported in an enclosed carriage where no one could see her. The once-vivacious and lovely woman was a prisoner to a disease that was slowly killing her body whilst her mind remained sound.

It was a horrible and slow death sentence.

But Jasper didn't anguish over her condition like he used to. Much like Rosamund, he had become resigned to her condition even though they had sought the most expensive treatments and best physics available. Still, there was no relief and Rosamund was falling apart, bit by bit, day by day. Jasper couldn't even bring himself to look at her any longer because she had lost most of her nose and he didn't like staying in her chamber any longer than necessary for fear he would contract her condition. They physics had told him that it was contagious. Therefore, the conversations between them were always short.

"How may I be of service today, my dearest?" he asked politely.

Rosamund was sitting on her bed, some kind of sewing project spread out around her. The woman had exquisite talent in sewing and her masterpieces were on display in all of her husband's castles.

"Has Kathalin returned yet?" she asked. "You promised me that you would tell me yet I have not yet heard. Surely she is here by now."

Jasper stood outside of the filmy, gauzy curtain, seeing the muted figure of his wife through the fabric. "Nay, my dearest," he said patiently. "I told you that I would tell you when she arrived and I will not break that promise. You needn't fear."

Rosamund sighed faintly and set down her sewing into her lap. It was clear that her mood was pensive, depressed even, and her movements were slow. It wasn't difficult to sense an aura of sadness around her, the sadness of her wasted life.

"After all of these years," she ventured softly, "I wonder what kind of a woman she has become. I have often wondered, you know. I am glad we have decided to bring her home. No de Lara is going to serve as a nun, in any case. It is time for her to come home and accept her destiny as a member of the House of de Lara."

Jasper leaned against the bed post. "You thought it was fine enough to send her to St. Milburga's when you did not want her under foot," he countered. "Yet she is too good to become a nun?"

Rosamund didn't say anything for a moment. "You know I did not send her away because I wanted to," she said softly "It was necessary."

Jasper pushed himself off the bed post, rolling his eyes. "You did not want any of the children around, Rosamund."

"Because I did not wish for them to contract this horrific curse," she insisted, her normally calm tone filled with passion. "You *know* this, Jasper. The symptoms were appearing when the children were young and I did not wish for them to become diseased as I have become. Why must you always make it sound as if I did not want my own children? I *could* not have them here."

Jasper put up his hands. "I will not engage in this old argument with you," he said, eyeing the maid sitting in the corner who was also busy with her sewing. A maid he had taken to his bed many times. His gaze lingered on the shapely woman for a moment before returning his focus to his wife. "I am beyond discussing the reasons for sending our children away when we did. It is done and over. What did you wish to speak with me about?"

Rosamund had been shielded behind curtains and scarfs and shades for the past fourteen years, even so, she had very keen vision when it came to seeing what was going on around her. Through the gauzy fabric, she could see her husband as he eyed her maid. Once, Rosamund had seen the same lust in his eyes when he looked at her. *But no more.* She had no choice but to accept it. She couldn't even become angry or hurt about it. This was her world and the world was hers alone, and she had resigned herself to it long ago. But she did so long to see that spark of attraction in her husband's eyes, meant for her, just one last time.

But there was no point in wishing what would never be again. Now, they were a bitter and lonely couple who co-existed in their own worlds and those worlds rarely collided. Pushing her sewing aside, Rosamund climbed off of her bed with great effort, for it was painful to move with her affliction. She pushed aside the curtains and stood unsteadily on her feet.

"I wish to speak of Kathalin," she said as she shuffled in Jasper's direction. "I have been thinking on what we must do for her future. Since she will not go back to St. Milburga's, it is only logical that we find a husband for her. Therefore, I would like for you to arrange a grand celebration for her here at Hyssington and invite fine houses with eligible young men to come and celebrate. You will arrange games of skill and strength so that Kathalin may see the young men and the young men may see her. She will preside over the games and hopefully by the end of the celebration, we will have several marriage offers to choose from."

Jasper grunted, though he was not entirely unhappy with his wife's directive. It was a rather smart thing to do and, given the advanced age of their daughter, they didn't have much time before men would overlook her completely in favor of younger women. They had to find a husband for her in a hurry before she become too long in the tooth. No de Lara had ever become a nun and no de Lara had ever become a spinster, either.

"I have been thinking on the same thing," Jasper admitted. "She will make an excellent marital alliance, as my daughter. You and I have discussed this before."

"We have."

"But we must choose very carefully who we invite to the celebration you have suggested."

Rosamund waved a hand at him. "I will leave that up to you," she said, turning away and shuffling back towards her bed. It was painful for her to stand any length of time. "It is my suggestion that you find Marcher lords with eligible sons so we can keep the alliance near to home. That would make the strongest bond of all."

Jasper nodded, stroking his chin thoughtfully. "I have already given it some thought," he said. "Your cousin, Rhett, has an eligible son, and so does Henry de Lohr."

Rosamund turned to look at him, her bright eyes the only thing visible in the layers of fabric covering her face. Their beauty had never dimmed. "Alexander?" she said.

"Aye."

Rosamund cocked her head thoughtfully. "All I know of Alexander de Lohr is what you have told me," she said. "You have said he is strong and brave and true but you also said that he has a reputation with women."

Jasper shrugged. "He is young," he said. "Of course he loves women. He should."

Rosamund sat back on her bed. "Then if that is the case, what of Gates?" she asked. "You love the man as a son. Why not him?"

Jasper hissed. "Because he loves women *too* much," he said. "He has at least three bastards that I have heard of, possibly more. Nay, I do not want such a man for my daughter. As much as I love and admire Gates, I would like for my daughter to have a husband who does not have such an unsavory reputation."

"Yet you sent him to escort her home."

"Because there is no one in England I would trust the task to more than he."

Rosamund was puzzled. "Yet you do not trust him as your daughter's husband?"

Jasper shook his head. "Nay," he said, "because I do not believe he can remain faithful to one woman and if he shamed her, I would be forced to kill him. Nay, Rosamund, put Gates out of your mind. He is not meant for our daughter."

Rosamund didn't push, mostly because she didn't have much of an argument in support of Gates de Wolfe. She, too, had heard of the man's dastardly reputation when it came to women. *Dark Destroyer*, he was called, a nickname whispered among man and woman alike. To women, he was the dark destroyer of their hearts but to men, he was a knight of dark and destructive force.

He was a paradox, indeed.

"Unfortunate," she said as she settled back on her bed, grunting with the pain of the movement. "He is a fine knight from a fine family. His great-great-grandfather was the great Wolfe of the North, William de Wolfe. You told me this yourself. Imagine the sons he could breed with de Lara stock. We could have legendary grandsons, Jasper."

Jasper, seeing that Rosamund was settling back in her bed, took it as his cue that the conversation was over. He was eager to leave, eager to be free of the disease-filled room with its terrible, heavy smell. He began moving to the door.

"Put him out of your mind," he told his wife again, his hand on the iron door latch. "I would possibly consider Alexander, but not Gates. Rest, now. I promise I will tell you when Kathalin arrives. It should be very soon."

Rosamund simply nodded as she picked up her sewing and Jasper, receiving no reply, left the chamber in a hurry. He was always in a hurry to leave. Rosamund reflected back to the days when he had never been in a hurry to leave her bed but those days were long over with.

She wondered fleetingly if her daughter would know something better.

She hoped so.

CHAPTER SIX

"**L**ET ME FIX yer hair, m'lady," the wench said. "Ye say ye've never dressed yer hair before?"

It was dawn in the tiny inn on the edge of town and the de Lara men were just beginning to stir. Kathalin could hear them grunting and farting, calling for chamber pots and warmed water and food. Everything was cold and dark at this hour, men muddling through the early morning shadows. But Kathalin had been up well before dawn even though she had slept very soundly on her mattress on the floor. The cloyingly hot room, coupled with the warm bath, had been exquisite and wonderful, lulling her into a very deep sleep of more comfort than she'd known in her entire life.

It was this first taste of comfort that was beginning to pique her interest. Having grown up in the convent, she had slept on a rope bed and the only clothes she'd ever worn had been those of durable fabric as opposed to fabric of comfort. Her tender skin had suffered through years of scratchy wool and rashes because of it, but last night after her bath, she had put on one of the feather-soft shifts to sleep in and woke up in the morning without a rash or without scratching. It had been utterly remarkable and, if she were to admit it, a great relief. Was it possible that she did not have to go through life scratching herself until her skin bled?

The lure of finding out was too much to resist. In her bathwater, she had washed the brown woolen garment she had worn from St. Milburga's and put it by the fire to dry, but as she rose that morning and looked between the soft and comfortable things Gates had purchased for her and the brown wool that chaffed her terribly, her need for skin relief drew her to the clothes from Gates. No sooner had she started pulling them out of the basket than there was a soft knock at her door and when she opened it, a serving wench was there with food on a tray.

Kathalin admitted the wench and when the woman set the food down and saw all of the marvelous clothing, she struck up a conversation. One thing led to another and before Kathalin realized what had happened, the woman was more than happy to help her dress. Shifts were being pulled forth, and hose, and it was all being organized on the mattress on the floor. Curious, Kathalin simply watched and learned. It was an education on worldly protocol that she had never received but one she found she was increasingly eager to learn.

The serving wench started from the bottom, or literally, the naked flesh. She instructed Kathalin to remove the shift she'd slept in, which she did except for the fact that she kept the garment clutched in front of her to protect her modesty as the serving wench took some of the oil in the glass phial and smoothed it all over Kathalin's body. Skin that had been dry and cracked was eased and the permanent rash caused by the woolen garments was soothed; *exquisitely* soothed. The wench also took the calendula salve and, after rubbing it on Kathalin's damaged wrists, she proceeded to rub it against the rash on her back and on her thighs, which further soothed her. Kathalin had never been so utterly relieved in her entire life. No itching, no misery. Those two marvelous little miracle-workers, the oil and the salve, had seen to that.

There had been no relief like that at St. Milburga's and Kathalin was awed that such things existed. Worldly things that Mother Benedicta had said were evil. But they didn't seem evil to Kathalin; quite the contrary. After that, she was more than willing to let the wench helped her pull the soft shift over her head again but Kathalin had no idea what she wanted to wear so the wench drew out the unbleached linen with the rabbit fur cuffs and neckline.

It was a gorgeous garment, and warm, and the wench pulled it over Kathalin's head and then tightened the laces on each side of the torso until Kathalin's slender but lovely figure was greatly emphasized. The wench could see how shapely she was but Kathalin couldn't, and it was probably a good thing because she would have been grossly embarrassed by what could be perceived as a revealing surcoat – the scoop neck with the fur lining, long and cuffed sleeves, and snug bodice were quite clinging.

And quite alluring.

Hose went on next, tied with two pieces of twine that the seamstress had attached to them, and the silk slippers with the fur lining went on after that. Kathalin was quite overwhelmed with the beauty and warmth and softness of what she was wearing, shocked and guilty that she loved it so much and felt so incredibly content in it. *I believe God would be happy for you to be warm and comfortable.* That was what Gates had said and she wasn't hard pressed to admit that he had been right. However, she felt guilty that she wasn't putting the brown wool back on but not guilty enough to want to actually do it. The soothed skin was enough to keep her out of the brown wool and remain in what she was wearing because it didn't irritate her skin.

Fully dressed and chewing on a piece of bread, Kathalin sat on the mattress while the wench, on her knees, got up behind her with the comb and pins the seamstress had included and began to dress her hair. It was then that the question had come up about the preferred style of her hair, to which Kathalin had no answer. She'd only ever worn it modestly braided so she genuinely had no idea what the wench meant.

And so, the true transformation began.

"Let me fix yer hair, m'lady," the wench said. "Ye say ye've never dressed yer hair before?"

Kathalin shook her head as the wench began to comb it with the tortoise-shell, double-sided comb. "Nay," she replied. "I... I have had no need to dress it."

The wench didn't say anything as she combed the dark, shiny tresses with a hint of red to them. Kathalin's hair was well below her buttocks, very wavy because Kathalin had washed her hair with the rosemary soap the night before and then braided it to sleep in. The wench combed and combed before finally sectioning the hair off into two parts, split right down the middle, and she began to braid one of the sections.

"'Tis a shame, m'lady," the wench said as she braided. "Yer hair is lovely. Ye could wear it with gold ribbon or feathers!"

Kathalin had no idea what the wench meant but she instinctively put her hand up to her hair, touching it nervously, as the dark strands were braided.

"Why?" she asked. "Do women really wear their hair so?"

The wench nodded. "Sometimes fine women come here," she said eagerly, as if gossiping. "I watch to see what they are wearing. I have seen women with golden nets in their hair and one woman who had peacock feathers arranged in it. Ye would look stunning with peacock feathers in yer hair!"

Kathalin listened with some awe, quite intrigued, before discounting her interest. Only vain and worldly women would do such things... *wouldn't they?*

"I would have no use for feathers in my hair," she said. "A simple arrangement is all I need."

The wench suspected that so she wasn't about to do anything outlandish no matter how much she wanted to. She practiced on her sister, the other woman who worked for the innkeeper, and she was growing quite good at dressing hair. She aspired to be a lady's maid someday so she kept up on fashions and hair, hoping that one day the opportunity would present itself. But this lady seemed quite different; she had come in yesterday dressed in rags and being led by a rope, and now she was dressed in great finery and having her hair dressed. It was all quite puzzling and the wench didn't have much control over her curiosity.

"I will only braid yer hair, m'lady," she assured her, eyeing the woman with the long, white neck and snow-white shoulders that blended with the pale color of the surcoat she wore. "May... I ask where ye are coming from?"

Kathalin thought on St. Milburga's, struggling with the depression it provoked. "Ludlow," she said softly.

The wench finished braiding the right side of her head, secured the ends with a strip of twine from the calendula salve box, and then started in on the left side of the head.

"The knight ye came with," the wench ventured, nosy. "Is he yer brother, m'lady?"

Kathalin thought on the men who were her brothers, men she had only seen a few times in her life. In fact, she'd spent more time with de Wolfe than she'd ever spent with her blood brothers.

"Nay," she said. "He is a knight who serves my father."

"Who is yer father, m'lady?"

"You ask many questions."

The wench fell silent for a moment. "My apologies, m'lady," she said quietly. "I meant no harm."

Kathalin immediately felt bad, as if she had rebuked the girl too strongly. She was usually an excellent conversationalist and not rude in the least. In fact, she was usually quite friendly but she was very much out of her element at the moment and unbalanced by it all.

"I know," she said. "I did not mean to be rude. What is your name?"

The wench was surprised by the apology. "Ruby, m'lady."

Kathalin smiled faintly. "Ruby?" she repeated. "I like that name."

Ruby finished plaiting the right side of Kathalin's head and now began to wrap both braids around her head, up behind each ear, creating a rather elaborate work of art that encircled Kathalin's head as she pinned the heavy hair down with the iron pins.

"My sister's name is Pearl," she said. "My mother named us after things fine and beautiful."

Kathalin thought it rather ironic that plain, well-worn women in a small village were named after things fine and beautiful. "They are lovely names," she said, wincing as Ruby pushed the last pin into her scalp. "Thank you for taking the time to help me dress."

Ruby stood back to look at her handiwork, which was quite exquisite. All of the practice on her sister's bushy hair had paid off. She smiled at the utterly lovely picture before her.

"Ye look beautiful, m'lady," she said.

Kathalin stood up, gingerly touching her hair, not waiting to mess the careful dressing. Ruby motioned her over to the cold bathwater that, in the glow of the firelight, acted as a mirror and for the first time in her life, Kathalin was stunned at the reflection gazing back at her. Her hair was beautifully dressed and the garment she wore was flattering to a fault. Kathalin hardly recognized herself. As she looked into the water with wonderment, Ruby found the calendula salve and, using a finger, slicked some of it onto Kathalin's lips before the woman could stop her. As Kathalin mashed her lips together, unfamiliar with the feel of the salve, Ruby began packing everything away into the basket.

"The cold will crack yer lips if ye aren't careful, m'lady," she told her. "The salve will help them not to crack and bleed. Ye should put it on yer lips every time ye put it on yer wrists to heal the rope burn."

It was an excellent suggestion and one Kathalin never would have thought of. In fact, Ruby seemed to know a good deal about garments and dressing and hair and salves that Kathalin didn't.

"I will," she said, rubbing her lips together still. "Thank you for your assistance. It has been invaluable."

Ruby smiled modestly. "My pleasure, m'lady," she said, now appearing somewhat distracted as she packed up the last of the basket including Kathalin's brown wool garment from St. Milburga's and her worn leather shoes. "I... I have always wanted to be a lady's maid so I have learned much. I would make a very good maid if ye need one."

Kathalin's first instinct was to agree; she thought she might feel much more confident with Ruby along to help guide her through this strange new world, but on the other hand, she had no idea what her father wanted of her and if, in fact, she was heading back to St. Milburga's soon. If that was the case, then she certainly wouldn't need a maid.

"I am sure you would," she said. "But my... my future is uncertain at the moment; otherwise, I would gladly take you with me."

Ruby was both elated and crushed. "If ye change yer mind, then ye know where to find me, m'lady."

Kathalin smiled at the girl. "I do," she said. "Thank you for your offer. Now, can you tell me where the knight is who brought me here?"

Ruby nodded as she put the lid on the basket, securing it, before going to the cloak that was hanging on the peg behind the door. She shook it out as she went to Kathalin and swung it around the woman's shoulders.

"He was by yer door all night," she said. "He never left, but when I came up to yer room a short while ago, he was at the bottom of the stairs with the other knight. Should I get him for ye, m'lady?"

Kathalin looked at her with some surprise. "He... he was outside of my door all night?"

"Aye, m'lady."

"But why?"

Ruby shrugged. "To protect ye, I suppose," she said. "He sent all of his men to bed but he remained awake, all night, guarding yer door."

Kathalin was somewhat astonished by the information but in the same breath, she had a strange urge to smile again. Just like that urge she had last night every time she looked at the basket de Wolfe had brought her. What was it about the man that seemed to make her smile all of a sudden? More than that, her heart would beat faster and her insides felt queer and quivery. She'd never known such sensations before and therefore had no way of knowing what caused them, but the only common denominator was, in fact, de Wolfe.

The man is making me giddy!

It was a startling realization. There was no reason why Gates de

Wolfe should make her feel giddy, but he did. Only yesterday she had hated the man, hated him for dragging her out of St. Milburga's. But since last night, her hate had vanished, turning into something else, something unfamiliar but strangely exciting. She had no idea what to make of it, only that she found it confusing.

I am simply exhausted, she told herself. *That must be why thoughts of him cause my heart to race.*

... isn't it?

Taking a deep breath, trying to calm her unfamiliar thoughts, Kathalin fastened the top of her cloak and turned away from Ruby.

"Will you please find the knight and tell him that I am ready to depart after prayers?" she asked, moving to the half-eaten food tray. "I am sure he is eager to leave."

Ruby nodded, heading for the door, as Kathalin popped a piece of white cheese into her mouth. "Aye, m'lady," she said, opening the door to find three big soldiers standing outside. She eyed the soldiers warily before returning her attention to Kathalin. "Remember that if ye ever need a maid, I should be happy to assist ye."

Kathalin nodded as she chewed and swallowed. "I am grateful."

With a timid smile, Ruby quit the chamber as Kathalin finished what was left on her tray. But the lure of food was in competition with the fox-lined cloak she wore, for most certainly she had never in her life known anything so warm or so soft. She kept running her hands over the fox, enthralled with the feel of it, enthralled with the feel of everything she was wearing because it was exactly as de Wolfe said it would be – soft, warm, and comfortable.

Was this what worldly vanity meant? Wearing garments that didn't make her skin raw? If that was the case, Kathalin began to think that, perhaps, she might be in danger of being a vain woman because she liked the feel very much. She knew she could get used to it, and happily.

Mother Benedicta would be most displeased.

With that thought, she dropped to her knees, crossed herself, and began intoning the morning prayers for Matins. It was a habit she had been in since childhood and Catholic guilt dictated that she prayed very hard for her wicked lust for comfort. At least, Mother Benedicta would say that she needed to. She was nearly finished pleading for God's mercy for her evil thoughts when there was a soft knock at the door.

Finishing quickly with her prayers, she bade the caller to enter and when she looked up and saw de Wolfe in the dim light of the chamber, she would remember the look on his face for the rest of her life. She'd never seen anything like it before, ever. Something between surprise, awe, and pleasure.

She fought off the urge to smile at him in return but she couldn't quite manage it.

"DID YOU SLEEP at all?"

The question came from Stephan as he sat across the table from Gates, down in the inn's common room that was hardly bigger than a solar. It would seat perhaps twenty people at the most, and even now, the twenty people that were there were Gates' men, all breaking their fast.

Tables were leaning, some were broken altogether, and the entire room smelled heavily of smoke and urine, but Gates' men didn't particularly care, and neither did Gates. Men were coughing, waking up, ordering food, and gathering their possessions for the march to Hyssington as Gates and Stephan sat at the table nearest the stairs. Gates, who appeared pale and exhausted highlighted by a growth of beard, grunted to Stephan's question.

"We will be at Hyssington by late today," he said, avoiding an answer. "There will be time enough to rest once we have reached home."

Stephan who, in fact, had slept quite well most of the night, whistled low to get the attention of the lone serving wench in the room. He pointed to the table, silently telling the woman they required food, before continuing the conversation.

"I have never known you to sleep much," he said. "In fact, you are usually awake when I go to bed and you are still awake when I wake up in the morning. Do you not ever become tired?"

Gates smiled faintly, nodding his head. "I am always weary," he said. "But I have never been able to sleep well, even as a youth. My master did not sleep well and therefore had me up at all hours of the night, keeping busy. It is an unfortunate habit that has remained with me all of these years."

Stephan's expression suggested sympathy and understanding. He moved his arm off the table as the serving wench brought a pitcher of watered ale and two dirty cups. He wiped them both out before pouring.

"So we return to Hyssington today," he said. "What then? We will not be returning to France any time soon, so what is there for us now?"

Gates took the cup that the man offered. "Wales," he said flatly. "We have come home to fight off Welsh raiders who can be just as deadly as any French fighter. But I will admit that I do have a longing to return home and see my father."

"The one that taught you to curse?"

"The same. His father taught him, and his father before him."

"A legacy of insults," he said. "Let me hear something, then. I've not heard you insult the men since we returned from France. Have you forgotten how?"

Gates grinned, drinking his ale as the wench returned with a tray of bread and cheese and cold beef. "Of course not," he said. "I simply have not had any reason to insult them. This has been a short trip with seasoned men who do not deserve insulting – yet."

Stephan laughed quietly as he stabbed his knife at the beef, pulling forth a big hunk. "You had plenty of reason last night with the men fornicating in the loft in full view of de Lara's daughter," he said, rolling his eyes. "Come on, now – just one little curse."

"I cannot think of one."

"You can always think of one. Then you are a forgetful old fool."

Gates cocked an eyebrow. "Is that the best you can do?" he said. "If

I am a fool, then you are a clay-brained maggot."

Stephan burst out into snickers. "Ah, the famous de Wolfe talent for insults shows itself," he said. "You would do your father proud. Speaking of fathers, I'd hate to see de Lara's reaction when he finds out his men were fornicating in full-view of his daughter."

Gates took a big bite of bread, still warm from the oven. "I cannot say if he will care, to be truthful," he said, sobering. "He seems not to care much about his daughter. I am curious to know what her fate will be once we reach Hyssington. De Lara and his wife do not want her to take her vows as a nun which means they want to marry her off, I would think."

Stephan was chewing loudly as he spoke. "But de Lara seemed grateful at the thought of not providing her with a dowry should she have already taken her vows."

Gates shrugged. "That being the case, I have no idea what the girl's fate will be once we reach Hyssington," he said, wondering why he should feel the slightest bit of concern at that thought. He tried to shake it off. "All I know is that I wish to see my father, as I have not seen him in many years. Mayhap when the snow melts and spring arrives, I shall take a trip north to Castle Questing to visit him."

Stephen delved into the cheese. "You are his second son," he said. "Did you not tell me once that your older brother serves Northumberland and remained close to home?"

Gates nodded. "Gabriel was forced to stay close to home, as the heir to the earldom of Warenton," he said. "Me, however… well, I have wanderlust in my veins, as my father would say. Even so, I would like to go home and see my family."

Stephan took a huge swallow of ale. "It is a very big family," he said. "The entire north is crawling with de Wolfes just as the entire Marches are crawling with de Lohrs. Soon the two families will merge and take over the entire country."

Gates was back to grinning. "Mayhap I should marry a de Lohr and join the two," he said, "although Alexander's sisters are already wed.

Beautiful girls, in fact."

"Then why did you not pledge for one of them?"

Gates looked at him in shock. "Are you *mad*?"

Stephan laughed, knowing well that Gates de Wolfe and marriage were mortal enemies. As he finished up what was left of the beef, one of the serving wenches came down the stairs and approached the table. She curtsied nervously as she fixed on Gates.

"M'lord," she said. "The lady says to tell ye that she is ready to depart after prayers."

Gates simply nodded and the wench fled, disappearing back into the kitchens. Gates lingered on his cup a moment, thoughtfully, before speaking.

"I wonder if she will be true to her word today," he questioned.

Stephen looked up from the beef. "What do you mean?"

Gates lifted his eyebrows in a pensive gesture. "Her wrists are torn up from the rope over the past two days," he said. "She told me that I did not have to bind her again today as she promised not to try to escape. I was simply wondering if she would be true to her word."

Stephen put the last bit of food in his mouth, wiping his hands on his breeches. "You will soon find out," he said. "If you discover she is a liar, then you can tie her up until we reach Hyssington and then she will be de Lara's problem."

Gates shook his head. "Untrue," he said. "She will continue to be my problem as I can promise you that de Lara will tell me to manage the girl. Do you think he will want to keep an eye on her? Of course not. Therefore, the burden will continue to be mine."

Stephan didn't have much to say to that, mostly because he knew it was true. "It seems strange to have a child and not care much about her," he said. "I received the impression that de Lara did not much care for his only daughter."

Gates grunted. "You heard him say that he loves his dog more than his family," he said. "I would believe that. I do not understand it, but I believe it."

Stephan simply nodded, finishing up the last of his meal as Gates drained his cup and stood up, wiping at his mouth with the back of his hand.

"I will go see to the lady now," he said. "Make sure the men are gathered and ready to depart. I do not intend to linger in this place any longer than I have to. Hyssington is on the horizon and I am eager to get there."

Stephan nodded, standing up as well, and went to corral the men as Gates headed up the stairs.

It was dark on the second floor for the most part and Gates paused in the loft area, ushering commands to the men who were still there, men who were now moving very quickly at the sight of de Wolfe. When he uttered commands in a low tone, almost under his breath, it meant that the man was in no mood for nonsense. Men scrambled.

With the last of the troops gathering their things and heading down to the common room, Gates made his way to Lady Kathalin's door, excusing the three big soldiers who had been standing guard for the last hour or so. When the men moved away, Gates rapped softly on the door. He waited a few moments and, receiving no answer, rapped again.

"My lady?" he said. "It is de Wolfe. May I enter?"

He heard movement but there was still no reply. Concerned that she was in need of assistance, or quite possibly couldn't answer, he opened the door just in time to see her standing up from the bed. It was evident that she had been kneeling. In the faint light of the weak hearth, Gates fixed on the woman when she turned to him and, for a moment, he didn't recognize her.

Dressed in the fine dark blue cloak with the fox lining, and the pale linen dress peeking out from underneath, Gates honestly didn't recognize her at first. Her face was cleanly scrubbed, her red lips faintly glossy, and her hair was gloriously arranged around her head. He had never seen anything so utterly lovely. He just stood there and stared at her just as she was staring at him, and when she smiled timidly, he finally lifted his eyebrows in disbelief.

"Lady Kathalin?" he asked hesitantly.

Kathalin nodded, unnerved by his reaction. "Of course," she said, her hands flitting to her hair nervously, then her face. "These are the things you brought for me last night. You said I should wear them… that is, you told me to…."

Gates could see how uncertain she was and he hastened to reassure her. "Aye, you should wear them," he said quickly. "I did indeed tell you to. In fact… please forgive me my shock, my lady, for I have never seen anything quite so fine in all of my life. Are the garments comfortable?"

Kathalin flushed a deep shade of red; Gates could see it even in the weak light and it was clear to him that the woman had never heard a compliment in her entire life.

"Aye, they are," she said, looking down at herself and stroking the fox lining of the cloak. "I… that is to say, you were correct that they would be warm and comfortable. They are very warm and comfortable. And the serving wench dressed my hair like this. If it is too much, I can remove the braids. Mayhap I should not have let her do it."

She was beginning to rattle on nervously and Gates smiled, putting up his hands to stop her as he took a step or two in her direction. Truthfully, he just wanted to get a closer look at the beauty he was facing.

"Your hair is beautiful," he assured her. "There is no finer woman in all of England at this moment. The clothing and your hair… you look magnificent, truly. You are truly an earl's daughter now."

Flattery. Kathalin had never been given any flattery – of course, it was wicked and vain, so Mother Benedicta never flattered and she rarely gave praise. Therefore, the kind words coming from Gates were causing Kathalin's heart to race and her cheeks to flush. She felt like turning away from the man and grinning at him all at the same time. Having no idea what to say or how to react, she simply opened up the cloak to show him the dress beneath.

"The garment fits," she told him nervously. "The servant was able to cinch it up but it is too long. I will have to hem the bottom unless you do not want me to. Mayhap you want to take this back to the seamstress after I have had my use of it."

Gates didn't really hear much after *the garment fits* and she opened up her cloak to show him. After that, it was all a blur. To the strains of her voice saying nonsensical words in the background (although she was making sense; he simply wasn't hearing what she was saying), what he saw before him was a glorious figure of a slender waist, full breasts, and a luscious neck. He had never seen finer, and he'd seen many a woman in his time. But Kathalin... surely God had meant her for something greater in this life because she wasn't like any other woman, ever. She was exquisite and unique unto herself.

Something changed inside of Gates at that moment as he envisioned Kathalin's grandeur; he could feel it. He'd declared the woman off-limits for conquest but, in viewing that spectacular figure, he found his willpower wavering. But it was more than that; clearly, she was a beauty, but there was something very naïve yet strong about her, something he'd notice from the onset. He rather liked the fact that she wasn't jaded and that she had lived a sheltered life. It meant that she was a woman in her truest form, untouched and uninfluenced.

And then there was him.

Cynical, predatory, and selfish. Those words described him when it came to women. For the first time in his life, he was coming to wish he'd been a bit more careful and thoughtful with his private life. Surely a man like him... and a woman like her... nay, it was too foolish to even consider.

She is not to be toyed with! He told himself sharply. *Your lustful urges are not meant for her, you fool!*

"Did you want to take the dress back to the seamstress when I am finished with it?" Kathalin asked again, cutting into his thoughts. "I will not hem it if you wish to sell it back to her."

Gates quickly shook his head. "I will do no such thing," he said.

"The garment is yours. It was made with only you in mind. Surely no other woman could wear it after you and do it justice."

More flattery. Kathalin's cheeks flushed again just when they were starting to ease. She thought that perhaps she should thank him for his kind words but that was rather embarrassing, as if thanking him would acknowledge that she appreciated his flattery. Well, she did, but she wasn't sure she wanted him to know that.

"The servant packed everything back into the basket," she said. "I am ready to depart when you are."

Gates smiled at her as he bent over to collect the rather large basket. It was clear that Kathalin was nervous around him, especially in matters she was uncertain with like fine clothing and conversation, so he simply picked the basket up and opened the chamber door.

"My lady," he said, indicating for her to exit. "We may proceed."

With her new slippers and fine cloak and beautiful hair, Kathalin left the room timidly, with Gates right behind her, walking slowly and uncertainly until Gates finally took her elbow to help her along. She was shocked at the physical contact at first, wondering why he was touching her, but then she realized he was simply being polite. Or perhaps he was being possessive. Unused to the behavior between men and women, she really didn't know. All of this was a new world to her.

Down in the common room, Stephan was rallying the troops, forcing everyone outside into the new morning. The front door to the inn was open and beyond they could see a winter wonderland of white snow and blue skies. The storm that had whipped them most of the night had moved on, leaving brilliance in its wake. It also left extreme cold and as Gates took Kathalin outside, their breaths hung heavy in the morning air.

Kathalin pulled the warm and soft cloak tightly around her body as she stood on the step of the inn, watching the soldiers bring the horses around from the livery where they had been lodged overnight. Men were preparing their mounts, heaving their rucksacks over their shoulders, and generally preparing to depart. Gates handed the basket of items over to a soldier to either carry or fasten onto the back of a horse, since they had no wagon, and once he was free of the basket, he turned to Kathalin.

"At least the snow isn't blowing sideways today," he commented as he extended his hand to her. "Come along, my lady."

Kathalin started to take a step but suddenly came to a halt, looking at the muddy, wet ground. "These shoes...," she said hesitantly. "I fear they will be ruined if I walk on this ground."

Gates looked down to the sopping ground and, without a word, reached out and swept Kathalin into his big arms. She gasped at the unexpected action, quickly gripping his neck as he picked her up. He slogged across the horrible muddy road with the big ruts in it until he came to his steed, being held steady by a soldier. Gates swung Kathalin easily up into the saddle.

She was sitting sideways, holding the saddle for support, as he mounted behind her, lifted her up, and then placed her across his thighs. Kathalin felt rather like she was being manhandled as he moved her around to find a comfortable position and the soldier who had been holding the horse now tucked the cloak in around her feet so it wouldn't be muddied.

Meanwhile, Gates was tending to her like a father. He made sure she was sitting properly, fully cover, and put the hood of the cloak over her head for both protection against the cold and modesty. Kathalin simply sat there and let him fuss, oddly enough, thinking she rather liked a man fussing over her. She'd never had such a thing before. When Gates was finally satisfied, he lifted a gloved hand in the air and made a forward motion. The group of men began to move.

With the bright blue sky above and the snow-white blanket below, it made for enchanting scenery as they traveled north. In the fields, they could see tracks from foraging creatures who had dared to venture out into the snow and about an hour into their ride, they saw a herd of deer off to the east and Gates gave the order for some of his men to go hunting for meat for sup. Kathalin watched as the men rode off, pursuing the deer that were beginning to run.

"It is so beautiful out here," she said, her gaze on the white and blue horizon. "I cannot recall the last time I was out of St. Milburga's. It was so long ago that I have forgotten."

Gates, whose attention had also been on his men as they took off after the deer, glanced down at Kathalin. With the hood covering her head, all he could see were her nose and lips. *Such lovely lips....*

"Aye, 'tis beautiful," he said, but not with the awe that she had use. "And cold. And wet. I will be happy when we reach Hyssington."

Kathalin looked up at him, brushing the fur of her hood against his chin. "When will we be there?"

Gates glanced up at the sun's position in the sky. "Another few hours," he said. "We should be there well before sunset."

Kathalin fell silent as her gaze once again moved over the snowy landscape. "May... may I ask you a question, Sir Gates?"

"Of course, my lady."

"Will you tell me the truth as to why my father wishes for me to return home?" she asked. "I realize you are only the messenger and I respect that position, but will you not at least tell me what you know so that I am prepared? I feel as if I am about to face the executioner and it would help me tremendously if I knew what was in store for me."

Gates hesitated before answering. "My lady, I truly do not know what your father has in mind for you," he said, "and even if I did, it would not be my place to tell you. I hope you understand that."

Kathalin did but she was still disappointed. "I do not wish for my father to become angry with you," she said. "'Tis only that he has not recalled me home in the fourteen years I have been at St. Milburga's. Only after the missive was sent requesting permission for me to take my vows did he send for me, so that leads me to believe that he does not wish for me to take my vows."

Gates truly felt some pity for the woman facing an uncertain future. "If I were you, that would be a logical assumption for me as well," he said softly.

Kathalin looked at him, those bright blue eyes sucking him in. "But what else is there for me?" she asked, a hint of distress in her tone. "Am I to go home and be a companion to my mother in her old age, a woman who clearly had no use for me as a child? Is that what my life is to entail? Uselessness and boredom?"

Gates didn't have an answer for her. "We will be there in a few hours and then you shall know," he said. "Until then, it is a waste of time to think on it. Enjoy the ride and enjoy the scenery. As for your future… you will know soon enough."

Kathalin thought on his advice. "Your words are wise," she said. "But I cannot help the apprehension I feel. I want to go home."

Gates knew that but he was fairly certain he would not be escorting her back to St. Milburga's any time soon.

"Mayhap at some later date," he said, trying not to give her too much hope. "Meanwhile, I should think you would at least be agreeable to seeing your parents once again. They are, after all, your parents. Times change. People change. You should not fear seeing them again."

Kathalin shrugged, not having much of an answer for that. "Are your parents still living?"

Gates nodded. "My father is still alive," he said. "My mother passed away some years ago."

Kathalin turned to look at him, hitting him yet again with her big, furry hood. "Do you see your father often?"

Gates lifted his eyebrows thoughtfully, trying to remember the last time he saw his father. "Not as often as I would like," he said. "He lives far to the north at a place called Castle Questing. He is the Earl of Warenton."

Kathalin smiled with some understanding. "Then you are the off-spring of an earl just as I am," she said. "That did not matter at St. Milburga's, but I suppose it matters in the world a great deal. Do you find that it has given you position and power?"

He shrugged. "My family name has most certainly allowed me privilege," he said. "Being the second son of the earl, however, I have had to work hard for everything I have."

"What do you have?"

It was a perfectly innocent question but as Gates thought on it, he realized he didn't have much other than military might and a great family name. *What do you have*? Not as much as he would have liked. He frowned as he thought on his answer.

"I have earned wealth as a knight," he told her. "I have four hundred men that are personally sworn to me. I feed them and clothe them and keep them supplied even though I am personally sworn to your father. He pays me well for my strength and skill."

Kathalin listened with interest. "No wife or home?" she asked. "No children?"

He shook his head, now becoming uncomfortable with the turn of conversation even though he knew she wasn't deliberately trying to harass him. "Nay," he replied. "Not at this time."

Kathalin cocked her head curiously. "Would you not like a home and sons to carry on your name?" she asked. "I thought that was what most men wanted."

He found those bright blue eyes most unnerving as he looked at her, a smirk on his face. "Are you offering to provide me with sons, my lady?" he asked, teasing, watching her grin and avert her gaze. "This is so suddenly. I do not know what to say. We have not even had our first kiss yet and now you offer to provide me with sons. How shocking."

Kathalin could tell he was jesting at her and she giggled, embarrassed. "I did not mean it the way it sounded."

He was glad the focus was off of him and his lack of sons, now on to her and her curious questions. He rather liked watching her squirm.

"What's this?" he demanded lightly. "Now you are rescinding your offer? I am crushed. Deeply crushed. How could you hurt me so?"

He was being quite charming and overly dramatic, but it had worked the desired effect and deflected the conversation away from his lack of a wife and children. Even though Kathalin wasn't at all versed in the flirtations between a man and a woman, it seemed to come naturally to her and she responded to his charm. She had a natural sense of humor, much like Gates did, and she sought to give the man a dose of his own medicine.

"Very well, if you insist," she said. "But we must be married before I provide any children. I want a very big wedding that costs a great deal of money. And... and more of these soft garments. And I want golden rings on my fingers and peacock feathers in my hair. Will that cost terribly much?"

Gates eyebrows flew up. "Demanding enchantress!" he exclaimed softly. "You have yet to provide me with sons but you still demand I spend all of my money on you? I find that most insulting. This bargain is most definitely off."

Kathalin continued to snort, her gaze averted and her cheeks flaming red. She'd never in her life had such a conversation and she was giddy with it, feeling her heart flutter with the thrill. She was quite certain Mother Benedicta would not approve of the conversation but, at the moment, she didn't much care.

"Then I am devastated," she said. "I am going to tell my father what you have done and he will not like it one bit."

Gates guffawed, a sharp sound, and quickly shut his mouth. "Oh, my silly young girl," he said, amused. "You have no idea what your father would do to me if you told him that."

She was interested. "Truly?" she asked, looking at him. "What would he do?"

He cast her a sidelong glance. "Beat me at the very least," he said. "Turn his dogs on me. How would *you* react if your daughter, who had spent all of her life in a convent, was blatantly toyed with by the knight who was charged with her escort? That is abuse of a position of power and you would make sure that knight was properly punished."

Kathalin grinned. "You did not toy with me," she said. "You simply demanded I bear you sons."

"I did not. You offered to do it."

Kathalin could see a smile playing on his lips and she shook her head reproachfully. "I see we shall not agree on this," she said. "Mayhap it is for the best that we do not marry and I do not bear you sons. I will return to St. Milburga's, eventually, and you shall continue on with your warring ways, and our lives will go in different directions. But I do wish you well, Sir Gates. I shall say a prayer for your safety. Your kindness will not be forgotten."

The conversation had taken a serious turn and Gates looked at her as she gazed off across the snowy lands. It seemed to him that she had suddenly turned thoughtful and introspective, as if there were a good deal on her mind that she could not, or would not, discuss. He had rather liked it the other way, when she was willing to speak with him and even jest with him. Aye, he had liked that a great deal.

"It was not kindness I showed you yesterday or the day before," he said quietly. "I showed you my sense of duty. This entire venture has been my sense of duty. I hope you understand that."

Kathalin instinctively looked to her wrists, buried under the gloves the seamstress had provided, and thinking on the raw skin that had been immensely helped by the calendula salve. She thought on the past two days and how she had hated de Wolfe for doing what he had been ordered to do. She had fought him, and struggled against him, and all the while he'd remained stoic and determined. Never had he wavered or been cruel. Providing her with clothing and comfort had also been part of that duty but she had to stop fighting him before he could do it. She was coming to think that the situation between them hadn't all been his fault.

Hate.

She didn't hate him anymore. In fact….

"I understand," she said softly. "I cannot fault you for doing as you were told. I am not entirely sure you could have done anything differently given the fact I did not wish to go with you. I still do not. But here I am and there isn't much I can do about it."

Gates could hear resignation in her voice and it depressed him somehow. He suspected what Jasper had in mind for her purely from what he'd mentioned, but Gates still wasn't in a position to tell her that. *A political marriage.* She was a pawn to her father and that was probably all she would ever be – a burden and a pawn. In Kathalin's case, both would be a tragedy. It was a fate she did not deserve.

But he could not, and would not, interfere.

"That is a sensible way to look at the situation, my lady," he finally said.

They continued to ride on in relative silence with the cold breeze caressing them both, but the silence was not uncomfortable. On the contrary, it was rather warm. As if there was some manner of under-standing between them now. Kathalin was thinking on what would take place once she reached Hyssington and Gates was wondering why he didn't like the idea of Jasper marrying his daughter off. She was fine and pure and beautiful, three words he had very much come to associate with her, and certainly something to be treasured and not bartered with.

As Gates mulled over those thoughts, shouts began to come from his men up at point. Stephan, at the head of the column, was calling back to him, waving at him, and Gates spurred his steed forward as Kathalin held on for dear life. The horse was spirited and with a somewhat bobbing gait when he was excited. As Gates drew near Stephan, the big knight pointed to the road ahead.

"Look," he said. "I am not entirely sure what to make of that."

Gates peered up the road, the glare from the snow hurting his eyes. The road was wet and muddy from the melted snow, with big dirty drifts piled up on the shoulders, and he could see up ahead a solitary bundled figure walking along. But the figure was staggering, and at one point nearly falling, so Gates sent Stephan up ahead to see to the situation.

Holding up a gloved fist, Gates brought the entire column to a halt as Stephan raced up ahead. He saw clearly when Stephan engaged the figure in conversation and he further saw when the bundled figure fell back, onto the snow drift, and simply sat there as if exhausted. At that point, Stephan climbed off his steed and stood in front of the figure, obviously conversing with it. After an exchange of a few words, he waved over Gates.

Gates spurred his horse forward and, once again, Kathalin clung to the horse's mane to keep from falling because of the jaunty canter. They came upon Stephan expectantly.

"My lord," Stephan said, pointing to the figure on the snow drift, which turned out to be a sobbing woman with a red nose. "She says her children are very ill and is walking to the nearest town to find a physic."

Before Gates could open his mouth, Kathalin spoke. "What is wrong with the children?" she asked anyone who could tell her. "Where are they?"

Stephan looked at the woman sitting on the snow drift. "Tell the lady what you told me," he said. "Speak now."

The woman on the snow drift wiped at her nose with her ragged clothing, dirty brown wool that was well worn. "A fever," she said. "Both of me children have it, m'lady."

Kathalin was very concerned; St. Milburga's was a healing order, as Milburga was the patron saint of lepers, and she had been trained to heal since a very young age. It was something she knew a good deal about. "Where are your children?" she asked.

The woman pointed off to the west. "There," she said. "Me home is not far, m'lady. I was going to town to find a physic to tend them."

Kathalin shook her head. "That is not necessary," she said, turning to look at Gates. "I must go and see what I can do for them."

Gates wasn't apt to agree. "My lady, we are expected at Hyssington," he told her. "We do not have time to make any detours."

She fixed him with those bright blue eyes. "Hyssington can wait," she said in a tone he'd never heard from her before. "If there is illness, then I must see to it. That is what I have been taught, de Wolfe. St. Milburga's is a healing order and that is what I know, so if I can help, I am obligated to do so."

He just looked at her. His sense of duty told him to get the woman to Hyssington as soon as possible but the part of him that was the least bit swayed by her passion and firm words was inclined to grant her request. He knew St. Milburga's was a hospital order; he'd seen the big dormitory where they'd kept beds for patients because they had passed through it on their search for the Prioress. *The Refectory*, it had been called. Indecisive, he made the mistake of showing it and Kathalin took advantage of his state.

"Please," she said, lowering her voice. "We will not be long, I promise. But please let me help if I can."

With a heavy sigh, and thinking he was a fool to acquiesce, he simply nodded to Stephan. "Put that woman on your horse," he said, pointing to the disheveled figure. "Let her show us where these children are or we shall never make it to Hyssington on schedule."

As Stephan moved to help the woman onto his saddle, and unhappy in doing so because she smelled and was dirty, Gates turned to the soldiers mounted nearby and gave them a directive – the main body of soldiers was to remain on the road and wait for them while he took ten men with him as a guard just in case the weeping woman was leading them into trouble. His horse was fast, and he was certain he could get away if this was some kind of trap, but he wanted the main part of the escort to remain behind in case it was. Too many men caught up in a trap would make it chaotic and difficult to flee from it.

With the weeping woman mounted behind Stephan, she directed them onto a small path they had passed about a quarter of a mile back, a path that led through a snow-covered field, through a grove of snow-heavy trees, and emerged out the other side to a small farm. It really wasn't far off the main road at all and, so far, there had been no signs of a trap.

Still, Gates was cautious and his senses were heightened as the woman riding behind Stephan led them to a small cottage amongst a cluster of outbuildings, all of them housing barn animals of some kind. With the melting snow and cold weather, it smelled terribly of animals and urine. The entire complex appeared dirty and run-down.

The woman riding behind Stephan slid off and rushed to the door of the cottage, pushing it open. Kathalin didn't wait for Gates to help her down from the saddle; she simply slid off as well and followed the woman into the cottage. With a grunt of frustration, for he had wanted to check out the cottage to make sure there was no danger inside before Kathalin entered, Gates bailed off his steed, secured the animal's reins to a post used for that purpose, and barged into the cottage after her.

The moment he entered the cottage, he knew something was very wrong. It was dark and freezing cold, and there was no fire in the hearth. He blinked his eyes, adjusting to the dim light, and he could see Kathalin over against the far wall, bending over a bed. As he stood in the doorway and let the cold air filter in behind him, Kathalin left the bed and scooted in his direction. She had both of her fine new gloves in one hand and was starting to unfasten the cloak around her neck.

"Both of the children indeed have fevers and I believe the grand-mother does as well," she said, indicating a very old woman sitting next to the bed. "This cottage is freezing. Can you please start a fire? We must warm it up."

Gates frowned. "It is not my job to start a fire," he said flatly. "Let the husband do it."

Kathalin looked at him, disheartened by his selfish reply, before turning to the peasant woman who was now bending over the bed, weeping softly as she spoke to her children.

"Where is your husband, woman?" Kathalin asked. "Where is wood for the fire?"

The peasant woman turned to look at the lady and the knight standing in the doorway. "Me husband died two weeks ago of illness," she said, wiping her nose with her hand again. "It has been snowing and we've not had the means to cut wood."

Kathalin's brow furrowed with concern. "So you have been without fire for two weeks?" she asked, aghast. "In this weather?"

The woman merely shrugged. "Everyone is ill but me," she said. "I cannot leave, even to cut wood. And the snow has been very bad. Even leaving this morning to seek a physic was difficult. It has been the first clear day in weeks and I had to go."

Kathalin was horrified by the story. Turning to Gates with a look of such sorrow in her expression, he didn't even wait for her to ask him again. He was already on the move. Turning around, he began barking orders to the soldiers that had accompanied them and soon, men were beginning to move, off to find an axe or some other way to cut wood. Things were in motion. Gates watched his men move and, in particular, Stephan taking a lead role in the search for an axe, before returning his attention to Kathalin.

"We will start a fire," he said. "I will have my men chop enough wood to see them through for a while. Do you require anything else?"

Kathalin nodded. "Provisions," she said, looking around the dark, cold cottage. "If they've had no fire then they've had little food, and certainly not hot food. Bring me the remainder of the provisions you had for the army on their journey to Ludlow. If Hyssington is not far off, then surely we do not need them. These people need food."

It made sense to Gates and he nodded without hesitation. "It will be done," he said. "If there is anything else, do not hesitate to ask."

"Willow bark," she said as he turned around to leave. He paused to look at her curiously and she continued. "I need willow bark. Certainly you know what a willow looks like?"

He nodded, cocking an eyebrow. "What do you need with willow bark?"

Kathalin finished unfastening the cloak and she carefully laid it across the old, broken-down eating table near the hearth. "I will make a brew to ease their fevers," she said. "She says the children have been sick for several days so I am not entirely sure I can help them, but I will do what I can."

She was businesslike and confident, and Gates realized he was seeing a completely different side of her. The lady who had fought him, resisted him, and who was so incredibly naïve in the world outside of St. Milburga's seemed to have finally found something she was quite confident in – healing. She was in her element now and Gates, initially reluctant to allow her to help these peasants, wasn't so reluctant any longer. In fact, he was rather interested in watching her work.

"Very well," he finally said, eyeing the peasant woman over by the bed. "Before I go hunting for willow trees in the snow, ask her if she knows of any."

Kathalin nodded, returning to the bed where the woman and her children were gathered, and she asked the woman about willow trees in the area. Immediately, the woman pointed off to the west and, as Gates watched, evidently gave Kathalin some manner of instructions. Kathalin listened and quickly returned to him.

"There is a stream behind the house and the woman says that the white willows grow there," she said. "You must cut out squares of the surface bark and bring it to me. Please bring me as much as you can."

She was holding up her hands to demonstrate the size and thickness of what she required. Gates bobbed his head in acknowledgement.

"Aye, my lady."

"And hurry."

"Aye, my lady."

Kathalin offered him a timid little smile of gratitude as he headed out of the cottage and Gates was bold enough to wink at her. *That sassy, bold wink.* Kathalin's smile turned genuine as she watched the man walk out and close the door behind him.

Giddy, she thought. *He makes me quite giddy.*

Smile still on her face, she turned back to the woman and her children, huddled in the bed, and promptly went to work.

WHEN THE FARMER'S widow had set out for the nearest village that morning in search of help for her children, she never imagined that the day would turn out as it did with the fortuitous meeting of the soldiers from Hyssington. It would seem that God had decided she'd had enough pain over the past few weeks and was determined to send her angels of relief in the form of a well-dressed lady, two knights, and several burly soldiers.

It started when the two knights had gone off to harvest willow bark per the lady's instructions. Outside, the soldier searching for an axe had managed to come across two of them in the larger outbuilding that served as a barn for several sheep, two goats, two horses, and a cow who were quite hungry from having not been fed. With the death of the farmer and the sick children, the widow hadn't been able to tend them as well as she needed to.

Therefore, while four of the soldiers went off to cut wood for the fire, the rest remained behind with the stock and released them from the barn so they could wander the muddy, frozen yard. They found a stash of hay in a smaller outbuilding, part of which had been damaged by a leaking roof, and while a pair of soldiers tossed bundles of hay to the hungry animals, another soldier fixed the roof so the rest of the hay could remain in good condition, at least for a while. When they finished pitching the hay, the de Lara soldiers wandered the farm to see if anything else needed tending or fixing. When they found something, they took care of it.

The little farm had a good deal of help that day.

Meanwhile, the four men who had gone off to chop wood from a nearby copse of trees returned dragging saplings and other not-quite-mature trees because they didn't have the means to haul anything bigger. The wood was mostly wet although there was some of it that was dry, and the wood was cut up and brought into the woodshed next to the cottage, stacked up so it could dry. Meanwhile, Kathalin had admitted one of the soldiers into the cottage so the man could start a fire. Soon enough, a blaze began to burn in the darkened hearth and for the first time in days, the sad little cottage saw light and warmth.

And that was when Kathalin could do more good for them. Gates had sent a soldier back to the road where the bulk of the army was and the man collected what provisions he could carry on horseback and brought it back to the farm. There were two sacks of sand-colored flour, barley, dried vegetables, salt, and dried beef. Having managed the kitchen at St. Milburga's, Kathalin knew what to do with the items.

Soon, a thin but tasty soup made from dried vegetables, barley, and the dried beef was bubbling over the hearth and Kathalin made little dough balls from a small measure of the flour, dropping the balls into the simmering soup to make dumplings. It would be difficult to make bread without any yeast so she mixed some of the water and flour together and set it in a pan by the warm fire, knowing that on the morrow there would be yeast to make bread from it.

As the soup bubbled, she had noticed that the farmer's cottage did have some ingredients about, small barrels of grain and a salt bin. There were also bundles of dried flowers and herbs hanging from the ceiling near the hearth, undoubtedly to use in the wintertime as additives to food, and she came across dried roses and rose leaves, dried bundles of rosemary, and what she thought to be chamomile flowers. She inspected the bundles closely, drawing upon her training for medicinal uses.

Mother Benedicta had been an expert in herbs and gardens and had schooled her wards well; consequently, Kathalin knew a good deal about herbs and other plants. There were other bundles of dried things, one of which was clearly wild mint, and Kathalin knew what she could do with what she had. Therefore, she took to boiling the chamomile and roses with the mint to soothe the children and possibly help the fever.

The children, two youngsters no more than four and six years of age, respectively, weren't eager to drink the tea but with the help of their mother and grandmother, they sipped at it. Even the grandmother, who was clearly ill, was given the tea and she eagerly drank it. The soup soon became ready, or at least the dumplings were cooked and the beef fully hydrated, and Kathalin doled the liquid out, finding the children were more apt to eat now they were able to put some tea in their bellies. Warm and soothed bellies were more receptive to food.

Gates returned to the cottage a short time later to find the children, mother, and grandmother eating the soup and dumplings that Kathalin had prepared for them. He was quite cold from having been pushing about a snow-laden willow tree on the edge of a frozen stream, cutting off squares of bark with his dagger, and he and Stephan barged into the cottage with their arms laden with chunks of the bark they had cut from the tree. Both men carefully dumped the bark onto the tabletop, shaking out bits of snow with it.

"There," he told Kathalin as she swooped over the bark to inspect it. He brushed off his hands, feeling the warmth from the fire sting the frozen flesh of his face. "Due to the fact that the tree is very close to the stream, it leans towards the water, and there is growth all around it. It was difficult to get what we were able to manage. I hope it is enough."

Kathalin nodded. "It should be," she said as she carefully inspected it. "It looks as if it is excellent quality, too."

Gates sighed, removing his gloves so he could warm his hands. "That is good to hear," he said. "We must leave as soon as possible, my lady. Do what you need to do so we can make it to Hyssington before nightfall."

Kathalin simply nodded as she began to work with the bark, brushing it off and making sure it was free of vermin. As Stephan pulled off his gloves and put his hands up against the fire, steam rising from his frozen and ice-caked clothing, Gates began to look around the small cottage, realizing that something had changed since he was last here.

There was a lovely-smelling soup bubbling on the hearth and the farmer's family was slurping it up from bowls. The floor was swept, there were bags of provisions from his army neatly stacked up against the wall, and there was a big fire burning in the hearth. It began to occur to him that Kathalin had prepared food for the family and taken care of the cottage. God only knew what else she had done. Aye, she'd been quite busy while he was out hunting willow bark.

A seed of respect began to sprout.

"Did you do all of this?" he asked her, gesturing to the hearth and the food in general.

Kathalin glanced up from the bark. "Aye," she said. "They had very little by way of food. I do not know what they had been eating for the past several days but with the fire, I was able to make them a good soup that should last them for a few days. And the provisions from the army will keep them supplied until the woman can get into town and buy more. It was very kind of you to give them your provisions."

He only gave them to the family because Kathalin had asked and for no other reason than that. Gates simply nodded, unwilling to absorb her accolades because it seemed oddly out of place to do that. It was clear that Kathalin had done a great deal of work for the destitute family and he was quite impressed with not only her skill but her willingness to help people who were clearly in need. It seemed to make no difference to her that they were poor and ill; she simply wanted to help. That spoke of a true and open heart to him, something that couldn't be taught. That kind of generosity and compassion was part of one's character.

That measure of compassion was rare, just as she was, and his respect for her grew.

But then there was him, who had virtually no compassion for the impoverished. He'd seen so many needy families in war-torn France over the past year that he'd become hardened to it. He began to feel guilty for thinking that helping this family was all one great inconvenience, especially when Kathalin was trying to do something good and helpful. She didn't see the needy the way he did.

But he should have.

Given that she'd spent the past fourteen years with a healing order, it made sense that Kathalin viewed things differently than he did. Even now, Gates watched her as she collected a small pot that was stacked near the hearth and went to the water barrel to fill it with some water. She then put it on an iron rack over the hearth to boil, taking pieces of bark and putting them into the water. Her movements were fluid and lovely, her fingers slender and white. She had callouses on her palms from the manual labor at St. Milburga's, but it didn't detract from the loveliness of her hands. It didn't detract from anything about her. The more Gates watched her, the more entranced he became with this woman of multi-facets.

"Once the bark boils and I strain it, they will drink the brew and it should help the fever," she told him, breaking into his thoughts. "We can leave as soon as they are able to drink the liquid. I will hurry."

Gates simply shook his head, sighing faintly as he did so. "It was wrong of me to rush you," he said quietly. "Forgive me. You are trying to help these people and I am trying to rush you out. Take your time and do what you need to do. Your father will have to understand."

Surprised at his turn of heart, for he had been clearly impatient about this entire endeavor, Kathalin looked at him with a rather wide-eyed expression, unsure what to say to him. But there was something in his gaze as he looked at her that was warm and gentle. She'd never seen that from him before and her heart, that silly and naive thing, began to beat just a little faster.

Warmth.

She felt warmth from him. Was it possible he felt it, too?

"I will be finished as soon as the bark boils," she said, hoping her voice didn't sound as tremulous as she felt. "I know that you are anxious to return to Hyssington and I do not want my father to become cross with you because I delayed the return."

Gates smiled at her words. "He will not become cross with me," he said, but then he wriggled his eyebrows. "Not much, anyway. We can usually soothe any anger he might have by speaking on subjects he is eager to discuss. We distract him as easily as one would an angry child."

Kathalin smiled at his impish statement. "We?" she asked. "Who is 'we'?"

Still by the fire, nearly smoking his clothes because he was so close to the flame, Stephan spoke before Gates could. "He means the knights, my lady," he said, glancing at her. "Your father is easily distracted with talk of warfare. Remember that should he ever become angry with you."

Kathalin laughed softly. "But I do not know any tales of warfare," she said. "I do not suppose I could distract him with talk of healing herbs or flour measures? Unfortunately, that is all that I know."

Stephan shook his head. "He would become positively irate should you speak to him of healing herbs," he said flatly. "Gates and I will tell you of great battles so that you may discuss them intelligently with your father. It is your only hope."

Kathalin, still smiling, looked at Gates. "What great battles will you school me on?" she asked. "Can you teach me the entire military history of England between now and the time we reach Hyssington?"

Gates snorted. "You would die of utter boredom if we tried," he said. "What can we tell her of, Bear? Something quick and deadly."

Stephan grinned as Kathalin cocked her head curiously at Gates. "Why do you call him Bear?"

Gates nodded, smiling because Stephan was. "An old knight started calling him that many years ago when his beard first came in and he refused to shave it off," he said. "He also refused to cut his hair, so between the hair and the beard, he looked like a bear. He is also the size of one, in case you have not noticed."

Kathalin looked at Stephan, who merely shrugged. "My mother likes me this way," he said.

Gates rolled his eyes. "Your mother is blind," he pointed out. "She cannot see anything at all. You tell her what she likes and she simply agrees with you."

Stephan pretended to be quite insulted. "Women like men with hair," he said, looking at Kathalin. "Is that not so, my lady? Women appreciate a good beard, do they not?"

Kathalin giggled. "I would not know," she said. "It all seems rather... bushy to me."

Gates swung a hand back at Stephan, slapping the man in the shoulder. "Do not ask Lady Kathalin such things, you impudent puttock," he scolded. "She has spent her entire life in a convent, or did you forget that? She would not know what women like about men."

Stephan, rubbing his shoulder where Gates smacked him, was properly contrite. "My apologies, my lady," he said, pulling his gloves on. "Mayhap I should go outside and wait before I say something that will cause Gates to put a fist in my mouth. He is not beyond that, you know."

As Gates cast him a very nasty look, Stephan moved to the door, making a face at the man when Gates was too far away to do anything about it. He then slipped from the cottage quickly as Kathalin giggled.

"He is very humorous," she said. "Has he been your friend a long time?"

Gates thought on the life and death he and Stephan had shared together, years of serving de Lara and years of battles.

"Aye," he said after a moment. "I could not do without him, as foolish as he is. He is a very good knight and a good friend."

Kathalin could hear admiration in his tone. "I envy that," she said, her gaze moving over his handsome face. "I had a few friends at St. Milburga's but most of them have left. Their parents recalled them home to marry when they came of age. But I remained. I am, in fact, the oldest ward at the priory."

Gates watched her as she spoke, the way tiny dimples in her chin formed when she said certain words. It was really quite charming, as was the rest of her.

"Surely there were some women you could speak with or confide in?" he asked.

She shook her head. "Not really," she said, tearing her gaze away from him to check her pot of bark, now boiling away. "The younger wards are all too young and the nuns... well, they did not really form friendships. They are all very kind but they viewed me as not equal to them in the eyes of God."

He regarded her. "Yet you love St. Milburga's," he said. "You call it your home."

She nodded as she took an iron spoon and stirred the bark. "It is," she said. "It is the only home I have ever known. Like any other home, it is not perfect, but it is home."

He didn't say any more, watching her as she stirred the willow bark.

The liquid was becoming a deep red; he could see it when she lifted the liquid in the spoon. Soon, he was helping her take the pot off the fire and pouring it whilst she tried to strain out all of the bark, leaving a steaming red liquid in a bowl. As it cooled, she continued to pick out pieces of bark, not having any cloth to strain it with, until the liquid was mostly clear but for a few bits of sediment.

When she was finally satisfied, she took a cup and dipped it into the liquid, taking it to the farmer's widow and explaining that she should have her children drink some tonight, tomorrow, and the next day, for as long as it would last. The willow bark potion should help ease the fever but she explained that they mustn't drink too much of it at once. Gates stood back and listened to Kathalin's kind and careful explanation of what must be done, and the farmer's widow was so grateful that she took Kathalin's hands and kissed them, thanking her profusely.

Given that Kathalin had been taught by her order that healing was better without the vanity of gratitude, she was uncomfortable with the woman's thanks. She simply nodded her head and moved away from the bed while the mother gave the liquid to the children, who didn't like the taste, and the grandmother, who drank it right down.

Leaving the family behind, and knowing she had done all she could to help, Kathalin approached Gates.

"I am ready to leave now," she said as she gathered her cloak off the eating table. "Do you think we will still make it to Hyssington by nightfall?"

Gates reached out to take the cloak from her, shaking it out and laying it across her shoulders. "Aye," he said, politely helping her settle the heavy cloak as she tied the fastens around her neck. "We should be just in time for the evening meal."

Kathalin couldn't help but be very aware of his big hands on the cloak, courteously straightening the hood, as she finished securing it. She then pulled on her gloves, noticing that the red welts around her wrists were hardly noticeable, but as she secured the gloves over her fingers, she realized that her hands were rather quivery from Gates' close proximity. She'd never been so close to a man in her life as she had been to Gates de Wolfe these past few days, literally and figuratively. When all of the fighting between them had died down, they'd had some very pleasant conversations and he had been quite attentive to her. But he was only following orders, she knew. She was quite sure his attentions had not been anything more than that regardless of the warmth she had so recently felt from him.

She was a task and nothing more, and her heart sank just a little bit to realize that.

You are a fool!

It was better not to dwell on such thoughts, for they were dangerous. Once the gloves were secure, Kathalin gave one last look to the family on the bed before exiting the cottage with Gates on her heels. His horse was tethered right outside the door and Stephan was standing there, waiting, as were most the soldiers who had escorted them. Two of the soldiers, however, were still repairing a section of the barn roof but when they saw Gates and the lady emerge, they hastened off the roof. As Stephan gathered his own horse, Gates lifted Kathalin onto his saddle. He gazed up at her a moment before joining her.

"What you did today for that family," he said, seemingly unsure of his words. "I just wanted to say that it was an honor to witness what you did. You have a good heart, my lady. That is a rare thing in this day."

More flattery, she thought. But no… it was more than that. It was a genuine statement of admiration, something she had never really heard before. And the warmth… it was there again in his expression and she struggled not to give in to it. *You are a duty to him!* She reminded herself sharply. *Cease with your foolish and giddy thoughts of the man!*

"I did what I have been taught to do," she replied after a moment. "It needed to be done."

Gates could see that she didn't seemed pleased by his compliment; he'd meant to tell her of his esteem but being modest, and without any vanity whatsoever, she didn't quite understand him. Or so he thought.

To him, the lack of vanity made her all the more charming. It was a rare thing indeed to meet a woman who didn't expect flattery or wasn't swayed by it. In fact, he'd never met one in his life.

Until now.

"I know," he said, finally mounting up behind her. He didn't try to lift her up this time but left her in the front of the saddle as he simply slid in behind her. He rather liked it that way better, with his thighs around hers, holding her fast so she wouldn't move around. Her left ear was by his mouth and he spoke softly into it. "But it was still an honor to watch. You have done the de Lara name proud today."

His hot breath on her ear nearly sent Kathalin into fits. The heat of it sent a bolt of excitement through her, a hand flying to her ear as if to touch the spot his breath had licked against. She could hear Gates laughing softly, no doubt because he felt as well as saw her quivering reaction. She should have been embarrassed in her reaction but she couldn't seem to manage it. Her response had been unmistakable, the naked thrill of the first time a man whispered to her.

She was certain Gates hadn't meant to make her tremble, but he had. The entire ride to Hyssington, Kathalin could only think of one thing.

She had very much liked his hot breath in her ear....

CHAPTER SEVEN

Hyssington Castle

S HARP, CRYSTAL-CLEAR STARS blazed against the cold night sky as Gates and the escort entered the bailey of Hyssington Castle. The entire fortress was illuminated by torches, all along the enormous walls, on poles in the bailey, and settled into iron sconces on both the exterior of the great hall and all around the exterior of the keep. The entire place was lit up like daylight when the escort from St. Milburga's arrived.

Oddly enough, Jasper wasn't in the bailey to greet them as they arrived but Alexander was. The big, blond knight emerged from the hall, making his way across the bailey as the escort party was coming to a halt next to the gatehouse. As Gates dismounted into the prolific mud left from the melting snow, he saw the man approach and his surprise was evident.

"What in the world are you doing here?" he asked Alexander as the man drew close. "Did I not just see you off to Lioncross?"

Alexander nodded, reaching out to grab the bridle of Gates' exhausted, excitable horse as the animal swung its head around. "Aye," he said, holding the big, gray head still. "What happened at St. Milburga's? We heard the Welsh attacked it."

Gates reached up to lift Kathalin out of the saddle, trying not to set her down in the worst of the mud. "They did," he said, surprised. "How did you know that?"

Alexander struggled with the horse. "Because one of the soldiers from Ludlow came to Lioncross to tell us what had happened and ask for reinforcements," he said. "Were you at the priory when it was attacked?"

Gates nodded, holding on to Kathalin's arm to keep her out of the way of the excited horses and the surrounding swamp of mud. "We walked right into it," he said. "The Welsh were tearing the priory apart when we arrived and we were able to subdue them fairly quickly, enough so that St. Milburga's didn't lose too much in the raid. Still, the Welsh were rather desperate and quite unwilling to be subdued. It was a bit of a battle."

"But you are uninjured?"

"I am fine, my friend. Your concern is appreciated."

Alexander let go of Gates' horse when a groom came around to collect the animal. Turning his full attention to Gates, it was then that he noticed the lady standing beside him, a lady that the horse had partially blocked. Clad in a deep blue cloak with a fur-lined hood covering most of her head, Alexander had nearly the same reaction that Gates had upon seeing Kathalin de Lara's face for the first time. He saw the bright blue eyes and the angelic features and, for a split second, his eyes widened. But he was cool and in control, as always, so his flash of surprise quickly vanished.

"Lady Kathalin de Lara?" he asked the obvious. "My lady, welcome to Hyssington Castle, although that seems strange considering it is your home."

Kathalin gazed back at the handsome knight with the short, blond hair. "It is *not* my home," she clarified. "It is my father's home."

"Very true, my lady. My apologies."

"Who are you?"

She sounded rather unfriendly and Gates fought off a grin. "You need not fear this man, my lady," he said. "This is Alexander de Lohr, a very close friend of the House of de Lara and excellent knight. You will not find a finer man anywhere in England, I assure you."

Kathalin eyed Alexander, who seemed rather gallant and full of himself. He just had that air about him. "Sir Knight," she greeted. Then, she looked at him curiously. "De Lohr? I have heard that name before."

Alexander was struggling to overcome his shock at what an astounding beauty Kathalin de Lara was. Much as Gates had upon meeting the de Lara daughter, Alexander was having a hard time believing that heavy-set, pale-haired Jasper de Lara bred something as fine as this woman. It didn't seem possible.

"My family is from Lioncross Abbey Castle, about thirty miles south of here," Alexander told her. "We have a connection to Ludlow Castle and the garrison there. You may have seen our banners or our men passing through town. My mother does some of her shopping in Ludlow, I believe. There is a woman there who supplies her with herbs and flowering plants for her garden."

As he spoke politely, Kathalin was a bit more at ease with him. "St. Milburga's sells planted herbs at the market there," she said. "It is how we make money. I, myself, have planted herbs and flowers for sale."

Alexander smiled; much like Gates, he had an attractive and devilish smile that women found quite alluring. Once Gates saw the smile come out, however, he hastened to intervene; he had been watching the exchange between Kathalin and Alexander, struggling to ignore the feelings of jealousy it provoked. He had no right in the world to feel such things but the fact of the matter was that he was indeed feeling them. He also felt very protective, as if he wanted to keep her safe from the ills of the world, including Alexander de Lohr. That both frightened and concerned him. As soon as Alexander flashed the captivating de Lohr smile, Gates could stand it no more.

"Where is Jasper?" he asked Alexander, pulling Kathalin along with him as he began to head towards the hall. "Does he know about the Welsh raid on St. Milburga's? And why are you here, anyway?"

If Alexander sensed any sharpness from Gates, he didn't let on. He simply followed the pair as they walked across the bailey and headed towards the great hall illuminated by the smoking torches.

"As I said, a soldier from Ludlow came to Lioncross to inform us of the Welsh raids," Alexander said. "Knowing you were at St. Milburga's in Ludlow, my father sent me to Ludlow to see if you needed assistance but when I arrived, I was told you had already left to return to Hyssington, so we went by way of the Lydham road to find you. We arrived here about three hours ago and Jasper was concerned that you'd not yet arrived. We were discussing sending out a search party."

Gates shook his head. "We went by way of the Brampton road," he told him, "and we stopped to help a family in need along the way. That is why we were delayed."

Alexander looked at him strangely. "You stopped to *help* a needy family?"

Gates caught his expression and shook his head, almost imperceptibly, as if to silently tell the man not to ask any further questions. When he flicked his eyes towards Kathalin's covered head, Alexander understood somewhat. At least he understood enough to keep his mouth shut about it.

"Jasper should be here any moment," Alexander continued on as if he'd not questioned the need to help a destitute family, which would have been completely out of character for Gates. That was not the man he knew. "He was summoned by one of the sentries a short time ago and left the hall, but I am sure he heard the alarm when your escort came through. He should be here shortly."

Gates simply nodded his head as they approached the hall entry. There were a few soldiers milling outside, men who moved aside when the two knights and the lady approached. The great Norman arch of the entry with the herringbone pattern around the frame and the corbel above that bore the de Lara crest carved in stone all loomed in front of them in a great and impressive display, but Gates couldn't help but notice that Kathalin had come to a halt. When he looked down at her, he noticed that she was looking up at the stone corbel overhead.

"My lady?" he said politely, gesturing towards the door. "It is warm inside. Let us go in."

Kathalin heard him but she was still staring up at the stone. "I remember this doorway," she said after a moment. "I remember playing in this hall with my younger brother whom I've not seen in many years."

Gates and Alexander stood on either side of her as she reacquainted herself with her family's home from long ago. There seemed to be something wistful in her tone.

"I hope they are happy memories, my lady," Alexander said.

Kathalin nodded. "They are," she said. "I suddenly missed him a great deal as I remembered those times. We played together constantly and it was difficult when I was sent away and... well, it does not matter. Will my brother Jeffrey be here any time soon?"

Gates pushed the door open and ushered her inside as Alexander followed behind. "I do not know for certain, my lady," he said. "Your brother is in London. I do not know of any plans to return him home."

The heat and smell of the great hall cleaved any further conversation about Jeffery de Lara. The shock of the scent hit Kathalin right in the nostrils and she immediately put a hand to her nose. The hall was only half-full of men at this point, of soldiers eating an early meal before they assumed their posts for the night. Even so, it was a loud place and well-lit as food was placed upon the feasting tables and ale flowed.

Men were either sitting on the benches, or on the tabletop, or even kneeling on the floor near the hearth where they rolled bones. A few men were even pissing into the hearth in full view of Kathalin. Shocked, she turned to look at Gates with eyes full of horror at the carrying-on of the men, with absolutely no manners whatsoever. Gates, who was used to these sights but knew she wasn't, reached behind her and thumped Alexander on the arm.

"Help me tame these wild animals," he muttered. "There is a lady present."

Alexander nodded grimly. Leaving Kathalin standing just inside the door, Gates and Alexander made their way into the hall, bellowing to the men who were pissing or gambling or generally being loud. Demands for quiet echoed against the stone walls of the hall, startling the men into near-silence as Gates demanded that they cease their obnoxious behavior and still themselves, as Lord de Lara's daughter had arrived.

The men knew that Gates was to be obeyed, in all cases, and they quickly quieted down and moved to take their seats for a polite meal with a woman in their midst. Since Lady de Lara never attended meals, they were unused to feminine company. Gates and Alexander prowled around the room, ensuring the men were prepared to behave, and when Gates was confident his men were at least moderately capable of being around a woman, he turned towards the entry where he had left Kathalin only to find it empty

Kathalin was gone.

IT HAPPENED SO fast that Kathalin barely realized what had occurred until she was nearly halfway across the bailey.

Someone, smelling heavily of alcohol, had grabbed her from behind the moment Gates and Alexander had left her side in order to tame the room full of drunk and lively soldiers, and whoever had grabbed her was strong. He put his dirty hand over her mouth and lifted her up, carrying her from the hall and out into the night before she realized what was happening.

But once she became aware of the fact that someone was trying to take her away, abduct her no less, she came alive with kicking and screaming. She bit the hand that was over her mouth and the man grunted angrily, letting her go and dropping her to the muddy ground as he cursed loudly.

"You little chit!" he exclaimed. "You'll not bite me again, do you hear? I will kill you if you do!"

On the ground, Kathalin had quickly scrambled to her feet, running away from the very drunk and very big soldier, an older man with a bushy red beard. They weren't too far from the hall, thankfully, and she ran back for it as he thundered after her, unable to keep pace with her because he was so drunk. By the time she reached the entry door and shoved it open, Gates and Alexander were barreling out and Gates collided with her, knocking her backwards. She would have fallen onto her arse had he not been fast enough to grab her.

"My lady!" Gates said, surprised with Kathalin in his grip. "Where did you –?"

Kathalin wouldn't let him finish. She pointed at the drunk soldier, now having come to a halt in his pursuit of her. "He grabbed me!" she cried, her voice quivering. "He put his hand over my mouth and carried me out here! He was trying to take me away!"

Gates turned to look at the soldier accusingly but Alexander was already moving to the man, coming up to him and grabbing him around the throat. The soldier, being choked by the big knight, fell to his knees as he struggled to breathe.

"You abducted her?" Alexander growled. "Did you do it?"

He was squeezing the man's throat, shaking him, and the soldier was turning shades of deep red. "Aye!" he managed to gasp. "I thought – she was another whore! I thought –!"

Alexander let go of the man and slugged him squarely in the face, sending him to the ground. Meanwhile, Gates held on to Kathalin, unwilling to let her go at that point. Truth be told, his heart was still racing from the fright he'd had when he realized she was missing. Therefore, he let Alexander punish the soldier, watching as his friend pummeled the man unconscious. Kathalin, who had been watching the scene with terror, turned away and clutched at Gates, her head against his chest.

"Please," she begged, in tears. "I want to go home. I want to go back to St. Milburga's!"

Gates put his arms around her, taking her in the direction of the keep. "Come along," he said, forgoing the usually polite protocol between them. The woman was frightened, seeking comfort, and he couldn't help himself from giving it. "Mayhap I should not have taken you into the hall. It can sometimes be difficult around soldiers who do not know limitations when it comes to women."

Kathalin gasped, trying to pull away from him. "Do not know *limitations*?" she repeated, horrified. "You would knowingly bring me to such a place? Is that what happens here at Hyssington? Men have no restraint?"

He shook his head, retaining his grip on her. "I did not mean it that way," he said calmly. "'Tis simply that Hyssington is a fortress without women for the most part. There are serving wenches, and your mother, and that is all. Men become accustomed to men for companionship and when they see a woman, it tests their control. I am very sorry I left you alone. I should not have, but I truly did not think someone would take the opportunity to abscond with you."

Kathalin wouldn't let him move her towards the keep; she was still in his grip, that was true, but she was trying to pull away from him, digging her heels in because she didn't want to go with him. The expression on her face was one of great distress.

"Then this is a terrible place," she hissed at him. "How could you take me out of the safety of St. Milburga's and bring me to a place where men would think I am a whore?"

Gates grabbed her by the other arm, now holding her with both hands, and forced her to stop pulling away from him. His gaze was intense.

"Lady," he said quietly, "you must calm yourself. I realize you were raised in a place where men did not live, but understand that what happened just now is not unique. Hyssington Castle is not unique. There are men all over England, in any given castle or tavern or establishment, who might have done the same thing to you. The soldier who grabbed you has been properly punished and the reasons behind his punishment will serve to show every man here that you are not to be trifled with. It was an unfortunate occurrence but one that will have a greater end. Men will be too fearful of the punishment, and of my wrath in particular, should they so much as look at you. Do you understand what I am telling you? Kathalin, I would never have knowingly placed you in danger. I hope you would have more faith in me than that."

Kathalin. He called her by her name, without the courtesy title of "lady" before it, and Kathalin was quite sure she had never heard her name sound so sweet. In fact, it was enough to bring her some pause in her distress and she looked up at him, seeing something of warmth and hope in his features. *Rescuer... great protector...* was it possible he would be all of these things to her in her time of need? Was it possible that this man who had carried her out of St. Milburga's under duress would turn out to be someone she could always depend on?

Someone she could love?

Love!

The word struck a chord in Kathalin so strongly that she gasped as it reverberated through her body. Dear God, she could not love him! *Would* not love him! He was the only man she had ever known so it would have been natural to feel some kind of attachment towards him... wouldn't it? He had been kind and gentle at times, firm when she needed it, and humorous when the situation called for it.

What wasn't there to love about him?"

Frightened by her thoughts, exhausted from the trip, and upset by being grabbed, the tears came and Kathalin lowered her head, struggling not to weep. Gates, still holding on to both of her arms, loosened his grip.

"I am sorry this happened," he said softly. "Please let me take you to a chamber where you can rest and where you will feel safe. Will you allow me to do that for you?"

"I want to go home," she wept softly.

He rubbed her arms gently, trying not to appear too comforting or too solicitous. It was dangerous for him, on many levels, and that voice inside his head was beginning to scream at him as he bordered on impropriety.

Don't touch her, you fool! It shouted. *Don't let her get under your skin!*

"I know," he said softly. "But you cannot go home right now. Will you please let me take you to your chamber so you may rest?"

Kathalin simply nodded and he pulled her along, holding her elbow tightly as he guided her towards keep. They were nearly to the door when a voice came from behind.

"Gates? Where are you going?"

Gates knew the voice before he even turned around. With Kathalin still in his grip, he turned to see Jasper a few feet behind him, his bearded face full of curiosity and confusion. Before Gates could answer, Jasper's gaze moved to Kathalin, who was wiping tears from her eyes, and his entire expression changed.

"Kathalin?" he murmured incredulously, inspecting her hooded features with the same shock Gates and Alexander had shown upon meeting the woman. Jasper, too, could hardly believe what he was seeing. "Kathalin, is that truly you?"

Gates spoke before Kathalin could. "We looked for you in the hall, my lord," he said. "But it is full of men and Lady Kathalin has just suffered a distressing experience, so it may be best to allow her to rest first before engaging in any meaningful conversation. May I have permission to take her to her chamber, then?"

Jasper couldn't take his eyes off his daughter. Ignoring Gates' question, he moved towards his daughter, reaching out a hand that came near her head. Kathalin visibly flinched, her eyes big at her father, but all Jasper did was peel back the hood of the cloak to get a good look at her. When he did, he sighed.

"God's Bones," he said softly, with awe in his voice. "You look just like your mother did as a young woman."

Kathalin gazed back at her father, reacquainting herself with the man. Truthfully, she didn't have much memory of him. She had been so young when she had been sent away that all she really remembered of him was dark hair and a booming voice. Essentially, she was looking at a stranger.

"Greetings, my lord," she said, unsure what more to say.

But Jasper shook his head at her, grasping her by the shoulders and pulling her away from Gates. "My lord, is it?" he said, looking her over in detail. "I am your father. You will kiss me."

Before Kathalin could protest, Jasper kissed her loudly on both cheeks, insisting she do the same to him. She did, timidly, and he laughed. "It will become easier, with time," he told her, completely oblivious to her hesitant behavior. "God's Bones, I cannot get over how beautiful you have become. Isn't she, Gates?"

Gates was looking at Kathalin with concern, knowing Jasper's booming voice and loud manner was probably not having a good effect on her. "She is indeed, my lord," he said quietly.

Jasper simply grinned. "It is good to have you home, Daughter," he said. "Your mother and I have a grand event planned to celebrate your return. Many houses will be coming to Hyssington to meet you and that means many young men as well. I am sure you will be quite excited by that. All young women love parties, do they not?"

Gates was somewhat chagrinned by what he was hearing. More than that, he was downright opposed to it. A celebration with young men? Men to gaze upon Jasper de Lara's grown daughter? Damnation, he didn't like that idea one bit but in the same breath, he knew that such things were beyond his control. What Jasper did wasn't up to him. He was sworn to the man and therefore sworn to obey any whim or command, including an idiotic party with young men that Kathalin was clearly uncomfortable around. As Gates stood there and held his tongue, Kathalin seemed to have found hers.

"It is kind of you to arrange a celebration, Father," she said, "but I do not require nor need one. I have come home because you summoned me and I would like to know why I am here. If you would be kind enough to tell me, I would be grateful."

Jasper, undeterred by her stiff and formal manner with him, waved her off. "There will be plenty of time to discuss such things," he said, grasping her by the hand and pulling her towards the hall. "Come,

Daughter. Allow me to introduce you to Hyssington. Everyone will want to meet you."

As Jasper pulled, Kathalin turned pleading eyes to Gates, who intervened on her behalf. He found that he had to. He could no longer remain silent.

"My lord," he said, putting himself in front of Jasper so the man couldn't move forward. He pointed to Kathalin. "Look at her; she has had an exhausting journey. She endured an attack at St. Milburga's and snowstorms before arriving here, so it would be my strong recommendation that you allow the woman to rest this night. There will be plenty of time to introduce her to Hyssington in the days to come. At least for tonight, have pity on what she has endured to get here. It has been a very long and trying day."

Jasper, now in doubt of his plans for his daughter, looked at Kathalin to see that she did, indeed, appear weary. She seemed pale and her eyes were red-rimmed. Disappointed he would not have the chance to sup with her, he sighed greatly. Not normally a selfless man, it was difficult for him to think of another's needs before his own, but he managed it.

"Very well," he said reluctantly. "Her mother has ordered the big chamber on the second floor prepared for her use. Take her there and make sure she has all that she needs, Gates, and when you are finished, I will see you in the hall. I want to hear what happened on this journey to St. Milburga's that has you both so weary that you cannot stand to sup with me."

Gates didn't want to get into a verbal confrontation with a man who was clearly being rather petulant about the situation. Therefore, he simply nodded and took Kathalin away from Jasper, quickly leading her towards the box-shaped keep. The structure had a big iron grate as an entry door, a grate that was always kept locked, so he called to the majordomo inside, the Tender of the Keep, who happened to be a woman. The old servant appeared from her room near the entry door and unlocked it.

The sound of the iron grate locking behind them made it sound as if they were in a prison. Hollow sounds of iron reverberated off the stone walls. That uneasiness was evident in Kathalin's expression as Gates took her up the narrow spiral stairs to the floor above where there was one large chamber and two smaller chambers. Servants slept in the smaller chambers but the larger one was used for guests, and it was into this spacious bower that Gates took her.

The chamber door was a very heavy oak panel, reinforced with iron, and made creaking sounds as it was opened. Kathalin stepped into the chamber and was immediately hit by the smell of fresh rushes, no doubt cut from the tree that very day. But as the smell filled her nostrils, she was caught off-guard by what she saw; an enormous bed was in the center of the chamber, facing the hearth, and there were furs and pillows and resplendent luxury all around it on a colossal scale.

Shocked, Kathalin looked further into the room. There was a lounge of some kind beneath a lancet window, something cushioned and long and without arms on it, and there was also a separate area with a small, painted table and two matching chairs, all made from pale wood, that was evidently an eating or refreshment area of some kind. A long, slender table nearby held a precious glass carafe half-filled with deep red wine and two small glasses. It was clear that someone had gone through a great deal of trouble to make this room very luxurious and comfortable.

Gates didn't seem to notice any of the decadence as Kathalin stood there and gaped. He moved into the chamber as if it all meant absolutely nothing to him, which it didn't, and went to the hearth, pulling forth peat and wood in order to begin a fire. Kathalin managed to close her mouth and wander into the chamber after him. Her initial surprise was turning to awe at the finery she was witnessing. From the austere halls of St. Milburga's to the wealth of the de Lara's, it was as if she had opened the door and stepped foot into heaven.

The first example of wealth was the floor – since stepping into the room, she hadn't walked on the floor once – there were cow's hides and sheep's skins covering most of it. The next example was the bed – she was almost afraid to touch it. It had a silk coverlet that was finely embroidered with hummingbirds and flowers, and there were several pillows on the bed that had also been exquisitely embroidered. In fact, the entire bed was the most beautiful thing Kathalin had ever seen and she inspected it with great care.

"I have never, in all of my life, seen such a bed," she said, timidly putting her hand on it to feel the softness. "It looks as if angels sleep here."

Down on one knee in front of the hearth, Gates had the peat and wood neatly stacked and was in the process of striking the flint. In spite of the fact that he had declared to Kathalin back at the farmer's hut that he did not start fires, he did indeed start them and he could do it very well.

"Your mother is responsible for the finery," he said. "She sews things of such beauty, you cannot even imagine."

Kathalin looked at him. "Truly?" she said, wonder in her voice. "I can sew very well but I never learned to embroider such as this. Mother Benedicta considered it a foolish waste of time."

"Why?"

"Because embroidery serves no purpose other than to flatter vain women."

The peat was beginning to catch fire and Gates blew on it to spark it up. "It seems to me that Mother Benedicta had very strong views of the world and those in it," he said. "She convinced you that anything other than brown woolen clothing was vain and sinful, yet you are wearing fine clothing this night and I do not think it is sinful in the least."

Kathalin smiled faintly, looking at the cloak she was wearing. "It is warm and comfortable, as you said it would be," she said, her gaze returning to the bed. "And, if you wish to know a secret, it has not turned my skin red. For that alone, I am thankful that I am wearing it."

Gates glanced up from the hearth, envisioning her resplendent beauty. Strong words of admiration came to mind but he chased them away. It hurt his heart in a way he did not understand to be unable to say such things to her.

"It suits you," he said simply. As the fire in the hearth began to blaze more strongly, he stood up and brushed off his hands. "You will be safe here while I go and retrieve your possessions. I will also have food sent to you, as I can imagine you must be hungry. Is there anything else you require?"

Kathalin shook her head, still running her hand over the coverlet. "Do you know who I will be sharing this bed with?"

He looked at her, confused. "What do you mean?"

Kathalin shrugged, pointing to the bed. "I mean am I to share this with someone?" she asked. "This is such a big bed. Mayhap I will share it with my mother's maid? Or a servant?"

Gates shook his head. "You do not seem to understand that all of this is for you," he said. "You will not share the bed with anyone. It is yours."

Kathalin's eyebrows lifted in surprise. "But it is so big!"

He gave her a half-grin. "You are the daughter of an earl," he said as he moved to the chamber door. "You must become accustomed to the fact that big chambers and fine clothing are your lot in life."

Bewildered, Kathalin's attention was drawn to the bed once more but she realized that Gates was leaving, so she hastened after him.

"Wait," she said, catching up to him. "You... you will return, will you not?"

He stood with his hand on the iron door latch. "I told you I would," he said. "I am going back to the bailey to retrieve the basket with your possessions in it."

She didn't say anything for a moment. It seemed that there was something on her mind but she wasn't sure how to voice it so Gates lifted the latch and opened the door, preparing to leave, but Kathalin stopped him again.

"After this," she said, struggling to find the correct words. "After tonight, I mean. Will... will you remain here? That is to say, will I see you? You are not leaving Hyssington?"

He shook his head. "Nay," he said. "I am not leaving Hyssington. Why do you ask?"

Kathalin wasn't sure why she had asked; all she knew was that the thought of him leaving her alone in a castle full of strangers terrified her. *Rescuer... great protector...* he had been all of these things to her since leaving St. Milburga's. But there was more to it and she knew it. It wasn't simply the fact that she didn't want to be left with strangers.

She didn't want him to leave her at all.

"Because...," she stammered. "Because I do not know anyone here and... what I mean is that I know you and you are the only person I *do* know, so I am hoping you will stay with me as I become accustomed to Hyssington. I do not want you to leave me."

I do not want you to leave me. Gates could have read a great deal into that statement and it was difficult not to do so. He didn't want to leave her, either, his protective instincts very strong when it came to her, but he, too, knew it was more than that. Something much more, something that frightened him. That fear caused his manner to harden somewhat in a purely self-defensive posture.

"Unless Lord de Lara sends me away, I will remain at Hyssington," he said formally. "I will be here. You need not fear. I am at your service, my lady."

Somehow, that wasn't what Kathalin wanted to hear. She wasn't exactly sure what she wanted to hear, but a generic statement of service hadn't been it. She felt a bit saddened by his stiff reply and a bit disappointed. There had been no warmth in his words at all and that was what she had been hoping for, in hindsight.

Warmth from his eyes again.

Warmth from him.

"Thank you," she simply said, putting her hand on the door because he was already halfway through it. "I will bolt this door after you leave. I will not feel safe otherwise."

He nodded, sensing something gloomy and moody to her manner

all of a sudden. She had been open and wistful only moments early, but now she was seemingly saddened. He was curious about her swift change in mood but he wouldn't dwell on it nor would he ask her why. It was probably safer if he didn't. He didn't want to give himself any false notions to feed his attraction to her.

God help him if she was attracted to him, too.

"Of course," he said. "I do not blame you for your fears. In fact, it would be wise not to open this door for anyone but me. I will bring food to you myself."

"No one?"

"Not a soul. Not even your father."

She fought off a grin. "Especially my father," she said. "He seems to want to put me in the middle of everyone you are trying to protect me from. I… am grateful, Gates."

Gates. His name never sounded so sweet, spoken in her gentle voice. Not one to give in to giddiness or the thrills of attraction, he nonetheless found himself feeling somewhat flighty as he gazed into her eyes. Foolish, even.

Dear God, he had to get out of there!

"It is my pleasure, my lady," he said, resisting the urge to call her by her name. *Kathalin.* It was such a beautiful name. "I will return."

Kathalin simply nodded and Gates had no more reason to stay. Quickly, he quit the room, listening to the door shut softly behind him and hearing the bolt thrown, as he made his way down the spiral stairway. The old woman guarding the grate door down at the entry unlocked the iron grate and allowed him to pass into the bailey beyond.

Even as Gates made his way across the muddy, half-frozen bailey, his thoughts continued to linger on Kathalin. It wasn't good for him to think on her beyond what was required for him to carry out his duties, but the fact of the matter was that he *did* think about her. He'd been thinking about her fairly steadily since last night, since he'd spent the entire night outside of her chamber door in the tiny inn, guarding it against any danger. That beautiful, fine, and pure woman was increasingly on his mind and as much as he tried to push her aside, he couldn't seem to do it.

Something was stirring within him, something unfamiliar, and it scared him to death.

When he finally tried to sleep that night, he found that he couldn't, for his thoughts and dreams centered around one thing...

Kathalin.

CHAPTER EIGHT

"**I** WILL NOT be kept from my own daughter, Gates," Jasper said sternly. "I have ordered you to bring her down to the hall. Since when do you refuse an order?"

It was early in the morning the day following Kathalin's arrival at Hyssington. The clouds were heavy this morning, pewter in the sky, threatening another dump of freezing white particles, and the castle grounds were just becoming alive with men going about their duties.

In the great hall, however, there was a potentially explosive situation happening as Jasper, demanding his daughter's presence, had been denied by Gates. *Denied.* Jasper was having great difficulty comprehending his knight's refusal to produce his own flesh and blood.

"My lord," Gates said patiently. "May I speak candidly?"

"You had better."

Gates, who had hardly slept all night, lifted a displeased eyebrow. "You must understand something about your daughter," he said. "She has lived most of her life in a convent where there were no men about. Men make her extremely uncomfortable. I told you last night that she had been molested the moment she reached Hyssington and for that reason alone, she is terrified to come out of her chamber. She has been living a spartan, quiet life at St. Milburga's. It is the only life she has ever known, one imposed upon her by you no less. You cannot suddenly demand the woman place herself in the midst of parties and feasting and the scrutiny of men because she does not know any of this. It would upset her greatly. You must allow her time to become accustomed it."

Jasper was listening seriously, understanding what the man was saying but unwilling to agree. "She is going to have to become used to her surroundings eventually," he said. "There is no better time than the present to start. Bring her to me, Gates."

Gates was growing increasingly frustrated with Jasper's lack of compassion. Under normal circumstances he would not have cared in the least, but after a sleepless night, he was coming to realize that he cared a great deal whether or not he wanted to. *God, I'm such a fool,* he thought. More than that, his feelings towards Kathalin were about to get him into trouble with her father.

"Shall I ask Lady de Lara what she thinks of bringing her daughter into a hall full of leering men?" he asked, cocking an eyebrow. "Let us see what she has to say about it. If she agrees, then I will do it."

Jasper's mouth flew open in outrage. "You would not *dare* do such a thing!"

Gates' reply was to turn on his heel and head for the hall door, leaving Jasper to bellow after him. "De Wolfe!" he yelled. "Do not leave this hall, do you hear? Come back here, I demand it!"

Gates made it to the entry before stopping, pausing long enough to turn around and see that Jasper was on his feet, moving towards him. The old man pointed at him.

"Since when are you so concerned about a woman?" he demanded. "Women mean nothing to you. Do you know why I did not greet you and my daughter in the bailey when you arrived last night? It was because a woman claiming she had borne your bastard son had come to the kitchen gate demanding money. It is true! I went to see her because she was creating quite a fuss and the sentries summoned me. I saw the child, Gates. He looks just like you. She calls him Wolfie, after you. I paid her a few silver coins and told her to go away."

Shocked, Gates considered what he had just been told carefully before replying. There wasn't much use in denying the possibility because he knew it would have been a lie for him to even attempt it. Therefore, he simply accepted it.

"Did she give her name?" he asked.

Jasper nodded but, in the same motion, his head began to wag back and forth in a reproachful gesture. "Helene of Linley," he said. "God's Bones, Gates, you bedded Lord Linley's daughter? Have you no sense?"

Gates remained cool. "Linley is a drunken old fool with less than fifty men sworn to him," he said quietly. "He lives in a dilapidated manor home, the last son of a once-great baronetcy, and drinks himself to death every day. I met Helene on an errand for you, in fact, and fed the woman because she was starving. She was in town trying to sell the last of her family's valuables. Did you know that about Linley? He uses all of his money for drink while his family starves."

Jasper did know that, in fact. His angry stance was suddenly not so angry. He waved Gates off, as if the background of the House of Linley made no difference. "Be that as it may, it does not give you the right to bed his daughter," he pointed out. "Now you have given them one more mouth to feed but more than that, the woman will never know a decent marriage to lift her family out of poverty because you bedded her. That is the third bastard that I know of from you and God only knows how many more there are out there. What on earth am I going to do with you, Gates?"

Gates looked at the man, seeing how flustered he was, and did what he usually did in these situations – he charmed himself out of it. He and de Lara rarely had cross words but when they did, Gates knew that honey worked much better with Jasper than vinegar. That, and stories of war. Either one had been known to work. He forced a smile.

"I know that I am a terrible lad," he said, trying to lighten Jasper's mood. "I refuse to let you see your own daughter and then I produce armies of bastard children all over your earldom. At the very least, you should beat me into a bloody pulp but then there would be no one to lead your armies to victory. I am your greatest pride and your greatest embarrassment. Whatever are you going to do with me?"

Jasper, who had been righteously upset, was struggling not to smile as Gates came over to him and clapped him on the shoulder, grinning devilishly. It was difficult to be cross with such a smile. He shook his head in disgust.

"You are a wicked bastard," he said, although by the tone of his voice it was obvious that he wasn't truly angry. "Between you and Alexander, it is as if you are led by your manhoods and not your common sense."

"I know. But it is much more fun that way."

Jasper snorted, easing out of his anger. "Naughty!"

Gates laughed softly. "Naughty and thrilling," he said. "I never know when an irate father is going to try and challenge me, and that makes life very exciting."

Jasper couldn't help but laugh at Gates, a man he truly adored. "You really are dastardly," he said. "Will you ever cease this behavior, Gates? Will you become a responsible man someday and marry a woman?"

Gates immediately thought of Kathalin, an idea that hit him so hard he actually had to suck in his breath. Suddenly, the situation wasn't so funny anymore. He felt anxiety and confusion. The smile faded from his face.

"I doubt any decent family will want to have their daughter married to me," he said, half because it was the truth and half because he wanted to see Jasper's reaction. "I will have to find a bride from a country far away where they have not heard of me."

As expected, Jasper agreed. "That is true, lad," he said. "I am not sure we could find you a bride from a decent family in all of England. No woman wants to marry a man who has bastards running around. Most shameful. But, on the other hand, you are a de Wolfe and you bring the de Wolfe name with you. You are a knight beyond compare. Mayhap a good family will take that into consideration."

Gates almost asked the obvious; it was on the tip of his tongue, begging to be spoken: *would you*? But he couldn't bring himself to say it, to give a clue as to what he had been thinking and feeling for Kathalin. Was it marriage, then? Did he want to marry the woman? Gates wasn't sure. All he knew was that he couldn't stand the thought of her with someone else. The very idea ate at him like a cancer.

"Mayhap," he was all he could manage to say. "But I do not have to worry over it today. Meanwhile, may I make a suggestion regarding your daughter?"

In a better mood now, Jasper shrugged. "Go ahead," he said with resignation. "You will, anyway."

Gates smirked, a half-grin on his face. "Allow me to suggest going to her chamber and speaking with her in private," he said. "She is a different young lady than you have imagined. Being raised in St. Milburga's has seen to that. But let me say that she has the de Lara strength. When we rode into St. Milburga's, it was overrun with raiders. I happened into the kitchen, where your daughter was, and she nearly beat me to death with an iron pot before she knew who I was. Strength and bravery like that is indeed a de Lara trait. So give her time to become accustomed to her new surroundings before you parade her around in front of men. She will do you proud but it would be better if you allowed her to do it on her own terms."

By the time he was finished, Jasper was listening seriously. "She beat you with a pot, you say?"

"She did, indeed. Me and another Welsh fool."

Jasper chuckled. "Indeed," he said, respect in his tone. He eyed Gates a moment before speaking. "Very well," he said. "I will go to her chamber this morning and become acquainted with her. I would also like to take her to meet her mother."

"I am sure she would be agreeable to that."

Jasper nodded. "Excellent," he said. "Will you come with me to see her, then? She knows you well by now and I am sure she would be comfortable with you in the room."

As Gates nodded, Alexander entered the hall. Dressed in a heavy fur cloak against the cold, his face was pinched red from the chill outside. When he saw Gates and Jasper standing there, he beat at his arms as if to drive warmth back into them.

"God's Bloody Feet!" he exclaimed. "I have never felt such cold!"

Jasper was already moving for the entry with Gates in tow. "Come with us, Alexander," he said, tugging on the man. "We are going to meet my daughter. I've not truly spoken with her since she was a child and even then, what is it possible for children to say? She was a silly little girl. I would like to see what a fine and obedient woman she has become."

Jealousy reared its ugly head in Gates' heart once again at the thought of Alexander interacting with Kathalin. It was a struggle not to show it. He didn't even want Jasper speaking with the woman much less Alexander. *Damnation, man, what is happening to you?* Frustrated, and trying to keep his composure, Gates had no choice but to follow Jasper, and now Alexander, out of the hall.

"I met your daughter last night, my lord, briefly," Alexander said as they entered the frozen bailey. "A lovely girl, in fact. She does not look like the de Lara side of the family."

Jasper grinned at the insult. "Nay, she certainly does not," he said. "She looks like the du Bois side, the half-Welsh side. They all have dark hair and bright blue eyes. Kathalin looks a good deal like her mother did as a young woman."

The three of them slogged through the freezing, slick mud as they approached the keep. Jasper kept trying to shake it off his fine boots even though it was a futile effort; the dark mud clung like clay.

"My lord," Gates spoke up before they could reach the iron-grate entry of the keep. "You should know that Lady Kathalin has brought up her request to take her vows as a nun more than once during the journey home. It is possible she will bring it up again when you speak with her. She is quite disappointed at being summoned home rather than remaining at St. Milburga's and being allowed to pursue a holy vocation."

Jasper frowned as they reached the keep entry. "She will *not* take her vows," he said flatly. "A de Lara is not meant for the cloister. She has a bigger destiny to fulfill."

Gates nodded patiently as the old Tender of the Keep unlocked the grate and pulled it open. "I realize that," he said. "But she is quite attached to St. Milburga's and has her heart set on becoming a nun. If I were you, I would be gentle when informing her that she will be denied her wishes. She is likely to become quite emotional about it. In fact, I had to carry her, bound, out of St. Milburga's because she did not wish to come with me, so be aware that her presence here is not by choice. It was by force."

The three men pushed into the lower level of the keep, which was cold and somewhat dark. Jasper was the first one up the spiral stairs, followed by Gates and Alexander.

"I see," Jasper said. He did not sound pleased. "Then her desire to join the cloister is not a whim."

"Not at all."

He fell silent a moment as they reached the top of the stairs. "That is unfortunate," he finally said, heading for the chamber door where his daughter was housed, "because my plans for her are much different."

Gates didn't say anymore as Jasper reached out a meaty fist and banged on Kathalin's door. He had to rap twice before a nervous voice on the other side asked for identification. Gates, knowing she would not open the door to her father, primarily because he'd told her not to, answered.

"My lady, it is de Wolfe and your father and Sir Alexander," he said. "May we please enter?"

The bolt to the door was thrown. They could hear it sliding against the wood. The chamber door jerked open and Kathalin stood in the doorway.

Her attention was only on Gates and his attention was only on her; she was wearing the heavy lavender wool gown, a simple garment that emphasized her lovely figure, and her dark hair was simply braided and draped over one shoulder. It was clear that she hadn't any help in dressing not only because of her simple hair, but for the fact that the lace-up ties on the back of the dress were somewhat awry. Gates only saw that when she managed to tear her attention off of him and step back into the room, ushering her father forth.

"Good morn to you, my lord," Kathalin said politely, her attention once again returning to Gates. "It is a lovely morning."

Gates didn't smile at her; he was terrified to do it, terrified that Jasper would see him do it and then read into the gesture of his interest in Kathalin. That could not happen, under any circumstances. But the fact that she was only half-dressed spurred Gates into action. He could see that she was tugging the neckline of her dress up so that it would not fall off.

"Greetings, Daughter," Jasper said. "I have come to see how you are faring this morning. I was hoping we might have a discussion."

Kathalin nodded, tugging at her shoulder again so her garment would not fall down. Before she could reply, Gates put himself between her and Jasper, pointing to the basket that had contained the possessions he purchased for her. The basket lid was ajar and garments were half-in, half-out of the basket.

"My lord," he said, distracting Jasper and Alexander. "Lady Kathalin did not have any possessions, or any acceptable clothing, because of her humble existence at St. Milburga's. I took the liberty of purchasing some items for her and I wish for you to inspect them. She may need more. You may wish for her to have something else. In any case, will you please inspect what I have spent your money on? I felt it was important for the lady to dress as a daughter of an earl."

Thankfully, Jasper was diverted. Talk of money always diverted him. He headed straight for the basket as Gates swiftly turned around, got in behind Kathalin, and began quickly and nimbly tightening up the laces of her surcoat. Jasper was digging into the basket as Kathalin grunted, sucking in her breath with surprise as Gates pulled the ties tight so her garment wouldn't fall off.

Alexander, of course, was watching the whole thing, biting off laughter as Gates cinched up the lady's dress and she tried very hard not to make any noise of it. He didn't think it odd that Gates would do such a thing considering how well versed the man was in removing ladies' clothing, so it was quite humorous to him as all of this went on behind Jasper's back. Jasper, quite oblivious, pulled out the shifts, peering inside at the fine slippers.

"Where did you get these things, Gates?" he asked.

Gates kept his eyes on Jasper as he tightened. "In a town not far from here," he said. "The wife of the local merchant was a seamstress and she had many fine garments already half-sewn. I simply purchased them."

Kathalin gasped as Gates pulled tight the top of the lacings, nearly pulling her off the ground in his haste. But Jasper didn't notice; he was still focused on the possessions he had paid for, unaware when Alexander moved next to Gates to make sure the man had laced the woman up properly. Silently, Alexander nodded his approval and both men moved away from Kathalin, quickly, as Jasper turned around with a bar of soap in his hand.

"What?" he demanded of Gates. "No jewelry? Why did you not buy her any jewelry?"

Gates was quite casual in his behavior, as if he hadn't just laced up the back of Kathalin's surcoat. They were all standing a respectable distance away from the lady, as if nothing had happened.

"There was none available," he said. "I would be happy to take the lady to Shrewsbury to purchase jewelry for her."

Alexander chimed in. "An excellent idea," he agreed. "I will accompany them. Shrewsbury is only a day's ride from Hyssington. And it will be imperative that the lady be properly dressed if you intend to show her off at the coming celebration."

Gates struggled not to scowl at Alexander, who seemed quite eager to accompany them to Shrewsbury. As Jasper considered the suggestion, Kathalin, who was feeling quite overwhelmed by the course of the conversation, and all of the male chatter, spoke up.

"My lord," she addressed her father firmly, wanting to be heard above the forceful knights. "You mentioned a celebration yesterday. Although I appreciate your generosity in planning such a thing in my honor, I can assure you that I do not need or want a celebration. I simply need to know why it is you have summoned me home. Won't you tell me?"

Jasper faced his daughter, trying to keep in mind what Gates had told him about her. *She has her heart set on becoming a nun.* The more Jasper looked at her, the more distaste that idea provoked. Now that he'd seen his daughter, he knew she would command a fine price with a fine family, and that was truthfully all he could think of. It didn't matter what *she* wanted; it was what *he* wanted. He indicated the small table and two chairs near the window.

"Please, Kathalin," he said. "Sit down. There is much to discuss."

Dutifully, Kathalin sat in one of the chairs. It was now difficult to breathe because Gates had cinched her ties so tightly. She shifted around in the chair, attempting to find relief from her squashed ribcage.

Jasper sat in the opposite chair, unaware of Kathalin's discomfort as he took a moment to gaze upon her. Then, in a surprising move, he reached out to take her hand. Kathalin watched him with a mixture of apprehension and curiosity.

"My dear," Jasper said, trying to sound gentle. "I understand that you wish to commit yourself to the cloister."

Kathalin nodded eagerly. "I do," she said quickly. "You received my missive about it?"

Jasper nodded. "I did," he replied. He hesitated a moment before continuing. "I have discussed the issue with your mother and we have come to the conclusion that you would better serve this family by fulfilling your destiny as the wife of an ally. The House of de Lara is a powerful Marcher lordship and it is imperative that we make allegiances. Since Roget is no longer with us, God rest his soul, the earldom will pass to your brother, Jeffrey, and he will make a political marriage someday. We must make one for you as well. It is important to the survival of our family. Do you understand?"

Kathalin was looking at the man with such a fallen expression that it was difficult not to notice it. She sighed heavily, great anguish on her face. "But I do not wish to marry," she said, her voice soft and pleading. "My brother will have children to carry on the de Lara name. If I marry, I will not be carrying on the de Lara name at all. I will be perpetuating my husband's name."

Jasper shook his head. "Untrue," he said. "Your children will have de Lara blood in them. That is a very important factor."

Kathalin was heartbroken. Now, she realized the true reason why she had been summoned home, to face a future she did not want. In hindsight, she supposed she knew it all along but to hear her father speak so callously of something that meant so much to her was truly disheartening. Part of her wondered if Gates, too, had known it all along and simply hadn't wanted to tell her. She looked at him, then, distress on her face only to see that his features were like stone. There was no discernable expression. No warmth, no sympathy. Her heart sank even more.

"But... I do not want to do that," she said, more sorrow in her voice. "You sent me to St. Milburga's as a child and I grew to love it. It is my home. It is the only home I have ever known. I want to become a nun and serve God. You have ignored me for fourteen years and I find it ironic that after all of the years of pretending I did not exist you should suddenly find my life important to you. You want me to marry and establish family ties with another house? You are condemning me to something I never, ever wanted to do. You are condemning me to a life of unhappiness."

Jasper let go of her hand; so much for trying to reason with her. "I am sorry you feel that way," he said. "When I sent you to St. Milburga's, it was for your protection and education. It was not to groom you to become a nun."

Kathalin gazed at him steadily, though there was disgust in her expression. "Then why did you send me to a convent to begin with?" she asked, rather passionately. "You could have sent me to any number of fine houses to foster, but you did not. You sent me to a House of God and I grew to love it. I want to make it my life. Why are you now taking that away from me?"

Jasper was becoming increasingly frustrated with her attempts to argue. "Your life is not your own," he said strongly. "Or have you not yet figured that out? No woman has a say in her life. That is up to her father or husband."

He was definitively cutting her off and Kathalin was becoming more distraught by the moment. "You are a stranger to me," she said quietly. "A stranger who has never cared for me, yet you have control over my life. You already have Jeffrey to perpetuate the family. You do not need me."

Jasper didn't like having his wishes refuted and it was a struggle for him to keep his temper with her. She most definitely had the de Lara stubborn streak, just like he did, and the truth was that he found that rather frustrating. If he didn't gain the upper hand in this conversation, it could end up quite unpleasant for them both. He wasn't about to let the woman make demands of him.

"There are times in our lives when we are forced to do distasteful things because of the need of the family," he said. "This is one of those times. You will not be returning to St. Milburga's. You will remain here, at your family's home, and when we give the grand party for you in two weeks' time, you will be introduced to some of England's most eligible and powerful men. I am sorry if that is distasteful to you, but that is what will be. Now, I am sure your mother would like to speak with you this morning. She has been most eager to see you. Will you please come with me so that I may reacquaint the two of you?"

Kathalin was sitting back in the painted chair, feeling overwhelming hatred for the man who was her father. Hatred and anger and bloody disappointment. She felt as if her guts were being ripped out. She simply looked away from him.

"Nay," she said. "I do not wish to see her and I do not wish to see you, either."

Jasper hardened. "Do not be foolish, girl," he growled. "I can force you to my will. I can force you to do anything I want you to do. Why do you think Alexander and Gates are here? If you do not obey my wishes, they will force you to do what I tell you to do. Do not test me, lass – you will lose."

Kathalin was pale by the time he finished his speech, still looking away from him, her face taut with emotion. Without another word, and without looking at either Gates or Alexander or Jasper, she stood up and marched to the door, obviously waiting for her father to take her to her mother. Jasper sighed heavily, stood up from his seat, and went to open the chamber door. Taking Kathalin by the arm, he turned to Gates and Alexander.

"Go downstairs and wait for me," he said quietly. "I will not be long."

Gates simply nodded, watching as Jasper, his fingers digging in to Kathalin's upper arm, took her from the chamber and directed her up the stairs to the level above where her mother's chamber was situated. When they quit the room and the footsteps faded up to the third floor, Alexander turned to Gates.

"Is she truly so difficult?" he hissed. "Jasper will not hesitate to punish her."

Gates couldn't let on just how emotional he was feeling about what he had just witnessed. That sense of protection towards her was nearly out of control, made worse by Jasper's threats. God help him, he was having difficulty thinking straight at the moment. He wanted very badly to follow Kathalin and Jasper up to Lady de Lara's room but didn't dare move in that direction.

He had to remain cool and in control.

"I know," he finally muttered, realizing there was sweat on his brow as the result of his inner turmoil. "Let us go down to the entry as he instructed. We will wait for him there."

Alexander preceded Gates out of the chamber and both men took the stairs down to the entry where the Tender of the Keep was smoking up a storm by stirring up the embers in her black, sooty hearth. When she saw the knights, she moved to unlock the iron grate but Gates waved her off. He simply stood next to the grate, feeling the cold air blow through, unsure what more he should say to Alexander or if he should try to start a conversation that took them off the subject of Kathalin and Jasper, for certainly, he wasn't entirely sure he could even keep up a calm conversation when it came to those two.

Calm wasn't something he was feeling at the moment.

As Gates stood in moody silence, Alexander sensed that something was wrong with the man although he truly had no idea what it was. Perhaps it was disgust that he'd had to go to St. Milburga's in the first place, or perhaps it was because he found himself in the position of nursemaid to a grown woman. Contrary to Gates' normal behavior with women, he didn't seem particularly attracted to this one. Perhaps it was because she was his liege's daughter or perhaps it was because she was not a particularly pleasant person.

In any case, Gates seemed distracted and upset about the situation, as if he wished he were anywhere but in the keep at that moment. As Alexander watched the man, he could see something odd in his expression, something distant and pensive. He wondered if his observations were incorrect and Gates was actually feeling some distress on the lady's behalf rather than experiencing distaste for her behavior. With Gates, it was difficult to know sometimes. He had no involvement in women other than conquest.

As far as Alexander knew, he'd never truly even come to know one. But maybe, in this case, he'd come to know Lady Kathalin on the journey from St. Milburga's and wished he hadn't. Either way, Gates wasn't acting like himself, and that was puzzling.

As Kathalin and Jasper entered Lady de Lara's chamber two floors above them, Gates and Alexander waited in silence.

CHAPTER NINE

"**L**ORD DE LARA already gave you money, woman," a de Lara sergeant with a bushy, red beard said. "Why have you returned?"

A small, pale woman with a pretty face and a baby bundled in her arms stood at the kitchen gate of Hyssington, a sectioned-out piece of the wall that looked as if it were made for midgets. It was only about four feet tall, making it difficult to pass through, but if one was being attacked and the gate was breeched, it would make it difficult for the enemy to pass through bending over. One could get a head lobbed off at that angle, which was exactly the point.

"Your lord cannot pay me enough money to go away," the woman staunchly said. "I told him that. I must speak with Gates de Wolfe and no amount of money will change that."

The soldier eyed the woman and the baby in her hand. He'd been on duty last night when she'd come around and he'd heard tale, from de Lara himself, what the woman's business was. It wasn't uncommon for a man to have a bastard or two about but Gates de Wolfe seemed to have a knack for it. He was fearless on the battlefield and commanded his men's utmost respect as a knight, and as a man who seemed to be rather prolific and careless when it came to women, he also commanded a good deal of respect, mostly because most men wished they had the comely looks, skill, and resources that Gates de Wolfe had.

The man was a legend and not all of it related to his blade.

Therefore, de Lara's men, men under de Wolfe's command, defended and supported their commander and this was one of those occasions. The bushy-beard sergeant shook his head at the woman.

"You'll not speak with him, woman," he said. "You have been fairly paid. Do not come back here."

The young woman's features hardened. "I will not go away," she said flatly. "If you send me away from this gate, I will simply go around to the front gatehouse and beg. I will create such a storm that you will not be able to hide from it, do you hear? This is Gates de Wolfe's son and he shall know of it."

With that, she held the infant up, who had been sleeping, now disturbed. As the baby began to wail, loudly, the sergeant was coming to re-think his strategy. He didn't want the woman creating a scene and embarrassing de Wolfe.

"Have you no decency?" he demanded. "You spread your legs for de Wolfe if, in fact, this is truly his son and now you show up to shame him in front of his men? If you had any respect for the man at all, you would simply go away from here and bear your shame in private. *You* bore the child – it is *your* responsibility."

The young woman's cheeks flamed. "Are you going to send for de Wolfe or not?"

"I am not."

The young woman's features stiffened with rage. "Then I shall come back here every day and scream for the man until you send him to me. And I will make sure and tell everyone that it is *your* fault that I am screaming for him. If you will only send for him now, this will cease to be your problem and become de Wolfe's. Now, *send* for him."

The sergeant believed her. He also knew he had little choice. Greatly annoyed, he had a kitchen servant unlock the gate and allow the woman into the kitchen yard as he sent another servant for de Wolfe. Then he stood by, glaring at the young woman as she now tried to soothe the yelling baby, and hoped de Wolfe wouldn't be too upset with him for bothering him with such a trivial thing. De Wolfe was an amiable man, good to his men, but his temper could be unpredictable at times. The sergeant hoped this wasn't one of those times.

So they waited as the morning deepened and the clouds began to shift around overhead, being pushed eastward by a strong breeze. The sergeant kept glancing up to the sky, concerned that it would begin to snow on them at some point as the wait dragged on. But no snow was forthcoming and the baby eventually quieted down and went back to sleep. Almost an hour after sending a servant running for de Wolfe, the knight finally made an appearance.

He was coming from the direction of the keep, heading into the corner of the fortress where the kitchens were located. Although there was a wall around the kitchen yard, the sergeant could still see the man's approach because of his line of sight through the kitchen gate. De Wolfe was walking with a purpose, slogging through the mud that was still frozen in places, as he reached the kitchen gate and yanked it open. Even from a distance, the sergeant could tell by de Wolfe's pinch-cold expression that he was vastly displeased.

"My lord," the sergeant said as de Wolfe approached. "The young woman would not leave. She has been demanding...."

Gates cut him off, his hazel-gold eyes boring into the young woman like hot steel. "I know," he said, reaching out to grab the woman. "With me, Helene."

He continued walking, away from the sergeant, yanking Helene of Linley with him. Tiny, slender, with a pale beauty about her, Helene was overjoyed to finally see the father of her child.

"Gates!" she gasped. "It has been so very long! I had heard rumors that you returned and I had to come and see you!"

Gates' jaw was ticking furiously as he pulled her all the way to the curtain wall before coming to a halt. Then he released her arm and faced her.

"Aye, I have returned," he said, unfriendly. "What do you want?"

Helene's face fell just a bit. She had been expecting a warm and happy welcome from the man she had given herself over to. "I... I have been waiting over a year for you to return from France," she said. Then, she began to quickly pull back the swaddling on the baby in her arms, exposing the sleeping face. "Look – your son. He was born six months ago. His name is Wolfe of Linley. I named him for you, Gates. He is a strong and healthy boy, worthy of your legacy."

Gates looked at the child, fighting off a sense of aversion. It was true that he had at least two bastards that he knew of and now he was gazing upon a third. He knew this because the child looked just like his father. Still, he would not acknowledge it. That sort of thing never came out in his favor.

"So you have had a son," he said. "Congratulations. What do you want me to do about it?"

Helene blinked. That was not the answer she had come for. Her mood fell further. "He is *your* son, Gates," she said softly. "I should think... he is a fine boy and worthy of you. I should think that you would want to claim him."

"Claim him?"

Helene nodded, receiving the distinct impression that Gates was not thrilled to see the child. Struggling not to become distraught in his reaction, she decided to push her agenda. It was something she had been practicing for since the night Gates had bedded her. With the man's son in her arms, she had a strong case to plead.

"My father is Lord Linley," she said. "I realize I may not be worthy enough for a de Wolfe wife, but I swear to you that I would be faithful and true. I would make a very fine wife, Gates."

Gates knew this had been the intention behind her appearance all along. This wasn't the first time he'd heard those words. *I will make you a fine wife and we can be a family.* Nay, not the first time at all. He'd heard them before.

Therefore, there were two ways he could handle the situation; either throw Helene out on her arse or try to charm his way out of it. Much like he did with Jasper, he found that honey often got him his wants more than vinegar did. With women, it was easy to show them a little honey. They were vulnerable to sweetness from a man, and Helene was no different. The night he'd bedded her, she had melted to his will like hot butter. It had truly been no feat at all.

"Helene," he said softly. "I am sure you would make a very fine wife. But you know that marriage is not for me. You and I discussed it… well, the last time we saw each other. You were in need of kindness and food at the time and I was more than happy to provide both. But I cannot marry, sweetly. You *know* this."

Helene swallowed hard, struggling against her great and vast disappointment. "I will be no trouble," she insisted. "Wolfie and I eat very little and we do not take up much space. If you could only consider it, Gates. My father… he does not know the baby is a de Wolfe. If I tell him, he will make outrageous demands of you and your father. Please… I do not want to tell him."

Gates cocked an eyebrow, suddenly seeing her angle in all of this. She was going to try and force him to it. *The little vixen!*

"Are you saying that if I do not marry you, then you will tell your father the child is mine?" he asked.

Helene shrugged, looking down at the infant in her arms. "He looks just like you," she said. "My father would not like it if you refused to marry me."

"Is that so?"

She nodded. "He might send word to your father, demanding money," she said, sounding casual about it. "He might even send word to the king and tell him of your careless behavior. There is no knowing what my father would do."

Gates didn't like being threatened. His initial resolve to charm his way out of marriage took a harsh turn and he quickly decided to fight back. More than that, he would beat her at her own game.

"The child looks just like any number of men here at Hyssington, men whom I can swear to you will attest that they bedded you at one time or another," he said grimly, watching her eyes fly open in horror.

"Is that what you want, Helene? To threaten me? Because I can guarantee you that it will make you look far worse than it will me. Shame will be upon *you*, not me."

Helene gasped. "You will not accept this child as your own?"

"I will not accept you trying to coerce me into marriage."

Her mouth flew open in outrage. "So you would slander me?" she gasped. "You are an honorable knight. You would not do such a thing!"

Gates didn't waver. "Are you willing to take the chance?"

Helene's outrage lasted a few moments longer before she burst into quiet tears when she realized what he was saying. *Shame will be upon you*. So much for trying to force the man into marriage. Weeping, she lowered her head.

"Why would you do this?" she whispered. "You... you told me I was beautiful. You told me I was special. You spoke of wonderful things that you promised to show me. Don't you remember?"

Gates wasn't moved by the tears. In fact, he was growing impatient. "I tell every lass she is beautiful and special," he said coldly. "What you heard was not unusual. But I will tell you this; had you not threatened me, this situation might have gone much better in your favor. But your greed has left you without recourse. You will go now and you will not return. Is this in any way unclear?"

Helene's head came up, tears on her face. "It is true what people have said about you," she hissed. "You *are* the Dark Destroyer, destroying women's lives for your own pleasure. You are a terrible man!"

"If I am so terrible then why do you demand I marry you?"

That caught Helene off-guard for a moment, but only for a moment. She came back in torment. "How can you be so callous towards your own child?"

Gates' jaw ticked. "You cannot prove it is mine," he said. "As I said, I can produce ten other soldiers at Hyssington who would swear they bedded you should you try to force me to accept this child. You would have done much better had you not threatened to tell your father in order to force me into marriage. See what your treachery has cost you?"

Helene was devastated. "But he is yours," she wept. "He is *your* son! No other man has ever bedded me. You are the only one!"

Gates reached out and took her arm, pulling her towards the kitchen gate. "So you say," he said cruelly. The woman had angered him and now he was behaving poorly, miffed with anyone who would try to blackmail him. "Go, now. I do not want to see you again."

Helene yanked her arm away from him, sharply, startling the child in her arms so it started to wail. She staggered towards the kitchen gate as Gates shepherded her in that direction, making sure she went through the gate and then ensuring it was locked behind her. He watched her wander off, her weeping fading as she moved away from the castle through the snow-topped trees. He couldn't even manage to dredge up any sympathy for her, greedy woman that she was.

But he knew, instinctively, that it would not be the last time he saw her.

THE FIRST THING Kathalin realized about her mother's chamber was the smell; clove and something else, permeating everything around them. It was quite heavy. Upon entering the lavish and warm chamber, Jasper sneezed twice and even Kathalin's nose wrinkled up at the pungent smell.

"Jasper?" came a soft voice. "Is that you?"

Jasper had a grip on Kathalin's arm, pulling her to a halt just inside the door. "Aye," he said. "I have brought our daughter. Come and greet her."

Still embittered from her conversation with Jasper, Kathalin truly wasn't in any mood to be social but as she stood there, she couldn't help but notice her mother's luxurious chamber. Although her room was quite glorious, this chamber was far more lavish with great embroidered tapestries hung from the walls, covering the cold stone. Kathalin caught sight of the one nearest to her, back by the door, and she gazed up at the magnificent piece that seemed to depict a biblical scene. There was an angel and animals in it, all finely woven works of great detail. As she studied the tapestry, she heard movement over on the enormous bed.

"Kathalin!" a woman's voice gasped and the bed began to twitch. There were heavy curtains all around it, making it impossible to see what was taking place on the bed, but whatever it was had it moving about a great deal. "I am so glad you have finally arrived. It is terrible weather to be traveling in, but thanks to God that you made it."

She seemed quite excited. Jasper, having his iron grip on Kathalin, stood a couple of feet away from his daughter.

"Thank Gates for ensuring she arrived safely," he said to his wife. "It is by his strength and skill alone that she made it intact. It seems that there was much turmoil in her coming here."

They could hear feet on the floor, shuffling, and the bed stopped moving. The shuffling was growing closer, coming around the end of the bed, and suddenly a swaddled figure appeared. Covered from head to toe in dark fabric except for around her face and hands, which were covered with pale fabric, only the woman's eyes were visible. Nothing else. But those eyes were of a brilliant blue, crinkling when she caught sight of Kathalin.

Kathalin, however, couldn't help but be curious and the least bit apprehensive about a woman who was covered completely with fabric except for her eyes. Her anger with Jasper faded somewhat as she focused on the figure; this wasn't the mother she remembered, at least not in whole, but the eyes... there was something familiar there. They stirred something deep in her memory.

"Turmoil?" Rosamund repeated, her voice muffled through the fabric across her face. "What happened?"

"Welsh," Jasper replied. "They raided St. Milburga's and had Gates not arrived when he did, I am not entirely sure we would still have a daughter. It is more fortuitous that we sent him when we did. God was merciful."

Rosamund couldn't take her eyes from her daughter. She came close to her but not too close. She could see Jasper backing away and she realized she must have been moving in too closely. She stopped a few feet from Kathalin, the bright blue eyes moist.

"Then I am grateful for God's mercy and for Gates and his skill," she said. "Kathalin, do you remember me? I am Rosamund, your mother."

Kathalin nodded, although she seriously wondered why the woman was covered from head to toe. More than that, she had noticed Jasper backing away when the woman came close. That seemed very odd to her. It was enough to ease her anger at the situation, momentarily, as her curiosity took hold.

"I remember you," she said.

Rosamund's eyes crinkled as she evidently smiled beneath her veil. "I am glad," she said. "It has been a long time."

"Aye, it has."

Rosamund warmed to her daughter. "I am very glad to see you again, my dear," she said. "Welcome home."

The anger abruptly returned. Kathalin thought her mother's statement was particularly offensive and she wasn't in a forgiving or pleasant mood. So it was good to see her again, was it? After fourteen years of silence, suddenly, it was good to see her again? Kathalin knew the only reason the woman was glad to see her was because it would complete some manner of political marriage she had in mind. It had nothing to do with Kathalin personally.

It had everything to do with being a de Lara pawn.

"This is not my home," she said after a moment. "My home is St. Milburga's. My last memory of you is when you screamed at me and then sent me away. You have spent the past fourteen years ignoring me. Why in the world should you be happy to see me again?"

Rosamund was taken aback by the venom of Kathalin's words. The smile vanished from her face because her eyes grew wide. Next to Kathalin, Jasper growled.

"Insolent girl," he chastised. "You are a wicked child to speak to your mother so."

Kathalin stepped back, away from Jasper and away from Rosamund. "Why?" she demanded, exasperation in her tone. "Why, in God's name, is either of you happy to see me? Do you not understand? You abandoned me as a child and I find it incredibly offensive that you expect me to forget about that. You act as if you have done nothing wrong while I am made to look ungrateful and hateful because I resent the fact that I have been taken from the only home I have ever known by two people who are strangers to me. How did you think I would feel about this? If you think I am happy to see you, then you are grossly mistaken. I am not happy about any of this. The only reason you want me is to cement some kind of political alliance so I would appreciate it if you would both stop acting as if there is some affection between us and treat me as you would any other person under your command. For you to try and become parents to me at this point in my life is ridiculous."

Jasper's jaw flexed dangerously and he took a step towards her but Rosamund threw out an arm, stopping him.

"Nay, Jasper," she commanded softly. When she was sure Jasper was stilled, she returned her attention to Kathalin. "I am very sorry you feel that way, Kathalin. There were reasons why you were sent away, my dear, and you will simply have to trust that they were good reasons. It was not to abandon you."

Kathalin had hoped when she had this conversation with her parents that it would have been with a cooler head, but at this moment, that was not to be. She was far too emotional, feeling hurt and anger well up in her that she thought had been long buried. As she had those years ago, she began feeling the pain of abandonment, the realization that she was unwanted. They were horrible things to feel again.

"Then what do you call it?" she asked, her voice tremulous with emotion. "I was five years old, Rosamund. You sent a five-year-old girl away with a soldier who kept pinching my arse. When that wasn't enough, he would put his hands between my legs and laugh when I screamed. He dropped me off at St. Milburga's and the nuns took me in, soothed my tears, fed me, and taught me everything I know. For the first few years, I prayed that you would come and take me home but when that did not happen, I prayed for a kind word from you. But you never sent me a missive, not ever. You ignored me for fourteen years and had de Wolfe not removed me from St. Milburga's by force, I would have never come back to Hyssington, ever. As far as I am concerned, I do not have parents."

A family reunion that should have been a joyous happenstance had become something cold and tense. Jasper was so angry that his lips were white and it was only by Rosamund's hand that he wasn't grabbing Kathalin by the hair and dragging her downstairs where Gates and Alexander could throw her in the vault. Insolence never went over well with him and, at that moment, he was struggling with his temper. Rosamund knew this. Quietly, she indicated a cushioned chair near the hearth.

"Will you sit, Kathalin?" she asked politely. "I do not mean to be rude, but it is difficult for me to stand any length of time. Will you please sit so that we may continue the conversation?"

Kathalin had no intention of sitting. "Nay, I will not," she said. "You may sit if you wish. I will converse with you from where I am standing."

Rosamund went to the chair and sat down, heavily. She grunted a great deal, as if she were in pain, and her maid, who had been seated in the corner, ran over to help her adjust pillows behind her back. When the little maid scooted back into the shadows, Rosamund turned to Jasper.

"Leave us, please," she said to her husband. "I will speak with Kathalin alone."

Jasper was glad to leave. He didn't like women and he certainly didn't like their drama, so he left without another word. If he'd remained, he knew he couldn't have guaranteed his composure. As

Jasper fled the chamber, Kathalin remained in her spot by the door, unmoving. She watched her mother carefully.

"Now," Rosamund said softly. "You feel abandoned. After you have explained your feelings to me, I can understand why you would feel that way. I am very sorry to hear it. It was not my intention to abandon you. But I... well, sending you to St. Milburga's was necessary."

Kathalin was unforgiving. "Why?"

Rosamond's eyes turned to her. "Because you had to be removed from my presence."

That was not a helpful answer. In fact, it only served to hurt and anger Kathalin more. More exasperation bled forth as she threw up her hands in frustration. "Then why did you ever have children if you found us so offensive?" she demanded. "Moreover, why must you ruin my life by bringing me back here for your political games? I do not want to be a wife. I want to take my vows as a nun. Lord de Lara said he received my missive requesting such a thing so I know you must be aware of it, too. Why torture me by forcing me to do something I not wish to do?"

Rosamund fell silent a moment. When she finally spoke, it was barely above a whisper. "It is not that I found my children offensive, my dear," she said softly. "It was because my health could not take the excitement. I am quite sure by your manner and your words that you do not care about my health, but I do not tell you this to gain sympathy. I tell you this for your understanding. I could not have children about. It only inflamed my condition. You said that your last memory of me is of me screaming at you... I will not deny it. I was in a good deal of pain. I had not yet learned to manage it."

In spite of her anguish, Kathalin could feel her guard going down a bit at Rosamund's softly uttered words. Naturally, she was curious. It was an unexpected factor in the history of her resentment towards her parents, perhaps a reason behind everything. Had she even been looking for a reason behind her parents' abandonment? It wasn't something that had crossed her mind but now that Rosamund spoke of such things, Kathalin was lured towards the possibilities.

"What pain?" she asked. "What is your affliction?"

Rosamund looked at her, the bright blue eyes glimmering. It was a moment before she spoke. "St. Milburga's is a healing order, is it not?"

Kathalin nodded. "It is," she said. "But surely you knew that when you sent me there."

"I did."

Kathalin nodded, a confirmation of understanding. "I have been trained by the nuns in healing ways," she said. "I learned a great deal from them. What is your ailment?"

Rosamund looked away, down at her lap as if contemplating a response. She reached out a wrapped hand, touching her arm through the fabric, perhaps considering what she should say.

"You must understand," she murmured, "this is not common knowledge. I do not wish for anyone else to know."

Kathalin's curiosity grew. "I will swear to you that I will not tell a soul," she said. "But you brought this up. You mentioned that you have an affliction. If you did not want me to know of it, you would not have mentioned it."

She had a point. Rosamund sighed quietly before replying. "Will you come to me, please?" she asked politely. "Not too close."

Driven by interest, Kathalin moved towards the woman, slowly, coming to within a couple of feet of her. *Not too close.* As she watched, Rosamund unwrapped one of her hands, pulling off the pale fabric, and her flesh suddenly became exposed to the light. Kathalin immediately saw the lesions, the discoloration, and the loss of two fingers. They were stubby and rounded at the tip. Deeply curious, she leaned forward to get a better look and as she noticed the particularly bad lesions on the palm of the hand, Rosamund whispered.

"I am a leper, my dear," she said. "It was just starting to show itself when you were very young. I sent you and your brothers away so that you would not become infected with it."

The hammer dropped and suddenly, Kathalin couldn't breathe. It was as if a thunderclap had deafened her, evaporated her senses, because all resentment and anger within her heart suddenly vanished. Her jaw dropped as Rosamund quickly covered her hand again, tucking the appendage back into its cloth covering, but it couldn't erase the memory of that horror from Kathalin's mind.

It couldn't erase what she had seen.

Everything, all of it, began to make sense to her now; Rosamund had been given a death sentence with this horrible affliction and she had children to protect. Now, all Kathalin could see was an ailing woman who had made the ultimate sacrifice. Dear God, was it really true? Had she spent all of those years resenting a woman who did not deserve it?

Distraught, she collapsed onto her knees before Rosamund.

"My God…," she breathed. "Is it true?"

"It is."

"But… did you know that Milburga is the patron saint of lepers?"

"I did, which is why I chose it to protect you."

I chose it to protect you. Kathalin was stunned. It was too much information, overwhelming her, but also helping her to see the situation clearly for the first time. Now, things were starting to make some sense.

"Then… then you have had this condition for many years," she said softly.

Rosamond nodded, her blue eyes moist. "Aye," she said quietly. "Many years. The finest doctors told me I had a dreaded disease and advised me to send my children away so they would not contract it. They advised Jasper to leave as well, or at the very least, take me to a home where I would be with others of my kind, but Jasper would not do it. He did not want rumors to get around that his wife was a leper, so I remain with him and he is a very unhappy man. Do not judge him too harshly, my dear. His life did not turn out as he had hoped, nor did mine."

Kathalin was flabbergasted. Stunned, her head swimming, all she could do was stare up at her mother and feel more pity than she had ever felt in her life. But along with the pity, she felt tremendous guilt, guilt for hating her parents for all of those years, guilt for believing they had not wanted her. *Abandoned her.* Emitting a loud, harsh gasp, she hung her head.

"God's Bones," she said with understanding. "I can hardly believe this. You sent me away to protect me."

"I did."

Kathalin's head came up, tears in her eyes. "If that is true, then why did you not send me any missives?" she wanted to know, struggling with her hurt and guilt. "For all of those years, you never once contacted me. I thought you had forgotten me. Why did you not send me any word?"

Rosamund's brilliant eyes were laced with sorrow. "Because I did not want you to remember me," she said. "I know it sounds foolish, Kathalin, but I wanted you to become accustomed to your new life and grow to love it, and forget about me. I wanted you to forget about ever coming home. Mayhap it was foolish, but I did not know what else to do."

Kathalin couldn't accept that explanation. "Yet you have sent for me, now," she said, rising to her feet and moving away, agitated. "You have brought me home so that you may marry me off to an ally. That is not fair to me! I came to love St. Milburga's as you had hoped, but now you want me back? I am an adult, Rosamund. My life is at the priory and I want to go back!"

Rosamund could see that. Now it was she who began to feel confused and anxious at the situation, understanding that her daughter was her own person. She had found the life she wanted to live and all of that was now threatened.

"I can see that," Rosamund said. "It did not occur to me that you would not be happy to return to your family and fulfill your duty as a de Lara daughter."

Kathalin simply looked at her, pain in her expression. "I have not been a de Lara daughter for many years," she said, trying not to be so harsh. "I have been a ward of St. Milburga's. I have learned to heal, I have learned to read and write, and I manage the kitchens. I am not a lady of refinement, one that would be expected in marrying a de Lara ally. Do you realize that? When you sent me to St. Milburga's, you sent me to learn the ways of the church, not the ways of a refinement. I would embarrass myself in a great household, as things would be expected of me that I know nothing about. Did that ever occur to you, either?"

Rosamund shook her head. "It did not," she said. Her gaze lingered on her daughter a moment. "You are not suited for the life we expect from you."

Kathalin shook her head slowly. "I am not," she said. "But that is your fault. Did you truly think that sending me to a convent would produce a fine and skilled lady?"

Rosamund fell silent, looking to her lap again. She could see, clearly, what her daughter was telling her and it was the truth. Kathalin would not know how to run a household or how to behave in noble and proper society. All Kathalin knew was prayer and kitchens. She truly hadn't thought of any of that until now and her heart sank; *why* hadn't she considered it?

She was a fool.

"I did not think on it," she said after a moment. "I knew you would receive an education and the truth of the matter is that I did not think I would live long enough to see you as an adult."

Kathalin regarded the woman a moment. "Yet you sent de Wolfe to bring me home," she said. "I am coming to see that it was my request to take my vows that prompted it. You do not want me to take them."

Rosamund shook her head. "Nay," she said. "No de Lara is meant for the cloister."

"Yet you still sent me to one."

Rosamund lifted her head to look at her. "It never occurred to me that you would want to pursue life as a nun," she said honestly. "And, as I said, I did not believe I would live long enough to see you into adulthood. But here you are, and her I am, and we have a problem between us. You wish to take your vows and I do not want you to. I want you to become a wife and mother and give me grandchildren. Is that such a terrible thing, Kathalin?"

Kathalin shook her head. "Nay," she said honestly. "But it was never anything I wanted to do. Being raised around women who were kind and generous and pious, they were the only women I knew. I always wanted to emulate them. You made a mistake sending me to St. Milburga's those years ago; you would have done better had you sent me to a great house somewhere to be raised as a fine lady if that was what you truly wanted me to become."

Rosamund nodded. "I see that now," she said. "I fear my lack of foresight has brought us to this point."

In spite of everything, Kathalin was starting to feel sorry for the woman. Ill with a disease, she had made the best decision with her children that, at the time, she could. Now, the future had changed and so had her decision about her daughter's future.

"What will you do?" Kathalin asked quietly.

Rosamund seriously pondered the question a moment before speaking. "You wish to take your vows because it is the only life you have ever known," she said. "I want you to become a wife, something you do not know anything about. Would it be fair, then, to ask you to at least see something of that life and consider it before making your final decision?"

Kathalin cocked her head curiously. "What do you mean?"

Rosamund rose stiffly, painfully, from the chair. "I will make you a proposal, Kathalin, and you will decide if it is a fair one," she said. "For now, allow your father and me to have a celebration in honor of your returning home. Meet people and become exposed to a world that you never knew. At least give it some time. Then, at the end of the celebration, if you still wish to take your vows as a nun, I will consider it. I promise that I will. But I feel that mayhap you must give consideration to a side of life you never knew. It is quite possible that you will like it."

Kathalin didn't want to agree to any of it but she thought of her alternative if she did not; they were going to force it on her anyway. She truly had no choice no matter how her mother made it sound. But the hope that Rosamund would consider her wishes if, in fact, she saw nothing agreeable with becoming a wife caused Kathalin to consider the proposal. Not as if she had any real choice, but still, for the fact that it seemed to mean a good deal to her ill mother, she would agree to it.

But in her heart, she knew her decision would never change.

"Very well," she said. "If you promise to consider allowing me to return to St. Milburga's, I will attend your celebration and see the world for myself."

Rosamund sighed heavily with relief. "Excellent," she said. "If you allow yourself to enjoy it, my dear, I am sure you will not be sorry."

Kathalin merely shrugged, unwilling to commit one way or the other. Her mother seemed pleased and at least there was the potential of her returning to St. Milburga's now, and that was all Kathalin cared about. As the situation was settled between them, Kathalin's focus began to lean back towards her mother's affliction. As a woman who had been trained in healing, Kathalin was most interested in it.

"May... may I ask you about your affliction, then?" she asked. "May I ask how you manage it? May I ask what you have tried to soothe it?"

A conversation that had started out harsh and tense turned to one of interest as Rosamund graciously agreed to speak on something she never spoke of. It was embarrassing to her, and tragic, and the only people who knew about it never asked. Neither Jasper nor her maid ever asked her how she was feeling; they simply reacted to her and her symptoms. Now, Kathalin was asking and it was awkward for Rosamund to speak of it at first, but Kathalin was genuinely interested without being judgmental or put off by it. Her daughter, a virtual stranger who had existed in a world that Rosamund knew little of, turned out to be a woman of compassion and understanding when it came to Rosamund's disease.

For the next hour, the two of them spoke of it and Rosamund even showed Kathalin both hands and arms, which the young woman carefully examined. Kathalin seemed to understand the physical burdens of the disease and she was sympathetic to what Rosamund had suffered through. When all was said and done, it had been one of the more surprisingly pleasant hours of Rosamund's life. Kathalin's, too.

But that trust would eventually be betrayed.

CHAPTER TEN

Three Days Later
Shrewsbury

S HREWSBURY WAS THE largest marketing town along the Marches, a
city on a massive scale compared to most, with street after street of
merchants and shops. It was distinctively known for everything from its
wool market to its specialty cakes, called Shrewsbury cakes, fruity and
brittle creations that gave the city a culinary flare.

It was into the southern edge of this city that Gates, Kathalin, Alexander, and twenty de Lara soldiers entered. In fact, the city could be
seen for miles in the distance and they had been approaching the burg,
in full view, for over an hour. The closer they came, the bigger it
became, until they finally entered the city limits.

Kathalin, of course, had been greatly awed by it. Coming from the
smaller village of Ludlow, and having never traveled out of that town in
her entire life, to see a city on this scale was quite overwhelming for her.
Astride a gray palfrey on this sunny day, and clad in the elaborate blue
patchwork surcoat that Gates has purchased for her, she appeared every
inch an earl's daughter but inside, she was still a naïve cloister ward.
She had to make a conscious effort to keep her mouth from hanging
open as she viewed the sights and smells and sounds around her.

From the cold and snow of only days and weeks before, the sun had
come out for the past two days and the weather had oddly warmed,

which meant the snow was melting at a prodigious rate and rivers and streams were full to bursting. Streets that had once been lined with snow drifts were now swamps of mud as the oversaturated ground refused to absorb any more moisture and the water tried to find its way out. It hadn't been pooling long enough for it to smell rotten, but it was making for quite a mess in the streets.

In her fine cloak, Kathalin made sure to keep it up on the horse so the edges of it wouldn't get splashed when the horses walked. Gates rode up ahead of her whilst Alexander rode behind her and the soldiers on horseback essentially formed a circle around her, ensuring she was well protected. Hyssington was only a few hours' ride from Shrewsbury and the plan was to shop for the day, spend the night in a tavern, then, if necessary, shop more in the morning before returning home by nightfall. Kathalin had to admit that she was very excited by it all.

As Kathalin marveled at the sights around her, Gates rode up at the head of the column, directing them towards the Street of the Jewelers. He knew this town very well, as he'd spent much time here. Probably more time than he should have because of a certain merchant's daughter who had lived here before her parents sent her off to parts unknown. He never did find out what happened to the lovely Fyona, which was probably for the best. She had been a happy dalliance for him until her father had chased him off one night with a very long blade, something old and antique and undoubtedly passed down through the family. That had deterred Gates for the time being but he'd seen her a few more times before she disappeared. He'd heard through the rumor mill that her parents had married her off and sent her to Saxony, far away from a certain knight. The thought of that still made him chuckle.

But he pushed aside thoughts of Fyona as they came to a fork in the road. One fork led to the cathedral and the Street of the Merchants, while the fork to the right led off to the Street of the Jewelers and also the section of the city where the Jews lived. Money was exchanged there, and horded there, at a fairly colossal rate, and Gates took his party off to the right to find the best silver and goldsmiths along the Marches.

But the area was also downwind from the Street of the Bakers, and as soon as they entered the area, the heavy smells of baking bread wafted upon the cold afternoon air. Gates turned to look at Kathalin to see if she was noticing and he could see, immediately, that she was. Her nose was in the air, sniffing. They had not eaten anything since leaving Hyssington that morning so he could already anticipate her hunger.

His gaze lingered on her a moment. He hadn't really seen her for the past two days, as she had been sequestered in the keep in the second floor chamber that she had found so spacious and beautiful. Jasper had described his meeting with her, and the subsequent meeting with Rosamund, as unpleasant but no more than that. He did not ask Gates to guard her or watch over her in any way so long as she kept to the keep and the truth was that, as long as she indeed remained in the keep, there was no reason for him to contact her at all.

It was rather unfortunate for him. Gates wasn't hard pressed to admit that he had missed Kathalin, conversing with her, and experiencing the world through her naïve eyes. He'd come to see he was rather hard about things in general but with Kathalin, to whom every experience outside of St. Milburga's walls was a new and exciting one, he had come to like that about her a great deal. It was rather good to see the world as she saw it.

It was rather good to see *her*.

Therefore, this morning was the first time in two days that he'd not only seen her for more than a second or two at a time, but actually spoken to her. *Take her to Shrewsbury and buy her some fine pieces of jewelry* had been Jasper's command, a command that Gates had been eager to follow. But Alexander was along with them for the journey, unfortunately, so Gates kept clear of Kathalin for the most part because he didn't want to give Alexander any more ideas about his attitude towards the woman than he already had. He was afraid that if Alexander realized Gates was interested in Kathalin, then it would turn into a challenge to Alexander. The man would view Kathalin as a prize to keep from Gates. If that happened, Gates was fairly certain he would have to kill the man. Kathalin was no conquest to be had.

The stakes had changed between him and Alexander, and so had the mood as far as Gates was concerned. This time, it was serious.

But he ignored Alexander for the most part, or at least tolerated the man because, so far on the journey, he'd made little attempt to speak with Kathalin and had only been politely short with her. That was enough to keep Gates' suspicions down, as well as his dander, and he merely observed Alexander for the duration of the journey, speaking to the man only when necessary. Once they reached the city, that situation changed. Bringing the column of men to the mouth of the Street of the Jewelers, he waved Alexander and Kathalin forward.

"Alexander," he said as the two approached on horseback. "I would think a meal is in order after we make the jewelry purchase, so will you please do the lady the honor of searching out a place to enjoy a meal? While you do that, I will complete the purchase and meet you back here on the street."

Alexander nodded, although he was looking to Kathalin. "My lady, do you have any preference in what you wish to eat?"

Kathalin had no idea what he meant. "I...," she said, looking between the two knights in confusion. "Is there actually a choice?"

She sounded astounded and both men grinned. "Some places will have pork while others will have beef," Alexander explained. "What is your preference today? Pork or beef?"

Kathalin had never been given a choice of food in her entire life. She had eaten what she was given and nothing more. Therefore, she shrugged to the question.

"I am satisfied with either, Sir Alexander," she said. "Whatever you select will be agreeable with me."

Alexander smiled broadly. "I am deeply flattered, my lady, that you would be so trusting," he said as he turned his horse around, motioning to a few soldiers to follow him. "I will seek out a feast fit for a queen."

With that, he spurred his horse down the street, pushing aside pedestrians who weren't fast enough to move out of his way. Kathalin watched him go, wondering what delights he was going to track down for her. Even though she'd managed the kitchen at St. Milburga's, her meals were always simple and plain. That was how Mother Benedicta had liked it. When he disappeared around a corner, she averted her attention away from the lure of food and back to the street around them only to find that Gates was watching her. When their eyes met, he smiled.

"Would you like to climb down off that animal and walk with me, my lady?" he asked as he dismounted his horse. "We can see much more down here than on horseback."

Kathalin nodded, thrilled to realize that it would just be her and Gates at this point. With Alexander gone, they were now alone for the most part. At least, that's how she looked at it. She had been vastly disappointed when Alexander accompanied her and Gates on the ride to Shrewsbury; she hadn't really seen or spoken to Gates in two days, as she had been sequestered in the keep, so this precious time to spend with him was something she was very much looking forward to.

But there was something more to this journey into Shrewsbury as well. After her mother's confession regarding her affliction being the basis behind sending her children away at such a young age, Kathalin's resentment towards her parents had fled a great deal. In fact, the healer in Kathalin very much wanted to help her mother and she knew of some remedies for skin conditions that she thought to try on her mother. Of course, providing the woman was open to such things, and having lived with the condition for as long as she had, Kathalin could only imagine she had tried everything that money could buy. But Kathalin was still determined to help if she could.

Oddly, she felt very strongly about it, strange when she'd spent so much time resenting the woman. But with time, and a plausible reason behind everything, Kathalin was willing to forgive. At least, she was willing to try.

It was something she wanted to tell Gates about considering he knew how she felt about her parents. She wanted to explain to him the reasons behind her parents' decision to send her to St. Milburga's at such a young age. She wasn't entirely sure she would tell him of the leprosy, for Rosamund had made it clear she wanted no one else to know, but to at least tell Gates that the bitterness in her heart towards her parents had ended meant a great deal to her. Furthermore, after the visit to the Street of the Jewelers, she wanted the man's help in finding an apothecary. She hoped such a shop would have the herbs she would need to help her mother.

But she didn't speak of what was on her mind as Gates reached up and helped her down from the palfrey. She was more interested, at the moment, in relishing the feel of his big hands around her waist. When he set her on her feet, she smiled openly at him.

"So," she said. "It is just the two of us now. It seems as if it has been years since I saw you last."

He grinned, extending an elbow which she eagerly accepted. "It does," he agreed as they left the escort behind and began to walk along the street. "How long has it truly been? Three years? Four? Whatever are you doing with yourself these days, my lady? The last time I saw you, you were healing the sick and trying to fight off a bully of a knight who was forcing you to visit your parents."

She laughed softly; at this point, she was able to laugh at what had happened those days ago. It seemed so long ago, truthfully. She could hardly remember the animosity between them.

"I do not blame him," she said. "He was only doing as he was ordered."

"You did not think that at the time."

She shook her head as a jeweler's stall caught her attention. "Nay, I did not," she said. "But I understand that now. I am sorry it took me as long as it did to realize that."

Gates could see where her attention was and he turned her in that direction. "No need, my lady," he said. "I cannot say that if I were in the same position, I might have felt any differently than you did."

The jeweler's stall had three elderly men working in it and two very big guards who were standing by the door. Gates also spied another heavily-armed man by the rear of the stall, back in the shadows. Mentally sizing up the situation, he proceeded as Kathalin, oblivious to the guards, simply stepped inside.

It was somewhat dark inside, windowless except for gaps in the wall where the wall joints didn't quite meet up. The old men were small, with caps on their heads, each one of them engaged in some project on their own individual tables, which were covered with black wool felt. Even though Kathalin had walked quite boldly into the stall, she came to a halt once inside and eyed the men working. As Gates came up beside her, she whispered to him.

"I do not know what to look for," she said. "I have never purchased jewelry in my life."

Gates winked at her before speaking out to one of the old men. "You, there," he said in his authoritative tone. "My lady is the daughter of the Earl of Trelystan. She would like to look at your wares. Will you show her?"

Two of the old men stood up, prompted by Gates' loud voice, while the third simply looked over his shoulder at Kathalin and Gates and, disinterested, turned back to what he was doing. But the other two men were quick to be of service.

"My lady," one very skinny old man with bad teeth bowed humbly in her direction. "I am Asher. I would be happy to show you my work."

Kathalin watched the old man with great interest as he turned to the cabinet behind him and opened the doors. There were various boxes inside and he pulled one of them out.

"Work?" Kathalin repeated, genuinely quite curious. "You make jewelry yourself?"

The old man grinned, displaying the three yellowed teeth in his head, as he opened the box. "I do indeed, my lady," he said. "I was taught by my father, who was taught by his father. He learned his trade in Roma."

Roma. Kathalin smiled at the mention of the name. "Rome," she said. "Where our Holy Father lives."

The old man nodded as he began to pull forth chains of gold and laying them upon the black wool felt. "Indeed, my lady," he said. "The Holy Father lives there, but there are also a million other people who live there and go about their daily lives. My grandfather's life happened to be that of a goldsmithy. He would take jewels, or pearls from the sea, and make jewelry with it for the nobles."

Kathalin was looking at the gold he was laying in front of her with wonder. In fact, she could hardly look at anything else. "God's Bones," she declared, lifting up a hand to touch it but, fearful to do so, lowered her hand. "I have never seen jewelry such as this. You truly made these pieces?"

"I did, my lady."

Kathalin bent over the black felt, watching him set necklaces of garnet, of yellow stones, of green stones, and of amethyst upon it. He even had a gold and pearl necklace with matching ear bobs.

"Oh… goodness," she said as he set the pearls out for her view. "I have never seen pearls before. They look like… like angel's tears. They are white and shiny and perfect."

Gates, standing behind her, was touched by her excitement. It was as he'd thought of earlier – seeing the world through her eyes. Who else but a woman who had never seen the finer things in life would have described something as simple as a pearl as angel's tears? He leaned down next to her right ear.

"Beware," he whispered. "This is evil finery. Beware that Mother Benedicta does not burst through this door and tell you how wicked it all is."

His hot breath against her ear once again sent ripples of excitement bolting through her body, although she refrained from lifting a hand to her ear as she had done before. She did, however, tremble with the thrill of it. She looked at him with a grin.

"It may be wicked, but it is beautiful nonetheless," she said. "I am coming to think that Mother Benedicta has never seen anything beautiful like this, or touched any fine garments, in her entire life. If she had, she would not have told me that they were wicked."

Gates winked at her as he straightened up, fighting off a grin. "Would you like to try any of these on?" he asked her. Then, he looked at the old man. "Do you have a mirror for the lady to see her reflection?"

The little man nodded eagerly, opening his magic cabinet again and withdrawing a polished bronze mirror. It was shiny enough that the likeness was fairly true. Before Kathalin realized what was happening, Gates had put the pearl necklace on her as the old man held up the mirror.

A woman of unparalleled beauty, now with a pearl necklace around her throat, gazed back in the shiny bronze. Awed at the sight of her reflection with the jewels around her neck, Kathalin leaned forward as if to gain a better view, running her finger along the bronze as if disbelieving what she was seeing. Her finger left a streak across the pristine bronze.

"I... I do not even recognize myself," she said quietly, looking down to her bosom to finger the pearls. "I cannot help but wonder who the woman is that gazes back at me."

Gates watched her as she lovingly fingered the pearls. "A woman who has had her life opened up to her," he said softly. "A woman who is seeing the world outside of the priory for the first time. I rather like what I see. Do you?"

Grinning with embarrassment, Kathalin removed the pearls from her neck and moved to touch the amethyst necklace. "I am not sure," she said. "I do like the fine clothing, for my skin has been eased by it, and the pearls are most becoming, but... but it is hard to say if I am comfortable with all of it. It is still all very new to me."

Gates knew that. It was part of his attraction to her, a woman who had never known such beauty or such pleasure, now becoming acquainted with it all. There was such naked joy in her expression and he liked telling her of things she did not know of. It made him feel as if he were useful and mentoring. He picked up the amethyst necklace because she seemed afraid to do it, holding it up so the deep purple stone caught the light.

"Hopefully, you will grow to like it very quickly," he said. "Although I have nothing against life in the cloister, the world at hand offers so much more by way of life and love and experiences in general. I should have thought you would realize that by now."

She nodded as he got in behind her so he could put the necklace on her. "I have realized that," she said, once again seeing herself in the bronze mirror now with the fingerprint on it. "It is all quite... overwhelming."

Gates stood back, watching her as she examined her reflection. "Then mayhap you are to be like your mother," he said. "She does not like the world, either. She remains sequestered in her chamber and does not come out. There is nothing wrong with preferring solitude, of course, but it could get a bit lonely."

Kathalin touched the purple stone around her neck. "Wouldn't you come and visit me?"

He grinned. "If you were in a convent, I could not," he said. "I am sure Mother Benedicta would have a crossbow meant only for me."

Kathalin laughed. "She is not so violent."

Gates watched her laugh, thinking he liked it a great deal. She had such a charming smile. "She would be violent if a knight kept trying to visit one of her novice nuns," he said. "For my sake, you should not return to St. Milburga's. You should remain at Hyssington where I can see you without fear of having an arrow lodged in my chest."

Kathalin was still gigging as she removed the necklace. She laid it back in the box when the second old man, who had retreated into the rear of the stall, reappeared with a larger box. It had a lock on it and, once he unlocked it with a tiny iron key, he opened up the lid to reveal a collection of precious rings carefully set upon more black wool felt.

Kathalin forgot about the necklaces for a moment as she fixed on the magnificent jewelry.

"Good heavens," she gasped, reaching out to timidly touch one, a gold ring with a scarlet stone in it. "Such beautiful rings!"

Gates leaned over her shoulder, looking. "Indeed," he said. "You could use those as weapons if needed. One good hit and you could put someone's eye out."

Kathalin was back to giggling. She ended up picking up a dark gold ring that had a big diamond set in it. It was truly awe-inspiring. "Who would wear such a ring other than a queen?" she wanted to know.

"Ladies often wear them as symbols of marriage, my lady," the second jeweler said before Gates could reply. He was a round man with dirty gray hair and foul-smelling breath. "I notice you do not wear a ring, my lady. Mayhap your husband should like to buy one for you."

He meant Gates, as he was gesturing at the man. Surprised, Kathalin looked up at the jeweler. "But I am not married," she said. "I do not need a ring."

Over her shoulder, Gates spoke softly. "You may have a need one day," he said. "Remember this place so that you may return to select the ring you want."

The shopping mood abruptly left her. It reminded Kathalin of the conversation with her parents, on how they were attempting to force her into a marriage she wanted no part of. Gates' words only seem to further distress her. Was it possible that her parents had told him to convince her that the marriage they wanted to arrange was for the best? Was it possible that the real reason behind this errand to purchase jewelry had an ulterior motive?

More than likely, it was not only possible but probable. Gates did serve her father, after all, and was sworn to do the man's bidding. There was instant frustration in Kathalin's manner as she moved away from the boxes of jewelry, heading for the door. She felt betrayed by a man she thought was her friend.

Nay... more than a friend.

He was much more than a friend.

"I do not want a ring," she said to Gates angrily. "You cannot force me to purchase one."

Gates followed her, grabbing her arm before she could get out of the door. "Wait," he said, holding her fast. "No one is forcing you to purchase a ring, my lady. Wherever did you get that idea?"

Frustrated, hurt, Kathalin frowned at him. "Did my father tell you to do this?" she wanted to know. "Was it your directive to take me to Shrewsbury and suggest a wedding ring?"

Gates shook his head steadily. "Your father said no such thing to me," he said. "I think you know me better than that. I do not hide behind subversion."

She held his gaze a moment longer before looking away, visibly forcing herself to relax. He was right; since she'd known him, he'd been upfront and truthful with her. In her experience he had never been the subversive type. Now, she was starting to feel foolish that she'd ever thought such a thing. She took a deep breath.

"Nay, you do not," she said. "Forgive me. After the conversation with my mother and father, I naturally assumed you came with me to Shrewsbury to do their bidding. They could not convince me into marriage so I thought mayhap they had sent you to try."

Now, she was starting to speak of those two days when he hadn't seen her nor spoken to her, when she had kept close to the keep. He knew that Jasper and Lady de Lara had spoken with Kathalin and could only guess at the contents of the conversation, but now he was starting to hear the reality of it. The truth was that he was not surprised; he had expected as much. Jasper had already told him that he wanted marriage for his daughter and it was evident they had told her as well. Her reaction was just as Gates expected it to be; she hated the idea.

He hated the idea of her being married to someone else, too.

"My only directive in coming to Shrewsbury was to purchase jewelry for you," he said after a moment. "I am not here to further your parents' agenda."

She eyed him, her anger fading. "Then I apologize."

He met her gaze, studying the shape of her bright blue eyes. They were most beautiful. "No need," he said. "But if you must know the truth, I do not agree with what they are doing. Now that I have come to know you and understand your wants in life, the fact that your parents are trying to force you into marriage is not something I approve of."

Her face slackened and he swore he detected hints of hope in her expression. "Truly?" she said. "I wish you would tell them that. I wish you would tell them to let me return to St. Milburga's."

He regarded her a moment. "Is that really what you want?"

She was puzzled. "What do you mean?"

He looked around the stall as if to indicate the world at large. "You have admitted you like fine clothing," he said. "You have admitted that worldly things are not as evil as you have been taught. Do you truly wish to return to woolen clothing that irritates your skin? Do you truly believe you could forget all of this and return to the priory?"

Her brow furrowed as she thought on his words and he could see how badly the question confused her. "I have wanted to become a nun since I was very young," she finally said. "It is my mindset. But... but you are correct in a sense. Now that I have seen the world outside of the priory, there are things about it that are quite pleasant. And I have come to meet you and you have been quite pleasant. Do you know that other than the priest, I have never known a man other than you?"

He smiled happily. "I am honored."

She returned his smile, timidly. "I am still astonished that you do not have a wife or family, de Wolfe," she said. "You are such a kind and noble man. I do not understand why you have not selected a wife to honor you. A woman would be very fortunate to have you for a husband."

Now they were back onto the subject that unnerved him so badly. His gut reaction was to jest his way out of it, which he'd done before with her. He would do it again now because it was dangerous ground they were walking upon, at least as far as he was concerned.

"You must not really think that," he said, rather dramatically. "You offered once to bear my children but then you rescinded that offer and left me devastated. Do you remember?"

Kathalin's giggles returned. "Of course I do," she said. "But you never once mentioned marriage. It would seem that all you want is a woman to bear your children without benefit of marriage and I would not do it. Why are you so opposed to marriage?"

"Why are *you*?"

He had her cornered and the giggles turned into laughter. "You know why," she said, sobering. "I do not want to marry because I want to join the cloister."

"But if you do not join the cloister, why are you still opposed to it?"

She put up her hands as if to push away any suitor that might come near her. "Because I do not want to marry someone I do not know," she said. "Would you?"

He shrugged. "You know me and yet you will not bear my sons."

"I will if you will marry me."

"And if I agree?"

She pointed to the box of rings. "Then you must purchase a very big ring for me, big enough to put an eye out."

He laughed. "That seems like a fair bargain," he said, realizing with shock that he had just agreed to marry the woman and hoping she wouldn't realize it. Or maybe he hoped she would. Either way, the rapid-fire jesting between them had turned into something unexpected and he struggled to get off the subject. "But in the interim, go and pick some jewelry so we can be done with this. I am famished and if we do not find Alexander soon, I will have to eat *you*, so pick your jewelry and let us be finished."

Kathalin was looking up at him, smiling broadly. She had, indeed, realized that he agreed to marry her, or at least he was thinking on it. That was all she could ask for. Having no tact or sense of restraint when it came to emotions, and most especially when it came to Gates, she didn't move for the jewelry boxes as he'd commanded. She was still standing there, gazing up at him and feeling that warmth that she had come to associate with him. It was warmer, and stronger, than ever before.

She had to tell him what was in her heart. There was no stopping it.

"De Wolfe," she said softly. "*Gates.* If you were the man my parents chose for my husband, I would not want to return to St. Milburga's. I think I would like being married to you."

He just looked at her, shock rippling through his veins. He'd heard words like that before, in many variations from many women, but never in his life had they actually meant something to him. In fact, he could feel a distinct sense of joy; was it possible that she actually had feelings towards him? Dear God, he knew very well he had feelings for her. Nay... more than feelings... something deep and powerful and fluid. But hearing her softly uttered words gave him such hope and joy that it was all surging through his body at an alarming rate, causing his limbs to tingle and his palms to sweat. He'd never experienced anything like it.

But on the heels of such joy came the cold dousing of reality. Jasper would never agree to a marriage between them and he knew it. Jasper wanted a man with a noble reputation, a man who didn't have bastards all about England, and man who would bring joy and honor to Kathalin. Gates couldn't do that. He'd lived a life free to do as he pleased, free to bed whom he pleased, and that was the way he'd wanted it. At least, until now.

Now, Gates was quite sure he would only bring Kathalin shame if he married her and, as much as it killed him, he had to accept that he could, in no way, become her husband. He would never knowingly shame the woman. He adored her... aye, he did. He adored everything about her.

Never in his life had Gates known his heart to break.

Until now.

God, this hurts!

"I... I am flattered," he said hoarsely, wanting very badly to take her in his arms but dared not do it. "You honor me greatly, Lady Kathalin.

You will never know how greatly it pains me to explain to you that I shall never marry. I am not the marrying kind. But I thank you for your kind words. I shall cherish them, always."

Slapped. That is what Kathalin felt like. She felt as if he'd reached out and slapped her across the face. Ashamed, she lowered her head, feeling her cheeks pinken and feeling her chest tighten up with shame and disappointment. Nay, it was more than that – it was sorrow. She had opened herself up to him, told him what was in her heart, and he had refused her.

Dear God... such shame.....

"Then... then I shall have to return to St. Milburga's," she said, trying desperately to grasp the light mood that had been there only moments earlier. "I was not serious about marriage to you, de Wolfe. I was only jesting. I have only always wanted to return to St. Milburga's and you know that. Now, let me look at the jewelry again. I... I do believe I want the pearls."

She moved away from him, back to the boxes of necklaces, and Gates let her go. He could tell from her expression that she had, indeed, been serious about marriage and he'd shut her down, hurting her. He wouldn't have knowingly hurt her for the world but in this case, he had no choice.

When he had wanted to declare his desire to marry her as well, he'd had no choice but to deny her. It was for her own good, he told himself. It would be no life at all for her to be married to a man who would only bring her shame. A man who would change his spots for her, become a devoted husband only unto her, but a man who would never be able to escape his past. A man who would never be worthy of an honorable wife.

For the first time in his life, he was deeply sorry for a reputation he'd never given a second thought to. God, it was killing him. As he stood there and watched her finger the necklaces in the box, he saw her bring a hand up to her face, twice. His heart sank when he realized why.

Tears.

CHAPTER ELEVEN

Linley Manor
6 miles east of Hyssington

"I KNEW IT was de Wolfe!" Linley screamed. "I knew it was him!"

In the only habitable room of Linley Manor, the great hall that had known grander days, the big, heavy-set drunkard known as Lord Linley was in a rage. His daughter, weeping, had finally confessed the father of her six-month-old son and, devastated, told her father that the knight refused to marry her. Now, Linley was in a rage and there was no way to stop it.

"Papa, please," Helene wept. "I do not need your anger. I need your help. Will you not help me?"

Linley, who had been stumbling around the room in his rage, came to a halt and threw up his hands. "What is it you expect me to do?" he nearly screamed at her. "If the man refused to marry you, all I can do is kill him! I will challenge him and I will kill him! It is a matter of family honor now!"

Helene shook her head. "Papa, *no*," she insisted. "He is a knight, one of the most powerful on the Marches. He will kill you!"

Linley was inflamed by what he considered slander against his skill and, in a rage, he rushed at his daughter and slapped her several times across the face as she screamed. In her struggle to get away from him, she ended up falling backwards over her chair, ending up on the dirty floor and crawling away.

"Silence your foolish mouth, girl!" Linley said, trying to kick her as she crawled away. "When you named your son Wolfe I should have known. You told me it was because you liked the name but I knew better. I knew Gates de Wolfe had somehow managed to steal your innocence but now that you have confirmed it to me, I will kill the man, I swear it!"

Sobbing, Helene was over by the wall, huddled in a fearful ball. "Mayhap you will not have to kill him if you can convince him to do the honorable thing and marry me," she said, wiping the mucus from her nose with the back of her hand. "Mayhap he will change his mind if you ask."

"You already said he refused!"

She nodded, wiping at her eyes, hoping he didn't charge her again and try to slap her. "He did," she said, sniffling. "But... but should you approach his liege, mayhap it would be different. De Lara can command Gates into marriage or punish him!"

Linley pondered that a moment, coming to an unsteady halt. He was weaving unsteadily, the result of drinking cheap ale that had been made from grain with mold on it. It had a tendency to make him see things that weren't there and give him horrible nightmares. But when one was dependent upon drink, one was not too particular where one got it from.

"Mayhap," Linley agreed, scratching at his louse-ridden head. "I will see de Lara, then, and demand he force de Wolfe to marry you. It is the only honorable thing to do and surely de Lara will not stand for a dishonorable knight in his service, especially when I tell all who will listen how disgraceful de Wolfe is. Imagine the man seducing my vulnerable daughter. I will not have it, I say!"

Helene remained huddled against the wall, listening to her father rant, hoping for two things – that Gates would, when challenged, kill her father and that afterwards, he would feel so terrible about it that he would agree to marry her. Aye, those two things were her wish because, for certain, living with a father such as Huw Linley was worse than a death sentence. He'd sold everything of value from the manor to support his drinking habit and any money that came up after that was also used for drink. He bargained with local brewers, trading them servants and livestock for stores of cheap and toxic ale, and sometimes the ale was so poisoned by bad grain that he saw his daughter as a demon and tried to beat her. Once he even tried to throw her in the fire.

Aye, living with the man was hell, which was why marriage to a knight had held out such hope for Helene. In her view, there was still hope now that her father intended to challenge de Wolfe. Perhaps Gates would not want to fight the old man, believing it a dishonorable thing to do, and simply give in. It was among the many hopes that Helene had at the moment.

The last hope that her son would indeed have his father.

The last hope that she would know a better life than this with the only man who had ever been kind to her.

⁕

WITH THE PEARL necklace, the amethyst necklace, a gold necklace adorned with crimson stones, and a bejeweled hair piece of emeralds packed safely away in a locked box that they had purchased from the jeweler along with the jewelry, Gates and Kathalin emerged from the stall to find Alexander and the men waiting for them. It seemed that Alexander had found an establishment on the Street of the Bakers that produced little pies with chicken and gravy, something that had smelled decadently delicious, so the group had proceeded across the avenue to the Street of the Bakers to partake.

The smells of baking bread and roasting meat were coming fast and heavy as they entered the street but Kathalin wasn't much interested in it. She was not very hungry, in fact, since Gates had turned down her marriage proposal. Well, it wasn't exactly a proposal but certainly he'd discounted her offer. She'd never known such disappointment in her life, and heartache, for at St. Milburga's she had been insulated against such things. Now, she wanted to go back more than ever. She didn't even want to look at Gates de Wolfe any longer.

She wanted to go home.

Oblivious to what had happened in the jeweler's stall between Kathalin and Gates, Alexander was his usual congenial self. He had reserved an area between stalls on the Street of the Bakers with upturned logs and a few benches where patrons could sit whilst eating their food. Normally, it was a pleasant place to eat but with the melting snow, it was a bit of a swamp. Still, Gates gathered his men there as Alexander and a few of his soldiers went to purchase food for a midday meal.

But there was brooding silence all around after he departed. It wasn't difficult to notice that Kathalin had fallen silent since their visit to the jewelers. She sat on one of the wooden benches, wrapped up in her blue and fox fur cloak, staring at her hands for the most part. Gates, who had been acutely aware of her silence all along, couldn't get more than one or two word answers out of her. It didn't take a great intellect to realize that she'd become this way after he'd turned down her suggestion of marriage and her shift in mood told him, increasingly, how serious she had been.

His heart, so hardened against women, wasn't hardened against her. The more she ignored him, the worse the tightening in his chest became. He very much wanted to explain the reasons behind his answer to her but he was afraid if he did, it would open him up to a confession he didn't want to make to her. A confession that would have him telling her what a terrible man he'd been at times, deflowering virgins and running from responsibility. Nay, he didn't want to tell her that at all. Of all people in the world, he wanted her to think of him as a strong and upstanding man, with no vices and of great moral character. He didn't want her to know of the Dark Destroyer, the destroyer of women's hearts.

He only wanted her to know Gates de Wolfe, the man she'd known kindness from.

That was the only legacy he wanted with her.

... *could* have with her.

So he kept his mouth shut, not speaking to her as they waited until Alexander finally returned with enough food for, literally, an army. He had more than two dozen small pies with dark brown crusts and a filling of chicken and gravy, or filled with mutton and carrots. There was also fresh bread and almond pudding in dried-out gourds, but before the men could jump at them, Gates gave Kathalin her choice and she selected, without enthusiasm, a chicken pie. That was all. Once she took it for herself, the men dove in and it was a feasting frenzy beneath the cold, clear afternoon sky.

"Is the plan still to remain here tonight?" Alexander asked as he walked up to Gates, shoving pie into his mouth. "There is a festival going on later today, you know. It should go all night."

Gates was eating his own pie. "What festival?"

Alexander, chewing, pointed off to the square where the big cathedral was. "Some kind of pagan celebration local to the town," he said. "Something about a sheep queen or a snow queen. I do not recall what I was told. In any case, they will have fires and food and dancing, so I am told. It might be fun to attend. There will be women there, after all."

Gates looked at the man. "In case you haven't realized it, we are guarding a woman right now," he said. "I will not go off and leave her unattended."

Alexander's gaze lingered on Kathalin's lowered head. "I did not mean to leave her unattended," he said. "She may like to attend."

"Having come from a convent where festivities like that were not allowed? I doubt it."

Alexander could see his point. He continued to watch Kathalin as she picked at her pie. "I heard that Jasper and Lady de Lara intend to throw a party for her in honor of her return home," he said. "My parents have been invited, in fact. By next week, we should have families here from all over the Marches to welcome Lady Kathalin home."

Gates simply nodded, taking another bite of his pie, unaware that Alexander was watching her closely. "She is a beautiful woman," he continued. "Rumor has it that de Lara is looking for a husband for her. Have you heard that, also?"

Gates heard something in Alexander's voice, something he didn't like. If he hadn't known better, there was a hint of interest there but he remained wisely silent even though what he really wanted to do was throttle the man. Jealousy, something he wasn't used to in the least, began rearing its ugly head again.

"What de Lara does with his daughter is no concern of yours or mine," he said. "I would suggest you not speak of the man's daughter in front of him, in fact. That would be an excellent way to garner his wrath."

Alexander looked at him. "Why?"

Gates lifted his eyebrows to emphasize his point. "If she was your daughter, would you not be protective over her from hot-blooded knights?"

Alexander conceded the point. "Mayhap," he said. "He should not worry over us, however. We are sworn to him and to the family. We would not take advantage of that trust."

Gates didn't say anything for a moment; he was starting to feel sick to his stomach, confused with Alexander's words. *Is that what I've done?* He asked himself. *Have I taken advantage of de Lara's trust by having affection for his daughter? By getting to know her and letting her get under my skin?* As he wrestled with that terrible thought, Alexander spoke again.

"I will tell you a secret, old man," he said to Gates, lowering his voice. "My parents have been harassing me to marry. No sooner had I arrived home then they were demanding to know when I intended to wed. If de Lara is truly looking for a husband for his daughter, and my parents know it, I have a feeling they will try to press my suit. I cannot say that the thought disturbs me because it does not. She is an exquisite creature. She would make a fine wife upon my arm."

Gates' jaw ticked faintly, increasingly disturbed by Alexander's prattle. More than that, he was greatly disturbed by the subject – was it possible that, of all men, Alexander would actually be pledged to Kathalin? God's Bones, the mere thought made him ill. He tossed the rest of his pie to the ground, unable to finish. His bitterness in Alexander's interest in Kathalin began to come out.

"De Lara will not want you for her for the same reason he will not want me," he said in an attempt to curb Alexander's interest. "You have been known to bed a woman or two, much as I have, and you have a history of romantic conquest. De Lara knows this."

Alexander looked at his friend, wondering why the man sounded so cynical. "That may be," he said, "but my legend isn't nearly as bad as yours is. Moreover, most young men our age have some manner of reputation with women. They would be odd if they didn't."

Gates didn't want to speak with Alexander any longer. He was afraid he might say something nasty if he did, jealous as he was. He simply couldn't control it. Without a word, he left Alexander and went to where Kathalin was sitting. Now, his focus became her, swiftly forgetting about Alexander. He stood next to her and cleared his throat softly.

"May I sit, my lady?" he asked politely.

Kathalin was jolted by the sound of his voice, so much so that she jumped when he spoke. Her mind had been lingering on a future without him, his refusal of her marriage suggestion, and any number of other sad and disappointing thoughts involving him. She had been wrapped up in her own world, the pain of his refusal building within her. But Gates had been speaking to Alexander; she knew this because she had heard their voices. She was hoping he would remain with Alexander so she would not have to speak with him. She was too terribly embarrassed and disappointed to speak with him. Therefore, his request to sit next to her was met with only a shrug.

Gates took the gesture as an affirmative and planted himself next to her on the wooden bench, hearing it creak under his weight. "God's

Bones," he complained, looking down at the bench. "I hope I do not collapse it. I will apologize in advance if I end up dumping you on the ground."

Kathalin smiled weakly but said nothing and Gates couldn't stand the silence between them. It was beginning to eat at him, consuming every thought in his head, and he knew he had to make things right. This was all his fault, anyway. Perhaps if he explained his position against her marriage proposal, she might not be so hateful towards him.

Now, the situation between them was about to become quite real.

He prepared himself.

"My lady," he said softly. "Kathalin. May I speak freely between us?"

Kathalin. She closed her eyes to the sound of her name coming forth, turning her head away and squeezing her eyes together tightly to stave off the tears. After a moment, she shook her head.

"Nay," she whispered.

His brow furrowed. "Why not?"

She abruptly stood up, hissing at him. "Because there is nothing to say."

With that, she stormed off, out of the eating area and out into the street. Gates quickly followed, grasping her by the arm as she made her way down the street. She didn't get very far. When he latched on to her, she tried to pull away.

"Hold, lady," he said, his voice stern but soft. "Where are you going?"

She was trying to yank her arm out of his grip. "Let me go!"

In response, he grabbed her with both hands, his grip like an iron vise. "I will not," he said, his voice less soft and more firm now. "What is the matter? Why are you running off?"

It took Kathalin a moment to realize she was making a fool of herself. Already, she'd made a great fool of herself by betraying the fact that she was embarrassed and hurt by his refusal. Now he knew, or at least he suspected. She wasn't sure she could cover for her behavior and try to throw him off the scent, but the truth was that she didn't want to try.

She wasn't clever or practiced in the ways of men and women. All she knew was honesty. Perhaps it was time for her to be honest.

Perhaps then he would leave her in peace.

"Because… because I said something to you that I should not have," she finally said, her struggles against him easing. "When I said I would marry you, it was the truth. But I should not have said it and I am sorry."

Her words were like arrows to his heart, each one doing more damage than the one before it. It was sucking the breath out of him, hurting him in ways he never knew he could hurt. Quickly, he looked around to see if there was someplace more private they could speak because he was quite certain there was about to be a good deal of honesty between them whether or not he wanted it.

Still, the time had come.

When he saw a gap between two baking establishments off to his right, he pulled her over in that direction and wedged them both in between the buildings. It was a narrow space and he was pressed up against her, too close, but it was necessary. What he had to say was for her ears only.

"I want you to listen to me carefully, Kathalin," he said, his voice quiet. "You must never be sorry for something you feel and you must never be sorry for speaking the truth. You cannot know how honored and thrilled I am to hear you say such things. It is the most wonderful thing I have ever heard."

Kathalin, very close to him, couldn't bear to look up at him. She kept her head lowered. "It was foolish," she said. "Silly and foolish. Please, de Wolfe… I want to go back to St. Milburga's. Won't you please take me there?"

He shook his head. "I cannot and you know it," he said, looking down at her bowed head and feeling her turmoil. "But know this; if I could marry you, I most certainly would. Your parents intend to seek a husband for you and the mere thought of you being married to someone else fills me with anguish such as I have never known. I would rather see you back at St. Milburga's than see you married to anyone other than me."

It took a few moments for his words to sink in but when they did, her head shot up and she looked at him, wide-eyed. "You... you do not wish to see me married to anyone else?" she repeated, laboring to comprehend what he had just told her. "You... you *would* marry me?"

He nodded, sorrow evident in his face. He put a hand beneath her chin, forcing her to keep her eyes on him, feeling the soft texture of her skin. It was like silk.

"When I told you that I could not marry you, it was not because I did not want to," he said. Then he shook his head, dropping his hand from her chin and averting his gaze as he struggled for the correct words. "There is something you must know about me, Kathalin. I have been a foolish man when it comes to women for most of my adult life. You see, I have always viewed women as conquests or prizes, something to be won, and used, and then forgotten about when I move on to the next one. I have spent my life disrespecting women and using them for my own needs. Since you are to be around Hyssington for some time to come, you will probably hear men refer to me by the moniker I have earned because of my reputation. I have been called the Dark Destroyer because of my prowess off the battlefield as well as on it. Do not be distressed when you hear it; it has followed me for many years."

Kathalin's brow was furrowed as she listened, trying to process what he was saying. Being as naïve as she was, she didn't immediately realize what he meant. "I do not understand," she said. "You have thought women to be conquests?"

"Aye."

"But... but how should you conquer them?"

He just looked at her, hoping he didn't truly have to explain that aspect to her, but he could see that she really had no idea what he meant. "As a lover, Kathalin," he said. Then, he lowered his voice. "In their beds."

Realization finally dawned and Kathalin looked at him in both denial and shock. "I do not believe it," she said. Then, more strongly: "I do not believe it! You are not a man who would do such things, de Wolfe. If you do not want to marry me, simply say so. You do not need to create some sordid reason behind your refusal. All you need do is tell me the truth!"

"I *am* telling you the truth."

"You are making this worse!"

He paused, mostly because she was becoming agitated and he didn't want it to turn into a shouting match. The last thing he wanted to do was shout at her.

"Unfortunately, every word is true," he said, softening his tone so she would hopefully calm. "I have never wanted to marry, ever. At least, that was true until I met you. You are so fine and pure and beautiful, Kathi... you are everything a man could hope for in a wife. You are, to me, perfect, and I am so completely unworthy of you. My past would only bring you shame and sorrow, and I could not bear it. I could not do that to you. I adore you too much."

Kathalin calmed a good deal with his latest statement, starting to realize that he was, in fact, telling the truth. She could see it in his face. And with his last words... *I adore you...* her heart both swelled and shattered.

"You adore me?" she whispered, stunned.

He nodded with great sincerity. "I do," he murmured. "Very much."

As he watched, her eyes instantly filled with a lake of tears, spilling over onto her pale cheeks. "Oh, Gates," she breathed. "I adore you, too. I love you dearly. I cannot remember when I have not loved you. Except when I was hating you in the beginning, of course, but after that, I... I fell in love with everything about you."

They were both grinning by the time she finished her rambling statement and Gates couldn't help it; he reached out and pulled her against him, hugging her so tightly that she grunted when he squeezed all of the air out of her lungs. But her soft warmth against him was the greatest thing he had ever known, emotional satisfaction that was greater than any physical satisfaction he had ever experienced.

"My sweet girl," he whispered against her hair. "I have never in my life heard words that have meant so much to me. You have made my entire life worth something."

Having never been held by a man before, Kathalin was at first shocked by the intimate embrace but, very quickly, it became the most astonishing and magnificent gesture she'd ever known. Her arms were around his torso tightly, holding him just as snuggly as he was holding her and she knew, at that moment, that she had no intention of letting the man go no matter what he said.

He adored her… that was all she need know.

"I do not care about your past," she said, muffled, into his chest. "All I know is that I love you, Gates. Please marry me. The alternative is too terrible to bear."

Gates released her, gently, cupping her face in his big hands. He simply had to look at her, and touch her, stricken with grief and elation that she loved him as he loved her. It was tragedy beyond belief.

"I cannot," he confessed. "I *will* not. Kathi, I cannot bring such shame to you. Don't you realize this? You must have an honorable husband with an honorable reputation. Off the battlefield, my reputation is less than stellar. You will be a laughing stock."

Kathalin, moved to tears by the feel of his hands on her face, shook her head. "I do not care," she said, her voice tight. "Gates, will you swear to me that you will be true only to me forever? If you tell me this, I shall believe you, and nothing else matters."

Gates looked at her, considering the bigger implication of her words. In truth, there was nothing to consider. He loved her and he always would. For a man who had spent his entire life running from woman to woman, at this moment, he couldn't ever imagine touching another woman as long as he lived. Kathalin was in his heart and soul and he would never be untrue to her. Ever.

There was no question.

"Married or not," he said hoarsely, "I will always be true to you. I will never know another woman ever again, Kathalin. Not ever. It is you and only you, forever."

"Do you mean that?"

"Upon my oath as a knight, I do."

Her tears spilled over and he swooped on them, kissing them away, tasting the salt upon his lips with the greatest of pleasure before very gently kissing her lips. Kathalin was uncertain at first but quickly warmed to him, responding to him in her first true kiss as if she had been kissing him her entire life. Nothing else had ever been so remarkable or so right. It was as if they were made for each other, kiss to kiss, heart to heart. When he finally pulled away from her, it was to gaze deeply into her eyes.

"Only you," he whispered. "I swear it."

Kathalin, overcome by his kiss and his words, swallowed hard. "Please," she begged softly. "Marry me, Gates. I do not care about the past, only the future."

She was pleading with him, trying to break down his resolve, but he couldn't let her. Gates had never known anything so painful in his entire life. His insides were eating themselves out, anguish over a situation he never thought to face. He opened his mouth to say something when he heard his name being called. Instantly recognizing Alexander's voice, he shifted so that Kathalin was in front of him and he gently pushed her from the confined space between the buildings, emerging behind her at a respectable distance. He could see Alexander off to his right, evidently looking for him, but Alexander's back was turned to them so Gates took Kathalin's elbow politely and came up behind him.

"I am here," he said, watching Alexander whirl around to face him. "What is the matter?"

Alexander was looking between Gates and Kathalin but he was mostly looking at Kathalin. "You disappeared," he said, looking at the lady full-on. "Is everything well, my lady?"

Kathalin kept her head down. "It is," she said. "I am simply feeling... unwell."

Alexander looked at her with concern, noting that the direction she was running was a public privy. Then he realized what she meant. Or, at least he thought he did.

"I see," he said, clearing his throat to avoid saying something embarrassing regarding the lady's pressing needs. "Mayhap we should find lodgings for the night so that the lady can rest."

Gates nodded. "An excellent idea," he said. "There is an inn at the end of this boulevard called The Raven. I have stayed there before. Gather the men and we will head down there."

Alexander nodded, turning for the men, but not before he passed a lingering glance at Kathalin. Gates saw it and his displeasure with the man grew. His relationship with Alexander had always been close, friendly competition, and all that. It was a difficult concept to him that it might be changing and Kathalin was the cause of that change. He thought it rather ironic that a woman could come between them or, at least, cause him to view Alexander as something other than a friend. Ironic, indeed.

In silence, he took Kathalin back to the area where they had left their horses at the mouth of the street and he helped her mount the small gray palfrey that he'd personally selected from the stables for her. He checked the cinch on the saddle, making sure it was secure, before handing her the reins. She made sure to brush his hand, just a little, and when he looked up at her, she was smiling faintly. He returned the gesture, just a little, and turned for his own steed.

With a heavy heart, he mounted his horse, motioning his men forward and making sure to stay near Kathalin as they made their way up the street, towards the end of town where The Raven was situated. All the while, he was coming to wonder if he shouldn't just run away with Kathalin and marry the woman, whisking her off to the north of England where he could serve his father and stay far away from de Lara. It seemed like a plan, in any case, unless one considered how dishonorable it was and what a bad light it would put Kathalin in.

Nay, he couldn't do it, as much as he wanted to. He'd done a lot of things in his life that he wasn't proud of but to run away with de Lara's daughter... it wouldn't matter if he loved her or not. Any chance at reclaiming his honor as a man would be lost if he did it and he couldn't bring that burden to bear on his own father, who would probably not understand. His father, Edward, was a wise and even-tempered man, grandson of Scott de Wolfe, who was the eldest son of the legendary William de Wolfe.

Gates' own grandmother, who knew Scott, said that Edward had Scott's temperament, which was collected and in control. Gates possessed it, too, but if he were to bring home a woman he had married without permission, there was no telling how Edward would react. His actions would shame the de Wolfe family. It was difficult enough to live up to the reputation of such a family without him doing something as terrible as absconding with a woman.

As the de Lara party approached The Raven, Gates began to think that he'd never had much of a chance to live up to the de Wolfe name. Maybe he'd felt pressure from the onset and, rebellious, fought against that name rather than try to honor it. Only in his personal life, of course, because as a knight he was every inch a de Wolfe. But as a man, and in his behavior towards women, there had been something left to be desired.

Maybe in this one instance, he wouldn't go with his sordid reputation. He loved Kathalin and wouldn't dishonor her by stealing off with her. Maybe on this one occasion, somehow, he could actually be proud of his actions as a man. He would not shame the woman he loved.

But he was quite certain the effort was going to kill him.

Already, he felt dead.

I will be true, only to you, forever....

CHAPTER TWELVE
~ THE SHADOWED HEART ~

SHREWSBURY'S ANNUAL SNOW Queen Festival was something of a paradox considering the heavy snow that had blanketed the land for months had, over the past few days, virtually melted away. Still, the villagers were eager to celebrate the ancient festival that was supposed to ensure spring would come early and as the sun set that evening in the west, people came out to the streets in droves.

The Raven was packed to overflowing. As the sun set and the sky turned shades of purple and blue, the windows of the two-storied inn were open, as well as the front door, emitting light out into the busy, darkened streets. A man with a torch went up and down the street, lighting other torches on poles that would give more light to the gloom, and it was all quite festive as men and women danced and sang in the streets.

Standing at the window of her rented room, Kathalin could see all of it below. Most people seemed to be wearing some kind of mask on their faces, most crudely fashioned but a few of them were actually quite lovely. Women had poles with flowing ribbons attached and they waved them about in a symbolic gesture of spring breezes, and men carried about small, wooden shields, ornamental only, and would ram them at each other when passing each other in the street, to great laughter.

Kathalin had never seen anything like it. From the austere halls of St. Milburga's to the party in the street in Shrewsbury, it was yet another reminder of what she had been missing outside of the old priory walls. She could smell food as vendors walked beneath her window, lauding their hot wine for sale or some kind of meat on a stick. She thought she might like to try the hot wine but she didn't have any money and she would have to ask Gates to provide her with coin, but she didn't want to bother him. In fact, after what had happened that afternoon, she wasn't sure she wanted to speak with him at all.

Thoughts of Gates brought thoughts of sadness. She didn't understand his sense of honor, the confusing reasons he had given for not wanting to marry her. He swore that he would be true to her and only her, didn't he? That was good enough for her. She didn't care about a humiliating past but the truth was that she really didn't grasp what he meant.

She had no idea how deep his shame ran.

Having lived such a sequestered life, she couldn't imagine the reality of having a bastard child thrown in her face or perhaps the reality of a spurned lover making a scene. Having only been kissed by a man, once, and that had been earlier in the day, that was the only sexual thing she really understood. It was true that she knew the mechanics of coupling from fellow wards at St. Milburga's who would gossip and giggle about such things, but other than that, she was completely naïve of the act. Of what it meant to couple with a man. Of what it meant to be man and wife.

Nay, she didn't understand much of it. But she wanted to learn of it from Gates and he refused to teach her.

So she was left sad and ashamed, hating this new world that she was being forced to be a part of. Sighing heavily, she sat on the open windowsill, watching the people in the street below, seeing their joy and being envious of it. She wanted to know that joy, too. She didn't understand how Gates could tell her that he adored her yet not want to give in to those feelings. She felt such anguish at his rejection that it was difficult to grasp it. Refusal that cut her to the bone. As she sat on the windowsill, her thoughts lingering on a future that was never meant to be, a soft rap at the door distracted her.

"Come," she said softly.

The door opened and she didn't even look to see who it was. Gates had said something when they'd arrived at the inn about sending a meal up to her so she assumed it was the servant bringing her food. But then she heard footsteps that sounded heavy, not like a servant's shoes should have sounded, so she turned to see that Gates had entered the chamber. He smiled hesitantly and, with a painful heart, she quickly turned away.

"What is it that you want, de Wolfe?" she asked.

Gates could hear the sorrow in her tone. He'd been downstairs for the past three hours in the common room, pretending to be focused on other things when what he was really focused on was Kathalin. Having left off where they had earlier, when Alexander had interrupted them when Kathalin had been begging him to marry her, he knew he simply couldn't leave it like that. He knew he had to speak with her privately again, to reason with her, and hope she could understand his point of view. He'd waited all of that time for Alexander to decided he was bored sitting in the common room of a tavern when there was a party going on outside. As soon as Alexander had left for the streets, Gates had headed upstairs.

Now, he was face to face with Kathalin, hoping to continue their earlier conversation but from her question to him, she didn't sound as if she was willing to discuss it. He took a deep breath before answering.

"I came to see if you would like to go down into the streets and join the party," he said. "Alexander is already out there, somewhere, so I thought you might like to experience the madness."

Kathalin shook her head. "Nay," she said. "I will watch it from here."

Gates had expected that answer. He moved over to stand on the other side of the windowsill, watching her as she looked to the crowd below. "Alexander wanted to escort you to the festival, you know," he said. "I told him to go alone and that no one but me would escort you. Now, do you still wish to stay here and watch from above?"

She nodded, feeling her heart twist with anguish. "I do," she said, feeling the sting of tears. "I do not wish to go anywhere with you."

Gates sighed sadly. "Kathi," he started. "You and I must come to an understanding. I realize you are hurt, sweetheart. I am hurt, too. I just wish you would understand that I never meant to hurt you, in any fashion. I swore to you that I would be true to you and only you, forever. That should give you some comfort."

She whirled to him, eyes blazing. "Comfort?" she repeated, appalled. "Why should it? I love a man who will not marry me. Instead, he will willingly see me married to another. Why should anything you say give me comfort?"

His jaw ticked. "I wish I could make you understand," he said quietly. "What I do, I do for you. I do it to protect you. I do it so you will not be married to a man who will bring you shame. Why can you not comprehend that?"

Frustrated, grieved, Kathalin turned around and put her hands to her ears. "Because I cannot," she hissed. "You told me that you adore me. You know that I adore you. I do not understand why love cannot overcome everything you are afraid of. You are a coward, Gates, a coward! You will not fight for what you love!"

It was difficult for him to hear those words from her mouth. "I can understand how you would see it that way," he said as his anguish mounted. "But it is not…."

She came out of the windowsill. "It is the truth," she cut him off. "You are a coward, afraid to stand up to your past. Instead, are willing to forsake me so that you may hide from it, bury it, and not suffer the consequences. You say that you will not marry me because you want to protect me. Well, I do not believe you. You do not wish to marry me because you do not love me enough to overcome your fear of the past."

He wasn't going to argue with her. She didn't understand. He couldn't make her understand. All he knew was that he was feeling more turmoil than he ever had in his life, now with his bravery taking a hit. Was it possible that she was correct in some ways? Was it possible that he wasn't brave enough to overcome his past, by accepting how he'd lived and now unwilling to face it? He didn't really know. All he knew was that her words hurt him, this pure and fine and beautiful woman that he so admired.

This woman he could never have.

"Mayhap," he said softly. "Mayhap I am more afraid that even though you declare that the sins of the past do not matter to you, mayhap they will after all. Mayhap I am afraid you will be the one running from them when they become too much to bear."

It was the second time in the day when she felt slapped by his words. Now, he was doubting her word of honor, her declaration that she would stand by him regardless of his past indiscretions. He was doubting that she believed love could overcome everything. Feeling wounded, she turned away.

"Mayhap that is true," she said, sounding hollow. "But we will never know if neither of us are strong enough to face the truth, will we? You have already made that decision for me as well as for you."

Wise and true words. He'd already decided they shouldn't face such a thing, so who was to say if they would have the courage to overcome all of this? Gates was feeling defeated, confused, and sickened. Without another word, he turned for the door. Quietly, he crossed the room and lifted the latch, only to hear Kathalin's soft voice behind him one last time.

"Gates," she said. "If you must relay information to me in the future, have Alexander do it. I cannot... I cannot see you anymore. I cannot continue to go through this every time we speak."

He sighed heavily. "You don't mean that."

"Aye, I do. Please respect my wishes."

He didn't move for a moment. Slowly, he shut the door and came back into the room. "I am the commander of your escort," he said. "If you do not permit me to speak with you, it will look very strange to everyone, including Alex. The man is already...."

He suddenly stopped himself and turned for the door, swiftly, but she came towards him, stopping him. "Wait," she said, noticing he wouldn't look at her. "What is this about Alexander? The man is already... *what?*"

He was vastly unhappy with the question and even more unhappy with the answer. "Nothing," he said. "But be aware that Alexander de Lohr also has a few conquests under his belt no matter what he tells you. He has bedded more than his share of women."

She was puzzled. "What do you mean 'no matter what he tells you'?" she asked. "Why should I care what he tells me?"

Gates simply shook his head. Throwing open the door, he nearly bolted through it before she could stop him.

Kathalin stood there a moment, indecisive, wondering why he had run out as he had. Something to do with Alexander, something in his words... in his tone... but she wasn't very good at reading men, or understanding them, but something told her that something was amiss. Gates had more to say about Alexander but wouldn't say it. Curiosity had the better of her and she threw the door open, rushing out after him.

The Raven had several sleeping rooms on the second floor plus a loft, and the common room below was crowded with people eating and drinking and laughing. Gathering the heavy blue brocade skirt, she made her way down the narrow stairs into the smoky, smelly room, her gaze seeking out Gates. It was so crowded, with a heavy haze of smoke in the air, that it was difficult to see those at the far end of the room and as she came to the bottom of the narrow stairs, she became apprehensive of all of the people around her.

It was the first time she'd been away from her escort, without anyone protecting her, and she suddenly felt fearful and vulnerable. *The world is a wicked place*, Mother Benedicta used to say. As she looked at the unfamiliar faces and listened to the loud laughter, she found no comfort or joy in it. In fact, she was increasingly uncomfortable. Perhaps it was best if she returned to her chamber and remained there until Gates decided to make another appearance.

Something told her that he would.

Unfortunately, she didn't get very far. No sooner as she turned around to retrace her steps back up the stairs than someone grabbed her by the arm.

"Lady, do not go!"

With a shriek, Kathalin turned to see that a big soldier had her by the arm. He was clad in mail, and a woolen tunic of blue, and his dark hair was plastered against his forehead from dirt and sweat. He smiled leeringly at her with teeth that had a green line on them against his gums.

"Come and share my meal," he said, tugging her right off the stairs. "I saw you come down the stairs, lady, and should enjoy your company."

Terrified, Kathalin yanked her arm away and made a break for the stairs again but he grabbed her by the skirt, which trailed out behind her, and yanked hard, throwing her off-balance so that she fell backwards and smacked her bum, and lower back, against the hard-packed floor of the common room. Stunned, she wasn't fast enough to stand up again before the soldier was scooping her up under the arms.

"Come along, lass," he said as those around them laughed at her failure to break free. "Come and talk to me whilst I eat."

Kathalin turned into a fighting, snarling cat. She began swinging her arms around, her open palms making contact with his head.

"Let me go, you fool!" she hissed. "Take your hands from me!"

The soldier was unimpressed. "So you found your tongue, did you?" he asked. "Good. I should like for you to use it on me later... in more appropriate places."

The crowd around them laughed loudly at his lewd comment as he made a swipe for Kathalin again but she lashed out, taking her nails across his face. His humor fled as he touched the three scratches on his cheek.

"You are going to regret that," he said quietly.

More terror filled her, terrified of what was going to happen now. Kathalin stumbled backwards again, trying to get away from him but she was not used to such a long, heavy skirt. As she fell to one knee, something rushed past her and she heard the soldier grunt. Men began standing up, all around her, as more men rushed in and, suddenly, there was a nasty fight going on over her head. Frightened for an entirely new reason now, Kathalin ducked underneath the nearest table and tried not to get stepped on.

There was a nasty fight going on over her head and she tried to stay beneath the table as it shifted around, being buffeted by men fighting around it. She held on to the legs of the table so it wouldn't get knocked over and her with it. But suddenly, a big, gloved hand reached under the table, grabbing for her, and she screamed until she saw Gates' face as he bent over, trying to pull her out from beneath the table.

Gates!

It was relief beyond description as she propelled herself out from beneath the table and into his embrace. Gates put his big arms around her, pulling her from the fight, but not before she noticed that the soldier who had grabbed her was bleeding out all over the floor. There was also a bloodied sword in Gates' hand. As he pulled her towards the stairs, it began to occur to her what had happened.

"Did you kill him?" she asked, pointing to the bleeding soldier even as he tried to take her up the stairs. "Gates, was it you?"

Gates didn't pause to see what she was pointing at. He knew. "Much was his mistake for putting his hands on you," he said. "One of my soldiers saw you come down the stairs and came to find me out in the yard behind the inn. I was just coming inside when that soldier grabbed you. I saw you fall. Are you injured?"

Kathalin realized she was halfway up the stairs at this point, herded by Gates. "Nay, I am not," she said, somewhat stunned at what had just happened. "But you... you clearly saved me from him. God only knows what would have happened had you not come when you did. That is not the first time you have saved me, Gates."

She had said it with admiration but he ignored the tone in her voice and the pleasure it provoked. He didn't say anything until they reached the top of the stairs. Then, his attitude was somewhat cold and professional.

"You should not have come out of your chamber to begin with," he said. "What was so important that you had to come out and risk yourself like that?"

She paused to look at him as the fight died down in the common room below. Why *had* she come? It was because of his comment about Alexander but, given the situation at the moment, she didn't want to bring that up. It seemed very foolish to do so. Feeling embarrassed, she lowered her head.

"I… I apologize," she said, turning for her chamber. "I will not do it again."

Gates watched her walk away. "Kathalin," he called after her softly. When she stopped to look at him, he lifted his eyebrows for emphasis. "Why did you come to the common room? Are you in need of something?"

She didn't want to tell him but she couldn't seem to stop herself. She was coming to realize she really wasn't very good at keeping her mouth shut where Gates was concerned.

"I came to find you," she said, shoving open her chamber door. "I came to find you and I do not know why I should have. I thought mayhap to say something to you but I do not remember what that was so I will bid you a good evening, Sir Knight. Thank you for coming to my aid and I apologize for the inconvenience."

She was in her chamber slamming the door before he could stop her. Once inside, she felt as if she was dying. All of her insides were twisting, her heart and soul were twisting, and she couldn't control the pain. God, she just couldn't control it. Every time she saw him, the pain became worse and worse. She just didn't know how to deal with it.

The tears came then, heavy wracking sobs. She collapsed next to her bed, sobbing her heart out, unable to withstand the burden of her love for Gates. She wept for the rejection, for the confusion of the day, and for the passion she would never know. There were so many things to weep over and she sobbed over feelings she never knew she was capable of. As she sat on the floor, leaning up against the bed, she didn't see the chamber door quietly open.

It was Gates.

When Kathalin had slammed the door she had failed to lock it; he knew because he had listened for the bolt and it was never thrown. He moved up against the door, listening for her, and hearing only tears. It was a crushing thing to hear and he knew he couldn't simply leave her like that.

She had told him she didn't want to see him and, at first, he had believed her because he had fled her chamber and had gone downstairs, into the yard behind the tavern simply to clear his head away from her and away from the noise of the tavern. But one of his soldiers had summoned him back inside almost immediately with news that Lady Kathalin had come down to the common room, and Gates had bolted in through the back of the tavern in time to see Kathalin being pawed by a drunken soldier.

After that, rage and fear took over and he had killed the man who had grabbed Kathalin. It had been the most natural of things to protect her from harm, something he would have done a thousand times over again, even for so ungrateful a woman. Then he had whisked her back to her chamber to ensure she remained safe. But even after she had gone back into her room, slamming the door in his face, he knew he simply couldn't leave her again. He was confused, and heartbroken, but still, he couldn't leave her again. He'd tried and it hadn't worked. Therefore, he was stuck – stuck loving this woman and having no idea what to do about it. He had no idea what to say anymore.

He had no idea what to think.

So he entered the chamber and made his way over to her as she huddled next to the bed, weeping. It broke his heart to hear her cry and he lowered himself down onto the floor next to her, his back against the bed. He simply wanted to be near her as they shared their mutual pain. It was an oddly unifying bond.

"I am here," he whispered so as not to startle her. "I will not speak to you and you do not have to speak to me, but please allow me to sit here. Do not tell me to go away again, for I cannot. I simply want to sit here, with you, if only to hear you breathe."

Kathalin initially jumped at the sound of his voice, startled that he had crept into the room, but his whisper was gentle and soothing, and it was something that gave her some comfort. She wanted him close yet she didn't. She didn't want to speak to him yet she did. God, she had no idea what she wanted. All she knew was that she loved him and their situation was as complicated as it was precarious.

As she placed her head against the side of the bed, weeping quietly, she reached a hand behind her, extending it, reaching for him even though she couldn't see him. She knew he was close for she could feel his warmth, his very presence close to her. When Gates grasped her hand, kissing it, it was the most comforting yet the most painful thing she could have ever imagined.

They remained that way all night.

The next morning, any further jewelry shopping and even the apothecary was forgotten. Kathalin had no more interested in shopping and was simply eager to leave, as was Gates. He'd spent the night holding her hand, knowing that his inability to keep himself from falling in love with Kathalin de Lara had cost him everything.

It had cost him the rest of his life.

The escort from Hyssington headed home before first light.

CHAPTER THIRTEEN

Hyssington Castle

"YOU SUMMONED ME, my dear?"

Jasper had gone through his obligatory sneezes after entering his wife's pungent-smelling chamber, now standing near the door in his usual place whilst Rosamund remained over on her bed, her usual place. He could see her outline through the sheer panels of curtain, silhouetted by a taper on the other side of her bed. The faint illumination gave her a surreal, other-worldly quality.

"I have," she said. "Thank you for coming so quickly."

Putting aside the sewing she had been working on, Rosamund rose laboriously from her bed. Her maid was there to help her, gently steadying the woman as she stood, and then releasing her so that Rosamund could shuffle over to where her husband was. Jasper watched his wife come around the bed.

"I came quickly because I assume you wish to tell me of your conversation with Kathalin," he said, sounding impatient. "You spoke with the woman three days ago and have yet to tell me the results of that conversation. I have sent her with Gates and Alexander to Shrewsbury so now we may speak openly about her for she is not here to overhear anything. What did you two speak of when I left you alone, Rosamund? I demand you tell me."

Rosamund moved for the chair near the hearth. "Why did they go to Shrewsbury?"

Jasper clearly had no time for idle conversation. "To purchase a few pieces of jewelry for her so she looks like an earl's daughter for the coming celebration," he said. "I will not have her looking bereft and poor if we are trying to attract a husband for her."

"And you feel dressing her in jewels will accomplish this?"

He nodded shortly. "I do," he said. "Now, what is it you wish to speak of? And why have you not told me of your conversation with Kathalin before now?"

Rosamund reached the chair, grasping it with her fabric-covered hand. "I apologize for not discussing my conversation with her after it happened," she said, "but there was much to think on. I wanted to have my thoughts straight before approaching you with my suggestions. Truly, our conversation was nothing you have not already heard from her. She does not wish to be married but I asked her to allow us to have a celebration with potential husbands in attendance. I told her that if she did not find any of the young men appealing then I would consider allowing her to return to St. Milburga's."

Jasper's cheeks flushed with anger. "How could you tell her that?" he said. "I will *not* send her back!"

Rosamund nodded, settling herself down in the chair. "Nor will I," she said. "I only told her I would consider it. I did not tell her that I would do it. But therein lies the problem, Jasper. I fear that we cannot wait to wed her to the son of an ally. We must do it immediately. The longer we delay, the more troublesome this situation will become, so it is something we must do right away. That way, she will never be able to return to St. Milburga's. It will be much more complicated for her to be accepted by the order if she is a married woman."

"It may not make any difference to her. She can still run away, you know."

"Not if her husband keeps her confined."

Jasper was frowning deeply. "The only way a husband will be able to keep her confined is to either throw her in the vault or lock her up for her own good," he said. "What kind of wife will that be for him? I will not permit her to shame me before an ally and sully the de Lara name because she tries to flee her husband."

Rosamund lifted a hand to quiet him. "I realize that," she said. "But I have an idea. It will take a strong ally, indeed, to help her see reason. To help her understand that the wife of a warlord is an important role."

Jasper rolled his eyes. "I know of no such ally, Rosamund," he said impatiently. "If you have an idea, I would hear it now."

Rosamund nodded. She considered her words carefully before continuing. "Lioncross Abbey is a massive fortress that would be difficult to escape from," she said. "I remember seeing it in my youth. Lady Elreda was once a close friend. She is a woman I would trust with convincing my daughter that marriage to her son is a fine and noble role in life. The de Lohrs would not permit Kathalin to escape; because she is a de Lara, and our child, they would look upon her as one of their own. They are close friends, Jasper. We must impress upon them the importance of a marriage between our daughter and Alexander. You once said you would consider Alexander, did you not?"

Jasper wasn't quite so impatient as he listened to his wife's plan. It wasn't a bad one at all. After a moment, he scratched his chin pensively. "Aye, I did," he agreed. "Alexander is a fine knight. And a marriage between our children would secure the entire southern section of the Marches."

Rosamund nodded. "Indeed it would," she said. "Instead of this celebration to parade our daughter before potential suitors, we should have simply sent a proposal of marriage to Lioncross. It would have solved the entire problem."

Jasper continued scratching his chin. "Henry and Elreda were sent a missive requesting their presence at the celebration," he said. "They should be arriving within days. We can simply make the proposal then. Moreover, they can meet Kathalin and inspect her for their son."

"True."

He suddenly frowned. "She will behave, won't she? She will not say something foolish to discourage them?"

Rosamond shook her head. "I think not," she said. "If Kathalin believes we will send her back to St. Milburga's should she not find any young man appealing, I believe she will behave herself. She will not want to jeopardize her chances of being sent back."

Jasper grunted. "You also know that if she believes we will consider sending her back to the priory, then she more than likely will find something wrong with every young man at the celebration, including Alexander."

Rosamond nodded her head in agreement. "She believes, for the moment, that she has a say in this matter," she said. "What she does not know is that she has no say at all. She never did. We shall cement a contract with Alexander de Lohr and have the wedding immediately whilst the guests are already here for her celebration. The party to introduce Kathalin to eligible young men will turn into her wedding feast."

Jasper wasn't feeling quite as anxious as he was when he had first entered his wife's chamber. Thanks to Rosamund's cunning plan, he could see an advantageous marriage for his daughter providing Henry de Lohr agreed. He couldn't imagine why the man wouldn't but he would make sure to produce his best wine and finest food when the House of de Lohr arrived. He would make sure to do all he could to convince them to marry their son to his stubborn daughter.

"Agreed," he said, thinking on things to come when Henry arrived. "I will make the necessary preparations for the Henry and Elreda. I should like for them to stay in the chamber Kathalin is occupying. It is our finest."

Rosamund nodded. "It is," she said. "Kathalin can stay in the chamber on this floor, the smaller one across the landing from me. It is my maid's room, but I will have my maid sleep in here with me for the time being."

Jasper thought on that particular sleeping arrangement because it meant he couldn't call upon the maid when he was feeling particularly lusty so long as the woman was sleeping in the same chamber as his wife. But no matter; that was secondary to what needed to take place in order to assure that the de Lohrs accepted the marriage proposal on behalf of Alexander.

Aye, Alexander de Lohr would make a fine son and a fine ally, and Jasper was pleased. More than that, Kathalin would cease to be his problem and become someone else's. A selfish thought, but Jasper was a selfish man.

Let someone else deal with her insolence.

Without another word, he left his wife's chamber in his pursuit to make arrangements for what was to come. The trap would need to be appropriately laid for Henry and Elreda with the bait being Kathalin when she returned from Shrewsbury. Jasper was quite certain that after Henry and Elreda met his daughter, they would heartily agree to the proposal.

He was quite certain Alexander would agree to it as well.

⁂

"WHAT DO WE do?" Tobias Aston asked. "If we do not let him in the gates, he's simply going to stand there and scream."

Stephan knew that. He and Tobias were in the great gatehouse of Hyssington, watching the scene below. Lord Linley was at the gate, drunk, and bellowing for Gates to come out and face him. It was very cold in mid-morning as they watched the man, beating upon the massive iron and oak gates, and it was something of entertainment for the soldiers. Lord Linley was making a spectacle of himself as he bellowed and threatened Gates de Wolfe for bedding his daughter and forcing his daughter to bear "his own spawn", as Linley put it.

"Linley is a drunkard and a fool," Stephan said with distaste. "This is nothing new for him, behaving like this for all to see, but if de Lara sees the man there will be trouble. He already paid Linley's daughter coinage to keep her mouth shut about de Wolfe's bastard, but if the father is here now to extract more money, he'll find himself in the vault – or worse."

Tobias watched Linley as the man slipped in the mud below, ending up on his knees in the midst of his ranting. "He is asking for Gates, not de Lara," he said. "Do you know when Gates is supposed to return from Shrewsbury? He shall be coming right into the middle of this if he returns any time soon."

Stephan shook his head. "I do not know when he is due to return," he said. "Far be it from me to criticize de Wolfe, but he should be more careful when it comes to bedding some lord's daughters. Linley sees money in all of this because of the wealth and prestige of the de Wolfe family."

Tobias continued to watch the drunkard below, considering the implications of the situation. He was very young, only twenty years and two, and somewhat of a prig when it came to women. He seemed a bit intimidated by them, as the older knights had seen, so this situation was somewhat serious for him. He leaned against the stone parapet as he watched the action below.

"He did not chase women whilst we were in France," he said. "I saw him with a few women, but he did not seem to have much time to carouse about."

Stephan snorted. "You are speaking of Gates de Wolfe," he said. "The great and mighty Dark Destroyer. Trust me when I tell you the man had plenty of time to seek out female companionship in France because that is what he does. We should all be so lucky to have the intelligence, the comely looks, and the wealth of Gates. No woman can resist him."

Tobias smiled faintly. "'Tis odd," he said. "I have seen him in battle. There is no one I would trust my life to more. At Poitiers, he was without fear. Men looked to him for courage. But when he is off the battlefield… that part of his life does not impress me so much. It is as if he has no self-control."

Stephan crossed his big arms, looking at Tobias. "I have known Gates for many years," he said. "It is not that the man has no self-control, for he has a great deal of it. To me, it has always seemed as if there was desperation to his actions when it comes to life outside of the battlefield."

Tobias looked at him curiously. "What desperation?"

Stephan shrugged, trying to put his thoughts into words. "He lives as if every day is his last," he said. "I have never seen him idle; if he is not fighting, he is bedding a woman, or laughing with the men, or celebrating in one way or another. Most of us have the ability to stop and rest at times, but I have never seen Gates do that. He lives as if he is going to die tomorrow."

Tobias considered that seriously. "So he beds women to stave off that fear?" he said. "Surely there are other things he can do in order to feel vital and alive."

"Like what?" Stephan shrugged. "Roll bones? Play games? Nay, lad, Gates is a de Wolfe, and that is a big name to live up to. He lives like he fights; with all of the passion in the world, which in his case means women. They make him feel alive."

It was an interesting take on Gates de Wolfe, one of the greatest knights that young Tobias had ever seen. He liked Gates, too, a great deal. All of the men did. And if it made Gates feel more alive to chase women, so be it. Therefore, to see Linley rolling around in the mud below was an unhappy observance because it was a direct insult to Gates. At least, that's how Tobias looked at it. As he pondered the enigma that was Gates de Wolfe, some of the soldiers up in the gatehouse decided to use the murder holes as a latrine again and aimed right for Lord Linley. The man was the recipient of a shower of urine as he stomped around in the mud below.

The entire gatehouse erupted in laughter as Linley roared with disgust, now covered in piss. Stephan, shaking his head at the antics of his men, made sure to bellow at them to scold them for what they had done, but he was unfortunately grinning when he did it so his reprimand was not taken too seriously. After that, no one took Linley seriously, either.

As the soldiers of Hyssington went about their duties, Linley spent the rest of the morning bemoaning his daughter's situation and demanding to see Gates. During the spring, summer, and fall months, Hyssington's gates were open to those wishing to do business within her walls – smithies, hunters who had leather hides to sell, farmers with their produce, and even men who would sell peat for fires and dried grasses for the livestock. But in the winter, the gates remained closed for safety reasons, mostly because starving Welsh might take advantage of it. Therefore, Lord Linley was kept outside the gates, left to his drunken temper tantrums, as those inside the walls ignored him.

That included Stephan and Tobias, who went about their duties once they were certain Linley wasn't going to cause trouble or do anything more foolish than he was already doing, like trying to climb the walls. They went about securing posts, dealing with problems among the men, repairing weaponry that needed refurbishment, and other duties that had been assigned to them. Stephan was in the armory, in fact, inspecting some of the weaponry they'd brought back with them from France when he heard a commotion around him. Since the armory was in the gatehouse, all he had to do was stick his head out of the door to see what was the fuss was about.

He saw it soon enough. At mid-afternoon during this sunny day amongst melting snow, Gates and Alexander were returning from Shrewsbury with Lady Kathalin and twenty men riding escort. And Lord Linley, who was closer to the incoming party than the sentries were, was running out to greet them.

Ordering the gates opened, Stephan ran after him but he wasn't fast enough. He could hear Linley swearing at Gates already.

"You... you *bedswerver!*" Linley was screaming. "You devious bastard! You are the father of Helene's child! *It is you!*"

After a very quiet ride from Shrewsbury, Gates hadn't expected a confrontation at the gates of Hyssington. He had seen Linley running at him from a distance and, to be truthful, it wasn't as if he didn't have suspicions about the man's intentions. In fact, he was quite certain what the man's intentions were but there wasn't much he could do about it.

Gates would have bet money that Helene had finally confessed to Linley who the father of her son was, perhaps in another attempt to coerce Gates into marriage. Whatever the case, Gates knew why the man was here, knowing that his indiscretions were about to be shouted for all to hear. For Kathalin to hear. He had warned her of moments to come like this, and here one was, unexpectedly, right on his doorstep.

He braced himself.

"Greetings, Lord Linley," he said evenly. "What brings you to Hyssington?"

Linley had come to halt, as had the escort, but Linley had eyes only for Gates. "What do you have to say for yourself?" he demanded. "What do you have to say before I cut your belly open and laugh at your misery?"

Gates just looked at the man. He wasn't about to admit to anything, or play any manner of game with Linley. He could be verbally brutal when he wanted to be, as Helene had discovered when she tried to force him into marriage. Now, Helene's drunkard father was embarrassing him and that didn't sit well. But before he verbally speared the man, he thought to give him the chance to quietly make his point. As he opened his mouth, Stephan suddenly came shooting through the gates, racing towards him.

"I am sorry, Gates," Stephan said as he came up to them, putting himself between Gates and Linley. "He has been here all morning. I had hoped he would go away before you returned from Shrewsbury."

Gates simply nodded. "It is no matter, Bear," he said steadily, focusing on Linley. "The man obviously has something to say to me. Did you wish to speak with me about something, Lord Linley?"

Linley was trying to move away from Stephan so he could have a clear line of sight to Gates, but Stephan kept moving, kept putting himself in between them. Gates finally called him off and Linley shook a fist at Gates.

"You are the father of Helene's son," he said angrily. "She told me so!"

Gates remained quite calm. "My lord, I have no idea what your daughter told you," he said. "I have been in France for nearly a year and a half, so clearly I have been out of the country for a very long time. That would make it rather impossible to do what your daughter has accused me of doing."

"It happened before you left!"

Gates merely shrugged. "If that is what you believe, I would be more than happy to escort you into Hyssington where I may hear your grievance in private."

Linley stomped his boot, which was foot covering in the purely academic sense of the word. It was really the remains of a shoe that had been wrapped, and rewrapped, over his foot. When he stomped it in the mud, half of the shoe started to come apart.

"You will hear them now, de Wolfe," he said. "Just as everyone else will. They will know what kind of a man you really are!"

So much for remaining cool. "Oh?" he said, preparing his verbal attack. "And how would you know what kind of man I am? I see that no tankard of cheap ale has escaped you this day. I can smell you from here. Moreover, if you wish to speak on your daughter, then I am sure there are ten or twelve men here who would know more about her than I would. Are you sure this is something you wish to discuss for all to hear?"

The verbal arrows hit their mark and Linley's anger took a dousing. He appeared astonished that Gates would say such a thing and his mouth, that great gaping thing that smelled of rot and ale, popped open.

"You *slander* her?" he hissed, incredulous.

Gates turned around, waving Alexander and Kathalin and the escort through. He even motioned to Stephan to leave them. Whatever was to be said was between him and Linley, and he was already greatly perturbed that the man was shouting accusations for all to hear. When Stephan, Alexander, and the soldiers began to move, Gates returned his focus to Linley.

"Listen to me and listen well," his said, his tone no longer friendly. "Whatever your daughter has told you cannot be proven. She has already come to Hyssington, twice, to demanded money and I will tell you what I told her – I can produce a dozen men from this fortress that will gladly swear that they have had their way with your daughter and they will do it before the priest, so unless you want your daughter to be dragged down into the depths of rubbish that you are attempting to drag me into, I would suggest you look elsewhere for a husband for your daughter and for money to pay for your drunken habit. You are the sad remnants of a once-great house so if anyone is to be embarrassed by all of this, it should be you. Your need for drink above all else has driven your daughter to do some very desperate things for money."

Linley was shocked to the bone, devastated and infuriated by Gates' accusations. Not that some of them weren't the truth, but no one around him had ever had the courage to say it to his face. With a roar of pure rage, he rushed Gates, who was still astride his big war horse. It was a very easy thing for Gates to lash out a booted foot and kick Linley squarely in the head with it. The man fell like a stone.

As Linley toppled over, Gates heard a gasp behind him. He turned, swiftly, to see Kathalin dismounting her palfrey and rushing to Linley's side. Gates was off his horse in an instant, pulling her away.

"Nay," he told her, his voice low and severe. "Leave him be. I told you to go into the castle with the others."

Kathalin was looking at the man who was now sitting up, rubbing his forehead. "You did not tell me anything," she said. "It was your men you ordered about. Who is this man, Gates? Is it true what he said about his daughter and you?"

Gates faltered. He didn't want to lie to her, considering he had warned her of this exact situation, but he wasn't about to admit fault in front of Linley. Taking her by the arm, he turned her towards the gatehouse. Stephan happened to turn around before entering the gates and Gates caught his attention, waving him back over to escort

Kathalin.

"Go inside with Stephan," he told her quietly. "I will not discuss this with you at this moment."

Linley, still rubbing his head, looked up and saw Kathalin. He pointed at her. "You *dare* to bring another woman into Hyssington, de Wolfe?" he demanded. "My daughter is the only woman you should be thinking of!"

Gates was trying to push Kathalin in Stephan's direction but she wouldn't move. She was looking at Linley.

The truth was that Kathalin was genuinely curious about the situation. She had heard the man accuse Gates of fathering a child with his daughter; it had been difficult not to hear it. But as she listened, something occurred to her; this was the exact situation Gates had warned her about, the fears of his past humiliating her. But she didn't feel humiliation in the least – in fact, she felt a good deal of protectiveness over Gates. Perhaps this was a chance for her to prove him wrong and to show him that his past, in all of its ignoble glory, truly didn't matter to her.

The ride that morning from Shrewsbury had been filled with a terrible, tense silence between them. She had fallen asleep last night holding his hand and had awoken the same way, but very little had been spoken between them. It seemed as if there was nothing left to say, as if everything they could have said to each other had already been spoken. What was left was a heartbreaking and terrible stalemate. But now... a drunken man accusing Gates of fathering a child... perhaps she could, indeed, show Gates that his fears were unfounded.

Perhaps this was the opportunity she had hoped for.

She wanted to take it.

"Your daughter has a child, my lord?" she asked. "Am I to understand you believe it to be de Wolfe's?"

Linley frowned, waving her off. "Speak not to me, harlot!"

Kathalin's eyebrows lifted. "Harlot?" she repeated, but offended and amused by his accusation. "You have the gall to call me a harlot when it is your daughter who bore a child out of wedlock? I should say you have misdirected that accusation."

Linley's features tightened angrily. "Be gone!" he bellowed. "I will not speak to such vermin!"

Kathalin could hardly believe the nerve of the man. "I am Lord de Lara's daughter," she said frankly. "You are not only a drunken fool but you are an ignorant one as well. At least my father raised me properly and respectably, for it is not I who bore a child out of wedlock but your own daughter. Instead of blaming Gates, you should be blaming yourself. *You* were the one who raised a woman too willing to warm a man's bed. It is your fault alone."

Linley was looking at her with much the same rage and offense that he used when looking upon Gates. He struggled to get to his feet but with his drunken state and the blow to his head, his balance seemed to be elusive.

"I will not hear this from you, woman," he said, rolling to his knees. "This is between de Wolfe and me. Be gone with you!"

Kathalin snorted. "You stood there not two minutes ago and declared that you would have everyone hear your business," she said. "Now we have all heard it. You come to accuse the man of fathering your daughter's child when it could just as easily be any other man at Hyssington. You have insulted Gates for all to hear and I will not stand for it. This man has recently survived the big battle at Poitiers and he has not come back to England to be challenged by the likes of you. You are not worthy to even speak to him. Be gone, you old fool. Be gone before I run you out of here myself."

Linley was on his feet by now, weaving dangerously. The expression on his face was pure venom. "No woman will tell me what to do."

Before Gates could stop her, Kathalin took a step towards the man and shoved him, hard, on the chest. He fell over again, back into the mud.

"I just did," she snapped, feeling Gates as he took her arm and gently tried to pull her away. "Get out of here and do not come back. We will hear no more of slander you cannot prove."

Linley was on his belly on the ground, trying to push himself up, as Kathalin turned away from him, being pulled along by Gates. He had her by the arm still, moving her away from the confrontation. She was upset, that was true, but not overly so. In fact, she felt rather pleased with what she had done. How she had proved to Gates that whatever had happened in his past did not matter to her. But it would be up to him whether or not he could figure that out for himself. There would be no more talk from her, no more trying to convince him that his past was of no consequence. Now, she would leave it up to him to decide.

She would let her actions speak louder than her words.

"I can walk by myself," she said, though not unkindly, as she removed her arm from his grip. "Come inside the fortress now. Waste no more time with that idiot."

Gates let her go, watching her walk back through the gatehouse with Stephan by her side. He simply stood there, watching her go, and realized that he had a smile on his face. She had handled Linley quite ably and had taken charge of the situation as a de Lara would. He'd never seen that side of her until now, a growing moment in the life of a secluded convent ward. She was secluded no longer and command came natural to her, as a de Lara.

But more than anything, Gates had been witness to how she had defended him against Linley's accusations. She had been poised and collected, and she had ably defended him when another woman would have run. Was it possible, then, that she had meant what she had said? That his past didn't matter to her? Only time would tell, as this was only the first test out of what could possibly be a few. Perhaps she would continue to defend him... or perhaps she would come to understand just how terrible his past had been.

He began to pray it wasn't the latter. He was starting to see that, perhaps, she was true to her word.

Gathering the reins of his steed and her palfrey, he followed without another glance to Linley, still in the mud.

CHAPTER FOURTEEN

I T WAS A cold, blustery day nearly a week after the return from Shrewsbury. The snows had virtually vanished, leaving a winter-dead landscape that was icy and brown. Spring was on the horizon, but not close enough.

Wrapped up in her lavender wool surcoat and heavy fur cloak, Kathalin stood out in a walled area with Rosamund's maid, a small, plain-looking woman named Mary. She was very kind and had a terrible stutter, which made her rather quiet. It was difficult to get answers from the woman, or any kind of information, even though Rosamund had sent her maid to assist Kathalin in her new life here at Hyssington. So far, the little maid had been a good deal of help.

Today, they were out in the small walled garden that Kathalin had seen from her window. She walked around the garden, kneeling down next to plants that were desperately trying to come back to life in the cold, as Mary followed closely.

"An herb garden, you say?" Kathalin asked to clarify what she'd been told about the walled section of dead foliage in a very small area next to the kitchen yard. "Is this for the cook or is it used for medicinal purposes?"

"The c-cook planted the garden, my lady," Mary said. "She d-does not have m-much time to keep it up, however."

Kathalin squatted down next to a host of dried, dead plants that were starting to show signs of green, new growth now that the snow had melted away and the sun had come out. She bent down, examining the plants because she knew a good deal about herbs and flowers from St. Milburga's extensive garden. Breaking off a piece of greenery, she smelled it.

"Rosemary," she said. "It will grow up in bushes. What's this?"

She rubbed her fingers along a hint of greenery on the plant further down the line, bringing her fingers to her nose to smell. She inhaled deeply.

"Sage," she said.

Mary, following behind, pointed to an entire section over near the wall. "L-lavender grows there, my lady," she said. "It will grow m-most year around although the s-snows have c-curbed it somewhat."

Kathalin stood up and went over to the lavender area where she could see dead sprigs intermingled with new growth. She smiled in approval.

"This is lovely," she said. "There will be many wonderful plants to come. I will cultivate this garden as my own. Do you think the cook will mind?"

Mary shook her head. "N-nay, my lady."

"Would you mind asking her for me?"

"N-nay, my lady."

Mary scurried off. Pleased, Kathalin moved to another section of the garden, finding some other new, green growth and smelling it. *Thyme*, she thought. It seemed as if there was an abundance of growth coming forth that simply needed to be cultivated and weeded, and she was more than up to the task. It was something she had done back at St. Milburga's and she was well versed in gardening. Additionally, it gave her something to occupy her time and mind. It was a diversion that was very much needed.

It was the fifth day after her return from Shrewsbury and the fifth day that Gates had stayed away from her. Well, that wasn't entirely true, because she had seen him on occasion when she had been walking the grounds under escort, which Gates had thoughtfully arranged, and last eve she had eaten her first meal in the great hall with Jasper and Gates had been there. His eyes had been warm upon her but his conversation had mostly been with his men and his knights, in particularly Stephan, Tobias, and Alexander.

Alexander, in fact, had spoken to her more than Gates had. He was young, and rather arrogant, but he was a well-read and well-educated man, and able to discuss a variety of subjects, including horticulture and biblical stories. Kathalin had found the man rather interesting and she appreciated that she'd had someone to talk to, but the entire time, her attention had been on Gates.

Sitting across the table from her, he and Stephan had been in deep conversation most of the night. In fact, Kathalin was hurt that he hadn't chosen to speak with her. He didn't go so far as to ignore her, but he definitely didn't want to converse overly with her. Sad, Kathalin had been forced to speak with Alexander, who seemed to want to discuss the morality of the tale of Job. Not exactly what Kathalin wished to speak of but she was able to keep pace with Alexander and his quick mind. The man talked very fast and she simply went along with him.

But the evening had been pleasant and she had retired with quiet young Tobias escorting her to the keep. After sleeping soundly in the new chamber she had been moved to, across from her mother's chamber, she had awoken to a view of a dead garden and that was where she now found herself. She was in her element now and feeling more cheerful than she had in quite a while.

Pacing the garden, she was making a mental note of where the herbs were located. She would ask her father if he would provide her with a couple of servants to help weed out the garden and till the soil. She needed to remove the new, green sprigs that were popping up so that she could replant them once the soil was tilled and broken. She had big plans for the garden, already laying out where she planned to plant things, when the garden gate screeched open.

Hearing the noise of the old iron, Kathalin turned to see Alexander enter. Dressed in heavy wool and mail against the cold temperature, he smiled brightly at her when their eyes met. Kathalin smiled weakly in return, wondering what he was doing here. He was a handsome man with his blond hair, blue eyes, and white smile and the truth was that he was rather charming, but she simply wasn't attracted to him, not when her heart belonged to Gates. He lifted a hand as he approached.

"Greetings, my lady," he said. "I had heard you had come to the garden on this fine day. Not much of a garden, however."

Kathalin's smile turned genuine as she looked at her surroundings. "It will be when I am finished with it," she said. "I plan to grow it into a fine, proud display."

Alexander came to a halt a respectable distance away, looking at the dried weeds around him. "Is that so?" he asked. "I wish you luck, then. You will need it."

Kathalin turned to him with a mock scowl. "Did you come to criticize my project?"

He laughed softly, shaking his head. "I did not, in fact," he said. "I came because one of the palfrey's is about to give birth and Gates thought you might like to claim the foal for your own. You do not have a horse and he thought you might like this one."

Kathalin's face lit up. "I would, very much," she said. "Is she giving birth now?"

Alexander nodded. "She is trying to," he said. "I will let you know once the foal has been born."

Kathalin was already moving around him. "I want to see the birth."

He reached out to stop her. "A nasty business, my lady," he said. "The mare is well-tended. You do not need to be present."

Kathalin puckered her lips at him wryly. "Do you think I have never seen a birth before?"

"Have you?"

She looked at him as if he were mad. "Of course I have," she said. "Many times. St. Milburga's is a healing order and that also means birthing children as well as birthing animals. I have seen quite a few in my time."

Alexander smiled, his gaze on her in an appraising fashion. "My, my," he said, rather teasingly. "Aren't we an accomplished lady? Not only do you plant gardens, but you birth children. My mother will be most impressed with you."

Kathalin cocked her head curiously. "Your mother?"

Alexander nodded, looking off over the garden as he spoke. "Aye," he said. "My parents have been invited to the celebration that your parents have planned in your honor. They should be here any day. My mother, in fact, is an avid gardener. She will like to speak to you of herbs and flowers and other things that are green. I hope you will indulge her."

Kathalin nodded. "I would be honored to," she said. "Does your mother have a garden, then?"

Alexander lifted his eyebrows as his focus returned to her. "Massive," he said. "It is four times the size of this little plot. She spends a good deal of her time tending it."

As he looked at her, Kathalin could feel something odd radiating from his eyes, something warm and curious. It occurred to her that she'd seen the same expression in Gates' eyes, too, but in his case, she had been receptive to it. In Alexander's case, she was not. Quickly, she averted her gaze and moved away.

"Then I look forward to showing her this garden and asking for her suggestions," she said. "I tended the herb garden at St. Milburga's but I was only one of many. I have never had a garden of my own."

Alexander watched her as she walked away, studying the dried weeds at her feet. "I am sure she would be more than happy to comply," he said. He hesitated a moment before continuing. "I… I would like to hear more of your plans for your garden. I would consider it an honor if you would allow me to take you on a walk where you can tell me of all of your great hopes for your plants. There is a fine walk next to the stream nearby and I noticed this morning that all of the snow had melted down there. It would be a fine place to walk."

A warning bell went on in Kathalin's head. She could just hear the interest in his tone, interest that went beyond mere politeness. She was very careful in how she responded, not wanting to offend him, for she truly liked Alexander. He was a pleasant and humorous man. But she was not interested in him romantically.

"I am honored, my lord," she said. "But not today, if you do not mind. My mother has asked to speak with me later this morning, so I will be occupied."

It was actually the truth and she was relieved that she had an excuse. Alexander simply nodded his head.

"Of course," he said. "Mayhap another time."

"Mayhap."

An awkward silence fell as Kathalin crouched down next to another plant, seeming more interested in the dead growth around her than in Alexander. He sensed that, of course, and tried not to feel slighted by it. It was time for him to leave.

"Then I shall look forward to it," he said. "Good day to you, my lady."

Kathalin looked up from her plant. "Good day, Sir Alexander."

He forced a smile and turned on his heel, heading out of the garden and feeling embarrassed about her rejection. He tried to tell himself that it was because she was in new and uncertain circumstances, but something told him that was not entirely true. He had been watching the interaction between the lady and Gates for several days now and the harder they tried to ignore each other, the more obvious it was that there was something between him. He didn't know why he felt that way, but he did. Lost in thought, he had just reached the garden gate when it swung back and nearly hit him.

Gates stepped through the opening, moving aside when he saw Alexander coming through. "There you are," he said. "I have been looking for you."

Alexander paused, his hand on the iron gate. "I came to tell the lady about the foal," he said. "What did you wish of me?"

Gates threw a thumb towards the gatehouse. "A party has been sighted about a mile out," he said. "They are flying the blue banners and yellow lion of de Lohr."

Alexander grinned. "My mother and father approach?"

Gates nodded. "They do," he said. "I thought you would want to ride out to greet them."

Alexander fled from the garden without another word, rushing in the direction of the stables. Gates paused a moment, watching him go, before inevitably turning his attention towards Kathalin, who was crouched down next to some dead plants, scratching at the dirt.

Alone. He was alone with her and the weight of the situation wasn't lost on him. He hadn't seen the woman alone in five days but now, here they were, just the two of them. Alexander was occupied, as was Jasper, but he knew that his time with Kathalin was limited. As soon as the House of de Lohr arrived, Jasper would want to show her off. He didn't blame the man. Therefore, he had to speak to her privately before she was taken from him.

There was much he had to say.

Five days of reflecting upon Kathalin's interaction with Lord Linley and five days of reflecting upon all they had said to one another in Shrewsbury had been weighing heavily on him. He couldn't think of anything else. He went to sleep at night with Kathalin on his mind and woke up the next morning with the same if, in fact, he was lucky enough to sleep at all. The woman was occupying his every moment, like a ghost talking over his body and filling him until he could hardly breathe.

Five days of weighing his options, of wrestling with his fears, of imagining a future with and without her. God, there was so much he wanted to say to her that he hardly knew where to begin. But he had to start somewhere.

He made his way over to her.

"Good morn to you, my lady," he said pleasantly.

Kathalin looked up from the dead weeds in her hand, her eyes lighting up at the sight of him. "Good morning, de Wolfe," she said. "I hear that I am soon to have a new foal."

He nodded, watching her as she fingered some tiny, green sprouts coming out of the dead earth. "Indeed," he said. "Did Alexander tell you?"

She brushed off her hands and stood up. "He told me that a mare was giving birth and that you offered the foal to me," she said. "I accept. May I go and see the birth? Alexander seemed reluctant to take me."

Gates gave her a half-grin. "I do not suppose I could discourage you, either."

She shook her head. "As I told Alexander, I have seen birth before," she said. "I find it fascinating."

He cocked an eyebrow, perhaps in disapproval. "You would," he said, watching as she grinned. "Digging in dirt, watching a live birth… are you sure I cannot direct you to some more lady-like pursuits?"

"Like what?"

He lifted those enormous shoulders. "Painting," he said. "And sewing. Your mother makes beautiful tapestries. Mayhap she can teach you. Those would be much more lady-like pursuits, my lady."

The smile was fading from her face as he spoke as she thought of her mother and the woman's affliction. She even looked up to the keep as if seeing the woman through the gray stone walls. Rosamund had told her that no one knew of her affliction and Kathalin understood the need for discretion, but the fact that they had not made it to the apothecary in Shrewsbury did not deter her wanting to help her mother's disease. In fact, the discovery of the dead garden had been fortuitous because Kathalin had been thinking on asking permission to start such a thing. She could grow the ingredients necessary to help her mother. But now, she didn't have to start a garden at all but she would need help in growing it. She thought to let Gates in on her plans because she didn't trust anyone else to tell.

Even if he wouldn't marry her, she still trusted him.

"May I tell you something, de Wolfe?" she asked quietly.

He nodded, a look of hope and longing on his face that was quickly gone. "Of course."

Kathalin had seen the expression and her heart beat faster, just a little. It was difficult to be around the man and not feel that pull between them, that attraction that was undeniable. It was so powerful at times that it literally took her breath away.

"It is about my mother," she said, brushing the hair out of her eyes when the breeze blew it in her face. "How long have you known her?"

Gates pondered her question. "Since I began serving de Lara," he said. "It has been thirteen years, at least."

Kathalin considered that. "When was the last time you saw her?"

Again, he thought on her question. "Not since I have returned from France," he said. "Before that, I cannot say when the last time was."

Kathalin looked up at the keep again. "But when you saw her last, how was she dressed?"

He wasn't sure what she was getting at. "Dressed?" he repeated. "I do not know, to be truthful. I do not pay attention to things like that. I am sure she was dressed as she is always dressed, with layers of fabric covering everything, even her face. Why do you ask?"

"So you have always seen her dressed like that?"

He nodded. "Ever since I have served de Lara," he said. "Why do you ask?"

Kathalin drew in a long, deep breath, her eyes still fixed on the keep. "Because I must tell you something and you must swear to me that you will never, ever repeat it. If you did, the consequences could be quite terrible."

Now he was concerned. "What do you mean?" he asked. "What have you to tell me, Kathi?"

Kathi. He'd used that sweet name before, murmured in his beautiful baritone. But this time, the way he said it made her think that he meant she, personally, had something terrible to tell him. She hastened to reassure him.

"It is not about me," she said. "It is about my mother. You see... my mother is very ill, Gates. That is why you have never seen her without every part of her body being covered. She is sick and, being that I have been trained in healing, I have decided that I must help her. That is why I am out in this dead garden. I want to bring it back to life and grow herbs and flowers that might help her. I would like to try."

Gates was listening to her seriously, digesting her words. But he seemed confused. "That is a noble desire," he said. "However, you made it a point of telling me on our journey from St. Milburga's that you resented your parents a great deal. Something must have changed your mind if you seek to help the woman you spent years of your life resenting."

Kathalin nodded, averting her gaze. "You and I have not really spoken about anything since we arrived at Hyssington," she said, trying not to touch on the delicate subject of their feelings for each other but realizing it was unavoidable. "When we went to Shrewsbury, we spoke of... that is, we did not speak of anything other than what was important to us."

"My love for you."

It was like a blow to the gut, hearing those words from him, and she struggled to stay on subject. "Aye," she whispered. "And of my love for you. There was no time or opportunity to speak of the meeting I had with my parents before we left for Shrewsbury. I spent time with my mother, alone, and discovered a great many things, Gates. I discovered that she sent me away because she was falling ill and she did not wish for me or my brothers to contract her disease."

Gates' brow furrowed as he absorbed her words. "Disease?" he repeated, very concerned. "What disease?"

Kathalin reached out and grasped his gloved hands, clutching them tightly. "You must promise not to repeat what I am about to tell you."

He held her hands tightly, too, pulling her to him so they were standing quite close to one another. The first physical contact with her after five days of virtually no contact at all was enough to drive him to his knees.

"I swear to you that I will not tell a soul," he assured her softly, gazing down into her lovely face and absorbing the warmth of her body into his. "I swear on my oath as a knight. What disease does your mother have?"

Kathalin tilted her head back, looking up at him, realizing how very much she had missed the man. "She is a leper, Gates," she confessed. "My father keeps her bottled up in that room because he does not want anyone to know. Fear of what it would do to the family name drives him, and fear of the panic it would spread if the people around here knew. My poor mother… she told me so much, Gates, how she never sent missives to me because she did not want me to keep fond memories of home. I think she wanted me to hate her so I would never want to come back because if I did, I might catch her affliction. It was very hard for her to tell me all of this and I do not know if she told my father at all of our conversation, but I get the impression there is not much trust or affection between them. In any case, St. Milburga is the patron saint of lepers. Did you know that? It is as if God has had a hand in me returning home so that I can help my mother. I *want* to do it, Gates. Will you please help me?"

He lifted her hands, kissing them tenderly. "You know I will," he said hoarsely. "What would you have me do?"

She smiled up at him, now pressed against his body as he held her hands to his lips. Her entire body was running wild with warm, fluid feelings, causing her knees to tremble. The glory of the emotions between them was not something she could ignore; she knew he could not ignore them, either. There was too much there, something deep, anchored within them no matter how much they tried to ignore it or pretend it did not exist.

"I want to regrow this garden for herbs to help her," she said softly. "I want to return to St. Milburga's but not for the reasons you think; it is not to stay. It is because I know they have the finest herbs and flowers on the Marches, and I want to bring some of them here, to my garden. I want you to ask my father if we can return to St. Milburga's to collect such things."

He smiled faintly. "He will think you are trying to trick me into taking you back there."

She shook her head, her focus on his full lips, watching them move as he spoke. "Alas, that was true, once, but no longer," she said. "I can never go back. You are here at Hyssington. Even if... if we cannot be together, as one, if I remain here, I will still be near you. That is all I can ask."

Gates kissed her forehead as he caressed her hands. "I have been a fool," he said, his voice raspy. "I must ask for your forgiveness. My fears for you... fear that the sins of my past would shame you... I was wrong, Kathi. I have never faced a situation like this before, finding love with a woman, and I was reacting the only way I knew how. To save you from my shame by refusing to marry you but the truth is that I am a weak man. I cannot stomach the thought of you married to someone else, for it would surely be the end of me. The torment would be more than I can bear. When we came home from Shrewsbury and you stood up to Lord Linley, I suppose I knew then that I had not given you enough credit for your bravery. I suppose I did not trust your word. But I will trust you if you will trust me. If you will not run from my past, neither will I."

It was everything Kathalin had wanted to hear from him and tears of joy popped to her eyes. "I will never run," she swore softly. "I will never run from you, Gates. I will be as strong and true as the strongest man ever could be. I am yours and only yours, my love, until I die."

She threw her arms around his neck as Gates swallowed her up in his massive embrace, a searing kiss for the ages sealing the love and desire and trust between them. In fact, Gates had brought his mouth down on hers so hard that he had driven his teeth into his soft lower lip, and he could taste blood upon their kiss. *Sealed in blood*, he thought. *My love for this woman is sealed in my blood.*

"Are you sure?" he whispered between fevered kisses. "Are you utterly sure, sweetheart?"

Kathalin nodded even as he kissed her cheeks furiously. "Aye," she said. "So long as we are together, I can face anything, I swear it."

He believed her. His doubt was gone; his fear in what his past might bring to their marriage. Whatever it was, they could face it. Now, he knew he could face anything. He stopped his frenzied kisses and held her face between his two big hands, looking deeply into her eyes.

"Then I must speak to your father right away," he said. "Given what he knows about me and my past indiscretions, I am not entirely sure I will be able to coerce a marriage agreement out of him, but I will not give up. I swear, by God, that I will not give up."

Kathalin touched his cheek with her small, calloused hand. "I know you will not," she said. "But if he does not give his consent, what will you do?"

Gates kissed her cheek one last time before dropping his hands. "Then we will flee," he said simply. "I will marry you at the first church we come to and we will head north to my father at Castle Questing. Although I would hate to break my oath of fealty to de Lara, you are more important than even that. You are the most important thing in the world to me."

Kathalin was greatly relieved at his words, touched by the sincerity of them. "When will we go?"

He shrugged, hearing the iron gate groan as it was opened and taking a step back from her for propriety's sake. "I am not sure," he said. "Your father has invited all manner of fine houses here in the quest to find you a husband, so I would say we will leave very soon if I cannot convince him. Let me at least talk to him and see what kind of response he has. If it is favorable, well and good, but if it is not...."

Kathalin understood. She glanced over at the garden gate and noticed that Mary had returned. Even so, she couldn't keep the utter adoration out of her expression as she looked up at Gates.

The man I love.

"I will pray that my father gives his consent," she said softly. "I should like to remain here, as your wife, and grow my garden and tend to my mother. It would be a wonderful life, Gates, so long as you are with me. But if we must flee to your father… do you think he will let me have a garden?"

Gates laughed, a joyful sound, just as the servant woman came upon them. After that, their conversation was cut short, but it didn't matter. It had been the best conversation of his life, one that gave him more hope and joy than he'd ever known possible. It almost didn't matter to him whether or not Jasper agreed to a marriage; either way, he would have Kathalin as his wife and the fulfillment he felt at that thought was something he'd never experienced before.

Gates stepped away from the woman, heading out of the garden and determined to seek out Jasper, but all the while, his mind was rolling with thought. He'd spent his entire life living dangerously, whether on the battlefield or in a woman's bed. He'd found such excitement in both, but as he thought on it now, only his prowess on the battlefield had been the part of his life that had been personally satisfying. He was confident in his abilities and he felt invincible.

But in his personal life, that was different… bedding woman after woman, treating them as disposable commodities, as if he were looking for that one woman who wasn't disposable to him. That one woman who would fill the big hole he'd been trying to fill for a very long time, the hole that spoke of loneliness and the fear of death.

Aye, death. Gates loved life. He loved the thrill of it, the accomplishment of it. Death frightened him because he knew he hadn't done everything on earth that he wanted to do, and that included finding love with a good woman. It had been a secret dream, one he never fully acknowledged until this moment.

Now, he was living that dream.

The Dark Destroyer had finally found his mate.

CHAPTER FIFTEEN

"H ENRY!" JASPER SAID happily. "Welcome to Hyssington, my friend!"

Henry de Lohr was climbing out of his luxurious wagon, the one he and Elreda traveled in for any length of distance. It was enclosed and cushioned inside, keeping them comfortable and protected from the elements. Henry disembarked the rear of his wagon only to be greeted by Jasper's big hug.

"I am so happy to see you," Jasper said, hearing Henry grunt when he squeezed. He released the man. "It has been too long. You are looking well."

Henry rubbed his ribs where the eager Jasper had nearly broken them. He chuckled at Jasper's exuberance. "Thank you," he said. "As are you, old friend. It has indeed been too long."

Jasper pulled Henry out of the way as Alexander helped his mother out of the carriage. "Lady Elreda," Jasper greeted. "You are looking quite well today. Welcome to Hyssington."

Elreda smiled weakly; traveling always made her ill and she wasn't feeling particularly well, so Jasper's comment was a noble lie. "Thank you, Jasper," she said. "It is very agreeable to see you again."

Alexander smiled at his mother, his arm around her shoulders. "How about me?" he asked. "Isn't it agreeable to see me again, too?"

He squeezed his mother and kissed her cheek, loudly, to which

Elreda put her hand over his mouth. "Alexander," she hissed. "Behave yourself."

Jasper and Henry laughed at Alexander's enthusiasm when it came to his mother. Alexander kept trying to hug and squeeze the woman, but she didn't want to be pawed at. She finally pushed her son away by the face to loud laughter.

"Henry," she said. "Do something about your son. He has gone mad."

Henry wagged a finger at a grinning Alexander. "Leave your mother alone for now," he said. "You know how traveling disagrees with her. All of the manhandling you are doing will only make it worse."

Alexander went to his mother. "Then let me carry you into the hall, Mother," he said. "I will not let your feet touch the ground."

Elreda rolled her eyes and pushed past him. "Madness," she hissed. "Get him away from me. I am going inside!"

Jasper and Henry, still chuckling, followed the woman towards the hall as Alexander, grinning at his parents, ordered the de Lohr escort disbanded and arranged accommodations for the men. Stephan and Tobias had come forth to assist and, soon, the big carriage was moving for the livery and the fifty-man escort was being directed towards the troop house near the north side of the fortress.

Meanwhile, Jasper and his guests retreated into the great hall, which was surprisingly clean. Jasper, not wanting his guests, particularly the female guests, to be offended by the odor of urine and dogs, had the servants scrub the tables and floors with ash mixed with pine needles at the cook's suggestion. Most of his servants were male and scrubbing floors and tables wasn't something they relished doing, as that was women's work, but they'd done a fairly acceptable job nonetheless. By the time Jasper brought Henry and Elreda into the hall, it smelled mildly of smoke, with a whiff of dog, and not much else.

Sending a servant for refreshments for his guests, Jasper took them to the feasting table reserved for him, one with table legs that were actually stable, and had his guests sit. Small talk bounced about as servants brought pitchers of tart red wine with cups, pouring the first of what would be many cups of wine for the day. Another servant threw peat and some wood into the hearth, starting a fire to bring about some warmth, as Jasper settled in with a cup in his hand.

"Was your trip pleasant?" he asked. "It has been a long time since I have traveled south towards Lioncross. I have not seen it in many years. Has much changed?"

As Elreda sipped at the rich wine in the hopes of settling her stomach, Alexander answered before his father could.

"Lioncross has not changed in over one hundred and sixty years," he said. "Ever since the Defender of the Realm, the great Christopher de Lohr, took charge of it. He is buried in the small chapel there, you know. I think that subsequent generations feared that if they changed the fortress too much that he might rise, displeased, from his grave."

Henry snorted at his son's vivid imagination. "It is not as bad as all that," he insisted, "although there are rumors that he haunts the place. I think I even saw evidence of that, once."

Jasper was very interested. "Is that so?" he asked. "What did you see?"

Henry was thoughtful. "When I was a very young lad, I thought I saw the image of a big man with a beard standing near the hearth. He was there for a moment and then he vanished. I described him to my father and he said that I saw Christopher."

Jasper liked stories of ghosts and phantoms; he believed in them when the church frowned upon such things. "Interesting," he said. "I should like to see his phantom sometime. Hyssington, of course, is without such prestige. It is a very boring place. No excitement at all."

Henry sipped his wine. "I am sorry to hear that," he said. "But at least your daughter has come home. That should be some excitement, shouldn't it? When will we meet the young woman?"

Jasper's thoughts shifted from ghosts of legends past to Kathalin and the entire reason for his eagerness to speak with Henry and Elreda before the other guests arrived. He was hoping to have more informal conversation first, however, setting a warm and pleasant mood before delving into the entire purpose for their invitation to Hyssington. But the subject of Kathalin had revealed itself and Jasper felt compelled to take it. He kept thinking on what Rosamund had said – *we must marry her off quickly* – and that fed his courage. There was no time to delay if he wanted Kathalin's situation settled.

It was time to set the trap.

Briefly, his gaze moved to Alexander. His first instinct was to send the knight out of the hall so that he could speak privately with the parents but on second thought, perhaps it was best if Alexander remained. After all, it was his life, too, and from what he had seen over the past week, Alexander had gone out of his way to be polite with Kathalin and to speak with her. Perhaps a marital arrangement might be agreeable to Alexander if he thought Kathalin attractive enough.

If the dowry was big enough.

Even though Alexander had something of the same reputation that Gates had when it came to women, Jasper surmised that if Henry and Elreda were anything like him, as a parent, they were probably more than anxious to see their son wed and settled, especially in lieu of his reputation. Jasper was fairly certain they didn't want their son chasing women for the rest of his life.

He had to take that chance.

"You will meet her very soon," Jasper assured them, his gaze moving to Alexander. "Your son has already met her. What do you think of my daughter, Alex?"

Alexander smiled. "She is an intelligent young woman and a fine conversationalist," he said politely. "I have enjoyed coming to know her, my lord."

Jasper grinned. "Is she beautiful?"

Alexander spoke without hesitation. "I have never seen finer, my lord."

Pleased, Jasper looked to Henry and Elreda. "You heard it from your son," he said. "Alex would not lie. My daughter has returned from

St. Milburga's a lovely and educated woman. She will make any man a fine wife, which is why I want to speak with you before more guests arrive for our celebration. Since Alex has spent time with her, properly of course, and has extolled her virtues, I would like to bring forth the subject of a marriage between my daughter and your son. Surely Alex would have no objections to marrying my daughter since he has just told you that she is a beautiful and intelligent woman, and you, as his parents, must surely be eager to find your son a wife now that he is growing advanced in his age. He is your eldest son, Henry. Surely you would like grandchildren and heirs."

By the end of Jasper's speech, Alexander's eyes were so big that they threatened to burst from his skull but, to his credit, he said nothing. He didn't dare look at his parents because he knew they were surely savoring this proposal as one would savor fine food or fine wine; he knew they were fairly drooling over it. After the conversation Alexander and his parents had engaged in those few weeks ago when he'd returned from France, he was quite certain his mother was about to shout in victory.

A wife for Alexander!

Truth be told, as shocked as Alexander was, he realized immediately that he wasn't resistant to the idea. In fact, he was quite interested in it. But there was the small matter of the lady having no interest in him and a good deal of interest in Gates, and he in her. He thought on what it would mean to his relationship with Gates should he marry that woman that Gates was interested in, but then he reminded himself that Gates simply looked upon Lady Kathalin as another conquest.

That was the way Gates' mind worked. But Alexander... he didn't look at her as quite another conquest. He was interested in her more than that. He wasn't quite sure *what* more, as there hadn't been the time to develop those interests, but the interest was definitely there. He wasn't hesitant to explore it. And, perhaps in some way, he would be doing Lady Kathalin a favor in saving her from Gates de Wolfe's sexual appetite.

Aye, perhaps he would be saving her, indeed.

As Alexander pondered Jasper's proposal and the implications therein, Henry coolly considered Jasper's offer.

"This is so unexpected, Jasper," he said, looking at Elreda, who couldn't hide her delight. "A marriage offer, you say? Certainly we are very honored that you would consider the House of de Lohr but I believe it is something I must discuss with my wife before giving you an answer."

"We accept!" Elreda couldn't control herself. "We would be delighted to accept a marriage contract between your daughter and Alexander. We have prayed for such a thing! God has heard our prayers!"

"Wait!" Alexander couldn't keep silent; he stood up, looking at his parents as if they had gone mad. "Can we not discuss this first before you already have me married and with children? Mother, I know you are thrilled by this offer, but may we please discuss it first before you accept?"

"I will provide her with a dowry of five thousand silver marks," Jasper said, his offer directed at Alexander as an outright bribe. "I will sweeten the deal with another twenty gold crowns upon the event of the marriage and the gift of Chirbury Castle, a small garrison near Trelystan. 'Tis not much more than a pele tower, but it would be a good place for a young couple starting off their lives together. It would be yours, Alexander, provided you marry Kathalin."

Alexander stared at him a moment as he processed the great riches Jasper was promising him. "I know Chirbury," he said. "I have been there, many times. It is built on an older site, in fact. I remember one of the locals telling me that the Romans had an outpost there."

Jasper could see he had the man's interested and he hastened to capitalize on it. "I would supply you with men, of course, as garrison for my holdings, but the castle would belong to you," he said, watching the gleam in Alexander's eyes. "Alex, you have been around Kathalin enough to know that she has had some difficulty adjusting to life outside of St. Milburga's. In truth, it was a mistake to send her there as a child and never bring her home, or send her to other fine houses to foster, because all she knows is the way of life of a convent. I have every confidence that you, as her husband, can help introduce her into society and help her to become the wife she was born to be. I know you can do this, lad. Will you?"

Alexander swallowed hard, realizing that everyone was looking at him. He was torn between the attractiveness of the offer and thoughts of Gates. *Gates!* Surely the man was only after another conquest with the woman, wasn't he? Alexander realized there was some doubt in his mind because he kept asking himself the same question. He had known Gates a very long time and knew how the man worked, and his behavior with Kathalin had been different. Was it possible, then, that Gates actually felt something for Lady Kathalin? If that was the case, then Alexander would be snatching the woman right out from under him.

Would he *really* be saving her from him? Or would he be separating two people who were genuinely fond of one another?

"Your proposal is extremely generous, my lord," he finally said. "But I... I must think on it. May I have until tomorrow?"

Next to Alexander, Elreda shushed him. "Nonsense!" she said. "Jasper, we accept your proposal. We are grateful that you approached us first about this marriage and we accept with all our hearts. How does Rosamund feel about this? And where is your wife?"

Jasper kept glancing at Alexander, seeing his uncertainty, even though he answered Elreda. "It is Rosamund who suggested this match," he said. "Her illness keeps her confined but, of course, she sends her affection and best wishes to you both. Now, may I have my scribe draw up the contract? I cannot tell you how thrilled I am to know that our children will be joined in marriage. We will not only be friends but family now."

Elreda held up her cup to Jasper, metal against metal to seal the deal, as Henry eyed his subdued son. He assumed, naturally, that it was simply Alexander's general reluctance to marry and soon found himself swept up in the celebration between Jasper and Elreda. Still, there was something in Alexander's expression that kept him from celebrating completely. He wasn't sure what it was yet, but he would find out.

"Now, Jasper," Henry said, forcing his focus away from his son. "When will we meet our future daughter? I am eager to come to know her."

Jasper downed his cup of wine and poured himself more. "Alex," he said. "Please fetch Kathalin and bring her here, but tell her nothing of our plans. I should like to do that personally."

Alexander nodded his head and stood up, heading out of the hall. He was silent in his actions, dutiful, but his mind was racing. He was still reeling from what had happened, therefore, it wasn't Kathalin he would seek first.

It was Gates.

He found that he had to.

THE TROOP HOUSE was already crowded with the addition of de Lohr's men and Gates, after he left Kathalin in the garden, found himself lured to the situation by Tobias, who was trying to deal with it.

The troop house was designed to hold about six hundred men in beds built in doubles, one on top of the other, and even more men should they sleep on the floor. With the men that had returned with Gates from France, and now the addition of de Lohr's men, Gates and Tobias were forced to do some reorganizing. Many more men were expected, so the rope and wood bunks in the troop house were moved around to create more space for the incoming escorts.

Gates was in the process of supervising the shift in sleeping space when Alexander entered the troop house. He asked the men at the door where de Wolfe was and, following pointing fingers, he found Gates about midway in the structure as men moved furniture all around him.

Gates, who was trying to figure out a way to cram a lot of bodies into a finite space, caught sight of Alexander as the man approached.

"Did your parents arrive safely, then?" he asked.

Alexander smiled weakly. "They did," he said. "They are in the hall with Jasper now."

Gates smiled. "The last time I saw your mother, she wanted to know why I had not yet married and I seem to remember that she harassed you fairly stringently about your lack of a wife, too," he said. "Has she started in on you already about being unmarried or will she wait a polite amount of time before laying in to us both?"

Oh, God, Alexander thought. *If he only knew how close he was in that lightly-uttered jest.* "She has started already," he said. "In fact... I have a need to speak with you, Gates. Privately. Can you spare a moment?"

Gates didn't sense anything out of the ordinary. He didn't even notice Alexander's pale features or tense expression; the dimness of the troop house negated such observations. Leaving Tobias in charge of the grunting, heaving men, he followed Alexander outside in the daylight, blinking his eyes and shielding them because he'd been inside the dark troop house.

"God's Bones," he complained. "The Light of God is shining into my face and I am blinded by it."

He said it comically and Alexander laughed softly. "God is scrutinizing you, my friend."

Gates lifted an eyebrow in resignation as he blinked his eyes, becoming accustomed to the bright winter day. "If He looks too closely He will not be pleased," he said. "I try to avoid His scrutiny at all cost."

"Is that why you stay away from church?"

"It 'tis."

Alexander simply grinned at the glib reply but almost immediately, his smile faded. "Sorry to drag you out into the brilliant light, but there are things we must speak of," he said. "I hardly know where to start so it is best I start from the beginning. You and I have been friends for many years, Gates. I treasure those years and I treasure you."

Gates nodded his head. "As I treasure you also," he said, still not particularly sensing anything odd. "You have been annoying at times, and even frustrating, but it is true that I love you like I would a brother."

He was smiling as he said it but Alexander couldn't give in to the humor, not now. There were serious matters at hand. He looked at Gates; *really* looked at the man, trying to figure out the best way to speak of such things. He realized that he was quite nervous about it Hesitantly, he continued.

"Please do not be offended by whatever I say, for I am only speaking frankly and honestly, friend to friend," he said. "Gates, I must ask you something and you must be perfectly honest with me. It is imperative. Will you do this?"

Finally, Gates began to sense that something was off. There was something in Alexander's manner and in his words that told him so. Curious but not yet concerned, he nodded.

"Of course," he said. "I would never lie to you."

Alexander nodded swiftly. "I know," he said. "But this is different. What I am about to ask you is personal."

"Then ask."

Alexander swallowed hard, hung his head, and then lifted his eyes to Gates in a manner that suggested he was truly reluctant to speak. But he did. "It is about Kathalin," he said softly. "Are you attempting to make another conquest out of the woman?"

Gates' expression flickered. It seemed at first as if he was startled by the question, which he was, but he quickly steadied himself. When he replied, his answer was slow and deliberate.

"I am not," he said. "Why do you ask?"

"Because I sense that you have interest in her and she in you," Alexander said. "Is this true?"

Gates didn't say anything for a moment. He sighed faintly and averted his gaze. "I will again ask you why you are asking me this."

Alexander could tell, by Gates' expression, that there was indeed something between Gates and Kathalin. He knew Gates well enough to know his moods and expressions, and he saw something in Gates' features that told him what he needed to know. Still, he wanted to hear the confirmation from Gates' own lips. He was starting to grow frustrated by the man's evasive answers.

"Because I must know," Alexander said, lowering his voice. "Gates, I have known you for many years. You are my friend. I have seen you bed woman after woman with hardly an afterthought when all was said and done. Lord Linley showed up last week announcing that his daughter had borne your bastard, an allegation that I can only imagine is true considering you took the woman to your bed before we left for France. I know this because I was with you when we found her in the streets of Churchstoke, starving to death. You have never, since I have known you, shown any serious interest in any woman. I must know if your interest in Lady Kathalin is serious or if it is simply a passing fancy. Will you please tell me the truth?"

Gates wasn't fully prepared to divulge the information, mostly because it was frightening and alien to him to realize that he was, indeed, actually in love with a woman. It was the first time someone had asked him that question and the first time he'd truly given thought to it. There was some embarrassment there, too, as if fearful he would not be believed given his reputation. He didn't want to be doubted or ridiculed. But he knew Alexander and knew that that the man wouldn't totally discount him, especially since he had sworn to tell him the truth.

The truth....

"She is not a passing fancy," he finally said, quietly. "You have asked me to be truthful with you and I shall. Alex, you know me – you know I would not say something unless I truly knew it, believed it, or felt it, and in this case I can tell you that Lady Kathalin is not a passing fancy. She has declared her love for me and I love her in return. I am not entirely sure how it happened, but it has. We were fighting each other one moment and adoring each other the next. You have asked for truth and I have given it to you. Now, will you tell me why you have asked?'

Alexander looked at Gates, a somewhat sickly expression on his face. "I see," he murmured. "And... you are sure of this, Gates?"

"Very sure."

"What do you intend to do about it? Do you intend to marry her?"

Gates nodded. "I was going to speak to Jasper today of it before the parade of potential bridegrooms arrive," he said. "Given what Jasper knows of me and my reputation, I am not entirely sure how receptive he will be, but it is my intention to ask for Kathalin's hand and not give up until I have it."

Alexander was looking at him with a huge amount of sadness in his expression. In fact, his hand was over his heart, unconsciously, as if to hold in his sorrow.

"And if you do not receive his blessing?"

"I will deal with that if the time comes."

Alexander held Gates' gaze for a long, tense moment before exhaling in a long, harsh breath. He nearly doubled over with it, bracing himself against his knees as he labored to catch his breath. Gates watched him, trying not to feel too much fear. Something was amiss with Alexander, something that had to do with his feelings for Kathalin, and he was increasingly concerned about Alexander's reaction to it. Finally, he could stand it no longer.

"Alexander, in the name of God," he said. "Why have you been asking about my feelings for Kathalin? I have asked you more than once and you have not answered me. What is amiss?"

Alexander stood up straight, looking at Gates with perhaps the most sorrowful expression Gates had ever seen. It seemed, when he spoke, that he was on the verge of tears.

"I did not know, Gates," he said hoarsely. "I suspected that there was some interest between you two, but I did not realize the depths of it. Please forgive me. I did not realize you loved her."

Gates took a few steps towards him, closing the gap between them. "Forgive you for *what*?" he hissed. "Alex, start making sense. What is going on?"

Alexander put out his hands and grasped Gates by the arms. "Jasper has made an offer of marriage to my parents," he said, gazing into Gates' stunned eyes. "A contract between me and Lady Kathalin. My parents have accepted."

Gates stared at the man, hearing his words, understanding them, but not truly grasping what he was being told for several very long moments.

"You... you are betrothed to Kathalin?" he finally asked.

Alexander nodded, anguish on his face. "Aye," he muttered. "It is true that I think she is beautiful and it is true that even though I saw of your interest in her, I thought you were only looking for another conquest. But it soon began to occur to me that your interest went beyond a conquest. That is why I had to find you and ask you, Gates. I will refuse the contract now, of course, but you must tell Jasper your feelings for her and you must demand her hand. We must go to Jasper now, together, and do this. That way he will know that I relinquish my claim."

Gates was starting to feel quite emotional about the situation. The shock of the betrothal and the realization that Alexander was fully willing to relinquish any claim on Kathalin, a legal claim that would supersede anything Gates had to offer, had him reeling. But it was then that he began to understand the depths of his friendship with Alexander, a man he had been viewing as a serious threat for the past few weeks when it came to Kathalin. He had seen how the man had looked at her and he had been nearby when Alexander had spoken to her, at least for the most part. Jealousy had filled his veins when it came to Alexander. But now, seeing how Alexander was willing to sacrifice his right for the sake of Gates' love for Kathalin, Gates was starting to feel like a monster.

"You would do that?" he asked, incredulous. "You would give up what was surely a very attractive offer because of me?"

Alexander nodded. "Aye," he replied. "Gates, I could not marry the woman knowing you loved her. It would not be right."

Gates lingered on the words, on the nobility of Alexander's attitude. He was deeply stunned but also deeply touched. "But...," he ventured, "I truly have no idea what to say to all of this. I am genuinely speechless."

Alexander simply lifted his shoulders. "If the situation was reversed, could you marry the woman I loved?"

Gates shook his head. "Of course not," he said. "But I... I must admit something. I have seen you with Kathalin over the past few days and I have seen when you've spoken to her, and I will admit that my heart was full of jealousy. I have never known such feelings before and they were difficult to stomach. I feel like such a fool for having been jealous. What you are doing now... this gesture of unselfishness... it is the greatest sacrifice I have ever known. But I must ask you a question, Alexander, for my own sake... are you sure you want to do this?"

"It would mean nothing to me knowing that I made you miserable. No bride, nor dowry, is worth that kind of anguish."

"Then you are positive?"

"Absolutely." Alexander eyed him a moment, trying to read his mood. "You are not angry with me? Or my parents?"

Gates shook his head. "Why should I be?" he asked. "None of this was done to spite me."

Alexander sighed, with great relief. "Nay, it was not," he said. "But I still thought you would take my head off for this. I was fully prepared to run for my life."

Gates could see how shaken Alexander was. This situation had him reeling just as it had Gates reeling. To share such a thing with Alexander was a bonding moment almost as much as battle had been. Truly, they were brothers in many respects.

"I would never be angry with you about this," he said. "You did not invite this betrothal. We know that this entire coming celebration has been to entice unattached men to vie for Kathalin's hand; Jasper has made no secret of his intentions. Nay, Alex, I cannot blame you for anything. But does Kathalin know any of this?"

Alexander shook his head. "Jasper sent me to fetch her to meet my parents but instead I came to find you," he said. "Jasper is expecting her in the hall."

Gates' attention moved towards the great hall situated on the south side of the fortress. "Are your parents still with him?"

"They were when last I saw them."

Gates quickly considered the situation and his options. "I do not want Kathalin to go into the hall just now, for obvious reasons," he said. "She is still in the garden. I will go and tell her to retreat to her chamber and then you will go to the hall and tell Jasper that I need his counsel. Bring him to me in the gatehouse, in my chamber there. We will speak with him then, in private and away from your parents. We must do it before he makes any announcements or arrangements."

Alexander nodded as the two of them began heading in the direction of the hall. "If I know my mother, she is already writing missives to relatives, inviting them to my wedding," he said, eyeing Gates. "She will be greatly disappointed, Gates. I am doing all of this at the risk of upsetting my mother, who has been known to become quite irate when provoked. You will have to stay away from her for a time when she finds out I refused this marriage for you."

They reached the point in the bailey where Gates would split off and head for the garden. He paused, facing Alexander.

"Mayhap she will understand that you refused on the basis of true love," he remarked, walking away, still facing Alexander, even as he headed for the garden gate behind him. "Not many men would do what you are doing. Surely she cannot become overly upset about that."

Alexander lifted his eyebrows ominously. "You do not know my mother very well."

"Then tell her I shall name my first daughter after her," he said. "Mayhap that will soothe her."

Alexander shook his head and turned for the hall. "It will not work," he said. "She will only say that your daughter should have been *her* grandchild."

Gates grinned as he came to a halt. "Mayhap," he said, his expression becoming soft with gratitude. "Thank you, Alex. For this... for what you are about to do... you have my deepest thanks."

Alexander, a normally arrogant man, seemed uncharacteristically reserved. "You would do it for me."

"Aye, I would."

Alexander simply smiled, as if that was good enough for him, and turned in the direction of the hall. Gates watched him go for a moment before turning around and making haste for the walled garden. He debated how much to tell Kathalin about the situation and opted, out of fairness to her, to tell her everything. She needed to know what her father had done, and who Henry and Elreda de Lohr were, so she would not be blindsided by any comments or confusion regarding a broken betrothal. It was only right she know the conflict she might be facing.

Nervous.

He felt nervous, edgy that Jasper had already betrothed Kathalin to his good friends and allies, the de Lohrs, and edgy that Jasper would not back down when confronted by him and by Alexander. Jasper was a stubborn man and did not like to be questioned, and Gates was more than certain he was going to have an uphill battle convincing Jasper that he would make a fine husband for Kathalin. Even without the de Lohr betrothal, the task was going to prove difficult. Now, he had even more of an obstacle than simply his roguish reputation.

Your sins will find you out.

He wasn't quite sure why he thought of those words at just that moment, but somehow, they seemed appropriate. He's spent most his adult life running from one sin to another, breaking hearts and leaving sadness in his wake. Perhaps those sins were about to catch up to him when Jasper denied his suit for Kathalin, punishment from God for all of those years of being selfish. He and God had never had a particularly good relationship, as he'd told Alexander, but it wasn't as if he hated God or had no use for Him. It was simply that he didn't much care so he went through life doing as he pleased.

Now, that lack of faith and respect for living a pious and clean life was about to catch up to him. He just had a very bad feeling about all of it.

A bad feeling that his sins were about to find him out.

And punish him.

CHAPTER SIXTEEN

WHAT DO GIRLS daydream for when they marry? A home? A handsome husband? Do they wish for babies? I think I would like to have a garden... and I would like for our home to be near a church where I can teach Bible stories to the children. And mayhap I would like for my mother to come with us. She does not seem happy here, confined as she is. Mayhap if she comes with us, I can help her affliction. Mayhap I will come to know her better... is there hope that we could even become close?

All of these thoughts were running through Kathalin's head as she crouched next to a sprig of lavender that was trying desperately to come to life. After Gates had left her, she had continued assessing the garden but her thoughts wandered to the inevitable ideas of the future with Gates. *He loved her.* She was still overwhelmed with their conversation, with the reality of the situation, and it was something that brought a smile to her face even as she fussed with the dirt and dead weeds.

It was true!

Never in her life had she dreamed of a home and family, or of a husband, but over the past few weeks her life had changed so drastically that she was now thinking of such things. Truthfully, it wasn't hard to feel happy about it, either. Even though she was not going to return to St. Milburga's to take her vows, she truly didn't mind at all. She considered Gates a fair trade-off. As she'd told him, she could never go back to St. Milburga's now that they had declared their feelings for each other. It was so strange that her entire outlook on life had changed so much to the point where St. Milburga's was no longer her location of preference.

It was wherever Gates happened to be.

Gates. Her smile grew as she thought of him, of his massive shoulders and powerful arms. He had a smile that lit up the room as if the sun itself was shining down upon them, and his voice... God's Bones, his voice was smooth and deep, like the finest wine. She could drink it all day and all night. She couldn't even remember the days when she had sworn to hate the man, when he had dragged her out of St. Milburga's bound hand and foot. At this moment, the man she had met at St. Milburga's seemed like a totally different person, certainly not the man she had warmed up to and fallen in love with.

Life was funny that way.

As she daydreamed of a future with her chosen knight and inspected the little, green growth in the dirt at her feet, the garden gate opened again. She could hear it creak and slam back against the wall. Turning, she saw that Gates had returned and she stood up, happy to see him once again, her heart fluttering wildly in her chest at the sight of him. He was back so soon but it also seemed as if he had been gone an eternity. Any time away from him now seemed like forever. Brushing the dirt off her hands, she made her way towards him.

"Well?" she demanded softly, conscious that Mary, the servant, was still in the garden, over in the corner helping identify the shoots. "Did you speak with my father?"

Gates looked at her, the hopeful expression on her face, and he felt incredibly sad. The entire walk over to the garden, he had felt nothing but determination and confidence, but now that he saw Kathalin's expression, that determination and confidence was joined by sorrow. He was so very sorry for what he had to tell her, sorry for the upset it would undoubtedly cause.

Even though he wasn't entirely sure how Jasper would respond to his plea for Kathalin's hand now that the de Lohrs held the marital contract, he was fairly certain Jasper wouldn't jump for joy. There was some doubt there, as there had always been, but he didn't want Kathalin to see it. It was imperative she see his positive attitude, as if they could conquer the world together, Jasper included.

Reaching out, he took her hand and began to lead her to a stone bench over near the western wall of the garden.

"Come with me," he said quietly.

Kathalin eagerly took his hand. "Gladly," she said. "What did my father say?"

Gates didn't say anything for a moment. "I have not yet spoken to him," he said as he took her to the bench. "I have not yet had the opportunity. I have, however, just come from a very interesting conversation with Alex that you and I must discuss. It concerns us both."

Kathalin held on to his hand tightly with both of hers. He didn't seem concerned as he spoke but she was naturally curious. "What do you and I have to do with Alexander?" she asked.

They reached the bench, partially shaded by a winter-dead birch tree. He indicated for her to sit. "As of an hour ago, quite a bit," he told her, sitting down beside her. He continued to hold her hand, gazing into those bright blue eyes and starting to feel some angst. It was a struggle to control it. "As you know, your father has arranged for a celebration in honor of your return from St. Milburga's with the purpose of finding you a husband. This is already an established fact."

The pleasant expression on her face faded. "I know," she said. "But why do you mention this? Has something happened to this regard?"

She was starting to get excited and he shushed her gently. "Nothing has happened as far as the celebration is concerned," he said, being careful in how he delivered the following information. "As far as I know, it is still going on as planned. In fact, Alex's parents arrived a short time ago and it would seem that your father has already made up his mind on who you should marry."

Her eyes widened. "He *what?*" she gasped. "How is this possible?"

"That is simple," he said, lowering his voice. "The de Lohrs have an eligible son. He has arranged for you to marry Alex."

Kathalin's reaction was instant. "*De Lohr?*" she said in outrage. "I cannot believe it!"

Gates held on to her hands tightly in an effort to keep her seated on the bench so she wouldn't run off in a fit. It was imperative that she remain calm and listen to him, as he was trying very hard to stay calm himself.

"It is true," he said quietly. "Alex came to tell me himself. He was there when your father made the offer to his parents and, according to Alex, his parents have accepted the contract."

Kathalin simply stared at him, her features a mask of grief and horror. It seemed as if she wanted to protest more, to yell more, to deny further what she had been told, but she couldn't muster the will. She knew that Gates would not lie to her about such a thing. As realization dawned, the horror left her expression and grief was all that was left. She shook her head, slowly.

"It cannot be," she said hoarsely. "Please tell me this is a mistake."

"It is not."

"A misunderstanding, then!"

Gates sighed, caressing her hands. "I wish I could tell you that it was," he said softly. "But it is the truth. You have been betrothed to Alex."

Kathalin held his gaze a moment longer before closing her eyes against the devastating news and hanging her head in sorrow. "Oh, Gates," she whispered. "This cannot be possible. I cannot believe my father has done this already. I thought we would have time… he spoke of finding me a husband but he never mentioned he already had someone in mind. And my mother – she said that she would give me the opportunity to give final approval over anyone they selected. Do you think she knows about this?"

Gates could only shrug his shoulders. "I do not know, sweetheart," he said, feeling the anguish radiating from her. The sorrow was in her very veins, flowing through her and into him as he held her hands. "But let me speak on what Alex and I discussed; he came to me after Jasper made the offer and wanted to know what my feelings were for you. It seems that I have not been very discreet in my attentions towards you, sweetheart. Even though he already suspected, I told him the truth, that we love one another, and he has told me that he will refuse the contract. He does not wish to interfere in our feelings for one another. It is now our intention to go to Jasper whereupon Alex will refuse the marriage and I will ask for your hand. Between the two of us, I think we can convince Jasper to give his permission for us to wed. That is the plan, in any case, so I do not want you to lose heart. Promise me you will not despair."

Kathalin was having great difficulty finding any hope in what he was saying. In fact, she was more upset over the fact that her mother gave her false hope that she would be able to approve a husband. That underlying fact seemed to eat at her.

"Then she lied to me," Kathalin said. "My mother told me that I would have approval over a husband. She lied to me about it."

Gates wondered if she even heard half of what he had said. "She may not have been given a choice," he said. "Jasper may have acted without her consent or knowledge. Until you hear her side of it, do not be too quick to judge. Meanwhile, I want you to go up to your chamber and remain there until I come for you. I must have this out with your father and I need to know you are safely tucked away. Can you do this for me?"

She looked at him, confusion now mixed in with her grief. "Why must I be safely tucked away?"

He lifted hands, kissing them. "Because I do not trust what your father will do at this point," he said. "He already surprised us with a betrothal to Alex and I do not want to return from my discussion with him to find out you have been stolen off to Lioncross Abbey. Technically, you belong to the House of de Lohr now and I do not want to find that they have taken you away. Therefore, go to your chamber, lock yourself in, and do not open it for anyone but me. Is that clear?"

She nodded seriously. "Not even Alexander?"

"Especially not him."

Kathalin nodded in understanding, feeling incredibly devastated and disoriented by the situation. "Very well," she said, depressed and struggling not to tear up. "Then I will go and await word from you. Do you really think you can convince my father to change his mind, Gates? You said once before that he might not consider it given your reputation, but now that he has approached de Lohr with a marriage contract...?"

She trailed off and Gates endeavored not to let his doubt show. *Confidence!* He told himself. He had to appear confident, if only for Kathalin's sake.

"Your father is rash at times but he is not daft," he said. "He will listen to reason."

"And if he does not, we will leave together and ride north, won't we?" she insisted, seeking an affirmative answer. "Ultimately, it does not matter what my father says. We will still run away and be married."

Gates heard his words reflected in her statement and, as she said them, he suddenly felt sick in the pit of his stomach. He had made that declaration assuming she would not be betrothed to anyone and most definitely not to Alexander. But the situation had changed, decidedly; were he to run off with the legal bride of Alexander de Lohr, the consequences could be devastating for them all.

First and foremost, Alexander would be shamed. It would be slander against him for another man, and especially a friend, to abscond with his bride whether or not Alexander wanted to marry the woman. The fact remained that she belonged to him. The House of de Lohr as well as the House of de Lara would have every reason to come after them, to wage war on the House of de Wolfe, and they'd have every right to take back what belonged to them. Gates could end up in the vault at Lioncross, or worse, and Kathalin would be returned to the

House of de Lara in shame. The House of de Lohr would not want her after that, assuming she was compromised. She would be returned to her father and there was no telling what Jasper would do with her after all of that.

A quick marriage could avoid some of that because not even the church would intervene to dissolve a marriage, but that would not prevent the House of de Lohr and the House of de Lara from forever being at odds with the House of de Wolfe. De Wolfe and de Lohr had been allies for over one hundred and sixty years, very close allies in fact. If Gates were to run off with a de Lohr bride, all of that would be ruined.

Ruined....

Gates' mind was swimming with the consequences of his actions. Would he shame a man who would willingly sacrifice a good deal for him simply to marry the woman that he loved? Would he destroy one hundred and sixty years of allegiance over a marriage? Torn, and increasingly distressed over the situation, he pulled Kathalin to her feet.

"I intend to make sure that we do not have to take drastic action if your father denies us," he said, evading her question because he really didn't have an answer. "For now, please do as I say. Return to your chamber and remain there until I return for you. In fact, I will walk you to the keep and watch you go inside. Come along, now."

Kathalin stood up as he gently pulled on her. "Will you speak with him now?"

"I will."

"And if he denies you?"

"I will not surrender, not in the least."

Kathalin didn't press him after that. He seemed resolute but he also seemed lost to his own thoughts. She held on to him tightly as they made their way through the dead garden, ignoring the chill breeze and the dark clouds that were now starting to gather overhead. The sun was disappearing behind the clouds as if to signify that all was not sunny or well in their world.

Now, the situation had markedly changed and there was a massive problem to overcome. Depression, and heartache, lingered between them even though Gates struggled to fight it off. He had a battle to fight, more powerful than any battle he had ever waged, and he was determined to come out the victor.

The stakes were high in this battle, much more than he'd ever faced. There was a prize to be had here, a prize held close to his heart, and he labored not to let his emotions get the better of him. Emotions, in battle, could be deadly, and this was a battle he fully intended to win.

God help him, there was no alternative.

"WHAT ON EARTH is the matter with you, Alex?" Jasper demanded as Alex practically manhandled him across the bailey towards the gatehouse. "What is so important that I must see Gates?"

Alexander was trying not to divulge too much about the purpose of the meeting with Gates. After he and Gates has gone their separate ways, Gates to the garden to find Kathalin and Alexander to the great hall to find Jasper, Alexander hadn't particularly wanted to see his parents again, or explain why he had not brought Kathalin with him, so he waited outside of the hall hoping that Jasper would, at some point, emerge. He stood there long enough to see Gates and Kathalin leave the garden, but still, no Jasper. He considered sending a soldier inside to bring the man to him.

As Alexander contemplated how to lure Jasper out of the great hall, he watched Kathalin head into the keep while Gates had headed for the gatehouse. Once Alexander saw Gates enter the gatehouse, he knew that time was growing short and he was seriously considering summoning a soldier to extract Jasper from the great hall. Fortunately, he didn't have to follow through on that plan because Jasper abruptly quit the great hall nearly the moment Gates disappeared into the gatehouse. He was alone, without Henry or Elreda, so Alexander immediately pounced and told him that Gates had an urgent need to speak with him.

Jasper had been somewhat reluctant, at first, to divert from his own plans because he was on his way to see Rosamund and tell her of the betrothal, but Alexander pleaded urgency in the case of Gates, who had something very important to speak with his liege about. Given that Gates was his commander, and wouldn't send Alexander with a message of importance if, in fact, it was not critical, Jasper switched direction and headed towards the gatehouse where the knights both slept and conducted business. It wasn't until he was near the gatehouse that he realized Alexander was holding on to him, leading him. He tried to yank his arm out of Alexander's grip with no success.

"Let go of me," he demanded. "Answer my question – what does Gates wish to discuss?"

Alexander didn't want to divulge anything, not until they were in Gates' chamber and Gates himself broached the subject, so he simply shook his head. "I am unsure of what, exactly, Gates intends to discuss first," he said, a lie. However, he was more concerned with maintaining his grip on his squirrely liege at the moment, fearful that the man would get away. "But he sent me to find you with the utmost haste."

Jasper grunted in frustration, giving his arm one last yank and pulling free of Alexander's grasp just as they reached the gatehouse. The structure had two staircases, one on either side of the entry area, and Jasper headed up the narrow spiral stairs on the north side of the gatehouse.

Passing through the skinny stairwell, he entered the second floor of the gatehouse, which was the portcullis room. There was a slit in the floor where the portcullis lifted to admit those passing through the gatehouse entry below. There were four chambers on this level on either side of the portcullis room and Gates occupied one of them.

The door to Gates' chamber was open when Jasper and Alexander appeared. Gates was standing near the thin lancet window that overlooked the main entry into Hyssington. There was a hearth that had just been kindled, kicking out bursts of smoke into the room as the flame caught on. Gates was in the process of removing his heavy woolen outer tunic when Alexander and Jasper entered.

"Gates!" Jasper boomed. "What is so important that you would have Alexander drag me across the bailey in his haste to bring me to you? Well?"

Gates pulled the tunic over his head. "Did Alex tell you anything at all?"

Alexander answered for Jasper. "I have not," he said. "I thought it would be best coming from you."

Jasper frowned at his knights. "*What* would be best?" he said, looking between the two. "Why are you two being so secretive?"

Gates tossed his tunic onto the bed and indicated the only chair in his chamber, a stool with a back built onto it. It wasn't comfortable in the least but it was enough to hold Jasper's weight.

"Sit, my lord," he said. "There is something of great import we must speak of. Please be comfortable."

Jasper was still frowning in exasperation. He put his beefy hands on his hips. "I will *not* sit," he said. "I have my own business to attend to, Gates, and have no time for foolishness. What is this all about?"

Gates didn't like that, already, Jasper was impatient. It didn't bode well for the conversation in general. "This may take more than a few minutes, my lord," he said. "Please sit for a moment so we may discuss the subject comfortably."

Jasper scowled. "*What* subject?" he said. "Tell me what you wanted to speak of *now*."

He wasn't going to make this easy. Gates didn't want to anger the man before the conversation even started but already it was heading in that direction! Jasper had been irked from the beginning and now it was growing worse with Gates' attempts to turn this into a calm and civil conversation. Already, Gates was feeling apprehensive and as he quickly determined the best way to broach the subject, Alexander spoke.

"My lord, I will tell you," he said. He could see how difficult Jasper was going to make this for Gates and he hastened to intervene. "This has to do with my betrothal to your daughter. Although I am deeply honored that you would consider me as a husband for Lady Kathalin, the truth is that I have no interest in a wife. My parents were hasty in accepting the betrothal for it is something that, after careful consideration, I must decline. I cannot, in good conscience, marry Lady Kathalin because she is in love with someone else. It would not be fair to me and it certainly would not be fair to her. My lord, if you wish for your daughter to be happy in the least, then you cannot marry her to a man she does not love. I will, therefore, not marry her."

Jasper's exasperation turned to surprise, suspicion, and back to surprise again. He faced Alexander with an expression of great confusion.

"What's this you say?" he said. "She is in *love*? Damnation, who could she possibly be in love with?"

"Me," Gates said softly, watching Jasper turn to him with wide eyes. "Your daughter and I are in love, my lord. Before you betrothed her to Alexander, I was summoning the courage to offer for her hand. My lord, I know that I do not have the most sterling reputation when it comes to women. I know that I have been reckless in the past, and even distasteful at times, and it was never in my mind or heart to marry any woman, ever. But your daughter has changed that for me. She is a kind, brave, and loyal woman and I would consider it the greatest honor in the world to be her husband. I swear to you that my wild ways would be ended. I would love her, and only her, until my death. I therefore beseech you to allow me to marry your daughter, as Alexander has relinquished his claim."

By the time he was finished, Jasper was staring at him in utter shock. Gates stared back, his heart pounding in his ears, more anxious at this particular moment than he had ever been in his life. Before Jasper could reply, however, Alexander spoke again.

"I cannot stand in the way of their love, my lord," he said, a hint of pleading in his tone. "Gates is a dear and close friend. I could not marry your daughter knowing that he loves her. Gates is a man of his word and if he says that he will be true to her until his death, then I believe him. He has never lied to me before. Men *can* change, my lord. I believe love can change Gates, if it has not already."

Jasper was truly stunned. He was still looking at Gates even as Alexander spoke on Gates' behalf, both men beseeching Jasper to consider Gates' offer. Oddly enough, considering his impatient stance since entering the chamber, Jasper seemed to cool dramatically. He finally averted his gaze and sighed heavily, planting himself in the chair that Gates had previously offered him. He leaned against the back of the chair, hand to his forehead in both a contemplative and overwhelmed gesture.

"You *love* her?" he finally repeated, looking to Gates. "Is this really true, lad?"

Gates nodded. "I do," he said. "And she loves me. We wish to be married."

Jasper was staring at him again as if hardly believing what he was hearing. "God's Blood," he finally hissed. "This is a surprise. I would have never expected to hear this, not from you. Gates, I trusted you with escorting my daughter from St. Milburga's and now that I hear you have feelings for her, I am extraordinarily concerned to know that you did not act on any feelings while you were in a position of power guarding my daughter. You may as well be honest with me now because, sooner or later, the truth will be known and if I do not hear it from your lips first, you will not like my reaction."

Even as he spoke, Gates was shaking his head. "Never," he said firmly. "Never at any time did I touch your daughter in the manner you are suggesting. My attentions towards her on the ride from St. Milburga's to Hyssington were strictly professional. I would never violate your trust in such a way, my lord."

"Swear this to me."

"On my oath as a knight, I swear it."

Being that Gates was an honorable knight, at least on the battlefield, Jasper believed him but he was still wildly off-balance with the entire situation. "It is well known that you are not one to pass over a lady you find attractive," he said. "You are an opportunist, Gates. I have known this for many years. God's Blood, Helene of Linley is a perfect example of that. Did you not tell me that you found her starving in the streets so you fed her? And to show her appreciation, she succumbed to her lustful desires?"

Gates cleared his throat softly. "It wasn't exactly like that," he said quietly. "What happened... it simply happened. I have no other explanation for it."

Jasper eyed him critically. "What of the sister of that knight from Halford?" he asked. "Did she simply happen, too? You were forced to kill that knight when he ambushed you, which brought an entire Welsh garrison down upon us for a week."

By this time, Gate was struggling not to become defensive. "I know, my lord."

Jasper waited for more of an explanation or apology to come forth but Gates gave no hint of either. In fact, Gates was rather stone-faced, which raised Jasper's ire.

"Have you nothing more to say to that?" he demanded.

Gates remained cool. "What would you have me say, my lord?"

Jasper was starting to become frustrated again. "Tell me something, de Wolfe," he said. It was rare when he addressed Gates by his surname, an indication of his annoyance. "If you had a daughter and a knight of your reputation asked for her hand in marriage, what would *you* say?"

Gates was struggling to keep his emotions at bay because he knew that if he didn't, this could very easily turn into a shouting match. He swallowed hard.

"I would not insult him by doubting his oath when he told me he would be true to her until his death," he said pointedly. "If it was a man I had known as long as you have known me, I would trust him."

Jasper snorted. "Trust him," he muttered, shaking his head. "My daughter's happiness is at stake and you ask me to trust you."

Alexander, who had been watching the exchange, wasn't happy about the way Jasper was ridiculing Gates' oath of honor. It was inexcusable as far as he was concerned. Gates had little honor where women were concerned, that was true, but as a knight of duty, he was flawless in character. It was a genuine paradox in one man, but such was the complexity of Gates de Wolfe.

"I am not entirely sure you are concerned with your daughter's happiness if you are willing to see her parted from the man she loves," Alexander said, watching the outrage on Jasper's face. "Is that not what you are attempting to do, now that you know she and Gates love one another? How happy do you think she will be if you force her to marry me?"

Jasper scowled at Alexander. "It is her future I must think of," he said hotly. "I must ensure she is married to a man who will not embarrass her, although I must say, Alex, that you have had a woman or two in your time. Still, you are marginally better than de Wolfe."

Gates sighed heavily, with great displeasure. He was genuinely trying to keep his mouth shut, to not say what was on his mind, but he couldn't quite manage it. His emotions were beginning to surface.

"You do not care for her happiness at all," he said. "If you did, you would have at least had contact with her while she was at St. Milburga's. You do not care for her at all so for you to say that you are concerned with her happiness is a lie and we all know it. You are more concerned in how your decision will bring shame upon the de Lara name."

Jasper cooled dramatically, holding up a warning finger in Gates' direction. "Careful, knight," he growled. "You border on slander. Insulting me is not the way to get what you want."

Gates took a deep breath and turned away, raking his fingers through his dark hair as he composed himself. "I apologize," he said. "I... I am quite emotional when it comes to Kathalin. Forgive me, my lord. I did not mean it."

It was enough to soothe Jasper, who was just as torn as Gates was. At least marginally he was soothed, but his guts were wrought with turmoil. He stood up from the chair, grunting, and obviously unhappy.

"Mayhap there is some truth in what you say," he admitted after a moment. "But whether or not there is, Kathalin is my daughter and I must do what is best for her. Gates, if I let you marry her, she will be a laughing stock. You *know* this. Everyone who knows of your reputation will think I have gone mad and pity her because she married a knight who has warmed women's beds from Dover to Carlisle. She will look like a fool and so will I. Do I trust your word when you say you will be true to her? It is a fact that I do. You are not a liar. You are a great knight, a powerful and cunning knight, one who has helped see my troops to victory on many occasions. I cannot get on without you. But allowing you to marry my daughter... I cannot say that I will agree to that. In good conscience, I cannot."

Gates' heart sank. As he scratched his head, pondering a reply, Alexander interjected. "I will not marry her, my lord," he said firmly. "Do not think that I will have her if you will not allow Gates to marry her."

Jasper looked at Alexander. "Then if not you, I will find another," he said coldly. "I offered the contract to the House of de Lohr because of my long affection for your parents, but if you refuse, I can just as easily find someone who will not."

Alexander knew that was true. Jasper could very easily do that. He looked at the man, pain in his expression. "You would truly do that to Gates?" he asked, sounding incredulous. "A man you love like a son? You would take away the only thing he has ever loved?"

Jasper looked at Gates, who was hanging his head, staring at the floor. "He knows why he cannot marry her," Jasper said, his tone hoarse with emotion. "It does not give me pleasure to deny him, for you are correct – I love him like a son. But I cannot let a man with such a reputation, with known bastards all over England, marry my daughter. It would shame the entire House of de Lara. I will therefore give you another chance, Alex. I will ask you one last time if you will fulfill the contract that your parents agreed upon. If you deny me, I will simply seek out any number of other young men to make the pact with. You are not special in that regard."

The pain in the room was palpable. Anguish was bleeding from every pore in Gates' body, filling the room like a fog. Alexander looked at his friend, seeing the slumped shoulders and lowered head, and his sorrow knew no bounds. He could hardly believe they had come to the end of this conversation and it had not gone in Gates' favor. He could not, would not, give up, but he wasn't sure what more could be said.

"What do you want me to do?" he asked Gates. "Tell me what you want me to do and I shall do it."

Gates was staring at the floor. He didn't look up. "Would it help if I begged, my lord?" he whispered to Jasper. "With God as my witness, I have never wanted anything so badly in my entire life. I will beg if you will only allow me to marry Kathalin. I will swear an oath of allegiance to you forever. I will do whatever you want me to do... only let me marry the woman I love. Let me marry your daughter."

He said it with such agony. Alexander, full of Gates' agony, hung his head as well, and Jasper, still standing near the chair, gazed at his knight with the most pained of expressions.

"Lad," he whispered. "I *cannot.*"

Gates suddenly whirled in his direction, falling to his knees and grabbing hold of Jasper's fine robes. He buried his face in them, holding on to the man as if fearful a loosened grip would send him into the pits of hellish despair.

"*Please,*" he begged, his eyes closed tightly as he held on to Jasper's robes. "Please, my lord, *please.* She is all to me and I am all to her. Please do not take this happiness away from us. Please grant us mercy and compassion and allow us our joy."

Jasper was horrified by Gates' actions; the strongest, most fearless man he had ever known was having the weakest moment of his life. Jasper reached down and tried to help him up, but Gates wouldn't move.

"Gates, *please,*" he said with great emotion in his voice. "Please stand up. Please, lad... do not do this."

Gates shook his head, unwilling to release him. "I beg you, my lord," he whispered. "Do not separate me from the woman I love."

Jasper was beside himself. He looked up at Alexander, silently begging the man to help him with Gates, but Alexander was watching the scene with tears in his eyes. When he noticed Jasper looking at him, he pointed to Gates.

"Can you not see what this means to him?" he demanded softly. "Look what he is willing to do in order to convince you of his sincerity."

Receiving no help from Alexander, Jasper returned his focus to Gates. "Rise, Gates, please," he said. "I understand your passion on the matter. I understand your wants. But you must let me do what I believe is best. Would you truly be so selfish to marry my daughter, knowing how she will be ridiculed? Do you truly only think of yourself in this matter?"

Gates suddenly let his robes go and nearly toppled over backwards. His emotions were reeling and so was he. "All I know is that I love her," he said. "If that is selfish, then I am sorry, but I believe we can overcome anything at all. Why do you have so little faith in me with your daughter when you have trusted your entire empire to my sword? I do not understand."

Free of Gates' grasp, Jasper stumbled over to the door. He simply couldn't handle the conversation any longer because he was becoming consumed by guilt and confusion. He had to get away from Gates and Alexander, who were turning his mind to mush and his heart to pulp. All he knew was that he hurt as they did, as Gates did, but he couldn't do anything about it. *Wouldn't* do anything about it.

He held out a hand to Gates as if to stop the man any further argument.

"No more," he demanded hoarsely. "I cannot discuss this anymore. Alexander, you will marry Kathalin and there will be no more discussion. I will tell your parents of this conversation. You will do what they tell you to do; therefore, you will marry my daughter. Gates, forgive me for denying you but I have given you my reasons. I am... sorry."

With that, he bolted from the room and hurried to the stairs leading down to the gatehouse entry. Gates was still on his knees, watching Jasper flee, his entire body wracked with pain. Behind him, Alexander spoke softly.

"I will go after him," he said, moving for the door. "I will make him change his mind, Gates. You will see."

Gates rocked back on his heels, exhaling long and deep. He was utterly, completely drained, feeling only the sting of Jasper's refusal. Not that he hadn't expected it, but still, the reality of it was almost too much to bear.

"Nay," he said to Alexander before the man could leave. "Give him time before you do... he will only become angry with you and mayhap even rescind his offer of marriage."

Alexander peered strangely at him. "I have already refused to marry her," he said. "He cannot make me marry Kathalin if I do not want to."

Gates looked up at him and the man's eyes were swimming in tears. Great tears of emotion glimmered in the weak light from the fire.

"Nay," he said again, his voice hoarse with emotion. "If he will not allow me to marry her, then I would be comforted knowing that she was married to you. You... you will be good to her, won't you? She is a great and wonderful lady, Alex. If I cannot have her, then I am comforted knowing you will take care of her. I could not bear it if she married another."

Alexander gazed at him with grief and bewilderment. He didn't even know what to say so, confused, he said nothing. Without another word, he left Gates' chamber, following the path that Jasper had taken out of the gatehouse. As Alexander's footfalls faded down the steps, Gates struggled to his feet and made his way over to the lancet window overlooking the entry.

A cold breeze blew in his face, spilling the tears over his face, but Gates didn't even notice. All he could think and feel, at the moment, was the pain of Jasper's denial, but he knew this would not be the last conversation they had on the topic. He was going to compose himself and go after Jasper once more, finding a reason to give the man that would make him change his mind. Their skirmish had been fierce and they had retreated to recover and regroup, but the battle was not over as far as Gates was concerned.

Not over in the least.

CHAPTER SEVENTEEN

S HE WAS ABOUT to disobey him.

Gates had watched her enter the keep as the Tender of the Keep opened the iron grate and admitted her. He'd even watched her as she mounted the stairs, at least the ones he could see, but he soon lost sight of her as she headed to the floor above. It was a good thing, too. She had plans other than seeking her chamber and bolting herself in. There was a certain woman on the floors above that she wanted to have a discussion with.

My mother lied to me....

Kathalin tried to remember what Gates had told her; that it was possible Rosamund knew nothing about the de Lohr proposal, but something told Kathalin that her mother had indeed known. She wasn't sure why she was of that opinion, but she was. Rosamund had known about the betrothal to de Lohr from the start and she couldn't seem to shake the thought.

So Kathalin continued up to the top floor of the keep where her mother lived in her lavish bower. As she mounted the steps, approaching that darkened level, she could already smell the heavy scent of cloves, the aroma that had set her father to sneezing. She could see why because it was most cloying in nature, permeating the very walls of the keep. She swore the stone at this level was oily with it.

It was dark on the landing as she knocked on her mother's heavy oak door. She heard a muffled voice, which sounded as if she was given permission to enter, so Kathalin timidly pushed the door open. More smells of clove and something else, something equally strong, hit her in the face. She made a mental note to ask about the smells in the chamber and what they were meant to accomplish. No doubt some physic told her to burn herbs daily to ward off the bad vapors associated with her affliction although Kathalin had never seen evidence that doing such a thing helped, at least not in her mother's case. Stepping into the chamber, she closed the door behind her.

"Lady Rosamund?" she called, looking around the dim bower. "It is Kathalin."

Something on the enormous, curtained bed over to her right stirred. "Kathalin," Rosamund repeated, pleasure in her tone. "How good of you to come and visit me, my dear."

Kathalin recognized her mother's voice and turned in the direction of the bed. The heavy curtains were drawn so she couldn't see anything, but she could hear the woman moving about.

"I came to see how you are faring," Kathalin said, although it wasn't entirely the truth. She simply wanted to lead off the conversation with more pleasant things and come to the interrogation later. "I was out in the herb garden this morning."

The bed shifted around some more and the maid came around, pulling back the heavy curtains to reveal the sheer coverings beneath. "Is that so?" Rosamund said. "I have not been in the garden in years. I was told that the cook keeps it up for her dishes."

Kathalin watched the maid as the woman finished pulling aside the curtains and then rushed back to the other side of the bed where Rosamund was evidently dressing.

"Who planted the garden?" Kathalin asked. "It looks rather old and established."

Through the sheers, the maid was wrapping Rosamund's hands. "That garden is very old," she said. "It was here long before I married Jasper. I believe there must be plants in that garden that are a hundred years old. Generations of de Laras have tended it."

Kathalin understood. "It is very overgrown in places," she said. "Although with the spring thaw, there is a good deal of new, green growth. I was hoping… that is, I would like to ask for permission to tend it. I think I could grow many things that might help your condition."

Through the sheers, Kathalin could see her mother falter, as if surprised by the statement. After a moment, the wrapping resumed, more slowly this time.

"I am afraid I am beyond help," she said quietly. "Your noble gesture is very kind, but I do not think there is anything that can help me."

Kathalin took a few steps closer to the bed. "Have you tried?" she asked. "I realize you have had this affliction for a long time, but what has been done for you in that time?"

Rosamund was silent for a moment as the maid continued to wrap. "Many things," she finally said. "A physic from Gloucester used to bleed me regularly, but it did no good. All of my bodily humors are infected and there was no use in trying to bleed it out. I have also been given gold to drink in the hopes of purifying my body, but to no avail."

Kathalin had been taught the four humors of the body; black bile, yellow bile, blood, and phlegm. She knew that physics believed that ridding the body of these humors in certain cases, and especially leprosy, could lead to healing, and she also knew that gold potions were popular with leprosy, as gold symbolized purity and was thought to help with diseases like this. But Mother Benedicta had proclaimed such cures towards lepers to be ineffective and believed in other healing measures that did not involve blood-letting and drinking metal.

"That is because such things only weaken the body," Kathalin said. "At St. Milburga's, we had people come to us with leprosy since St. Milburga is the patron saint of lepers. We had an entire room dedicated to them. Mother Benedicta would have them drink a brew of rotten tea and she would also rub their limbs with salve made from rotten bread and lavender oil. We had excellent results with it. I should like to try it on you, too, if you are willing."

The maid had finished wrapping Rosamund's hands and the woman stood up from her bed, unsteadily, as the maid held her fast to prevent her from falling. "That is a magnanimous gesture, Kathalin," she said, "but, as I said, I am beyond help. I do not believe it would do any good."

Kathalin was rather disappointed. "Will you not even let me try?"

Rosamund came around the side of the bed, gazing upon her daughter with her bright blue eyes. The expression in her eyes spoke of hope and perhaps even excitement, but the woman shook her head.

"It would not do any good," she repeated. "It could not undo the damage that has been done even if you did manage to stop the progression. I am grateful for your offer, however. Please know how truly grateful I truly am."

Kathalin took a step in her mother's direction. She didn't want to push, for the woman had been clear, but she was still disappointed.

"Mayhap you will reconsider sometime," she said. "In any case, will you give me permission to tend the garden as my own? I should like to care for it."

Rosamund nodded. "Of course you may," she said. "Generations of de Lara women will thank you."

Kathalin smiled weakly, thinking now that the matter of the garden and her mother's care had been settled, she had other things on her mind. Much more *important* things on her mind. Now that she'd proven herself to be a thoughtful and considerate daughter, she hoped it set the right mood for the next part of their conversation about her betrothal to Alexander. She wanted the truth and she hoped her mother would be truthful with a most sympathetic daughter.

"Thank you," she said after a moment, carefully bringing forth the next part of the conversation. "And speaking of generations of de Laras, I am not sure if you know that my father has already moved to make a marriage for me. Were you aware he had made an offer to Alexander de Lohr?"

Rosamund's gaze wavered slightly. "He did?" she said, sounding genuinely surprised. "He has already done this?"

Kathalin nodded. "He has," she said. "Lord and Lady de Lohr arrived at Hyssington earlier today and my father has already made them a marriage offer between me and their son. I was just told of it. Did you know of his plans?"

Rosamund didn't reply for a moment. She held Kathalin's gaze before turning away, going in search of her favorite chair. Her movements were slow and painful, shuffling as she did.

"Forgive me," she said. "It is difficult for me to stand."

Kathalin couldn't help but notice her mother not only hadn't answered her question, but hadn't outright denied her knowledge of such a thing. She followed the woman at a safe distance as she moved for her chair.

"Lady Rosamund," she said, suspicion reflecting in her tone. "Did you *know* about this betrothal?"

Rosamund heard the distrust in Kathalin's voice but she ignored it. She wasn't about to allow her daughter to gain the upper hand in this conversation, in any way. With a grunt of pain, she settled herself into the chair.

"You knew as well as I did that Jasper is seeking a husband for you," she finally said. "Why should you be so surprised by a marriage offer?"

There was a hint of self-defense in her tone and Kathalin could see, in that instant, that Rosamund had known. She had known all along. It was difficult to keep her outrage out of her manner when she answered.

"Aye, I knew he wanted to find me a husband, but you and I struck a deal in that I would be allowed to approve of a potential candidate before anything was offered," she said. "You told me that you would consider sending me back to St. Milburga's if I did not find a suitable husband from the guests you had invited to the coming celebration."

There was great reproach in her words, something Rosamund found infuriating. She would not let her daughter reproach her in any way and her anger began to rise.

"You are wrong," Rosamund said, her eyes flashing in a way that Kathalin found most intimidating. "You have utterly misconstrued the contents of our conversation for your own selfish wants. What I said, exactly, was that you should allow your father and me to have the celebration in honor of your return home. I asked that you meet people and become exposed to a world you have never known. I then said that if, at the end of the celebration, you still wished to take your vows as a nun, I would consider it. Never, at any time, did I give you permission to approve your husband."

Kathalin was stunned to realize that the woman was correct. She had remembered the conversation, or at least she thought she had, but now that Rosamund had repeated her words, Kathalin realized that, indeed, her mother was correct. Feeling sick and frightened, she struggled to recover.

"You led me to believe that I had a say in the matter," she said, hoping her voice didn't sound as tremulous as she felt. "What am I supposed to think when you ask me to experience a world I never knew? To meet the young men you have invited to vie for my hand? I was led to believe I would have some say in this matter."

"If that is what you feel you were led to believe, then you were mistaken."

She sounded so cold. Kathalin was truly taken aback, thinking this was not the same woman she had first met those days ago, the woman who had shared the details of her affliction and had been grateful for Kathalin's concern. This wasn't the same woman who had pleaded for understanding when she told Kathalin that she had sent her children away because she had been afraid her children would contract her disease. Kathalin had foolishly fallen for the woman's explanation enough so that she felt pity towards Rosamund and forgave her.

But that had been her grave mistake. Whether or not Rosamund's explanation was the truth, Kathalin would never know because the woman before her wasn't the same woman at all. This was someone cold and calculating, not to be crossed.

The true Rosamund was finally revealed.

Kathalin had been betrayed.

"Then you knew about this betrothal," she finally said.

Rosamund maintained her intense gaze. "Of course I did," she said. "I suggested it."

It was a blow to the belly as far as Kathalin was concerned. She thought she had an ally in her mother but she couldn't have been further from the truth. Now, it was all becoming clear; Kathalin had never had any say in her future in spite of what Rosamund had led her to believe. She was as she had always been, simply a pawn who also happened to be the daughter of a disconnected earl and his calculating wife. Now, it was out in the open. Kathalin had to accept the truth.

Her parents had never cared for her at all.

Feeling foolish, and sad, the resentment she had always felt for her parents began to make a return but Kathalin refused to give in to that old hatred. For now, she wanted something from her mother and she wasn't going to leave until she had it. Being angry and resentful towards Rosamund would not help her cause. She had to be as calculating as her mother was but that wasn't in Kathalin's nature. She hadn't any practice at it. Still, she had to try.

"Then I suppose I should thank you," Kathalin said. "Alexander is a very kind man and the House of de Lohr is very prestigious."

Rosamund's hard eyes eased somewhat. It had been clear that she had been gearing up for a battle, so Kathalin's instant agreement was rather unexpected. The bright eyes softened, but still, she was on her guard. With that in mind, she continued the conversation carefully.

"Elreda de Lohr, who is Alexander's mother, was a good friend of mine long ago," Rosamund said. "She and Henry are fine people. You should feel very honored that they are willing to accept you into their home."

Kathalin simply nodded. There was a stool near the hearth, a three-legged piece of furniture, and she moved towards it. She wasn't going to be leaving the room any time soon so she thought it best to get comfortable.

"Indeed I am," Kathalin said, although she didn't mean a word of it. "It was a wise choice."

"It was."

"May I ask you a question?"

"That depends. What is it?"

"You will not know until I ask."

Now, Rosamund was growing wary. "Speak, then."

Kathalin looked at her mother, cocking her head thoughtfully. "Have you ever been in love with a man?"

It was a question that caught Rosamund off-guard. Her brow furrowed for a moment before speaking. "Why do you ask?"

Kathalin was trying very hard to manipulate her mother into the direction she wanted her to go. She shrugged casually. "All of this talk of marriage has me thinking," she said. "Is love as wonderful as I have heard it is?"

Rosamund shook her head, averting her gaze. "A foolish question."

"Then you have never been in love?"

"I did not say that."

"Then you have!"

Flustered, Rosamund looked away completely. "Of course I have," she said. "Every woman has been in love at least once in her life."

"Are you in love with my father?"

Rosamund's head snapped up, her eyes flashing again. "That is none of your affair."

Kathalin could see she had the woman off balance, which had been her goal. She simply nodded, pretending to be sorry that she had asked the question.

"Of course, it is not," she said quietly. "But I thought that if you understood love, then you would understand my predicament."

Rosamund looked at her suspiciously. "What predicament?"

Kathalin gazed into eyes that were the exact same color as her own. "I am in love," she said quietly. "I have never been in love before, so this is something quite new and wonderful to me."

Now, Rosamund was intrigued. *Very* intrigued. She peered at Kathalin, surprised by the woman's statement.

"Who are you in love with?" she asked.

Kathalin sensed she had her mother's interest and she very much hoped to capitalize on it. *God, help me convince her that this betrothal to Alexander is not right!* In order to do that, she was willing to lie. She had to.

It was time to raise the stakes.

"Gates de Wolfe," she said softly. "And he is in love with me. Alexander knows this. I am definitely not opposed to marriage if it is to Gates. You must betroth me to him, Rosamund. Alexander will not want me, anyway."

Rosamund was deeply shocked; that much was obvious. "Gates?" she repeated. "He... he cannot possibly be in love with you!"

Kathalin's eyebrows lifted curiously. "Why not?"

Rosamund was very quickly growing animated in manner. "Because he cannot love any woman," she insisted. "Do you not know about him, girl? He will say anything to bed you. Sweet Jesus... *has* he? Did he tell you he loved you and then take you to his bed?"

Kathalin could see how much the very idea horrified Rosamund. She was going to strike back at the woman any way she could and do whatever she had to do in order to gain Gates as a husband. If this was the way then, God forgive her, she would take it. But she stopped short of a flat-out lie; with Rosamund, perhaps the intimation of as much would work the magic she hoped to work. Coyly, she looked away.

"He *does* love me," she said. "He told me so. I believe him."

Rosamund was struggling out of her chair, her outrage evident. "Has he taken you to his bed?" she nearly shouted.

Kathalin could see her mother attempting to stand from the corner of her eye. "And if he has?"

The shock was nearly too great for Rosamund to bear. She fell back into her seat. "Dear God," she whispered. "Please tell me it is not true."

"If I want to marry him, and he loves me, why would it be such a terrible thing?"

Rosamund clutched the arms of her chair, her nubby fingers gripping at the wood through the fabric wrappings she wore. "Let me make this perfectly clear, Kathalin," Rosamund said, sensing that her daughter was not taking this situation seriously. "If he has, in fact, bedded you, then I will make sure Jasper throws him in the vault and strips him of his honorable knighthood. I will then turn him over to the House of de Lohr so that they can punish him as they see fit. I will not let Gates get away with deflowering my daughter simply to satisfy his lust. I will make sure he is terribly punished. Do you comprehend me?

Kathalin looked at her mother and, suddenly, she realized that she may have raised the stakes of the game too high. She hadn't expected Rosamund to turn her anger on Gates. Concerned that she may have pushed Rosamund too far, she nodded.

"I do," she said. "But you needn't worry. He did not take me to his bed. He never even suggested such a thing. Rosamund, please... I love the man and wish to marry him. He has sworn to me that he will be a good and true husband, and I believe him. Please allow me my happiness; for once in my life, do something that will make me happy. I have spent so many years alone and sad, existing at St. Milburga's because I had to, but what I have discovered with Gates is that there is happiness in the world, happiness such as I had never even imagined. I have had a brief glimpse of this and I want to know it for the rest of my life. If you were in love in your lifetime as you say you were, then think back to that time and of how badly you wanted to be with the man you loved. That is where I am now. Won't you please let me know such joy?"

All of the manipulation, the game-playing, and the bargaining between the two of them fled and all that was left was honesty and anguish. Rosamund stared at Kathalin, seeing the raw emotion on her face, and it cut through the hardness and the control that the woman had been exhibiting. The look of pure hope cut through everything until Rosamund hardly had any resistance at all. What she saw before her was herself as a young woman, in love for the first time. What she saw was great anticipation for the future.

But much as Rosamund's hope had been destroyed, so would Kathalin's.

"I understand your plight," she finally said. "I understand that you wish to be with the man you love. But life does not always give us what we hope for, Kathalin. Sometimes it gives us absolutely nothing and it is God's will that we make the best of such things. I loved Jasper when I married him. I, too, had the great hopes that you do for our future together. But a terrible disease took my husband from me. You have only known love for a short time; it will be easier to forget. Alexander is a fine man and I am sure, someday, you will become fond of him and remember Gates only as a warm memory. Gates is a man with too many ghosts in his past, ghosts that will shame you and shame the name of de Lara, and it is for those reasons that I cannot agree to your marriage with him. You do not understand now, but in time, you will."

Kathalin was left feeling hollow and defeated by her mother's response. The course of the entire volatile conversation had been for naught. She was where she didn't want to be, refused marriage to the man she loved. Well, it would *not* end here. Much as Gates had sworn not to surrender, neither would she.

"You would deny me my happiness because you were denied yours?" she asked, pain in her words. "You have such power over everything about me... why can you not let me be happy?"

Rosamund didn't want to argue any longer. She was exhausted from the conversation and she finally shook her head at Kathalin, waving her away.

"I am sorry," she said simply. "You will leave me now. I must rest."

Kathalin was distressed that she was being cut short. "That is all?" she said. "You have nothing more to say to me?"

Rosamond waved her off again. "I do not," she said. "I have said all I intend to. Go, now. Please."

It was the end, at least for now. Kathalin stood up from the stool she was sitting upon and, without another word, went to the chamber door. She lifted the latch and paused, wanting to say something more, but she thought better of it when she watched her mother's maid practically lifting the woman out of the chair. It was clear that the woman was beyond exhaustion by the conversation. Perhaps it was best if she left now and let her mother rest and reflect upon their discussion. Perhaps if she thought about what Kathalin said enough, she might have some sympathy for her and change her mind.

With a heavy heart, she left the chamber and went across the hall to her own, bolting herself inside as Gates had asked. Dropping to her knees beside her bed, she lost herself in prayer.

Praying for a miracle.

CHAPTER EIGHTEEN

"ROSAMUND!"

Half-asleep and startled by the sound of someone hissing her name, Rosamund quickly covered her face as she rolled onto her back, struggling to see in the darkness. It was dark in her room as the black clouds had returned, blotting out the sun and threatening an icy downpour. Blinking her eyes, Rosamund could see Jasper standing over her bed, curtains in his hands where he had yanked them back.

"Rosamund!" he hissed again. "Do you hear me?"

"I hear you," Rosamund said, muffled, through the veil over her face. "Why have you come? What has happened?"

Jasper turned away from the bed, still gripping the curtains and nearly tearing them down in his haste. He ended up ripping one down and the maid rushed out of the shadows to pick it up from the floor, but Jasper was already across the room by that time. It was clear that he was agitated, pacing around like a man with a good deal on his mind.

"This betrothal with Kathalin," he said to his wife, wringing his hands in frustration. "I have just come from Alexander and Gates where I was informed that Alexander will refuse the betrothal because Gates is in love with the girl. Can you imagine? Gates de Wolfe being in love with any woman? It is preposterous!"

Rosamund struggled to sit up on the bed with her maid's help. Hearing such news from Jasper's lips did not surprise her, considering she had just heard the same information from her daughter.

"Kathalin was just here and told me the same thing," she said. "She says that she wants to marry Gates and swears that he wants to marry her as well."

Jasper threw up his arms in an exasperated gesture. "It is true!" he said. "Gates nearly wept as he told me, begging me to permit him to marry Kathalin. Can you imagine the outrageousness of such a request? I cannot believe he would be bold enough to even ask after the years I have spent paying off fathers and brothers of the women he has compromised. The man must have lost his mind!"

Rosamund affixed the veil across her face to the wimple that the maid was struggling to put on her head. When she lay down to rest, she had pulled both of the items off of her head, items designed to cover her horrifically disfigured face. Now she was quickly trying to put them back on again. She wasn't sure Jasper had even seen how ravaged her face had become in the darkness but she hoped not. She liked for the man she once loved to remember her as she was and not now how she had become, which is why she kept herself fully covered at all times.

It was for Jasper's sake.

"Gates came to you, did he?" she asked her husband, pondering that revelation. "I thought Kathalin was fabricating her story, but it seems as if Gates has confirmed it."

Jasper nodded, raking his fingers through his graying hair. "He very much confirmed it," he said. Then, his pacing slowed as he struggled to think clearly on what he had just witnessed in Gates' small chamber. "I will admit that he was quite convincing. He truly behaved as if he were in love with Kathalin and is devastated by the fact we have betrothed her to Alexander. And Alex – he was a martyr on his friend's behalf. He is willing to give up a good deal of money and a castle for Gates. Such madness!"

As Jasper ranted, Rosamund contemplated what he was telling her, coming to think that, perhaps, there might be something to all of this. Kathalin had pleaded with her to be allowed to marry Gates and, at the same time, Gates had evidently pleaded with Jasper the very same thing, which led her to believe that there was some truth to this surprising love story. Rosamund had been quite willing to discount it before but with this new information, she found herself wondering if it was all true. She eyed Jasper as the man paced around.

"Mayhap it is not such madness, after all," she said. "If Alex is willing to give up so much and both Kathalin and Gates have declared their desire to marry out of love, then mayhap there is truth to it."

Jasper frowned at her. "It does not matter if there is truth to it," he said. "Love or not, Kathalin will *not* marry Gates. We have had this discussion, Rosamund. His reputation as a scoundrel will not become our daughter's shame."

Rosamund simply lifted her shoulders and averted her gaze. "A grandson with de Lara and de Wolfe blood in him would be a powerful knight, indeed," she said, reminding him of what she'd said once before. "Is that not who you would wish to leave your legacy to?"

Jasper was coming to look at her as if she'd lost her mind. "And what of a grandson with de Lara and de Lohr blood?" he said. "Will he be any less great?"

Rosamund shook her head. "He would not," she admitted. "But Kathalin does not love Alex."

Jasper stomped over to the bed where she was sitting. "It does not matter who she loves," he declared. "She will marry Alex and that is the end of it. In fact, we must make haste with this wedding so that the deal will be sealed and there will be nothing Kathalin or Gates or even Alex can do about it. These foolish children do not know that we are doing what is best for them so it is time that we move ahead with it. I have no more time for nonsense; I will summon the priest from town and we shall have the ceremony by tomorrow."

Rosamund wasn't surprised by his directive; Jasper often made his decisions quickly and, at times, rashly. But there was something suspicious in her gaze as she looked at him.

"You do not trust that Gates will not take Kathalin and run away," she said, reading his thoughts. "Or you do not trust that Alex will not simply vanish, leaving us with no groom."

Jasper sighed heavily. "If you had seen the look on Gates' face when he was pleading for Kathalin's hand, you might think the same thing," he said. "And Alex is staunchly opposed to marrying the woman that Gates loves, so I would not put it past those two to conspire against us. Therefore, we must make this marriage quickly. You understand, of course."

Rosamund nodded. "Of course," she murmured. "But remember what it was like to be in love, Jasper. The sun rises and sets upon the wings of love. If Gates and Kathalin are truly in love, then this will be very difficult for them. It will be difficult for Alex as well and, ultimately, that could disrupt your knight corps. You have strong and loyal men in your service who are also friends. If Kathalin marries Alex, and Gates is in love with her, you may be dooming your army."

She had a point, and a very good one, but Jasper would not admit it. It wasn't as if he hadn't considered that himself, but he was convinced that his men would do as they were told regardless of any personal feelings on the matter. He was convinced that whatever feelings Gates held for Kathalin would eventually fade away. Such a man like de Wolfe, with a lover in every nearby town, would soon enough forget about a woman he once loved.

At least, Jasper hoped so.

"Pah," he finally said, flicking a wrist at his wife as if to brush her off. "Love is easily forgotten. Are you taking their side, then?"

Rosamund shook her head but she was hurt that he'd brushed off the suggested memories of the love they'd once shared whilst trying to make her point.

"Not at all," she said. "As I mentioned, I thought Kathalin was simply living in her own fantasy when she came to tell me that Gates wished to marry her, but hearing that Gates came to you as well… it simply confirms to me that Kathalin must have been telling the truth. Did you tell Elreda and Henry any of this?"

Jasper looked queerly at her. "How do you know that they are here?"

She nodded. "Kathalin told me."

Jasper understood in that brief explanation. Rosamund always seemed to have the pulse of the fortress, seeing and knowing much from her confinement in her room.

"They do not know," he said, answering her question. "But I must tell them. They will have to keep close watch of Alex and make sure he does not do anything foolish."

"Agreed."

"Then you support my decision to have the wedding immediately?"

"I do."

That was all Jasper needed to hear. He fled her chamber to tell Henry and Elreda of the news, leaving the door open in his haste so that the maid had to rush to close it. Rosamund remained sitting on her bed, her mind lingering on the situation between her daughter and Gates de Wolfe.

Aye, she knew what it was to be in love. She remembered that much of it and she had hoped that Jasper had, too, but if he did, he would not acknowledge such a thing. *Love is easily forgotten.* Now, she was starting to have some doubt as to whether or not she and Jasper were doing the right thing. Would it be so terrible to marry Gates de Wolfe, a man with a history of women? Men could change. Rosamund knew that first-hand because her loving husband, Jasper, had changed drastically when disease began to ravage her body. The man who had sworn to love her until death and be true to her, and only her, had broken that vow.

Rosamund eyed the maid as the woman tried to affix the curtain that Jasper had yanked off. She'd stopped resenting the quiet, plain woman long ago, knowing that the maid had not been given the option of refusing Jasper's advances. Still, when she looked at the woman, at her breasts and hips, knowing that her husband had touched them, it still hurt her as it did the first time she'd become aware of it.

Men could change, indeed.

THE SUN WAS setting in the western horizon, but one couldn't tell very much with the collection of tarnished silver clouds that crowded up the sky above.

Kathalin had been in her chamber most of the afternoon, having not left it since her conversation with her mother. The truth was that she didn't want to leave it, locked away from the world, because every time that door opened, something drastic happened. She wasn't sure she could take anything drastic again today but she was desperate to see Gates and to know of his conversation with her father. If it was anything like the conversation she'd had with her mother, then the future she had so hopefully dreamed about wasn't quite as bright as she had wished. In fact, it had turned stormy and uncertain.

The chamber she occupied now, the one that was located opposite her mother's lavish bower, was small but comfortable. There was a big hearth that kept the room very warm and a very comfortable bed she had slept soundly upon. Her possessions, the ones that Gates had purchased for her those weeks ago, had followed her into this chamber and were neatly put away in a slender but well-made wardrobe cabinet. The lumpy, white soap was sitting out next to a basin of cold water and the fur-lined cloak hung on a peg near the door. Everything in the room, from the soap to the cloak to the contents of the wardrobe, reminded Kathalin of Gates.

It was both a depressing and comforting sight. Kathalin sat on the wide sill of the lancet window overlooking the garden, the same window where she had first seen the dried, dead garden. She wasn't looking so much at the garden any longer because it reminded her of the conversation with her mother and the long line of de Lara women that she was now coming to hate because they reminded her of her separation from Gates. She had no emotional link to her family, and especially not now. Her only emotional link was to Gates and she prayed he would come to her soon to tell her of better news from his conversation with Jasper. In fact, she'd been praying steadily on that very subject since her meeting with her mother.

Please, God… let us be together!

As she gazed up at the darkened sky, watching the birds as they flew about, seeking cover before the storm broke, she caught movement down in the garden. Peering down, she could see that Gates was standing there, waving his big arms up at her. She stuck her hand from the window, waving back, and when she pulled her hand out she could see that he was motioning her to join him in the garden. Waving at him again to signal that she understood, she grabbed her cloak off the peg and fled her chamber.

Giddy with excitement, Kathalin took the stairs too fast and nearly tripped on her way down. The keep was dark as she made her way down to the entry level where the Tender of the Keep sat huddled up against the fire in her small room near the entry door. When the woman saw Kathalin, she stood up, tossed off the blanket that had been over her shoulders, and made her way over to the iron gate, unlocking it so Kathalin could leave. Kathalin bolted outside once the gate opened and dashed off in the direction of the walled garden.

The wind was picking up and big, fat, freezing drops of rain were falling as she rushed to the gate of the garden, only to be met by Gates. He was already there, opening it, and she threw herself into his arms as she entered. Gates held her tightly, off the ground and aloft in his arms, and carried her over to a corner of the walled garden where eyes from the keep could not see them. He needed, and wanted, privacy. Before she could open her mouth to speak, he slanted his lips over hers and kissed her deeply.

It was a kiss full of longing and promise, and Kathalin wrapped her arms around his neck, holding him fast as he suckled her lips. It was new and thrilling and exciting, a kiss of untold passion beginning to awaken, and he pushed her back against the wall, supporting her body with his as he reached down and pulled her legs up so that they were wrapped around his hips. Kathalin was so involved in the heat of his kiss, the newness of something she had never before experienced, that she hadn't realized the position he'd put her in. Her back was against the walled garden, her legs around his body as his pelvis rubbed up against hers.

It was an extremely intimate and naughty position but Kathalin, as naïve as she was, hardly recognized that. All she knew was that she was content in his big arms, his enormous body pressed against her as his lips devouring hers. Since her body was being supported by his as he held her against the wall, his hands moved to her face, cupping it, as he kissed her.

"Gates," Kathalin breathed between heated kisses. "I spoke with my mother. She is unsympathetic to our cause. She insists that I marry Alex but I will try again to convince her. I will not stop until I have the answer we seek."

He slowed his kisses, his hands still holding her face. Finally, he stopped altogether and looked at her. "I spoke with Jasper also," he murmured huskily. "He has denied me as well."

Kathalin's brow furrowed with worry. "Did Alex speak with him, too?" she asked. "Did he tell my father that he did not wish to marry me?"

Gates nodded. "He did," he said, his thumbs stroking her cheeks. "It is only the first battle in the war, sweetheart. Do not lose faith. I will approach him again tonight and see if I cannot change his mind."

Kathalin nodded, trying not to allow feelings of defeat to claim her just yet. "Was he angry in his refusal?" she asked. "Did he become angry with you?"

Gates shrugged, his hands moving from her face to her neck, his gaze turning towards her shoulders and the swell of her full bosom. "He was upset, of course," he said, drinking in his fill of her creamy white flesh. "He did not believe me when I told him I loved you."

Kathalin was watching his face as he gazed at her chest. "He is concerned with your reputation."

It was a statement, not a question, and Gates nodded as he bent over and kissed the swell of her breasts. "Aye," he said. "I am sure he does not think I am capable of such feelings. It is not surprising, Kathi – I told you that my past would be an obstacle. You knew we would come across this. It is simply a matter of convincing Jasper that the right woman can change a man, as you have done for me."

He pushed his face into her neck, kissing it softly as he inhaled her womanly musk. Kathalin's arms were still around his neck, her hands in his hair as he kissed her, but her mind was thinking on her parents and their refusal. As Gates said, it was only the first battle in the war. They both knew it would not be easy. She pulled him closer as he nuzzled her neck.

"I thought I could coerce my mother into giving her consent by intimating that you had taken me to your bed," she said softly. "She became quite irate about it and threatened to turn you over to the House of de Lohr if it was true. I was therefore forced to confess that it was not even though I wish it had been."

Gates stopped nuzzling her neck. He lifted his head, looking her in the eye. "For once in my life, I am glad it was not true."

She wasn't sure if she should be offended or touched. "Why?"

His brow furrowed in thought as he began to toy with a stray lock of hair on her shoulder. "I am not entirely sure I can explain it," he said. "You are so pure and untouched and lovely... to bed you now, before we are properly wed, seems dirty and wrong on so many levels. You are not meant to be soiled before the proper time, Kathi. You are meant to be kept pure and strong, just as you are, until the day I make you my wife. I have gone my entire adult life bedding women on my whim, using them to satisfy something inside of me that I could not quite comprehend. It was a need of sorts, a need to be fulfilled, but no amount of sexual contact could fill it. Now... when I look at you, that part of me is at peace, anticipating the time when I will join my body with yours because I know it will be the best possible experience of what such an act is meant to be. For the first time in my life, I will be demonstrating my feelings for a woman and not simply satisfying my male lust. Does that make any sense?"

Kathalin was listening closely. "It does," she said, "in a way. Marriage is meant to be consummated and in our case, because we love each other."

She didn't really understand what he was saying and he shrugged. "Sort of," he said. "When I finally take you, it will be the ultimate demonstration of my love. I have never done that before, with anyone."

She grinned. "Nor have I."

He laughed softly. "That is well and good," he said, gazing into her eyes. "I am looking forward to that moment more than you know."

Her body tightened around him, her legs around his hips and her arms around his neck. "I... I would not be opposed to sampling now what is to come," she said softly. "I give you permission to do as you will with me."

Gates looked at her; *really* looked at her. It was so odd that the first reaction he had was one of refusal. He had never refused a woman's offer in his life, yet here he was, about to refuse the offer from the woman he loved.

The only woman he *should* accept the offer from.

God, what is happening to me? He thought wildly, his mind whirling with inner thoughts and feelings of love and honor that he never knew he had. Thoughts of Alexander were coming to mind, thoughts of the House of de Lohr and the House of de Wolfe, and all of the complications such a thing would cause. The more he thought on it, the more confused he became. With a sigh, he unwound her legs from around his hips and set her carefully to the ground.

Kathalin sensed that something was bothering him, that something was very wrong indeed. His expression was full of distress and she peered at him as he set her down and turned away.

"What is the matter?" she asked. "What did I say to upset you?"

Gates wandered over to the wall and leaned against it, shaking his head. "It is madness, truly," he said. "I... I am not entirely sure I can explain my thoughts but I will try. I pray you will understand my side of it."

She was concerned. "Of course I will understand," she said. "What is wrong?"

Again, he sighed heavily, collecting his thoughts. They were scattered and he grasped at them, trying to form a reply that would make sense to them both.

"My life has been a paradox," he finally said. "As a warrior, I am honorable and loyal. It is very important to me to have the trust of my liege and of my men. I have built my reputation on it. But as a man off the field of battle, when it comes to women, I've not cultivated that same honor. I have not much cared. All I have cared about is satisfying the lust I spoke of and damn the consequences."

Kathalin nodded patiently. "I know," she said. "We have discussed this. I understand who you were before you met me."

He put up a hand as if to plead her patience for what he was about to say. "With respect to women, I have never been an honorable man," he said. "I have made promises I never intended to keep and took, from many, that which did not belong to me. Right now, by the church and laws of the country, you do not belong to me. You belong to Alex. Alex is my very dear friend, a man who is willing to make great sacrifices on my behalf, and if I sample you, as you have given me permission to do, I feel as if I am violating what belongs rightfully to Alex."

Kathalin wasn't quite following him. In fact, she didn't much like what she was hearing. "What do you mean?" she asked. "You love me and I love you. Alex knows this. Why would you be violating what belongs to him?"

He exhaled sharply. "Because I would," he said. "Kathi, think on it this way. Let's say that I sample you, as you have called it. Let us say I have my fill of you and take from you that which a woman values most highly – your innocence – and let us say that somehow, someway, we cannot convince your parents to allow us to wed. You must wed Alex. Now, you are not pure for him because I have stolen that away. I will have taken what rightfully belonged to him. I simply could not dishonor my friend so, not when he is willing to risk everything for my happiness."

Kathalin frowned. "What does this matter?" she asked. "If my parents do not agree to let us wed, you said that you would simply take me anyway and we would be married."

Gates looked at her with more pain in his expression than he had ever exhibited. He had been dreading this moment, knowing that, at some point, the question would arise. He didn't want to tell her the truth, but he had to.

"If I do that, I will shame Alex more than you can imagine," he said hoarsely, his voice full of emotion. "He does not deserve that shame, Kathi. It is true that he is willing to give up his claim to you in order for us to be wed, and that is the most selfless thing anyone has ever done for me. Do I reward him by running away with you when your parents deny us permission to wed? Do I shame the entire House of de Lohr with my dishonorable behavior? At what point do we stop thinking about ourselves and start thinking about others? As much as I do not want to see you wed to Alex, I cannot shame the man by running off with his bride, not when he has shown such selflessness towards us. Kathi, let me be an honorable man just this once by not doing something dishonorable such as running away with my friend's bride. Let me keep my honor, just this once. Will you let me do this?"

By the time he was finished, tears were pouring down Kathalin's face. The fact was that she understood what he was saying, very clearly, and it broke her heart.

"But...," she wept softly, "but I do not want to marry him. I want to marry you."

His instinct was to go to her and pull her into his arms but he fought it. "And I want to marry you," he concurred. "But I will not do it at the risk of shaming a man who has done nothing to deserve it."

She sobbed and hung her head. "Then you are choosing him over me."

Gates' guts were being twisted as he listened with pain, sorrow overwhelming him. "I am choosing honor over everything," he said. "Kathi, for once in my life, please let me do the honorable thing. If we run away and marry and leave Alex facing such humiliation, at some point, I fear I will start to hate myself. I cannot love you with all that I am if I hate myself for what I have done. I have a few regrets in life but none would be as big, or as terrible, as this one. I could not live with myself and I would not doom you to be married to such a man."

She shook her head, miserable. "Then you do not love me enough."

He smiled uncomfortably, thinking that to be an entirely ludicrous statement. "I am doing this *because* I love you enough," he whispered. "I will love you, and only you, until I die."

The only reply from Kathalin was of her soft weeping. There wasn't anything to say because, truth be told, she understood what he was saying. He had lived his entire life caring only for himself but in this instance, having been shown such generosity by Alexander, he was unwilling to show the man such terrible disrespect by stealing the man's bride.

Aye, she understood it well.

And it was, at that moment, she knew that she would never be Gates de Wolfe's wife.

CHAPTER NINETEEN

"ALEXANDER," HENRY SAID. "Jasper has told us of his conversation with you and Gates earlier in the day with regard to Lady Kathalin. We must speak on this, lad."

Alexander knew that his father was displeased for two reasons; the man had used his full name, Alexander, and also the tone of his voice suggested he was quite unhappy. Alexander knew his father well enough to know that the situation, already, was grim.

But he remained cool in spite of it. Alexander had been summoned to the great hall by a servant who had found him in the gatehouse, telling Stephan and Tobias of the situation with Gates. He felt that he had to because, sooner or later, the situation might get volatile and it was unfair for Stephan and Tobias not to know what was going on. Alexander explained the circumstances simply – that he had been betrothed to Lady Kathalin but that Gates and the lady were in love. Of course, Stephan didn't believe that Gates was truly in love with the woman and Tobias seemed rather fearful of the entire situation. It was then that the soldier appeared and Alexander made haste for the great hall.

Now, he stood in front of his parents and in front of Jasper in the cold and nearly-empty hall, seeing three very upset expressions before him. Rather than take a verbal beating from his parents, who were quite capable of such a thing, Alexander decided to take the offensive. He felt as if he had little choice.

"So now you know," he said, refusing to sit at the table as the other three were. He liked the position of power, which is what standing over them gave him. "Gates is in love with Lady Kathalin and she is in love with him. Love is not a crime, Papa, but marrying a woman who is in love with another man does a disservice to us all. Why is that so hard to understand?"

Henry scratched his head, grunting with annoyance at his son's attitude, but it was Elreda who spoke.

"Alexander, we do understand," she said. "We understand that you are trying to do something noble for Gates. But you seriously cannot believe that he is in love with a woman. How many women has he known since you have been his friend? And how many women has he believed himself in love with?"

"None," Alexander fired back softly, looking seriously at his mother. "That is why this is so important, Mother. Gates has never, since I have known him, expressed feelings for a woman. I cannot stress this enough. But he has expressed them for Kathalin and I cannot, in good conscience, marry the woman. How unfair would that be to us? She would be pining over a lost love and I would have a wife who wanted nothing to do with me."

Elreda, who wanted her son married more than anyone else did, understood the situation more than she let on. There had been a young nobleman back in her youth whom she had fancied herself in love with until her father, a Saxon prince, had married her into the powerful English de Lohr family. She'd forgotten about her lost love, eventually, but it had been a very difficult time. Now, listening to her son, she could fully sympathize with what he was saying.

"It would be difficult at first, I agree," she said softly. "But you and the lady would come back to live at Lioncross. You would serve your father and you would not see Gates, and neither would the lady. It would be easier to forget that way."

Alexander was struggling not to be harsh with his mother. "You want me wed so badly that you would do it at any cost?" he asked. "Because from my position, all I can see is that all three of you are so desperate to see the lady and me wed that you do not care about anyone else. It does not matter what I feel, or what the lady feels, or what Gates feels – as long as Lady Kathalin and I are married, that is the only thing that matters."

He was speaking rather passionately when he was finished, irked by the entire circumstance. He was irked that Jasper was being so stubborn and irked that his parents were going right along with it. He turned away from the table where Jasper and his mother and father were sitting, pacing angrily as he tried to gain a handle on his emotions. Behind him, he could hear Jasper speak.

"There is a fine line between lust and love, Alex," he said, his tone low and dull. "I have never known Gates to love a woman and neither have you. I am not entirely sure he knows what love is. He could very well marry my daughter and then grow bored with her after a week and return to his old ways. To be frank, that is my greatest fear."

Alexander simply shook his head. "I do not believe that would be the case," he said. "He says he loves her and I believe him. Did his pleading in the gatehouse not convince you, my lord? What more would it take to convince you that he is sincere? Shall he write of his love for her in blood?"

Jasper shook his head. "Gates is a great knight," he said. "He is a de Wolfe and performs in battle as a de Wolfe should. I trust him with my life. But I do not trust him with my daughter."

So much for trying to remain calm. Alexander threw up his hands in exasperation. "Up until a few weeks ago, you had not seen or spoken with your daughter since she had been a young child," he said. "I fail to see why she is suddenly so important to you. Gates is at least offering her love and his devotion. I should think you would be glad to accept his offer."

"Alex," Henry said sternly. "You will not question Jasper's relationship with his daughter, is that clear? It is not your place to do so."

Alexander knew he had pushed too far and he simply shrugged and turned away again, pacing over to one of the enormous hearths which was warm with glowing embers against the chill of the room. He took a couple of deep breaths, easing himself, trying to focus on saying something that would make them all understand what he had, so far, been unable to convey.

"If I marry Lady Kathalin, then I become part of the de Lara family in a sense," he said, calmer now. "Kathalin will be my wife and I will be concerned over every aspect of her, including her relationship with her parents. In that respect, it is my place to question Lord de Lara's motives. He seems very concerned over a daughter he has barely mentioned the entire time I have served him and I do not understand why."

Henry geared up for another scolding but Elreda called him off. She held her hand up to him, begging for silence, as she quietly stood up and went to her son. Alexander was distressed and she didn't like to see her son that way. She thought to soothe him before the discussion turned heated because it was obviously moving in that direction. As she went to Alexander, over near the hearth, Jasper summoned a nearby servant, muttered to the man, and sent him on the run.

Silence lingered in the hall for several minutes as Elreda calmed Alexander and Henry and Jasper sat in stillness to sip their wine. Henry eventually apologized for Alexander's behavior but Jasper waved him off, knowing that young men were passionate sometimes. Jasper well remembered his eldest son, Roget, and how passionate and outspoken the lad had been. He related a bit of a humorous story to Henry about Roget's outspoken nature, something about shouting at a French count and ending up in a fist fight, and the two men shared a chuckle over Roget's manners. Just as Henry started on a story about his youngest son, Baxter, and the young man's penchant for getting into trouble, Stephan appeared in the hall.

The big, hairy knight made his way into the hall, heading for Jasper, but not before noticing Alexander standing over near the hearth. He gave Alexander a quizzical look, and Alexander returned it in a most concerned fashion, but no words were spoken until Stephan reached the table where Jasper and Henry were sitting.

"You summoned me, my lord?" Stephan asked.

Jasper nodded. "Aye," he replied. "I want you to ride into town and bring back Father Wenceslaus. Tell him I have need of him immediately."

Stephan didn't hesitant. "Aye, my lord."

Jasper dismissed the knight with the wave of a hand. "Make haste, Bear," he said. "I would see the priest here by tonight."

Stephan simply nodded, casting Alexander another odd and questioning look as he quit the hall, but Alexander could say nothing, or do nothing, in return. When Stephan was gone, Alexander came away from both the hearth and his mother, heading back over to the feasting table where Henry and Jasper were sitting. There was great foreboding in Alexander's expression.

"Why did you send Stephan for the priest, my lord?" he asked Jasper.

Jasper looked at Alexander without any emotion whatsoever in his expression. "One needs a priest in order to perform a marriage mass."

Alexander blinked in shock. "A marriage mass?" he repeated. "When are you planning to have it?"

Jasper's irritation began to rise at the young knight who seemed to think he had any control over this situation. He slammed his cup onto the table, splashing out wine onto Henry, as he rose to his feet and angrily faced Alexander.

"I will have the wedding whenever I damn well want to have it," he snarled. "Is this in any way unclear? I have listened to you beg and plead and bark for the better part of the day, thinking you had some say in this entire situation. The truth is that you have no say in anything, Alexander de Lohr. I control this marriage and this household and even the knights within it, including you, and I am weary of having my wants and desires constantly questioned by you. Your parents have accepted my proposal of marriage so we are going to have this marriage immediately so there will no longer be any argument about Gates and Kathalin and the love they imagine for each other. You will marry my daughter this night and I will hear no more about it, from any of you. Do you understand?"

He was shouting by the time he was finished, which upset Elreda. As the woman rushed to Henry's side, needing comfort because Jasper was shouting at her beloved son, Alexander had no visible reaction at all. Strangely enough, the more Jasper yelled, the cooler Alexander became. When Jasper finally finished, Alexander simply stood there and stared at him.

"I understand, my lord," he said formally. "Will that be all?"

Jasper, now seeing the obedient knight before him and not the argumentative groom, was still riled up. "Aye," he said firmly. "We are expecting guests to arrive at any time for the coming celebration. For those who arrive by tonight, they will be part of the wedding feast so make sure that any new guests who arrive will know that. And you will not leave this fortress, is that clear?"

"Aye, my lord."

"And stay away from Gates."

"Aye, my lord."

"Go, now. I will send for you when the priest arrives."

Without another word, Alexander quit the hall, out into the afternoon beyond and skies full of pewter clouds and fat raindrops. He was so angry that he had bit his tongue, literally, in the desperate attempt to bite off words of refusal and anger as Jasper had yelled at him. All he could see before him was a tired, bitter old man who was trying to ruin his life just as he was trying to ruin the lives of Kathalin and Gates. They were all caught up in this maelstrom together, an unhappy trio of unhappy people, all controlled by the desires of one man.

But Jasper would not have the last word in all of this, Alexander quickly decided. He would commit his first act of disobedience by seeking out Gates. They had to make plans now that the wedding was quickly approaching, now that the arguments were finished and there was no more bargaining to be had. On a hunch, Alexander headed for the walled herb garden and found Gates and Kathalin just inside the entry, standing in the shadows of the western wall.

Gates was lingering a few feet away from Kathalin when Alexander entered, and Alexander didn't even notice the tears on Kathalin's face. He was focused strictly on Gates as he made his way to the man's side.

"Gates," he said, urgency in his tone. "I have just come from Jasper and my parents. We have a problem, my friend."

Gates looked at Alexander, feeling the man's sense of apprehension. It was enough, for the moment, to cause him to put aside the utter devastation of the conversation he was having with Kathalin regarding the fact that he was not willing to run away with her. One look at Alexander's expression and he was quite concerned with the man's manner.

"What is wrong?" he asked.

Alexander glanced at Kathalin before replying, noticing that she had her back to him and appeared to be wiping her face. He was coming to realize that he had stepped in to a private moment between the two of them but he couldn't concern himself with that now. He returned his focus to Gates.

"Jasper has sent Bear for a priest," he said. "He is furious that I have tried to back out of the betrothal and furious that we have tried to manipulate the marriage. He says that the marriage will be performed as soon as the priest arrives, which should be by sunset."

Gates was shocked. "So soon?" he said. "I thought we had days, or even weeks. What about this celebration that is coming? Will he not wait for even that?"

Alexander shook his head. "He will not," he said. "Gates, you must take Kathalin and go. Go as far as you can, as fast as you can. The time for trying to convince Jasper is over."

Gates looked at his friend for a moment before closing his eyes, tightly, and hanging his head. "And leave you behind to take the punishment?" he muttered. "I could never call myself a man again if I did that to you, Alex. I could never respect myself if I were to abscond with a woman that belongs to you and leave you here to suffer the consequences."

Alexander's brow furrowed in concern and confusion. "What are you talking about?" he demanded. "Gates, do you understand me? The priest is coming. If you do not take Kathalin and leave, now, there will never be another chance."

Gates reached out and grabbed Alexander by both arms, holding him fast, as he looked the man in the face. The expression on Gates' features spoke of untapped anguish from the depths of his soul. It was agony to simply breathe.

"Alex, listen to me," he said, his voice hoarse with emotion. "I have never done an honorable thing in my life where a woman was concerned. If I run away with your bride, no matter how much I love her, I will be dishonoring myself as well as you and Kathalin. You will be shamed, the House of de Lohr will be shamed, and the House of de Lara will be shamed. I can take Kathalin and go north to Castle Questing, but how do you think my father will react when I tell him what I have done? I am his eldest son but I am not the son he is most proud of. If I take a woman that does not belong to me, I have a feeling he will disown me completely, but more than that, I cannot do that to *you*, my friend. You have shown me what a true and selfless friend you are and I cannot dishonor you in such a way. I have been trying to tell Kathalin this but she does not understand. For once… for once in my life, Alex, I need to do the honorable thing. I do it because of my love and respect for you and for Kathalin. I cannot dishonor the people I love most."

Alexander was sincerely shocked by Gates' speech. His eyes widened as he looked at the man, seeing how pale and worn he was. It was then that he began to understand the gist of Gates' words and what it meant to all of them. He stepped away from Gates, breaking the man's hold on him.

"I will *not* marry a woman you are in love with," he said, looking to

Kathalin who had turned around to face the men. "I will not marry her, Gates."

Gates grabbed at him, clutching him by the shoulder. "If you do not, someone else will," he said. "Jasper will marry her to someone else and I could not bear it. You promised me that you would marry her if could not, Alex. I will hold you to that vow. To know she is with you... it will ease my mind."

Alexander was both torn and horrified by Gates' expectations. He hadn't expected this reaction from Gates when he'd entered the garden and now, he was disoriented from the path the conversation had taken. He could hardly believe what he was hearing. He exhaled, sharply, an indication of the turmoil in his heart.

"Gates, *please*," he begged softly. "Take her and go. I beseech you."

Gates simply shook his head. "I will not," he said huskily. "I cannot. I have given you my reasons. Please... for once, Alex, let me do the right thing."

Alexander was stunned. To realize that Gates wasn't going to take Kathalin and flee was almost more than he could comprehend. But in the same breath, he understood exactly what Gates was saying. To run away with Kathalin, to steal a de Lohr bride, would shame three families- de Lohr, de Lara, and de Wolfe. Gates was selfish, that was true, but for the first time in his life, he wasn't thinking only of himself. He was thinking of Alexander for his sacrifice and of Kathalin and her honor as a wife. Gates was making the most noble decision he could possibly make.

He was sacrificing himself, and his happiness, to save the honor of three families.

"Oh... God," Alexander finally muttered, wiping a weary hand over his face. "Are you truly serious, Gates? Is this really what you want?"

Gates, hoping that Alexander was finally understanding the situation from his standpoint, nodded his head.

"It is," he said quietly. "It is not what my heart wants, but it is what is right. I cannot take Kathalin away, not when it will ruin so many others."

"Then you will do nothing at all?" Alexander asked, simply to make sure he was understanding all of this correctly.

"I cannot. I *will* not."

Alexander didn't know what to say after that. He looked at Kathalin, who was looking at Gates. The abject sorrow on her face spoke volumes to Alexander and he wasn't quite sure who he felt more pity for – Gates or Kathalin. Or maybe he felt more pity for himself. He was about to marry a woman who was in love with his dearest friend. And along those lines, Alexander felt the need to make something perfectly clear. For his own sake, he had to.

"Very well," he said, his voice strangely weak. "If that is what you wish, then I will not argue with you. Just know that I gave you the chance to run."

"I know. And I am ever grateful for it."

Alexander nodded, addressing his next statement to both Gates and Kathalin. "Then so be it," he said. "But I will say this here and now to the both of you; I will marry Lady Kathalin and I will take her back to Lioncross Abbey. Gates, you are not welcome there. She will be my wife and I am telling you now to stay away from her. I will not marry a woman who fornicates with another man, love or no love, and if I catch you with her or anywhere near her, I will kill you. I will not be made a fool while you two carry on behind my back."

Kathalin's eyes filled with tears again as Gates nodded. "I would not do that to you, my friend," he said. "My love for her will never end but when she becomes your wife, that is where that love ceases to be spoken or acted upon. I swear to you upon my oath as a knight."

Alexander believed him. It had been hard thing for him to say, and for Gates to acknowledge, but it was something that needed to be said. He looked at Kathalin.

"Is this understood, my lady?" he asked.

Kathalin closed her eyes and tears spilled down her cheeks. "It is," she whispered tightly. "I would not dishonor my marriage in such a way, Alex."

"Swear it."

"I do."

Satisfied, but distraught and muddled, Alexander turned away from the pair. He had to get away, to collect his thoughts, and to come to terms with his future. He needed to do it alone. With a heavy sigh, this one of resignation, he headed for the garden gate.

"I have been ordered to stay away from you, Gates," he said as he lifted the latch on the old iron gate. "Do not tell Jasper that I came to see you. I fear it may cause… issues."

Gates watched the man as he opened the gate. "I will not tell him," he said. "And Alex… thank you. For everything you have done, and everything you will do for Kathalin, you have my undying gratitude."

Alexander didn't say anything as he continued through the garden gate, letting the thing creak shut behind him. After he was gone, Gates sighed heavily and turned to Kathalin.

They gazed at each other in the growing darkness, a thousand words of sorrow and love and anguish filling the air between them. Neither one of them wanted this moment in time to end, this very space of time that had been carved out for the two of them, but it was impossible to hold back the moments as they ticked away. Time was passing.

They were passing.

It was time to end it.

"I suppose this is the last time I will be able to speak with you alone," he said quietly. "It seems that things are happening rather quickly and I should not be seen here with you. It would cause you great trouble if we were discovered together."

His words were like daggers to Kathalin's heart, poking holes into her, causing her to bleed her emotions out all over the place. She was so drained, physically and emotionally, that it was difficult to stand much less think. But much like Gates, she realized that their time together was at an end. Everything between them was at an end. The pain she felt was unbearable.

"I am not worried about myself," she said. "But I am worried about you. My father is already angry with you. Finding us alone together would only make it worse."

Gates nodded, his gaze lingering on her, knowing it would probably be the last time he ever saw her. His heart, so recently awakened with feelings of love for the woman, was shattering into a million pieces. It would take him many lifetimes to collect all of the shards. He didn't even want to try. He had to get away from her because the longer he lingered, the more painful the separation would be. Taking a few steps in her direction, he grasped her by the arms and planted a chaste kiss on her forehead.

"Be happy," he whispered, his throat tight with tears. "Be good to Alex. He is a good man."

Kathalin burst into quiet tears, trying to grasp him but he pulled away from her. "I love you, Gates," she murmured. "Until the end of time, I will love you."

Gates had to turn away from her because, for the first time in his adult life, he realized he was fighting off tears. "And I will be true to you and only you until I die," he said hoarsely. "You are my heart, Kathi. Never forget that."

He was to the garden gate before Kathalin could say anything more. It seemed as if he were moving very quickly because by the time he reached the gate, he was nearly running. He opened the gate, nearly yanking it off its hinges, before charging through it. He was gone so quickly that that suddenly emptiness left in his wake was startling and painful. *Too* painful.

Kathalin sank to her knees and wept.

CHAPTER TWENTY

~ THE TENDER HEART ~

"I HAVE COME to see Lady Rosamund," Elreda said. "Is she availa-ble?"

After a soft knock on Rosamund's chamber door, Rosamund's maid had opened the panel to find Lady de Lohr standing on the landing outside. The maid remembered Lady de Lohr from visits to Hyssington in the past but she wasn't sure she should admit her until Rosamund, on her bed, heard the woman's heavily accented voice.

"Elreda?" she said. "Is that you?"

At the sound of Rosamund's voice, Elreda pushed into the chamber, nearly shoving the maid out of the way. Clouds of the heavy clove smell greeted her and she rubbed at her nose, avoiding sneezing as Jasper so often did.

"Aye, it 'tis," Elreda said, her attention eagerly focused in the direc-tion of Rosamund's voice, towards her great bed. "Is it you, Rosamund? It has been so long since we last spoke, my dear friend!"

Rosamund hadn't physically seen Elreda in fifteen years, ever since the symptoms of her disease started becoming apparent. Elreda and Henry had invited her and Jasper to Lioncross, many times, and Elreda and Henry had even come to Hyssington and Trelystan a few times, but in all that time, Rosamund had never made an appearance, pleading illness or some other manner of excuse. But now, Elreda was here, on

Rosamund's doorstep, and there was nothing Rosamund could do but try to stay away from her.

She didn't want the woman to see the truth.

"It is me, my dearest," she said, making sure to keep herself covered up and remaining behind her sheers. "Please do not come any closer. I am ill and it is contagious."

Elreda came to within a foot or so of the bed, seeing her friend, swaddled up like a baby, through the sheer fabric of the curtains. She studied the woman through the wispy material, reacquainting herself with her friend from long ago. From the vivacious dark-haired lass to this bound creature, times had changed, indeed.

"I am sorry to hear it," she said after a moment. "It is unfortunate that you have been so ill, so often, that you have not come to see me in so many years. I have missed you."

Rosamund could see her friend through the fabric, as well. Elreda was older in feature, but still as lovely as she remembered from their younger years. In truth, it did her heart good to see the woman.

"I have missed you, as well," she said. "But my health is very poor. You are looking well, my dearest. How are your children? I hear that we are to be related now. I cannot tell you how happy I am at such joyous news."

Elreda smiled faintly. She was increasingly curious at Rosamund's head-to-toe covered appearance, with only her eyes visible through a slit in the fabric covering her face. She wondered what terrible affliction her friend should have that would keep her so tightly wrapped and so utterly secluded. She thought to ask but then she assumed that if Rosamund wanted her to know, she would have told her. Still, she was very curious and concerned.

"I am happy, also," she said. "At least, I am happy at the prospect of becoming related to you. But that is why I have come, Rosamund. There is much turmoil surrounding this wedding and I am not sure if you know this. Have you been told?"

Rosamund knew immediately what Elreda was referring to. There was little doubt in her mind. "Do you speak of my daughter's love for another man?" she asked. "If so, I am aware. My daughter came to tell me herself."

She didn't sound particularly sympathetic as she spoke and Elreda was surprised. There was something in Rosamund's statement that suggested coldness. It was strange, considering she had always known Rosamund to be kind and compassionate. Still, perhaps the years had changed her. Having not seen or spoken to Rosamund in many years, it was possible that the woman had changed a great deal. That was a disheartening thought.

"What did your daughter tell you?" Elreda asked.

Rosamond paused before replying, as if contemplating what, exactly, to say. When she spoke, there was a disconnect to her words, as if she didn't much care for her daughter's problems. "She told me that she is in love with Gates de Wolfe," she said. "You know Gates, of course. He has led my husband's armies for many years. He and Alexander are close friends. My daughter also believes that Gates is in love with her but we know that to be false. Gates de Wolfe is incapable of loving just one woman. It is not in his nature. I am sorry that my daughter believes herself to be in love with the man, but she will get over it. You needn't worry. She will not shame your son or the House of de Lohr."

Frankly, Elreda couldn't believe the coldness she was hearing from her long-time friend. "But...," she began, stopped, and then started again. "Rosamund, you know what it is like to be young and in love. Sometimes you do not overcome such things so easily. Alex seems to believe that Gates is, indeed, in love with Lady Kathalin He was in the hall pleading his case not an hour ago. He does not want to marry your daughter because he firmly believes she is in love with Gates and he with her."

Rosamund looked at her friend, the bright blue eyes piercing through the sheer fabric. "That is of no consequence," she said. "Alexander is a much better match for my daughter than Gates de Wolfe."

"Why should you say that?"

"Because she will not be shamed by Alexander's past," Rosamund pointed out as if Elreda was a fool. She was beginning to grow annoyed. "Why is my daughter's misdirected love of such concern to you, Elreda? I told you that she will forget it. Gates will forget whatever he feels for her, too. I am sure he has felt what he thought to be love many times in the past. Knowing him, *too* many times. Jasper is arranging for the wedding to take place as soon as possible so this foolishness will come to an end. You put too much concern in the feelings of the young. They will forget soon enough and realize, in the end, that we knew what was best for them."

Elreda was speaking with someone she didn't know. The Rosamund from years ago would never have spoken in such a way about love or emotion. The woman before her was as hard as stone and just as cold. Elreda began to move, to come around the side of the bed, to where Rosamund was sitting. She didn't like the curtains up between them, shielding Rosamund from her. Shielding the woman she used to know. There was something odd and unfeeling going on here and she was determined to get to the bottom of it.

"You have changed," Elreda said. "The Rosamund I knew those years ago would not have discounted love so easily. I remember the days when you were very much in love with Jasper and he with you. Has so much changed, Rosamund, that you would forget young love?"

Rosamund could see that Elreda was moving closer and she tried to shrink away. "I have not forgotten it," she said. "It is wonderful while it lasts but when it ends, there is nothing more brutal. Mayhap, in a way, I am saving Kathalin from knowing such pain."

"Surely she knows it now."

Rosamund looked away. "It is for the best," she said. "Soon it will be but a memory as she comes to know Alexander. He is a likeable young man; mayhap she will even fall in love with him, too."

Elreda came to a halt, seeing her old friend very close and contemplating her next move. "No one wants Alexander to be married more than I do," she said. "But to marry a woman we know is in love with someone else... I am not sure that is right, not even in my eagerness for my son to wed. Can you not see this, too, Rosamund? Or have you changed so much that you are hardened to any matters of the heart?"

Rosamund sighed faintly. "I have grown up," she said. "I have come to realize that love is a fool's dream, Elreda. If you and Henry still share love at your age, then I commend you. But it is not always so with most people. It is not true with Jasper and me. Marriage can be a prison more than the four walls of this chamber when the love that used to be there is gone."

Elreda's features narrowed in concern. "And you would commit your own daughter to such a prison?"

"I am doing it for her own good."

Elreda shook her head. "Nay, you are not," she said, yanking back the sheers so she could see Rosamund without any material between them. "What is your motivation for this, Rosamund? Are you somehow punishing her for knowing love when you no longer do? Are you punishing her because she is young and passionate, and you can no longer feel the same way? There is something very wrong here for you to be so cold towards your own child. She loves a man who evidently loves her in return. Are you so bitter and jealous of that love that you would separate them simply because you have the power to do so? That is not the Rosamund I used to know and love. The woman I used to know was generous and compassionate, not petty and cruel. Is that what you have become?"

Rosamund's bright eyes flashed as she turned on her friend. "You have no idea what I have become," she growled. Suddenly, she yanked off the veil across her face, revealing a collapsed, flat nose and lips that were twisted with old scars and new sores. She ripped off the covers on her hands, showing that four of her ten fingers had been lost and stubbed by disease. Her flesh was gnarled and black, and she thrust her hands in Elreda's face. "*This* is what I have become! A monster, a creature who hides in darkness, a twisted relic who lost the only love she knew long ago because he could not bear to touch this gnarled flesh! Have I become cold and unfeeling? It is very possible considering that, for the last fifteen years, that is all I have known. How dare you come in here and accuse me of being cold and unfeeling, Elreda de Lohr! You live in your beautiful home with a husband who is still attracted to you while I live in the dank depths of a hellish existence. You have no right to judge me!"

Elreda was appalled at what she was seeing; her gorgeous friend was now decayed with a horrible disease that had robbed her of her physical beauty. Tears sprang to her eyes as Rosamund pushed stubby, black fingers into her face, but to her credit, Elreda didn't back away. She remained in place as Rosamund raged, her heart breaking for the truth behind Rosamund's years of absence. Now, some things were becoming clear but others were not. Her features were wrought with distress as she spoke.

"My friend," she murmured. "My dear and true friend. Now I understand why you have been captive in your own home. There is nothing I can say that will heal the scars left by this disease, for you have every right to show your agony. But I will say this – has this disease also robbed you of your good heart? You used to have one. You were so very kind and gentle, but it would seem now your heart is as twisted as your body. How could you become so cold and gnarled? How could you forget about love and blame your daughter because she has experienced it? That is not the Rosamund de Lara I grew to know and love. It is as if your very soul has left you!"

Rosamond sat back on her bed as if she had been struck, as if suddenly realizing she had just exposed her secret to the world. *To her beautiful friend.* Quickly, she lowered her head, struggling to put her veil over her face with fingers that didn't work correctly any longer. She pulled the sleeves of her robe over her hands, covering them, hiding them from Elreda, her embarrassment and horror filling the room like a cold, gray fog. Even Elreda could feel it, breathing it in, as Rosamund shrank away from her.

"You may go now, Elreda," she said, her voice sounding strangely weak after her outburst. "It was good to see you again. I pray your good health continues."

Just like that, Rosamund was shutting her off. No more conversation, conjecture, or the exhibition of pain. A simple shut-down of everything. Elreda stood over her friend as the woman tried desperately to cover herself, her heart breaking for the lovely woman that once was. In spite of everything, she didn't hate her. She didn't even dislike her. She felt a good deal of compassion and love for her old friend, now a mere shell of herself. Impulsively, she leaned down and wrapped her arms around the woman, squeezing tightly.

"And I pray you find your heart again," she whispered, kissing Rosamund on the top of her wimpled head. "No matter what was spoken here today, you are still my friend and I still love you. I pray that you find peace, Rosamund. I pray that you know happiness again. I will pray for many things for you, but most of all, I will pray that you reconsider your stance against your daughter's happiness. Remember what it was like to be in love with a man, Rosamund. Surely you cannot forget such a thing."

At the first touch of the embrace, Rosamond stiffened and tried to pull away. It had been fifteen years since anyone had touched her. But the moment she felt the warmth of human contact, and the love of Elreda's embrace, the tears began to come. She didn't realize how much she has missed such things, an embrace to tell her that she was still loved in spite of the fact that she had become a slave to the disease that imprisoned her. It was the most simple of gestures yet one of profound power. As Elreda gently squeezed, Rosamund couldn't help the tears from flowing.

She couldn't stop them.

The pain, the years of pain, washed down her face, dampening the veil that covered her twisted features. Elreda felt the woman sob beneath her and her tears quietly joined Rosamund's. She couldn't help it. Together, the old friends wept for the cruelty life had dealt

Rosamund and for the soul she had seemingly lost. Perhaps it was too late to reclaim anything; perhaps not. For the moment, the coldness from Rosamund was gone and, once again, she felt human.

She felt loved.

For the moment, it was simply her and Elreda, and a simple embrace that Rosamund needed so badly.

Elreda held her friend until the tears would no longer come, until, exhausted, Rosamund lay back on her pillows and closed her eyes as she was overcome by the emotion of the day. Elreda pulled the coverlet up around her friend, seeing the sunken face and black fingers but remembering the pert nose and exquisite skin instead. That was what she chose to remember.

That was what she chose to see.

As Elreda left Rosamund sleeping in her chamber, the beautiful face from fifteen years ago was, in fact, the only thing she *could* remember.

CHAPTER TWENTY-ONE

THE NIGHT WAS cold and the dark clouds that had gathered that day had finally started to shed some of their freezing rain. As Kathalin sat at the window, overlooking the now-dark herb garden, the wall of Hyssington beyond that, and then the landscape in the distance over the wall, there was so much in her heart that was frozen like the clouds and the rain, an indefinable coldness that had settled into her soul. She was numb against what was to come, numb against a future that would be determined on this night.

Gates wouldn't fight for her.

That was all she could think of. He refused to run, refused to take her and marry her. He gave his reasons and although, in theory, she understood him, the truth was that her heart was damaged and all she could see was that his honor meant more to him than she did. Or the honor of Alexander, and the entire houses of de Lohr, de Lara, and de Wolfe. So many people he was concerned with over her, or perhaps it was as he said – he'd never done anything truly honorable with regard to his personal life and felt strongly that he had to start somewhere.

So he started with her and in choosing this situation with which to regain his honor. Maybe it was true what she said, that he didn't love her enough to take her and flee. That was what it boiled down to, she thought.

He simply didn't love her enough.

Therefore, she sat and brooded, thinking back to the day she had first met him in the kitchen of St. Milburga's. She had been attracted to him, then, the very big man in the red de Lara tunic, fighting off the Welsh raiders who had invaded the priory. But that attraction had turned to hate when he had captured her, bound her hand and foot, and carried her off towards home. But the night before they'd reached Hyssington, when she'd seen the soldiers fornicating through the hearth and her wrists had been so terribly chaffed by the rope, he had softened his harsh stance against her and brought her so many lovely things. A peace offering, she knew, but she didn't care. It was then that the hatred had left and the emotions sprouting up in its place had turned into something warm.

Those warm emotions had turned into adoration for the man. He was strong, wise, humorous, at times, and honest. God's Bones, he was honest to a fault. She'd learned things about his past she probably didn't want to know, but in the course of honesty, he had told her. She knew a great deal about him and she still loved him, and he loved her.

… so why was this honor he spoke of worth more to him than she was?

Kathalin didn't know. She was muddled and distressed, too distressed to eat the food that the Tender of the Keep had brought her earlier in the evening. It now sat, cold and congealed, next to her bed. She couldn't even think of food at the moment, knowing that Stephan had ridden for a priest. A priest for her wedding. It had grown dark some time ago and she was coming to wonder if the priest would even come this night, as she'd been told.

The answer came soon enough.

A soft knock on her chamber door roused her from her thoughts. Timidly, Kathalin called out.

"Who comes?"

"'Tis Lady de Lohr," came a heavily accented Germanic voice. "Will you please admit me, Lady Kathalin?"

De Lohr. Kathalin knew that Alexander's parents had arrived so she

326

could only assume that it was his mother. She seriously considered sending the woman away but she knew it would be foolish to do so; it wouldn't delay or prevent anything. Even if she was to fight back, and perhaps grossly offend Lady de Lohr, that was no guarantee they would back out of the marriage contract. Even if they did, she could only imagine that Jasper would still not allow her to marry Gates and they'd be right back where they started. Many thoughts and many possibilities, rolled through her head, but none of them viable. It all came down to the truth of the matter –

She was trapped.

Her father intended marriage for her regardless of what she wanted, so if she wanted to look at the positive side of the situation, at least she knew Alexander. It would be horrific to be married to someone she did not even know, perhaps an old, smelly man or even a young, foolish heir, someone she could not stand to be around. At least she could stand to be around Alexander.

Perhaps this was the best she could hope for.

Resigned, she climbed off of the windowsill and went to the door. Throwing the old iron bolt, she pulled the door open.

A handsome woman with blue eyes, fair skin, and a pristine white wimple was smiling back at her. "Lady Kathalin?" she asked.

Kathalin nodded. "Aye."

"I am Lady de Lohr, Alexander's mother."

Kathalin stood back and admitted the woman into her chamber. "Please come in."

Elreda came into the chamber but her attention remained on Kathalin. In fact, she couldn't seem to take her eyes off her. "Sweet Mary," she sighed. "You look much as your mother did when she was young. Have you been told that?"

Kathalin shook her head. "Nay, my lady."

Elreda, in just the short few exchanges they'd had, could see how depressed Kathalin was. Now, the reality of all of the arguing Alexander had been doing against his participation in the marriage now had a face and a name in this lovely young woman. Elreda well understood what it was to have a broken heart, to be forbidden to marry the man you loved, but she also well understood a sense of duty. One had to do what one was told to do, especially when one was a woman. That being the case, it was impossible not to extend some measure of compassion to the girl.

"You look like her a great deal," she said, forcing a smile. "She was very beautiful in her youth. I have come to extend my welcome to the de Lohr family and to help you prepare for the ceremony. The priest has arrived so the mass will be conducted as soon as you are ready."

Kathalin's heart sank at that news. Not that she didn't know the wedding was coming, eventually, but to realize she was on the cusp of marrying Alexander in a matter of minutes made her nauseous. Still, there was nothing she could do. She couldn't fight back and she couldn't run off. For her, it was over.

Her entire life was over.

"Very well," Kathalin said, looking down at the lavender wool gown she was wearing. It was the garment Gates had purchased for her and even as she gazed at it, she fought off thoughts of him. "I suppose I am ready. Is there something more we must do?"

Elreda could see that the girl was dead in the eyes. No glimmer of hope, happiness, or excitement. A young lady should be thrilled for her wedding, but Lady Kathalin clearly wasn't. Although Elreda knew why, she would not say so. Some things were better left unspoken. Moreover, there was no reason to acknowledge pain that she could not help in any way. Perhaps it was as Rosamund said; perhaps Kathalin would forget about it, eventually.

Elreda had her doubts.

"Mayhap you will allow me to fix your hair," Elreda said, trying to sound positive and happy. "You have such lovely hair but it would be nice to dress it. Would you permit me?"

Kathalin had no desire to refuse or protest. She simply lifted her shoulders in a defeated gesture and Elreda took that as an affirmative. If the girl was going to be so apathetic, then Elreda would simply do what needed to be done. Gently, she pushed Kathalin down onto her small bed and went to work.

Elreda found the comb and iron pins on the same table that contained the soap and wash basin. Kathalin's hair was already in a tight, single braid, so she unbraided the hair and combed it vigorously before braiding it again and wrapping it around Kathalin's head, creating an elaborate hairstyle of braids that was exquisitely detailed. All the while, Elreda kept stealing glances at Kathalin's face, thrilled with the perfect beauty and imagining the magnificent grandchildren she would have from this woman. For the mother who had desperately wanted her son to marry, it was difficult not to think such thoughts.

But on the heel of thoughts of grandchildren also came thoughts of Rosamund, wondering how the woman could be so cold and callous towards this child. Surely the disease had something to do with it, but Elreda sensed that there was more to it. She wondered if Rosamund would ever return to the way she was before and if the compassionate woman Elreda had once known would make a resurgence.

For Kathalin's sake, she hoped so.

When the hair was finished, Elreda moved to inspect the surcoat Kathalin was wearing and noticed that the bottom of it was quite soiled. She asked Kathalin if she had any more dresses that would be appropriate for a wedding and Kathalin pointed to the slender wardrobe. Elreda opened it to find the blue patchwork brocade and the eggshell-colored wool with the fur around the neck and cuffs hanging on pegs inside. She withdrew the pale wool.

"This is a lovely garment," she said, holding it up. "Will you wear this? It would be better if this was pink or blue for your wedding, but the white will do. Will you put it on, my lady?"

Kathalin simply nodded and Elreda helped her from one garment into the next, tying up the laces in the back of the eggshell wool that cinched up the bodice. All the while, Kathalin ran her hands over it, smoothing it, remembering when Gates had bought it for her. *Gates....*

She closed her eyes, seeing his face, remembering when he'd produced the three garments at that tiny inn with no name, having purchased them from a business with a seamstress who sewed for the Countess of Shrewsbury. The dresses had been beautiful and it was then that something warm had begun to brew between her and Gates. Aye, she remembered that night well.

It had been the first night of the rest of her life.

Or so she thought.

Now, she was facing a different life as the mother of her future husband helped her dress for the wedding. Lady de Lohr seemed kind enough, quietly and efficiently helping her with her gown. Her touch was gentle but sure, but Kathalin had been completely silent through most of the process and she was coming to think that perhaps she might need to show some gratitude to the woman she was going to be related to for the rest of her life.

Even though her mood was heavy, and her heart broken, none of that was Lady de Lohr's fault or even Alexander's fault. The de Lohrs, through all of this, had not done anything wrong. It had not been these people who had separated her from Gates. Keeping that in mind, she tried to be somewhat polite.

"Thank you for your assistance, my lady," she said.

Elreda was surprised by the gratitude. She had been fussing over the back of Kathalin's dress but moved so that she could see Kathalin's face. She smiled timidly.

"You are very welcome, my lady," she said. "May I say that I am very happy to have you join our family? Alexander is our eldest son and his two younger sisters are already married. Strange thing that my boys do not have brides yet but my girls were married at a young age."

Kathalin could already see warmth in the woman, warmth she had hoped to see in her own mother but never did. "How old are your girls?" she asked.

Elreda went back to fussing with the hem of the gown, which seemed to be torn. She was trying to shore it up with what thread was still there. "Beatrix has seen twenty-four years," she said. "She already has two sons with her husband, who is part of the Cornwall d'Vant family, and Roxanne has seen nineteen years. She is pregnant with her first child."

It was clear that Elreda was thrilled to speak of her children. *Is it possible that women do love their children so much?* Kathalin thought. She'd often wondered.

"And you said that Alex has a brother?" she asked.

Elreda finished with the hem of the gown and let it fall to the floor. "Baxter is twenty years and two," she said. "He was in France with his brother at Poitiers, although we have not yet seen him returned. He serves de Montacute now and it is possible he has been kept with the earl. Ah, well... I am sure we shall see my boy very soon."

Kathalin couldn't help but be fascinated by a mother who should love her children so. "Do you miss your children, then?"

Elreda heard the wistfulness in Kathalin's tone and it nearly broke her heart, for she knew that the girl had known none of that from her own mother. Reaching out, she grasped Kathalin by both arms in a comforting, motherly gesture.

"I miss them all very much when they are away from me," she said, "and I take great comfort with the fact that you and Alexander will come to live with us at Lioncross Abbey after the wedding. It is a very big place and I am sure you will be quite happy there. I look forward to spending time with you and coming to know you, Lady Kathalin. You will be most welcome in our family."

Kathalin had never felt so wanted in her entire life and it was nearly too much to take. From parents who rejected her to people she didn't even know welcoming her, it was overwhelming. Confused, she nodded her head but just as swiftly burst into quiet tears. She simply couldn't help it. So much about this situation was agonizing, now with a future mother-in-law who spoke of her excitement for having Kathalin join her family. It was a wonderful thing to hear but it meant nothing to her considering Gates would not be part of that family. According to

Alexander, he wasn't even allowed to visit. Her hand flew to her face to quickly wipe away the tears.

"Forgive me, my lady," she said. "You are so kind. I... I am simply... this day has been quite taxing."

Elreda knew why the girl was crying. She needed no explanation. But Elreda could do nothing to help her; she had tried, so it was best now to simply get on with it. There was no use in delaying the inevitable.

"I know," she said, putting her arm around Kathalin's shoulders and turning her towards the door. "Let us go down to the hall now where the priest awaits. We will conduct the mass tonight and be done with it. Shall I tell you of Lioncross Abbey, which will be your new home?"

Kathalin simply nodded, allowing the woman to lead her to the door as she wiped away her tears. Elreda prattled on about Lioncross, a massive and important castle, but Kathalin wasn't really listening. She was reflecting on their conversation.

We will be done with it. Something in Lady de Lohr's tone suggested that she understood the situation, the reluctance of Kathalin. Perhaps she even knew about Gates. Kathalin suspected that she must know, being that Alexander must have told his parents. Surely everyone knew by now. And no one would do anything to help her or help Gates. They were determined to see a de Lohr/de Lara wedding, no matter what the cost.

As Lady de Lohr took Kathalin by the hand and led her out of the keep, Kathalin couldn't help but feel as if she were being taken to her own funeral.

The funeral that would bury any chance of her and Gates ever being together.

The funeral for a love that would never die.

"THE PRIEST IS in the hall, Gates," Jasper said. "I will expect you to attend Alex now. You will dress in your finest and stand by while he is married. You owe him that much considering how hard he tried to disobey both of his parents and me for your sake. The least you can do is not hide like a coward and pay witness to his wedding. It would show everyone that you do not bear a grudge. I would not have a knight in my stable that bore a grudge."

Jasper was standing in Gates' chamber in the gatehouse, dark now that the sun had gone down and lit only by the fire in the hearth. As Gates listened to Jasper's words of both threat and abuse, he lit a fat taper on the table near the window.

"I never considered hiding," he said, annoyed that Jasper had resorted to insults in his attempt to force him to attend Alexander and Kathalin's wedding. "Alex is my friend and I will support him in this endeavor which he did not choose to be a part of."

It was a volley back at Jasper for what he had done to all of their lives. Jasper inhaled slowly, displeasure on his face.

"Gates," he said, his voice low. "I realize that this entire situation with my daughter has been distasteful for us all. I am willing to forget about your behavior, as I always am, but do not cross me. Do not give me a reason to become upset with you. Am I making myself clear?"

Gates wasn't in any mood for Jasper and his veiled threats. He wasn't in any mood for the man, anyway. He was beaten, hollow, despondent, and struggling not to show it. After leaving Kathalin in the garden earlier that day, he had been lingering in a state of anguish. He thought about throwing himself on his sword or going into town and buying some poison from the apothecary. He even thought about getting on his horse and riding north until he came to Castle Questing and then remaining there for the rest of his life, living like a hermit. The more he gazed at Jasper, the more attractive the latter option became.

"You are," he said. "But to you I will say this; I can no longer stand the sight of you or of Hyssington Castle. I have had a belly full of the inequity and despair of this place. I will stand with Alex as he marries Kathalin but after that, I am leaving and I will never return. I ask that you release me from my oath of service to you but if you will not grant me a release, I will simply go anyway. There is nothing you can say or do that will change my mind, so it would be best not to try. I would rather part amicably from your service but I take no issue with parting with hostility. The choice is yours."

Jasper gazed back at him, steadily, trying to deduce whether he was bluffing. Jasper had known Gates for many years and he'd never known the man to lie, or bluff, but in this case, he couldn't tell. He thought perhaps it was the disgruntled lover in him speaking.

"For all of the husbands and fathers and brothers I have paid for the women you have compromised, you would show me no greater respect than this?" he asked, shaking his head with regret. "I thought you were a better man than this. You *owe* me, de Wolfe."

Gates could feel his temper rise and his jaw began to tick. "If you would give me a tally of what I owe you, what you have paid out on my behalf, I will be happy to repay you," he said. "But my service to you is at an end. You seriously cannot expect me to continue after what has happened."

"I not only expect it, I demand it."

Gates could see that Jasper was serious and he considered his options at that moment; if he continued to argue about it, he could very well end up in the vault for insubordination, but if he simply shut his mouth and let Jasper think he had the upper hand, then he would be able to slip away at some point and Jasper wouldn't know anything about it until it was too late.

Frustrated, and hurt, Gates opted for the latter. He would not argue with a man who not only dispossessed the capacity for understanding, but who lacked the reasoning to do so as well. A selfish, petty man. He had always known that but now, he was seeing it more than he ever had. He turned back to the wardrobe that contained his possessions, including clean tunics.

"I will be down to the hall momentarily," he said in a clear refusal to verbally engage Jasper. "Allow me to change into something clean. I will not go to a mass looking like this."

He wasn't dressed particularly badly but Jasper didn't argue with him. He was simply grateful that Gates wasn't arguing with him, that he was submitting to him, which is all Jasper wanted, anyway. Therefore, he turned away and left the room, heading down the narrow stairs that led to the entry level of the gatehouse. His footfalls faded, echoing off the stone.

When Jasper was gone, Gates emitted a heavily sigh. It was as if a weight had been lifted from his chest and he could breathe once again. But the weight of losing Kathalin was still there, like a vise around his chest, and it was a struggle simply to live. He had no idea he was capable of such emotion, something that literally drained the life from his body. He was dead already, in purgatory, soon to live out the rest of his life in the indentured hell of a man in love with a woman he could never have.

Gates knew that Stephan had returned with the priest some time ago. He recognized Father Wenceslaus as he had arrived with the big knight astride his small, elderly palfrey that hardly moved well at all these days. Gates knew that because Jasper had once offered the priest another horse to ride, a fine animal, but the priest had declined, stating he was quite attached to his old mare. As Gates had watched from his chamber window, seeing Stephan astride his big rouncey, and the priest riding, strangely, sidesaddle on the back of his elderly mare, he resigned himself to the inevitable.

The passage of the pair beneath the gatehouse had been something of a blow to Gates. He'd been hoping beyond hope that, somehow, this was all a nightmare and by some miracle, the priest would never come, Jasper would forget about the betrothal, as would the de Lohrs, and he could slip away with Kathalin.

Since leaving her in the garden, he'd done quite a bit of soul searching, knowing that he was doing the honorable thing by not abducting her, but as time passed, he wondered if he was doing something he could really live with. Had Kathalin been correct? Did he love his reclaimed honor, or at least the idea of it, more than her? It was quite possible that she had been correct and as the hours passed and the sky turned to night, he was coming to think that he had been wrong. In his angst, he was deeply confused.

Was he doing the right thing?

And then the priest had arrived with Stephan and the reality of what was to take place that night hit him like a hammer. He'd known all along it was coming but to see the clergyman arrive through Hyssington's big gatehouse brought it all home. Kathalin was being married that night and it would not be to him, yet he would be expected to attend the wedding as a show of good faith, that he held no hard feelings, in the hopes that Jasper and the de Lohrs and even Alexander might see that he was made of better things. He was a de Wolfe, after all, and he'd never in his life truly lived up to that name.

Now, he was hoping he finally would.

He was hoping the cost of redeemed honor was worth the price of a lost love.

"Gates?"

A soft voice came from the doorway and he turned to see Stephan and Tobias standing there. Tobias was already entering the chamber, looking at Gates with great concern.

"We came to see if there is something we can do for you, Gates," the young knight said. "We have not been invited to the wedding. We thought, mayhap, we could... *do* something for you."

Gates' eyes crinkled at the corners as he suspected what the man meant. In truth, he wasn't surprised that they knew. The four knights were quite close and there wasn't much they didn't know about each other, not even in a situation such as this.

"Like what?" he asked.

Tobias appeared uncertain, hesitant. "Anything," he said. "*Anything at all.*"

Gates cocked an eyebrow. "Are you offering to abduct Lady Kathalin and spirit her off so that I may come to her later, and then we will run away together?"

Tobias looked at Stephan with some chagrin because Gates wasn't pleased by their offer of service. Stephan chuckled softly. "Something like that," he said as he came into the room. Quickly, he sobered. "As you might have suspected, Alex told us everything. Gates, I cannot tell you how sorry I am for you, my friend. If you want our help, then all you need to do is ask."

Gates' initial reaction was one of embarrassment, embarrassed because his men knew of his weakness in his love for a woman. But he was deeply touched, and not at all surprised, that they would be willing to risk themselves on his behalf. Their bonds of brotherhood ran deep.

"Did Alex send you to ask me this?" he asked.

Stephan shook his head. "He did not," he said. "Tobias and I discussed it. You are our liege and, truth be told, much more of a liege than de Lara ever was. You have stood beside us in battle, have risked your life for us, and now it is time for us to repay the favor. We stand at the ready to do your bidding, my lord."

Gates looked between the pair; the big, hairy knight and his young, pure-looking counterpart beside him. They made quite the team, now intending to right the wrongs on behalf of Gates and Kathalin. After a moment, Gates simply chuckled and reached out, putting a big hand on Tobias' shoulder.

"I am honored and touched by your gesture," he said, "but I will tell you what I told Alex. I would not dishonor him in such a way as to abscond with his bride. The implications of an action such as that would be more far reaching than you know. It would not be a simple matter of running away with Lady Kathalin. To do so would shame Alex, his family, my family, and the de Laras. The greater implications could be staggering. I will not go into all of it, but you get the gist of my reasons. And I thank you for your offer. It means a great deal to me."

Tobias, who was young enough that he'd not yet learned not to wear his heart on his sleeve, was clearly upset by the situation. "Alex said that you and the lady are in love with each other," he said. "Alex said he did not want to marry her because of it, yet Stephan had to fetch Father Wenceslaus and bring him here. Is Lord de Lara going to force Alex to marry Lady Kathalin?"

Gates sighed heavily. Even the mere mention of what was to take place this evening left him feeling hollow and weak. It was one thing to think it, but to hear it… God, it was painful.

"Aye," he said. "The marriage is going through as planned."

Stephan, who had known Gates for many years, could see the anguish in his features. He'd never seen that from Gates before, not ever. It was enough to sink his spirit.

"Gates, are you sure there is nothing we can do?" he pleaded softly. "Anything, lad. If you want me to break down the door to the keep and steal your lady, I will do it. It doesn't seem right that de Lara is forcing this."

Gates looked at his old friend. "Bear, if I asked you to pull a wall down to get to a barrel of ale on the other side, you would do it for me," he said, watching Stephan smirk. "You are a true and loyal friend, but this is a battle you cannot fight for me. In fact, the war is over and de Lara has won. But I will tell you this and you must vow you will never repeat it, especially to de Lara – after this wedding, which I have been asked to attend, I am leaving for Castle Questing. I do not want any memories of this place after tonight. I am going home."

Stephan was saddened but he understood. "Of course," he said quietly. "Shall I have your horse ready for you?"

Gates nodded. "Aye," he said. "And if you would not mind packing my belongings and putting them on my horse, I would be grateful. Once the mass is completed, I am leaving for good."

Both Stephan and Tobias nodded. "Aye, we will," Stephan said. "Is there anything else?"

Gates thought on that a moment. Then, he went to his wardrobe and took out a clean, red woolen tunic along with a small leather purse at the bottom of the cabinet. He set the purse on the bed as he pulled the tunic over his head, settling it on his big frame, and then retrieved the purse. He pulled several coins out of the purse and handed them to Stephan.

"You will look in on Helene of Linley from time to time," he said. "Make sure she and the child are fed. Will you do this?"

Stephan took the money. "Of course."

Gates looked at the man a moment, a man he'd seen years of battle with. A man who was his close friend. He put his hand on Stephan's cheek.

"Thank you for your friendship and sword," he said softly. "If you need me, you know where to find me. But you will not tell anyone else. Understood?"

Stephan nodded firmly. "Indeed, my lord."

Gates was satisfied. He then turned to Tobias, putting a hand on the man's shoulder. "And you," he said, nodding his head in Stephan's direction. "Listen to this old man and you will live a long and healthy life. Will you do this?"

Tobias nodded. "I will, my lord."

"And you know my whereabouts, too, but you will tell no one."

"A thousand instruments of torture could not drag it out of me."

Gates smiled ironically. "Let us hope it does not come to that," he said, giving the lad one last pat before dropping his hands. "Good knights, it would seem I am expected at a wedding. Will you escort me to the hall?"

Stephan and Tobias did, gladly, but there was great sadness in their movements. Gates saw it but he hardly cared, mostly because it was taking everything he had simply to put one foot in front of the other, heading towards the great hall where the priest waited to join the woman he loved in marriage to another man. He kept praying it was a dream and that he would soon awaken, with Kathalin in his arms and the love between them growing deeper by the moment.

But he knew that was not the case. He was living a nightmare. He had fleeting regrets about not bedding Kathalin, simply because it would have been a demonstration of his love for her, but he knew it was better this way. He knew that once he had a taste of her flesh, his honor would leave him and he would become the dishonorable rogue who ran off with Alexander de Lohr's bride. He knew that any taste of her beyond what he'd already sampled would have turned him into a mindless primitive, a being led by feelings his common sense could not overcome. But in his case, it would be more than lust. It was love as he'd never known it.

And never would again.

Once the three of them reached the bailey, the great hall loomed before them in the darkness. The rain was growing heavy at this point and the long, lancet windows cut into the side of the building were glowing from the light and warmth emitting from inside. The entry door was open and he could see illumination beyond and he could also see figures standing in the doorway.

Of course, it was the priest and Jasper and the de Lohrs preparing for the ceremony at the door to the hall before proceeding inside and heading to the small chapel that was just off the west side of the hall. The chapel wasn't big enough to hold more than six people at any time, a tiny room where generations of de Laras had worshipped. Tonight, it would see a man's life ruined.

Stephan and Tobias moved away from Gates midway through the bailey and let the man continue on his own to the hall. Step by step, inch by inch, Gates felt as if he were going to his own execution. Everything for him would end on this night, the life he had never hoped for but found himself wanting.

The love he would never fully know.

Death, to him, would have been preferable.

CHAPTER TWENTY-TWO

I T WAS UPON her.

Kathalin and Lady de Lohr approached the great hall in the darkness of the bailey, through the cold rain that was falling on them, and Kathalin could see the men gathered outside the door of the great hall where the beginning of the marriage mass would take place. The priest would begin the mass at the entry before gathering the wedding party and proceeding inside, which was the normal protocol. As Kathalin drew closer to the door, which was emitting light into the darkness of the bailey, she realized that the time was finally upon her. No more pleading, no more bargaining or begging. Now, it was finished.

It was time to marry Alexander.

The realization was like a stab to her heart and the tears started, mingling with the freezing rain that was falling upon them with increasing strength. Her careful hair dressing was becoming wet, as was her gown, and by the time she and Lady de Lara reached the doorway, the priest was ushering everyone inside and out of the rain. It was beginning to rain in epic proportions and a change of location would have to be made. The mass would have to be started, and finished, inside.

The fire in the hearths were burning brightly and Lady de Lohr gently pulled Kathalin over to the closest one, now concerned with drying the woman out. It was very cold, and Kathalin was shivering violently, and Lady de Lohr sent the nearest servant for something hot for the woman to drink. The priest, seeing that the bride and the groom's family were gathered over near the hearth closest to the door, made his way to them.

"It is of no matter to begin the mass in here, my lord," the priest said to Jasper. "It will keep my book from becoming soaked if there is a roof over our heads."

Jasper, who had been drinking fairly steadily since having left Gates about a half hour earlier, simply waved the priest off. He had a fourth cup of wine in his hand and he wanted to be done with this entire situation, as stressful as it had been. After everything that had happened over the past few days, he was coming to regret ever having a daughter. His mood, therefore, was foul.

"Fine," he snapped. "We are waiting for one more guest and when he arrives, you will begin."

The priest nodded. "What of Lady de Lara, my lord?"

Jasper glanced at him, sharply, before grunting in disgust. "She will *not* attend," he said deliberately. "We are waiting for one more man only and not my wife."

Elreda, standing with Kathalin and trying to dry the poor woman off, heard Jasper's comment. "We could wait for her, Jasper," she said. "In fact, I will go to her chamber and escort her down here."

Jasper was shaking his head before she even finished. "Nay," he said shortly. "She does not come out of her chamber. She never comes out of her chamber. She stays in there and rots."

Jasper's drunken words were harsh. Henry, standing with Alexander, didn't want to get caught up in a tussle between his wife and Jasper. He put out a hand, mostly to interrupt any manner of argument that might be starting.

"Certainly we can conduct the mass and if Lady de Lara chooses to attend the feast afterwards, it will be most agreeable," he said, trying to lighten the mood. "Jasper, I forgot to tell you that I have brought four bottles of good red wine from Spain. I will bring them forth after our children are wed."

Jasper was interested in the wine, enough so that it forced him off the subject of his wife. As he and Henry began to discuss the region where the wine originated, somewhere in the Andalucia region, Kathalin held her hands out over the fire and tried to warm herself. Elreda was behind her, shaking out the back of her surcoat and trying to wring the mud out of it, and as Kathalin rubbed at her hands, she heard a quiet voice beside her.

"I see that you let my mother have her way with your hair," Alexander said. "You look quite lovely."

Kathalin looked over at the man standing next to her. He was smiling timidly at her, his handsome features reflecting the firelight. His golden hair had been neatly combed and he had even shaved. When he smiled, the dimples in both cheeks were deep. Aye, he was a very handsome man but all Kathalin saw when she looked at him was sorrow. She sighed heavily.

"Thank you," she said quietly. "Alex, please know how sorry I am that you are being forced into this. I am sure this is not how you ever imagined you would be married."

His smile turned ironic. "Nor you," he said, his eyes lingering on her a moment. "The situation cannot be changed, my lady. I will make the best of it if you will."

Kathalin nodded but her eyes were beginning to well. "Gates told me to be good to you," she said, choking up. "I promise that I will do my very best."

"I know you will."

"I hope… I hope we will at least come to like each other. I could not bear it if you resented me."

He shook his head. "Nor could I bear it if you hated me," he said quietly. "I swear to you, Kathalin, that I will do my very best to make you a good husband. It is the least I can do to make this situation pleasant for the both of us."

Kathalin nodded as the tears spilled over, and Alexander was seized with sympathy for the woman. He wanted to reach out and comfort her, but somehow, it didn't seem right. He didn't want this marriage and neither did she, but at least he didn't have the added burden of being in love with someone else. So he stood there, close to her, watching her weep and wishing he could say something to her that would bring them both comfort. As he stood there, wondering what he could say, he saw movement in the hall entry.

Looking over Kathalin's head, his eyes locked with Gates as the man entered. The storm outside was raging and Gates was fairly soaked, and his eyes found Alexander's right away. It was a poignant moment for them both, one full of a thousand unspoken words of thanks, of sorrow, and of friendship until Gates finally nodded, once, as if to acknowledge that he had arrived and that he was ready for what was to come. Perhaps not completely ready, but as ready as he would ever be. But then his gaze moved to Kathalin's lowered head and it was then that Alexander saw just how distraught Gates still was. By his sheer expression, the man was being torn apart. Before Alexander could move to him, however, Jasper caught sight of the knight.

"Ah!" Jasper said, thumping the priest on the arm to get the man's attention. "Our last guest has arrived. You may begin. Gates! Attend me!"

Kathalin's head shot up at the sound of Gates' name being shouted and she turned around to see the man as Jasper went to him, grabbed him by the arm, and pulled him up to the hearth. Gates' gaze found her, through the people and the smoke around them, and he gave her a small smile, an encouraging one, as if to silently tell her that everything was going to be all right. Of course, it wasn't going to be all right and they both knew it. Kathalin couldn't even manage to smile back.

In fact, she realized she shouldn't be looking at him at all. The sight of him threatened to destroy her composure completely so she quickly turned around and faced the hearth, telling herself that there was no use in thinking on the man. There was no use in looking at him or even acknowledging that he was standing behind her. For once, for just this once, she had to be strong and not think of him and pretend none of this mattered because, for certain, the alternative was a complete collapse which, in the end, wouldn't stop the wedding. It would only delay it, and there was no use in delaying the destiny that had been chosen for her.

A destiny without Gates.

So she faced the hearth, tears still streaming down her face in silent protest of what was about to take place, each tear representing a fragment of her heart that had been splintered away. So many fragments poured down her cheeks and she kept wiping at them, dashing them away, and trying not to be too obvious about it. It occurred to her that her tears might be an insult to Alexander, who was trying to be kind to her in this dismal hour. Therefore, she tried very hard to stop those fragments of liquid emotion that poured down her cheeks.

It was the most difficult fight of her life.

The priest, not oblivious to the weeping bride, had Alexander face him and then positioned Kathalin on Alexander's left side, as woman was created from Adam's left rib according to the church doctrine. Father Wenceslaus, a slender man with heavy, dark eyebrows and hair growing out of his nose, eyed Alexander and Kathalin seriously.

"We shall begin," he said. "I will ask the guests in attendance if any of them can show just cause as to why you two should not be married, and then I shall ask you the same question. Can anyone tell me why this couple should not be joined?"

The question went out to the group. Kathalin closed her eyes tightly, cringing as she waited for Gates to speak up. Perhaps she was praying that he would, hoping beyond hope that the man would denounce what was happening to the woman he loved. In fact, every person in the room other than the priest was waiting for the same thing, but Gates remained silent in the matter. He was staring at the priest without saying a word. Elreda and Henry sighed with relief as Jasper glared at Gates, who refused to meet the man's eye. The priest, not receiving any response, turned the question on Alexander and Kathalin.

"My lady," he said, "my lord? Do either of you have any cause or reason why you may not be joined in matrimony?"

Now it was everyone else's turn to hold their breaths as the question focused on Kathalin. Tears were still trickling from her eyes, less now, but she did nothing more than reach up and flick them away. She kept her mouth shut to the question because she knew that it would do no good for her to speak up. *I am in love with another man!* No one would care about that. She would be considered disrespectful and, in turn, make Alexander look like a fool. Gates had asked her to be good to him.

She didn't want to disobey Gates.

So she said nothing, sickened that no one would speak up for the travesty going on. If the priest sensed that there was an entire hall full of unspoken protests, he didn't let on. He simply opened the liturgy book in his hand and lifted his arm, open palm out, to the bridal couple.

"Let us pray," he said.

"Wait!"

The cry came from the back of the hall, near the door, and everyone turned sharply to see a swaddled figure standing there. Kathalin, Elreda, and Jasper recognized the person immediately.

"Rosamund!" Jasper gasped, leaving Gates' side to go to his wife. "What in God's good name are you doing here?"

Rosamund held up a hand to Jasper, forbidding him to come any closer to her. She was soaking wet and the veil around her face was clinging to her skin, transparently, making her sunken face fairly visible. She appeared feeble and twisted, but the bright blue eyes were strong. They were fixed on Jasper.

"I had to come, Jasper," she said quietly. "I... had to."

Jasper looked at her, perplexed, but also increasingly horrified. He could see his wife's face quite plainly through the wet fabric and, having not seen it for years, was stunned at what he was seeing.

"Why?" he asked again, disgust for her appearance marking his features. "You made no mention of wanting to attend this wedding."

Rosamund nodded. "I know," she said. "But I had to. I fear I must stop it."

Jasper's eyes widened. "What's this you say?" he said, shocked. "You intend to *stop* it?"

Rosamund nodded and her gaze moved to Kathalin, standing over near the hearth. Her gaze softened. "Jasper, it was wrong of us to do this to Kathalin," she said. "We have gone our entire lives wronging the child because she was born a girl. Do you recall how disappointed you were? You had wanted another son, like Roget, but when Kathalin was born, you refused to look at her for an entire month. When she was an infant, you did not even want her around. I told her that we sent her to St. Milburga's because I did not want her to contract my disease but that was not entirely the truth. The reality is that you did not want her here. It is the reason behind sending her away more than my disease was."

Jasper was turning red in the face. "Must we discuss this now?" he said through clenched teeth. "This entire room of people does not need to hear our business, Rosamund."

Rosamund looked at her husband, her veil lifting when she sighed with exasperation. "They already know our business," she said. "They know that you want to wed Kathalin to Alex to form an alliance with the House of de Lohr. They know that you have denied Gates' suit for Kathalin even though both Gates and Alex begged you to reconsider. Think, Henry; think back to the days when I was young and beautiful, and you were madly in love with me. Are you so old and hard that you cannot remember those days of glory? I can. I remembered them today when Elreda reminded me of such things. I remember when I was beautiful and you loved me still. I remember the joy of those days. It took a while for me to recall them, but I do now. I supposed I had shut them out, but this afternoon, I remembered. It all came back to me."

Jasper wasn't sure what to say or how to react. He was feeling increasingly embarrassed by the appearance of his wife, who was not only contradicting his wishes for this marriage but also showing her diseased face.

"Go back to your chamber, Rosamund," he said. "You are not well. Your mind is not well."

Rosamund chuckled ironically. "My mind is perfectly sane," she said, shuffling away from Jasper and heading in the direction of the people gathered at the hearth. She looked at Elreda, who was blinking back tears.

"You were correct, Elreda," she said. "I am not the Rosamund you knew. You said that you would pray that I found my happiness again but the truth is that my happiness is gone. I had my chance. But Kathalin has never had that chance. Do you know that she begged me to allow her some happiness? She begged me to allow her to marry Gates and I refused her, much as Jasper did, but it was not right that we did that. Kathalin has known absolutely no affection from her parents her entire life. She has lived within the cold walls of St. Milburga's, never knowing a mother's love or a father's affection. Jasper and I did that to her. We were about to do it to her again by wedding her to Alex. But I find that I simply condemn her to the rest of her life in misery."

Kathalin, who had thus far been standing in stunned silence, began to realize what her mother was saying. She stepped away from Alexander, moving towards her mother.

"Rosamund, what is your meaning?" she asked, suspicion and shock in her tone. "Did you truly come to stop this wedding? Or did you simply come to clear your conscience for the way you and father have treated me all of these years?"

Rosamund looked at her daughter. The bright eyes crinkled at the corners as the twisted lips smiled beneath the veil. "She looks like me, does she not?"

The question was directed at Elreda, who nodded. "She does, indeed."

Rosamund studied Kathalin's face for a moment. "I think she is much more beautiful than I ever was," she said to Elreda. Then, she focused on her daughter. "Kathalin, I must ask your forgiveness. For the years of neglect, for a loveless existence, I must ask your forgiveness. Although I still believe a marriage to Alex is a smart move, and would make a strong alliance, to force you into it not only makes your life miserable but also ruins Alex's life as well as Gates. And Gates... your father loves him like a son. It is true that his past is not as we would like it to be, but a true man would show his repentance by making a good and true husband to you for the rest of your life. Gates?"

Gates heard his name called and he straightened. Up until this point, he was much like everyone else in the hall, listening to Rosamund in stunned silence. In truth, he could hardly believe what he was hearing. He could hardly dare to hope, but when he heard her call his name, he answered without hesitation.

"My lady?"

"Come here."

Gates did as he was told. He moved past the priest, past Jasper, and went to stand next to the tiny woman in the wet clothing.

"Aye, my lady?"

Rosamund looked up at him with eyes shaped very much like Kathalin's. "Tell me that I am not making a mistake, Gates," she said. "Tell me that if I permit you to marry my daughter that you will make a fine and true husband for her for the rest of your days. Swear to me that your loyalty will be to her and only to her."

Gates didn't hesitate; he dropped to a knee in front of Rosamund in a gesture of fealty and service. It was a fluid, gallant gesture not lost on anyone in that room. It was a show of complete submission.

Of truth.

"With everything I am, I swear it to you," he said steadily. "With all that I am, I would endeavor to make as fine and true a husband as has ever lived. I would love her, and only her, until my death, and even beyond if God would allow it."

Rosamond looked at the knight, now nearly eye-level with her, and she could read his sincerity like a book. Reaching out, she put a damp, swaddled hand on his head.

"You love her, do you not?"

Gates had been in control until she had asked that question. Then, his control left him and his eyes grew moist. He swallowed the lump in his throat.

"With every fiber of my being, I do, my lady," he said hoarsely.

Rosamund smiled; the gesture could be seen through the damp veil. "I believe you," she said. "I am sure Alex would not protest if he switches places with you in this ceremony. Go and stand next to my daughter, Gates de Wolfe."

Astonished, Gates rose to his feet, looking at Alexander, who was gazing back at him with equal shock. But Alexander quickly moved away, clearing the way for Gates to take his place, as Kathalin stood there with her mouth open. She was so overwhelmed that she couldn't even speak. But standing back behind the group as Rosamund gave orders, Jasper let out a grunt.

"Rosamund!" he demanded. "What in God's name are you doing? Have you gone mad?"

Rosamund turned to him. "I have not," she said. "I have come to my senses and I am doing what we should have done in the first place. To the devil with our fears of Gates' reputation and the shame on Kathalin; the truth is that *you* are the only one who would be shamed by such a thing, and frankly, it does not matter to me if you feel shame or not. I would feel more shame knowing that, once again, we made our daughter miserable. She loves this man and he loves her, and that is the only thing that matters. Let them have their love, Jasper. Now, shut your pie hole. I have come to witness a wedding and I will not hear your voice again."

Jasper, mouth agape in outrage, started to reply but thought better of it. Rosamund might have been diseased and decrepit, but at the moment, she was the most powerful thing in that room and he wasn't about to tangle with her. She might become angry and wipe some of her disease on him while he was sleeping. Or, so he thought.

In any case, he kept his mouth shut because, truth be told, he knew he was in for a lifetime of utter aggravation if he didn't comply. And the truth was that he had been put in his place in front of a room full of people who now knew the truth about him and his attitude towards his daughter. There was nothing more he could say, so, at the risk of embarrassing himself completely, he simply shut his mouth.

Rosamund, as always, knew best.

Reluctantly, Jasper resumed his place near Elreda and Henry, who actually seemed relieved that their son wouldn't have to marry a woman who was in love with another man. It seemed that they, too, had second thoughts about the marriage contract and Rosamund's well-timed appearance had solved their dilemma. In fact, Elreda seemed quite thrilled by it, dabbing at her eyes as Gates took his place next to Kathalin and gazed down at the woman with enough love in his expression to fill the great hall of Hyssington and then some.

They all saw it. It was the look of a love that would finally be realized.

Kathalin latched on to Gates and refused to let go, holding the man tightly as if afraid she was living a dream, afraid he might fade away were she to relinquish her grip. For certainly, a moment like this could only be in a dream, a wisp of a thought so pure, so beautiful, that it was as if angels had spun it upon their looms of life. As the priest began to intone the mass, Kathalin reached over and pulled Rosamund to stand with her, clutching the woman with one hand and Gates with the other.

Rosamund, normally too weak to stand for any length of time, found the will to stand tall at her only daughter's wedding. Finally, Rosamund realized that she had, once again, found her happiness in the glowing expression of Kathalin's face.

She'd found her heart again.

A dream, Kathalin thought as she stood between her mother and Gates. *Surely such things as this only happen in dreams, when happiness is so complete that there is nothing left to wish for or hope for. I never thought I was destined for much happiness in life, but it would seem that I have been wrong. This must be what young women dream of when they imagine a perfect life. Now, I know. Finally, I know.*

A glance to Gates as the priest finished the marriage mass saw the man with tears in his eyes. When their gazes met, Kathalin smiled knowingly at him.

Finally, he knows, too.

The days of the Dark Destroyer and his roguish ways had finally come to an end.

EPILOGUE

THE SMALL CHAMBER was warm and the fire was low, white-hot, casting a golden glow into the room that spilled over the walls and bed. The Tender of the Keep had stoked the fire in the small chamber across from Rosamund's bower, the chamber that Kathalin had been sleeping in because Henry and Elreda occupied the larger bower on the floor below.

But Henry and Elreda were not in their room. They were still in the hall, having gone through the four bottles of fine Spanish wine that Henry had brought with them and more besides. Moreover, Rosamund was still in the hall, and she and Elreda had moved to their own private corner to discuss days past as the men gathered and drank. It was embarrassing for Alexander, actually, because his father and mother could hold more liquor than he could. After the wedding feast following the most unconventional wedding, Alexander decided he'd had enough and begged off to retire for the night.

Gates had gone with him simply to make sure he made it back to his chamber in one piece, but Kathalin followed because she, too, was genuinely exhausted, and both men ended up escorting Kathalin to the keep. Gates told his bride he would return to her shortly and as Kathalin went inside, Gates and Alexander walked arm in arm across the bailey towards Hyssington's enormous gatehouse.

The rain had eased up at that point, falling in a soft mist, as Alexander wept on Gates about the beauty of the marriage and how very happy he was for his friend. He also revealed that he was quite relieved. He was terrified that he wasn't ready yet to become a husband and terrified that he would fail Gates where it came to Kathalin. Gates assured Alexander that he was, indeed, a fine friend, the very best, and he swore that he would repay his kindness someday. Alexander became emotional and slobbery after that, and Gates tried to avoid the man's alcohol-saturated hugs to the head.

Fortunately, he was saved by Stephan and Tobias, who were on guard duty and saw the pair coming across the bailey. They came out to help Gates with Alexander but before Alexander was taken away by his grinning friends, he hugged Gates tightly and kissed the man loudly on the cheek, congratulating him on his marriage. Then he turned to Stephan and began weeping all over the man, reciting the story of Lady Rosamund's change of heart. Stephan and Tobias were naturally stunned to hear of such a thing, as the news hadn't made it out of the great hall until that moment, but their shock soon turned to joy on Gates' behalf.

After accepting their congratulations, Gates watched with a smirk on his face as Stephan and Tobias dragged Alexander off to put him to bed. A truer and more noble friend had never lived, for certainly, he owed everything to Alexander. As of tonight, he felt like the most fortunate man in all of England.

Perhaps his sins didn't find him out, after all.

Perhaps he had been forgiven.

But thoughts of his selfless friend and sins of the past were quickly pushed aside as Gates turned towards the keep, his mind moving to the night ahead, a night he never imagined to experience. His thoughts were full of the evening and what had transpired, no longer reeling from the shock of it but settling into the reality of what had happened. He was a married man now with the most beautiful bride he could ever imagine. He never thought he'd be happy to realize he was married, but he was. He was thrilled.

Lost in thought, he had entered the keep without even realizing it, now on the third floor outside of Kathalin's bower. Knocking softly on the door, it was almost immediately opened and Kathalin stood there in the warm glow of the firelight, smiling at him. Glowing, delicious firelight was all over the room, inviting him in.

"I half-expected you to spend time with your knights, drinking away your wedding night," Kathalin said. "There is a good deal to celebrate tonight."

Gates nodded as he entered the chamber and she shut the door behind him, bolting it. "That is true," he said. "But any celebrating I do will be with you and not a gang of smelly men that I have spent far too much time with already."

Kathalin laughed softly, gazing at him in the dim light. After a moment, her smile faded. "I thought I would be facing Alex at this moment," she said softly. "Is this real? Is it really you?"

"It is."

"I can still hardly believe it. It does not seem possible."

Gates smiled faintly. "Nay, it does not," he said. "I still expect to wake up tomorrow and discover it has all been a dream. I think it would kill me if that happened. I could not bear it."

Kathalin shook her head. "Nor I," she whispered. "I do not know what changed my mother's mind, but I will not question it. Something gave her a change of heart and I thank God for it. He must have heard my prayers."

"And mine."

She cocked her head. "Did you really pray, Gates?" she asked. "I did not know you were the praying kind. You have never seemed like one."

He shrugged. "Mayhap it wasn't praying so much as it was my heart screaming with pain," he said quietly. "Even God could feel it."

"Then God was merciful."

"He was."

Kathalin smiled in return and Gates reached out, taking her into his arms and slanting his mouth hungrily over hers. It seemed that he

355

couldn't stand it any longer. He had to touch her, taste her, and claim her for his own. On this night of nights, they'd been given an unexpected gift and Gates would not wait to take what was rightfully his. For the first time in his life, he would take what legally belonged to him. The mere thought of Kathalin as his wife was the most powerful aphrodisiac he'd ever experienced.

"Lady Kathalin de Wolfe," he murmured against her mouth. "My wife."

Kathalin's arms were around his neck, instinctively pulling him closer to her, her body pressed against his, knowing that on this night, he would claim her for his own just as she would claim him. Fleetingly, she thought of the women that Gates had taken in his time, faceless females with whom he'd had his way, but the thought, in fact, was only fleeting. After this night, she knew there would never be another. It would be her, and only her, in his bed for the rest of their lives.

"My husband," she whispered in return. "My love."

Gates picked Kathalin up and lay her upon the bed, his big body covering hers as the firelight reflected off their features. His mouth drifted away from hers, to her neck, to her delicate shoulders, trying to avoid the fur around her neckline as a free hand began to unlace the ties on her gown. His attentions were gentle and delicate as Kathalin lay there, eyes open, watching him. He must have sensed her attention because he lifted his head from the swell of her bosom, his gaze melding with hers.

It was a moment full of silent words of love, of gratitude for this moment they thought they'd never experience. Her surcoat was coming loose in his hands and he lifted himself up, kissing her nose, her cheek, as he slid the coat off her shoulders, kissing the flesh that came exposed the lower he pulled the garment. Gently, he pulled it off her body, leaving her clad only in her shift and hose, and bathed in the warm glow of the fire. He managed to pull all of that off of her as well. Flipping the coverlet onto her to cover her nakedness, he stood up and pulled his tunic over his head.

His gaze never left her face as his padded under tunic came off, revealing his magnificently muscular chest, thick neck, and broad shoulders. There was a fine matting of dark hair over his chest and Kathalin watched with a mixture of curiosity and apprehension as he removed his boots and breeches as well. Completely nude, and nearly full aroused, he faced her for a moment, allowing her to become acquainted with his naked form, before climbing beneath the coverlet with her.

Hot flesh against flesh met and melded, searing and scorching as Gates' lips latched on to hers again. She was so soft and warm, and to feel her against him with such intimacy was more than he could bear. He'd been with many women, and many times, and had experienced naked flesh against his, but not like this. Never like this. The sheer sensation of it overwhelmed him to the point of madness.

His mouth moved away from hers, down her neck, seeking a heated nipple. Beneath him, Kathalin bucked and gasped at the newness of the sensation but Gates held her slender body fast, hardly allowing her any movement at all. He didn't want her to squirm away from him as he greedily suckled her breasts, first one and then the other, using his body weight to keep her from moving too much as his right hand stroked her thighs. They were so very supple and he left her breasts to wedge his big body in between her legs so that he could put his mouth on her thighs and groin. He could smell her feminine musk and it was intoxicating, filling his nostrils until he could hardly stand it. As he lifted himself upon her body again, his manhood pressing against her virginal core, he put a hand between their bodies, touching her pink folds gently, easing his way inside her.

"Relax, sweetheart," he murmured against her cheek. "You will enjoy this, I promise."

Kathalin, who had so far been loving everything he had been doing to her, was suddenly apprehensive. His fingers, and his great shaft, were touching a place she'd rarely touched herself. It was very sensitive and as he stroked her carefully, her entire body quivered in a way she could not control.

"I… I am not afraid," she breathed, although it was a lie. "This is how children are born, how a husband touches a wife. This is how…."

He suddenly thrust forward, cutting her off, filling her with his fullness as she gasped at the sting of possession. The sting of losing her innocence. But it was truly no sting at all, more of a feeling of closeness and intimacy that she had never imagined. Gates was atop her, in her body, filling her with his manliness, and Kathalin forgot all about her apprehension. Already, she loved the warm possessiveness of it, the feeling of being impaled by a man. It was shocking, but true.

Already, she craved it.

Instinctively, her hands move to his buttocks, her nails in his flesh, and Gates groaned with pleasure as he began to move. She was tight, so incredibly tight as he thrust into her body, slowly and with measured force, lost in a world of fluid warmth that all revolved around the woman in his arms. Her hands on his buttocks were feeding his desire with a fervor he'd never before experienced, with anyone, and as he made love to his wife, one thought, and one alone, rolled through his head.

This is the first time I have truly made love to a woman.

The very first time.

Aye, he felt like a virgin. With the number of women he'd had in his lifetime, it was a foolish thing to think but he couldn't help it. Nothing he'd ever done like this in the past even came close to this moment in time when he bedded the woman he loved. It was more than a physical need; it was an emotional one, a spiritual one, and a need that overwhelmed his entire being. He kissed her deeply as he impaled her on his manhood again and again, the kisses infused with the love and passion he felt for her even as he filled her body with his. This was more than simply a coupling by any standards.

It was an awakening.

Exactly nine months later, on a cold October night, the result of that awakening was born after four hours of very hard and very fast labor. When Gates finally entered the chamber upon being informed by Rosamund that his fat and lusty son had been born, one look at his weary wife cradling the red-faced infant and Gates realized, at that moment, that nothing he had ever done in his life could compare with what he was envisioning. He could only feel light and love and happiness beyond anything he could ever comprehend. There was no longer any past for him; there was only the future. The Dark Destroyer, the destroyer of women's hearts and the rogue of epic proportions, finally knew what it meant to be a man.

A true man.

That night, Gates slept with little Liam Alexander Edward de Wolfe tucked safely in his arms.

Cʒ THE END ЬꝊ

The De Wolfe Pack Series:

The Wolfe

Serpent

Scorpion

Walls of Babylon

The Lion of the North

Dark Destroyer

ABOUT KATHRYN LE VEQUE

Medieval Just Got Real.

KATHRYN LE VEQUE is a USA TODAY Bestselling author, an Amazon All-Star author, and a #1 bestselling, award-winning, multi-published author in Medieval Historical Romance and Historical Fiction. She has been featured in the NEW YORK TIMES and on USA TODAY's HEA blog. In March 2015, Kathryn was the featured cover story for the March issue of InD'Tale Magazine, the premier Indie author magazine. She was also a quadruple nominee (a record!) for the prestigious RONE awards for 2015.

Kathryn's Medieval Romance novels have been called 'detailed', 'highly romantic', and 'character-rich'. She crafts great adventures of love, battles, passion, and romance in the High Middle Ages. More than that, she writes for both women AND men – an unusual crossover for a romance author – and Kathryn has many male readers who enjoy her stories because of the male perspective, the action, and the adventure.

On October 29, 2015, Amazon launched Kathryn's Kindle Worlds Fan Fiction site WORLD OF DE WOLFE PACK. Please visit Kindle Worlds for Kathryn Le Veque's World of de Wolfe Pack and find many action-packed adventures written by some of the top authors in their genre using Kathryn's characters from the de Wolfe Pack series. As Kindle World's FIRST Historical Romance fan fiction world, Kathryn Le Veque's World of de Wolfe Pack will contain all of the great story-telling you have come to expect.

Kathryn loves to hear from her readers. Please find Kathryn on Facebook at Kathryn Le Veque, Author, or join her on Twitter @kathrynleveque, and don't forget to visit her website at www. kathrynleveque.com.

41180655R00207

Made in the USA
Middletown, DE
06 March 2017